WHAT SAVES US

WHAT SAVES US

A SMALL TOWN SINGLE MOM ROMANCE

MAGGIE GATES

Copyright © 2024 Maggie C. Gates. All Rights Reserved

No part of this publication may be reproduced, transmitted, or distributed in any form or by any means including photocopying, recording, information storage and retrieval systems, without prior written permission from the publisher except in the case of brief quotation embodied in book reviews.

No part of this work may be used to create, feed, or refine artificial intelligence models, for any purpose, without written permission from the author.

This book is a work of fiction. The characters and events in this book are fictitious. Any similarity to real places or persons, living or dead, is purely coincidental and not intended by the author or are used fictitiously.

The author acknowledges the trademark status and trademark owners of various products, brands, and/or establishments referenced in this work of fiction. The publication/use of these trademarks is not associated with, or sponsored by the trademark owners.

This book is intended for mature audiences.

ISBN: 9798852526823

Cover design by Melissa Doughty - Mel D. Designs

To me.

CONTENT WARNINGS

What Saves Us deals heavily with the topics of postpartum depression, PTSD, self harm, harm to others, suicidal thoughts and ideation, and alcohol addiction.

In *What Saves Us* there are multiple scenes that explicitly depict these themes. Please know that this is not a subject that I write about lightly, but I believe it's an important story to tell. These characters are human, flawed, and have painfully real struggles.

Due to the explicit nature of themes in this book, *What Saves Us* may not be appropriate for some readers. Your mental health matters more than reading this book.

Motherhood is a unique experience for each person. No two journeys are the same. A positive experience does not invalidate a negative one, and vice versa. In this book, contested topics like breastfeeding are discussed. Please know that however you choose to feed your child(ren) is the best choice.

Should you have questions regarding content in this book prior to reading, please reach out to the author and/or publishing team.

If you are not in a place to read this story, please read the following message before closing the book:

You are not alone. You are valued. You are worthy of love. There is hope to be found even in the darkest moments of life. There is beauty and strength in rising from the ashes. You are not broken. There are people on your side.

And to the Mamas,

Beth's journey through new motherhood and her struggle with postpartum depression is very personal to me. Please know that asking for help does not make you unfit. I see you. I see you sacrificing yourself for your babies. They need the best of you, so please take care of yourself. It's not selfish. You are a priority.

Love,

Maggie Gates

PROLOGUE
BETH

DECEMBER

Two pink lines.

The stench of vomit lingered in the humid bathroom air. Steam rose from the shower as I clung to the toilet. The porcelain was cool to my sweaty palms. The spray from the showerhead harmonized with the ringing in my ears. My stomach lurched and I wretched again, confirming what I already knew.

Pregnant.

It hadn't even taken the full three minutes for the test to come back with a screaming positive.

That didn't stop me from taking the other two in the box just to be certain.

False positives happened, right? I held out hope even though it was accompanied by my period being late and non-stop nausea.

I groaned and slunk into the space between the tub and

the toilet. My head spun in an echoing haze. I needed to rinse the conditioner out of my hair before the water got cold, but I didn't have the strength to stand. Not if I didn't want to slip and crack my head open on the safety bar.

Falls Creek was a tiny little town. The last thing I wanted was to have to call 911 and be carted to the hospital in my birthday suit with half of the first responders knowing exactly what I looked like naked.

I tipped my head to the side and rested it against the bathroom wall, hoping my heart would stop racing.

This explained the bloating.

I thought I had just been stress-eating because it was the end of the semester.

Teaching and working on my doctorate were kicking my ass. Through the insanity of it all, Bradley and I had always managed to steal a little time away to see each other.

Oh God—

A roar of worry slashed through me.

How was I supposed to tell him that he had gotten me pregnant? We weren't even that serious.

Bradley Childers and I had hit it off immediately when I became his teaching assistant at the university.

Such a cliché...

Flirtatious glances turned into lingering chats in his office. Those turned to dinners under the guise of discussing teaching methods and the course load.

And then sex.

A lot of sex.

The first time was in his office. *Such a cliché.*

We both ended the tryst apologetically, promising to keep things strictly professional.

That lasted all of thirty-six hours.

Neither of us wanted rumors to float through the faculty. I

was vying for a full-time position and starting the arduous journey of earning my third degree, and Bradley was about to become tenured.

So, we kept it a secret.

Maybe the thrill of it all is what was keeping me tethered to him.

I wasn't in love with him. I was in lust, sure. Maybe a little enthralled at the idea of having a distinguished older man look at me like something he wanted to devour.

But it wasn't love.

I looked at the pregnancy test that had fallen to the vinyl bathroom floor when my stomach had revolted at the news.

Clandestine rendezvous intended to keep our relationship private became something that would be very public very soon.

Somehow, I managed to lumber back under the water to wash out the conditioner, but I skipped the rest of the "everything shower" I had been intending to take.

I stared at the illuminated screen on my phone as the text thread from the group of girls I had befriended blew up.

In the mix of those notifications, a text from Bradley popped up.

> PROFESSOR CHILDERS
>
> Thinking about your body. All the things I want to do to it. What does your weekend look like? I'll get us a place. How's Raleigh or Greensboro?

It was on-brand for us. We'd steal away to hotels or B&Bs for a weekend of sex and relaxation. He had been to my place twice, but I had never been to his.

It was better that way. Most of the faculty in our department had been to his place. We didn't want to get caught by an accidental pop-in.

Part of me wanted to go ahead and make plans for the weekend. Having him all to myself for forty-eight hours would probably be the best way to break the news.

Maybe he'd be excited.

Sure, we had never talked about the future beyond when our next weekend away would be. But maybe this didn't have to be a bad thing.

It was a surprise, but not all surprises were bad.

BETH

Are you busy?

PROFESSOR CHILDERS

I've got a three o' clock tee time with Dr. Branten.

Okay, surprising him at the golf course with baby news when he was with the head of the mathematics department was not the move to make, but this also wasn't the kind of news I could drop over a phone call.

Before I could decide better of it, I threw on a university sweatshirt, a pair of leggings—because jeans felt *awful* with the bloating—and boots.

On my way to the front door, I nearly tripped over the extension cord that snaked across my living room to the Christmas tree. It was more ornate than the one in Rockefeller Center.

For the briefest of moments, I imagined baby toys strewn about.

Little ornaments on the tree from preschool.

A stocking beside mine.

Two more stockings beside mine.

I crossed my fingers and said a prayer. Maybe he'd be excited.

———

I DOUBLE-CHECKED the address that one of the adjunct professors had sent me.

I told a little white lie to get her to forward Bradley's home address to me. If I had asked him directly, he would have given me a place in town to meet him—somewhere that would be plausible for the two of us to run into each other should anyone catch us.

But this wasn't a coffee shop or bookstore conversation.

In the margin between two pink lines, my life had changed.

A stately brick house with Christmas card worthy decorations was situated at the peak of a cul-de-sac. A shiny SUV and a sedan were piled up behind Bradley's sleek sports car.

Oh shit. He had company.

I looked at the time. It was a quarter past two, which meant he'd be heading to the country club soon.

But I wasn't chickening out.

I was going to own my decisions and deal with this like a fucking adult.

...Just as soon as I got through the mild panic attack that was raining down on me like a hailstorm.

I didn't even bother with my purse. I just cut the engine and grabbed the test that I had thoroughly wiped down. *I did pee on it, after all.*

A stretch of perfectly maintained asphalt looped in a semi-circle from the road to the front steps. The thirty feet between my car and the front door might as well have been a marathon.

Fueled by a burst of courage, I rang the doorbell, clenching my fist around the test. I needed the pressure of hard plastic to ground me.

My stomach jumped into my throat as footsteps approached, but it wasn't the sound of golf shoes and a man's gait. It was the tip-tap of stilettos.

The door whipped open and a woman fifteen years my senior appeared. "Can I help you?"

Weird. I didn't recognize her from the department... Maybe she was a neighbor.

I stammered for a moment before regaining my voice. "Hi—um. Is Bradley around?"

She scoffed as her eyes dropped to the university sweatshirt I was in. "I believe you mean *Professor Childers*." Her smile was derisive. "This is his home, sweetie. Crushes are cute, but they can come with restraining orders. I suggest you speak to him during class or meet with his TA."

A younger girl appeared behind the woman at the very moment the woman's gaze dropped to the pregnancy test clutched in my hand.

"Oh my god," she whispered. Her skin went white as a ghost.

"Mom?" the girl questioned as puzzle pieces fell into place for her. "What's going on?

Mom?! The girl was the spitting image of Bradley which meant that the woman in front of me was—

"You're his... wife." It slipped out of my mouth before I could stop it. Everything went numb.

Wife.

He was married.

He had a daughter.

A pitter-patter of feet carried through the house. A

smaller, boyish version of Bradley, who looked to be in middle school, appeared. "I'm hungry."

Two kids?!

Heavier footsteps approached. *Great. He had three kids.*

My eyes went wide and bile rocketed up my throat. A boy I recognized as one of my freshman students from the last semester appeared. "What's going on?" He looked at me with confusion. "Professor Hale?"

"Josh Childers?"

Oh my god. I had taught his son and had no idea.

Bradley knew the roster of students I had in my classes and he never said a peep. Not about having a son—*two sons*—or a daughter, or a wife.

A whole life…

I stumbled backward. "*I swear I didn't know*," I whispered as tears rolled down my cheeks. My heart pounded violently inside my chest. "I swear I didn't—I wouldn't!"

"Get out, you—*you whore*!" Mrs. Childers roared.

I wasn't his secret workplace love interest.

I was the other woman.

"I promise I didn't know he was married," I cried.

His daughter clapped her hands over her mouth. "Oh my god."

"What?" Josh, the oldest, said. "What's going on? Why is my math professor here?"

"Dad cheated on Mom and she's—" the daughter pointed at me "—pregnant."

My stomach roiled.

Mrs. Childers was hysterical, and I couldn't blame her. "Get out!" she shrieked, her face turning an unnatural shade of eggplant. "If I ever see you again, I'll—I'll have you arrested!"

A fourth set of footsteps thundered through the house.

I knew those footsteps.

"What the hell have you done?!" Mrs. Childers screamed.

But she wasn't screaming at me. Not this time.

"Beth!" Bradley bellowed with vitriol as I bolted for my car.

Tears blurred my vision as I dove into the driver's seat and cranked it up with a sputter.

"*BETH!*" Bradley was running down the front steps, a look of anger marring his otherwise attractive face. "Get back here and face me!" he shouted. The macabre was in his eyes.

The thinly veiled threat was an icicle stabbing my spine.

I gritted my teeth as I peeled out of the driveway and zipped down the road.

This was not happening.

I was the other woman, and I was pregnant with his child.

Bradley Childers had made his home in a house of cards, adding pieces from the deck as he went. He thought he had it all.

The picture-perfect family.

The career.

The lifestyle.

And me.

The mistress.

1

SHANE

EIGHT AND A HALF MONTHS LATER

"A little higher!" Brandie Jean Palmer screeched as she stood on the patio of the Copper Mule and eyed the bedazzled *CONGRATULATIONS* banner that Callum and I were holding up.

It was a scorcher—one of those wicked North Carolina summer days that felt like the inner circle of hell. The humidity was so thick it was like using Satan's ass as a snorkel.

Sweat trickled down the back of my neck, and my arms wavered as Callum and I looked at Brandie Jean for approval.

"Little to the left!" she hollered, pointing an inch-long acrylic nail at me.

I tugged the sign closer.

"No, the other left."

Callum huffed and rolled his eyes as he pulled it back his way.

"Y'all better hurry up," Layla said from her seat in the shade. "Austin and Caroline are gonna be here soon. Sloan just texted me from the school and said she heard screaming."

The aforementioned banner was to celebrate Austin Hale

and his soon-to-be fiancé, Caroline Tyree. The screaming was most likely a good sign. It meant Caroline probably said yes when he had popped the question.

Austin and I worked together to serve the living, breathing mayhem that was Falls Creek. While we shared a station, I was a paramedic and Austin was a firefighter.

The two of us had successfully cohabited for a few months before he found a place of his own and moved in with his girlfriend, Caroline. Living with Austin was great. He was a cool guy.

My former roommate's girlfriend... She was another story.

Caroline Tyree had a piece of me. Literally.

I fought back the bile that boiled up when I thought back to the dark days that had brought me to Falls Creek. The inescapable weight that nearly crushed me.

There were days I still wanted to succumb to the darkness. The depression. The addiction.

"Shane!" Brandie Jean snapped, bringing me back to the present. "I said higher!"

And there she was—my sparkly Barbie Doll sponsor who literally dragged me out of the depths of the worst days of my life.

I hoisted the banner to match Callum. "Here?"

BJ's arm-full of bracelets jingled as she tapped her chin in thought. "Maybe down a little."

Callum swore under his breath. "Gonna fuckin' die of heatstroke if she doesn't make up her damn mind."

"Hey, guys," a sweeter voice called.

I looked over my shoulder, wobbling on the wrought-iron chair I stood on. Beth Hale, Austin's sister, slowly loped onto the patio.

I still remembered the day I met Beth.

I had stopped at the Falls Creek Filling station for an energy drink before I went on duty. It was the morning after one of the nights where sleep played hard to get.

Beth had been inside, filling up a tankard of coffee.

It was one of the rare moments where I actually felt the urge to go up to the pretty girl debating between light roast and dark roast to see if I could get her number. She wasn't from around here—that much I knew for certain.

Her skin sported a deep, sun-kissed glow from a summer spent at the beach. Swimsuit tan lines wrapped around her neck, making the blazer and button-up duo just a little less professional.

It made my mind race about what kind of skimpy, barely-there bikini she would wear for a day in the sand and sun.

"You know, it's all the same," I said to her as I passed by to get to the drink cooler. "Barry just labels the percolators with different roasts so unassuming out-of-towners think it's fancy. It's not even Folgers. It's from the bulk food store in Chapel Hill."

She smiled, a dimple puckering the middle of her cheek as she looked me up and down. "And you're the authority on gas station coffee?"

I chanced a grin. "I'm just saying. Usually I'm on board with a little fun at the expense of motorists passing through."

She popped her hip out and rested her hand on it. "And you think I'm the exception to that rule?"

The newcomer to my morning gas station routine was most certainly the exception.

After leaving the military against my will, I quickly realized that alcohol was my numbing agent of choice. Drowning myself in booze was the quickest way to forget everything.

And it was the only way I actually slept.

But just because my days of substance abuse were behind me didn't mean I had fully recommitted to living.

Hence the reason I was standing in front of a stunning blonde with a killer body and hadn't asked her out yet.

Maybe it had been so long, I had forgotten how.

Her bottle green eyes studied the radio on my hip, my navy cargo shorts, and black station shoes. "You're a firefighter?"

I pulled open one half of my jacket and showed her the stitched logo on my station polo. "Paramedic."

Her lips pursed. "I suppose that's slightly better."

I met her with an arched eyebrow. "Don't tell me you have some hangup about EMS."

She laughed as she opted for the percolator that was falsely labeled to be the light roast. "My brother's a firefighter. I've been around your type all my life." She eyed me up and down. "You lot have a certain presence about you."

I wanted to show her my presence in all sorts of ways. In the bedroom. In the car. On top of her. Behind her.

But instead of manning up and asking the pretty girl out, I choked.

I grabbed an energy drink out of the cooler as she slammed a lid on her coffee.

"Thanks for the tip about the coffee," she said by way of a peace offering.

"No problem."

She swiped her card at the register to paid for her coffee and a half tank of gas.

"I'm Shane, by the way," I said as I stood in line behind her.

That damn dimple appeared again. "See you around, Shane."

I tipped my drink can toward the pretty woman who stole my breath with one smile. "Looking forward to it, Dimples."

My thoughts were brought back to the present by a whiff of Brandie Jean's god-awful perfume. That shit was worse than ammonia inhalants.

Beth paused. Her hand went to her lower back as she let out a worn breath.

Goddamn—she looked pretty today.

Her blonde hair was pulled up and knotted in a massive bun on top of her head. The dress she was in clung to every sexy curve from her breasts to her baby bump, and that ass...

Yeah. Today was a good day.

I had always been attracted to Beth. Before she got pregnant, I practically drooled at the sight of her.

But watching from a distance as her body changed over nine months...

I probably needed to go to confession for the thoughts that I'd had about her while she was carrying her child.

Then again, I'd probably get struck by lightning or turned into a pillar of salt if I ever set foot on church grounds again.

Her life had been turned upside down nine months ago when she found out she was pregnant.

The shit stain who knocked her up was the worst part of the whole situation. He lied to Beth about being married and having a family. When she cut him out and went no-contact, he harassed and threatened her until she finally filed a restraining order.

That ass potato was the reason Austin had packed up his life in the beach town he and Beth grew up in, and moved out here to be with her.

He had been on edge the entirety of her pregnancy, but especially when he lived with me. He would slip out in the middle of the night to check on Beth if she expressed even the slightest complaint.

I had tried to be that guy for Beth, but she never let me in.

Once upon a time, we had shared a flirtatious friendship, but all of that went to hell the moment she saw those two pink lines.

Beth's cheeks were flushed as she lumbered through the iron tables that we had commandeered for Austin and Caroline's surprise engagement party.

"Sorry, I'm late," she huffed, bracing one hand on the back of a chair and the other on top of her bump. She peered over her *very pregnant* belly. "I couldn't tie my sneakers." The laces were still untied, flopping through the pebbles that covered the restaurant patio.

I dropped the banner and jumped down.

"Hey!" Callum called as I left him hanging with his half. I faintly heard him swear as he tacked his side up, disregarding Brandie Jean's instructions.

"Dr. Hale," I said by way of a greeting, strolling over.

Beth's cheeks turned even redder. "I've told you a million times—"

"I know, I know," I conceded. "Not Dr. Hale *yet*."

"Ever," she countered.

"You're still working on it, aren't you?" Before she could argue, I knelt in front of her and tied her left sneaker. "Haven't withdrawn from the program?"

Beth huffed. "No."

I tied her right shoe and wondered if she could see me over her baby belly or if it looked like I had lost a contact, and was pawing around for it on the ground.

"Then it's *aspirational*," I said, looking up with a grin.

She won the battle against her lips, removing any hint of a smile aimed my way. But that dimple in her left cheek popped, and I knew I was the victor.

"You look nice today." *An understatement was the best I could do.*

Beth groaned as she lowered herself into a chair and closed her eyes. "I feel like a beached whale." She rested one hand on top of her belly. "I'm huge. Everything gives me heartburn. I can't roll over in bed without doing a four-point turn. It's so freaking hot in this damn state, I feel like I'm going to die."

Her belly flexed and moved on its own as the little one in there tumbled around. It was weirdly mesmerizing and kind of disturbing all at once.

She let out a heavy breath. "Sorry. Whenever I complain to my mom, she just goes on about how *magical* pregnancy was for her. And whenever I complain to Austin, he gets way too overprotective. God bless Caroline for making him fall in love and keeping him distracted."

I couldn't have stopped staring at her if I tried.

Was it weird to be this attracted to a pregnant woman?

I probably should have brought that up with my psychiatrist over one of the many sessions I'd had with him over the last eight months, but for one reason or another, I never got around to it.

But it wasn't just Beth's body that got me going. She was funny as hell. Sharp and sarcastic.

Considering she was working on her Ph.D., she was fucking smart too.

Beth had these sweet moments where her soft side showed. They were brief and brilliant. Then, of course, she'd follow it up with a quick-witted quip.

I chuckled as I knelt in front of her. "You never need to apologize to me, Dimples."

That earned me an actual smile.

"I'm so ready for this baby to be out," she whimpered.

"How much longer?" I asked.

Like the rest of Falls Creek, I knew the answer. The whole town was on baby watch. Beth had about two weeks left and everyone was on high alert.

It was the beautifully annoying thing about this little town.

Sure, there was a serious privacy deficit, but no one walked alone.

"Two weeks, three days, seven hours, and—" she looked at her phone "—thirty-six minutes."

I chuckled. "What are you gonna do if your little troublemaker decides he or she is cozy in there and doesn't want to leave?"

Beth laughed. "That, Shane Hutchins, is the beauty of elective C-sections."

It was good to hear her laugh. She hadn't been doing it much lately, and I missed it.

Brandie Jean stuck her fingers in her mouth and let out a sharp wolf whistle. "Alright, y'all! Places! Bea Walker just said she spotted them passing her house."

"Help me up?" Beth asked as she reached out for my hand.

I stood, wrapped my palm around hers, and slid my other hand to her back to help her out of the chair.

Beth heaved as she eased up. "Oh my god. Standing up is a workout." She fanned herself. "I'm sweating."

I studied her carefully. "Maybe you should step in the restaurant for a moment. Get in the AC. It's too hot on the patio for you today."

Beth waved me off. "I'm fine."

I grabbed her arm as she listed to the left. Without even thinking, my hand went to her bump. It was tight against my palm. Something thumped against my hand.

Holy shit.

I mean—I knew she was pregnant. That was pretty damn obvious. But feeling her baby kick... That was something else.

She looked up at me with wide eyes. Her brows were lifted in surprise.

"I think you should go sit down inside." My voice was

much gruffer and more intense than I had intended, but I couldn't help myself.

"*Congratulations!*"

Noise from the patio of The Copper Mule exploded as friends and family cheered when Beth's brother, Austin, and Caroline Tyree made their way up the sidewalk.

Beth moved into the middle of the craziness, her hands resting comfortably on her belly. As soon as Caroline was within arm's reach, she dragged her into a hug. "My baby's gonna have an aunt!" she squealed.

Caroline laughed as her ringlet curls spilled down her back. "How long have you known about him proposing?"

Beth squealed. "We've been scheming all summer."

A tornado of pink glitter ripped Caroline out of Beth's embrace and nearly tackled her to the ground. "Congratulations, my little moonbeam!" Brandie Jean shrieked. "Three down, one to go!"

Caroline spat out the strands of Brandie Jean's platinum extensions that had made it into her mouth. "Three?"

"You, me, and Layla!" BJ pointed to Beth. "Now we just have to work on that one."

Beth cackled. "Good luck with that."

"Wait ... *you're* engaged?"

At Caroline's exclamation, everyone looked at Brandie Jean.

"That's right!" She pointed across the patio to an old man doing a crossword puzzle. "He popped the question last night! You're looking at the next Mrs. Amos Johnston and the fifth Mr. BJ Palmer!"

What in the backwoods hillbilly...

"Congratulations, babe!" Layla threw her arms around Caroline. "I'm so happy for you!" She turned and hugged my former roommate. "It's about damn time, Hale."

Austin chuckled. "You can say that again. But the wait was worth it." He planted a kiss on Caroline's mouth. "So worth it."

Something tugged at my heart. Seeing Caroline happy and living life was something that—for a long time—was a long-shot. I elbowed my way in and pulled her into a hug.

"Thank you," she whispered.

"When are you gonna stop saying that?" I grumbled. I knew exactly what she was talking about, and it wasn't the hug.

She stepped back and wiped her eyes. "Never."

"Don't you dare make me fucking cry."

She sniffed, blinking at me. "I wouldn't be here if it wasn't for you."

Fuck me. Caroline knew some of it. She knew the parts of my story that were relevant to her. She knew the parts about me being her anonymous kidney donor.

She even knew some of the "why." It was going to be my final act of atonement—saving a life before taking mine.

But she didn't know all of it.

I swore under my breath and used the collar of my t-shirt to wipe the dampness in my eyes. "Same to you."

We took a few steps back to get some necessary breathing room.

"Happy for you, kid. Even if you stole my roommate."

Caroline laughed through the tears. "Sorry about that. I guess it was short-lived."

"No worries," I said, slapping Austin's back as he grabbed my shoulder and yanked me in for a bro-hug. "Happy for you both."

Beth sided up to Austin and threw her arm around him.

My intuition was immediately heightened. "You okay? You look pale."

She fanned herself. "Fine. It's just hot out."

I grabbed a chair and helped her sit down as Caroline pulled Austin away to give Beth a little breathing room. Tiffany waltzed by, carrying a tray of drinks. I didn't care whose drink it was supposed to be, I stole a glass of water that was piled high with ice and pushed it into Beth's hands.

"Drink that."

Beth looked up at me with doe eyes. "I told you—I'm fine."

Austin's shadow nearly overtook us, but Caroline dragged him away. "Shane's got it," she said quietly.

He argued like he always did when I reminded him that one of these days I was going to ask his sister out. "But—that's—"

Caroline practically grabbed him by the ear and yanked Austin down to her level. She pointed to me as I discreetly pressed my fingers to Beth's wrist and checked her pulse. "*See?* Shane's got it."

Austin groaned. "I'm gonna throw up."

Caroline laughed. "Breathe through it, babe."

"Fuckin' hate it," he grumbled.

"Come on," Caroline said, pulling him to the long row of tables that had been pushed together so that everyone could sit together. "Give her a little breathing room. She'll let you know if she needs you."

Austin glowered. "I hate that you two gang up on me."

"Doesn't feel so good, now, does it?" Caroline sassed.

I looked up at Beth. "How you feelin', Mama?"

She smiled into the glass of water as she took another sip. "Like I'd marry Caroline if my brother hadn't gotten to her first. I swear she's the only person on this planet who can distract him from turning into an overprotective Hulk when it comes to all this." She motioned around her belly.

My gaze flicked down to her bump. "You know you can call me if you need anything, right? Day or night."

She laughed. "I know. I've already got your number memorized."

My heart fucking skipped. "You, uh ... you do?"

"Of course." She grinned. "Three digits. 911. I'll have you and the rest of Falls Creek's finest at my beck and call."

Right.

2

BETH

The sky was an ominous gray. What had been a day of triple digits and swamp crotch had dropped thirty degrees to linger in the seventies.

That was never good.

My hips ached something fierce as I shifted uncomfortably on the couch. The pillow wedged between my legs did nothing to help me get the rest I so desperately craved.

My boobs ached, so I stuck a second pillow between them to take a little of the pressure off.

Guilt boiled up whenever I complained. I chose to keep this baby, so what right did I have to complain about it?

A stab of pain flashed up my leg and struck my pelvis like lightning.

Yeah, I wasn't going to miss that.

Great. I had to pee again.

I eased up, bracing my hands on the coffee table and the arm of the couch before heading to the bathroom.

At least my townhouse was blissfully quiet. The town was abuzz with news of my brother's engagement to Caroline, giving me momentary reprieve from nosey nellies popping in to see if I had exploded yet.

As if they wouldn't know the second I went to the hospital.

This was Falls Creek, after all. Gossip flowed like sweet tea.

There was a phone tree and a contingency phone tree in case the first phone tree didn't spread the news that I was going under the knife. There was a Facebook group dedicated to being the digital town crier. If I so much as left my house, there was sure to be a post asking if I was just going to the Copper Mule for mashed potatoes or if I was heading to the hospital.

It wasn't like I was going to spontaneously combust. When my obstetrician agreed to my birth plan, I hugged her so hard she probably thought she was being strangled.

Elective C-section. My favorite words in the entire English language.

Finding out I was pregnant with this baby had been surprising enough. I didn't need the surprise of my water breaking to force me to go to the hospital and drop whatever was on my calendar.

The only surprise I was willing to subject myself to was the gender.

I finished up in the bathroom and peeked in the nursery. Stacks of neutral onesies had been laundered and were in a basket on top of the changing table, ready to be put away.

The aroma of fresh paint still lingered. Just last week Caroline had finished the mural she designed for the nursery.

A magical woodland scene warmed the otherwise beige space. A canopy of stippled leaves and branches reached across the top of the wall. Glowing yellows and greens beamed down like sunlight peeking through. Toadstools and daisies added a touch of whimsy. An adorable bear snoozed against the trunk of a tree while playful squirrels scampered along the branches.

I had gotten a few decorations to bring it all together. There was a mobile of felt pinecones and leaves hanging above the crib. A blanket in crimson that matched the mushrooms in the mural was draped over the back of the rocking chair.

The teddy bear that sat on the seat of the rocking chair was arguably overpriced for what it was. I had almost walked out of the store without it, but the baby hormones got the best of me. Before I knew it, I was swiping my card as I shooed away a tear.

There were a million things on my to-do list that I just hadn't gotten around to yet.

I taught a full load of courses through the summer in an attempt to solidify myself as a dedicated and indispensable member of the math department faculty. Now that the summer term was over, I was officially on maternity leave and needed to get cracking on the long list of looming tasks.

Tiny clothes needed to be folded and put away. I had a stack of baby shower thank you notes that needed to be addressed and put in the mail. The car seat still needed to be unboxed and installed. Lucky for me, I had a firefighter brother who was trained in car seat safety. Austin could figure out how to get that engineering nightmare into my vehicle.

My hospital bag needed to be packed, and I needed to stock every room in the house with necessities so I didn't have to go from room to room to get whatever I needed for the baby.

The recovery from the C-section was going to suck, but I'd rather six weeks of hell than spontaneous labor.

That was the downside of doing this by myself. Nights

were the loneliest—especially when I was uncomfortable and couldn't sleep.

I had always imagined pregnancy being this blissful experience.

I would glow and beam, loving my body as it grew a tiny human. I would have a partner who doted on me and helped satisfy my middle of the night cravings. I would have someone to rub my back. Someone to hand me tissues when car commercials made me cry. Someone to tell me that I wasn't crazy when I most certainly was. Someone to help me remember what I was supposed to do when I walked in a room.

Pregnancy brain was no joke. I had started making voice notes to remind me of the things that floated through my mind; otherwise I'd never remember them.

But I didn't have that someone.

That someone was a cheating liar who had been put on administrative leave by the university after earning himself a DUI and the restraining order I slapped him with.

I'd rather miss all those things than be strapped with a monster like that.

Sure, I had my brother and his fiancé. They were my go-tos most of the time.

I had Layla Mousavi and her endless well of medical expertise. On more than one occasion, she talked me off the ledge when Google's suggestion for symptoms and pregnancy side effects was to start digging my own grave.

Brandie Jean would drop everything and be here in the blink of an eye if I asked. Same with Layla's fiancé, Callum. *Especially now that they were actually engaged and not just pretending.*

That list didn't even begin to cover the hoards of Creekers who would fight each other to help if I asked.

And then there was Shane.

My skin tingled when I thought about the way it felt when he touched my bump; the slow slide of his hand over the swell.

It was probably a knee-jerk reaction to me nearly passing out in the heat. Shane was a paramedic. He probably just didn't want me to make him work on his day off.

I leaned on the doorframe as my mind replayed the touch repeatedly.

I had wanted to lean into him that day. To close my eyes for just a moment and rest on his shoulder.

I met Shane around the same time that Bradley and I got involved in our ... *situationship*.

Flirting with Shane was fun. We had an easy rapport, but all of that changed nine months ago. It was unfair for him to be as attractive as he was. But beneath that fun, tattooed exterior, there was something haunted that called to me like a siren song.

But stringing him along and subjecting him to the insanity I had gotten myself into would be cruel.

But just because I had cooled off on how much I let myself linger in his presence didn't mean he had done the same. If anything, Shane had made himself a staple in my life over the last year.

I chalked it up to the fact that he was best friends, former roommates, and coworkers with my brother. But another part of me wanted his increasingly close proximity to be because he wanted to be close to *me*.

The pressure of his hand against my belly... God, it felt so good.

For some reason, people tended to think that pregnancy was an excuse to touch women without their consent.

Usually, little old ladies were the worst offenders, reaching out and groping my stomach in the middle of the fucking grocery store.

I had made it to month five without smacking a bitch in the cereal aisle. Now, I played whack-a-mole with the wandering hands that reached for my body.

But Shane's touch didn't make me want to cower away.

He hadn't meant to touch my stomach like everyone else did. It was a knee-jerk reaction when he sensed I was in trouble.

A knee-jerk reaction that had me busting out my vibrator when I got home.

Pregnancy was weird. One minute I'd want to rip someone to shreds if they looked at me the wrong way. But if my brother's best friend asked if I was okay, I'd be dying for a little battery-operated assistance.

Was this what my life was destined to be? Long days of teaching and parenting broken up with stolen fantasies I'd never be able to indulge?

The melancholy was shattered by a knock at the door, followed by a bark.

I knew that bark.

"Coming!" I called out as I waddled through the living room. Stanley would worry if I didn't holler.

Stanley Campbell was the adorable eighty-year-old man who lived in the townhouse next to mine. He was the best kind of neighbor—the kind who was quiet and abided by the mantra of 'live and let live.' Stanley and his geriatric bulldog, Arthur, checked on me twice a day when they stepped outside for the short walk that Arthur tolerated.

One time when he popped in, I had gotten stuck sitting on the floor of the nursery and it took me a little longer than usual to get up and answer the door.

Stanley was in a panic, mid-dial to the police department to come bust into my townhouse when I finally got out to him.

Now, I made sure I was within shouting distance when I heard his front door open and close.

I let out an exhausted breath as I yanked open the door. Folding baby clothes could wait. I had a hot date with a nap on my schedule.

"Hey, Stan," I said as I opened the door and reached for the bag of dog biscuits I kept on hand. Squatting was out of the question, so I dropped it in front of Arthur who snarfed it up without skipping a beat.

"Looks like a storm's rollin' in, Miss Beth. Anything I can do for you?"

I made a show of thinking it over. "I think I'm alright. I'm probably gonna use the rain as an excuse for a nap."

His wrinkled smile was kind. "Good. Good. That's good." He pointed a gnarled finger at my belly. "You get all the sleep you can. Lord knows even the best kids will steal your rest."

I sighed and stared at the gray storm clouds rolling across the sky. "Yeah, I'm trying to wrap my head around eighteen years of no sleep."

Stanley chuckled. "I'm going on fifty years of no sleep. The worry doesn't go away once they're grown. You just worry about different things. And you worry about your baby's babies, too."

I laughed. "Come on, Stan. Don't tell me that now." I rested my hands on top of my bump. "I'm just getting started and I'm already exhausted."

He chuckled. "You just come next door if you need a cup of coffee and someone to hold your little one for an hour."

My back throbbed and I held back a groan. "Thanks, Stan," I gritted out. "I really appreciate it."

He nodded kindly and backed away from the door. "Enjoy your nap, Miss Beth." Thunder cracked overhead, and he took another peek at the sky. "I might just turn in, too. I don't much like driving around in these conditions at my age. No need for me to be another person on the road in a gully washer to make life harder on the fire department."

"I'm sure Austin would thank you for staying home."

Our goodbyes were cut off by a slap of thunder that was so loud it rattled the windows. Stanley scurried over to his half of our duplex with Arthur on the heels of his slippers.

Heavy pelts of rain splattered on my toes as the sky opened up.

Definitely a nap kind of day.

I AWOKE to seizing pain in my lower back. "Fuck whoever Braxton Hicks was," I muttered as I groaned and three-point-turned onto my other side.

Maybe that would give the baby a little more wiggle room in the increasingly cramped living space that was my uterus.

I wrapped my arms around my belly and snuggled myself. "Just a little longer in there, baby bean."

A few names bounced around in my head, but I hadn't quite settled on anything yet.

Maybe I should have found out the baby's gender.

That probably would have been better than calling the little trojan "baby bean" for nine months.

But that's what it had looked like the first time they were able to pick up my pregnancy on an ultrasound. My little lima bean, lost in a mass of gray and black swooshes.

Something that I guessed was an elbow nailed me in the ribs as the not-so-little bean danced on my bladder.

Wind shook the townhouse. The lights flickered and my appliances buzzed.

"So help me—" I heaved myself out of the bed and padded to the bathroom "—if the motherfucking air conditioning goes out, I will be *so* pissed."

I had just stepped onto the bathroom's vinyl floor when I felt something warm trickle down my leg.

I didn't even have the energy to get angry about peeing myself again.

If the disgusting glucose drink I had to chug in my OBGYN's office was the Kool-Aid that made women think pregnancy was magical, I must have been born immune.

I pushed down my damp yoga pants and underwear and yeeted them into the hamper with a flick of my ankle. There was no bending over happening. Not with the way the baby was ramming my pelvis with whatever body part that was.

"*Fuck.*" I gasped as I grabbed the edge of the sink.

Fake contractions were no joke.

It's the body's way of preparing you for labor, Dr. Benoit had touted when I complained about Braxton Hicks contractions at my appointment two days ago.

I was prepared for labor.

I was prepared for the nice cocktail of drugs that would take the pain away, and a team of surgeons who would slice me open and get this baby out of me without any long-term damage to my lady temple.

No more surprises.

I dropped down onto the toilet to finish relieving my bladder before I tossed my pants in the washing machine.

As soon as I sat down, lightning crotch stabbed my pelvis like a pickaxe. At least sitting on the toilet gave my knees a little reprieve.

I grabbed my phone and texted Layla.

. . .

> BETH
>
> There would be fewer unplanned pregnancies if people knew how awful the third trimester is.

LAYLA

Aww, did you pee yourself again?

> BETH
>
> Yes. And these stupid practice contractions suck. And I can't sleep. Everything makes me angry. Or sad. I've clearly lost my mind. And dear God—lightning crotch is the worst thing ever. Don't ever get pregnant. It's a scam.

LAYLA

Well, I can guarantee that I won't get pregnant for at least fifteen hours.

> BETH
>
> What do you mean?

LAYLA

We got toned out before the storm hit. Odin can't fly back to base. We're riding out the storm at the hospital in Winston-Salem. Looks like we'll be hanging out in the EMS lounge for a while.

LAYLA WAS a flight nurse with the AirCare medevac team. She and her fiancé, Callum, had met when he was in a wreck and got pinned inside his police cruiser.

> BETH
>
> That sucks. Stay safe.

Before I could set my phone down and heave myself off my porcelain throne, a text from my brother came in.

AUSTIN

Got called in to the station. They're swamped. You need anything?

BETH

I need this baby to chill the fuck out.

AUSTIN

LOL. Sorry. Can't help you there.

BETH

I think I'm fine. Just uncomfortable.

AUSTIN

Caroline's going through a flare right now, so she'll probably be sleeping. If you need anything give me a call.

BETH

Will do. I'll call to check on her later. Are you working until shift change in the morning?

AUSTIN

Yeah. Looks like it's not going to slow down tonight. Thanks, kid.

I set my phone on the edge of the sink vanity and washed my hands.

Poor Caroline. The pressure changes during storms like this made her lupus flare up. I hated that she felt miserable.

I grabbed the hand towel draped through the loop on the wall as my phone lit up with a text from Brandie Jean. She was sporting a bright pink bikini with the combined coverage of three tortilla chips, while sitting on the power-scootered lap of Amos Johnston.

A honeymoon in the Bahamas was a far cry from a summer thunderstorm in Falls Creek.

For once in my life, I wished I was Brandie Jean. Tanned, tipsy, and totally relaxed.

Instead, I was pasty, pissed, and out of patience.

Rather than carting the half-filled hamper down to the washing machine like I knew I should, I decided to extend my pity party just a little longer and crawled back into bed.

3

SHANE

"You sure are handsome," Clarice Sherman said as we lowered the gurney out of the back of the ambulance we lovingly referred to as The Band-Aid box.

Missy, my right-hand woman for the shift, hopped down and closed up the back of the truck as we started through the sliding doors of the emergency department.

Sharp droplets of rain stung my skin as the wind whipped up beneath the sheltered ambulance entrance.

Sirens wailed in the distance with more incoming patients.

There was nothing quite like the chaos of a hellish supercell thunderstorm slamming into Orange County on the same night as a full moon.

Missy and I hadn't stopped running since we clocked in this morning. Most of the helicopter teams were grounded for the weather, which meant we picked up twice as many calls.

I chuckled as Mrs. Sherman felt up my forearm while we rolled her into the emergency department.

This was our third interfacility transfer of the day. Clarice Sherman had fallen when she tried to get out of bed at the assisted living facility she called home. I tried to take it easy as I navigated the ambulance through inches of standing water and downed branches, but the poor woman was hurting after being jostled around.

"Thank you, ma'am," I said with a customer service smile.

"Don't care much for tattoos—" she paused and gave my arms another look "—but I suppose they're not too bad on you."

I'd take it.

"I'm sorry about all this," she said with a tired huff. "You two really shouldn't be zipping around in the rain the way you are, but I'm sure thankful for ya."

"Just doing our job," Missy chimed in with a sweet smile.

I winked at Clarice. "You fall, we haul."

"You got boo boos, we bring the wee-woo," Missy chimed in, and we fist bumped.

The handoff to send our patient higher up the continuum of care went about as smooth as could be expected when the entire department was a dangerously understaffed circus. Finally, the nurses in the ED took Clarice into their care. We barely had time to make a pit stop in the hospital restrooms before we were back in the truck.

The radio traffic was non-stop as we buckled our seatbelts.

Missy reached for the opened box of granola bars we had wedged between us. She had just handed me one when our radios squawked.

Groaning, she slumped against the back of the seat. "I just want a damn nap."

"That's what you get for covering for Tommy yesterday," I pointed out.

She pinched the bridge of her nose and huffed. "He guilt tripped me, okay? I was trying to be a team player."

"Rule number one. Don't pick up extra shifts unless you

need the money. Act your pay grade. Do what you're scheduled to do and go home. Slow and steady gets you further in life than flooring it into burnout."

And with that wisdom nugget thrown out into the universe, I answered the radio. "Falls Creek Squad Two in service. Go ahead."

Heavy pelts of hail began to thump and rattle against the body of the Band-Aid box.

"Squad two, respond to 201 Pine View Court. Twenty-nine year old female called in an OB emergency. Thirty-eight weeks gestational age. Be advised, the patient is likely in active labor."

Pine View Court... That was Beth Hale's townhouse community. But she wasn't due for another two weeks...

Shit.

I burned rubber pulling away from the hospital. "Show me going," I clipped into the radio. "Central, has Engine 1 returned to the station? Last update was a request for mutual aid on scene from Hillsborough Station three."

"Negative. Engine 1 is still on scene at a structure fire."

I swore under my breath.

Beth's emergency plan was her brother, Austin, and he had picked up an extra shift today.

Damn overachievers.

"Is there anyone with an obstetrics background you can get me in touch with?" I asked dispatch.

Missy gave me a quizzical look as I took a back road to circumvent a downed tree that was tangled with a power line.

There was a pause before the radio crackled again. "I'll see what I can do."

"Why do we need an OB?" Missy asked as she wolfed down her granola bar and chased it with a glug from the water tower she called a bottle.

"Because it's a full moon," I said. "That's enough probable cause to take emergency measures."

Missy's eyebrows winged up. "Are we about to have an obstetrical emergency?"

I let out a heavy breath before reaching for my phone to call Beth. "I sure as fuck hope not."

Missy swatted my hand away. "Eyes on the road. If you crash and die, I don't want to have to deliver a baby on my own. Babies gross me out. Especially the new ones."

I tipped my head toward my phone. "Look in my contacts and text Beth Hale to see if she's okay."

Thunder rolled overhead and a bolt of lightning sliced through the sky. I glanced over as Missy's thumbs flew over my phone, typing out a message to Beth.

Dread boiled in my gut. I had that feeling... That prodding in the back of my mind that told me something was wrong. Very wrong.

"No response?"

"Not yet." She looked up at me. "Have you ever delivered a baby?"

Missy was still a rookie. She was talented and sharp, but there was something to be said about the hands-on experience of a call that the classroom didn't prepare you for.

"Once. I was new. The paramedic I was working with did all the heavy lifting."

She groaned as I sped through downtown Falls Creek. "Great."

I tried to keep my eyes on the road, but every half mile I'd glance over to see if my phone lit up with a response from Beth.

Nothing.

Beth was still two weeks from her due date, we were in the

middle of a hail storm, and every other first responder in the county was otherwise tied up.

There had to be a firefighter in the department who had delivered a baby before.

Surely, this didn't completely fall on my shoulders.

Then again, it was Beth...

Fuck.

She was my Achilles' heel.

The neighborhood came into view and I confirmed the house number with dispatch.

Beth's car was the only one parked in her two reserved spaces.

"Listen to me," I yelled to Missy as wind and rain whipped all around us.

She shouldered one of the med bags, and I grabbed the other.

"When we go in there, you're the most confident person in the room. You get me?"

Missy nodded and tossed her waterlogged ponytail to the side. "Got it. Fake it till you make it."

"More like fake it until we can send her up the chain of care."

She huffed as we trudged through pooling water to make it up to Beth's front stoop.

I swallowed the ache inside and knocked loudly on the door that sported a festive beach themed wreath. "EMS!" I called out. When there was no answer after ten seconds, I knocked and tried again. "Beth, it's Shane. Are you okay?"

Still nothing.

But the lights were on, her car was here, and I knew dispatch had sent us to the right house.

We were getting drenched in the downpour and I wasn't waiting another fucking second. "Hold this," I said as I handed off the med bag and reached into one of the many pockets in my navy uniform pants, producing a pocket knife. I flipped open one of the attachments and slid it into the lock, listening as best as I could through the howling winds to hear the *click*.

"Are you seriously breaking into someone's house?"

"Wouldn't be the first time; probably won't be the last."

Click.

I inserted the next pin until it stroked the locking mechanism and released. I folded the knife and dropped it back in my pocket. "Ladies first," I said, pushing the front door open.

Missy took one step inside and gasped. "Oh my god!"

"Nope. Not what you say when you walk into someone's house, Miss."

She stammered. "Uh, Miss Hale. We got a call about an OB emergency. What's going on?"

Shit. Maybe "oh my god" was better than protocol.

Beth, on her knees with her arms braced on the couch cushion, was covered in sweat and as pale as a fucking ghost.

Usually steel-stomached Missy looked like she was about to pass out.

I knelt beside Beth and brushed her damp hair out of her face. "Hey, Dimples."

Her eyes fluttered closed again as every muscle in her body seized at once. She groaned in agony, a fierce guttural noise reverberating her from her chest.

I glanced at my watch and timed the contraction while Missy donned a pair of gloves and rooted around in the bags.

Sixty seconds later, Beth's body relaxed and she took a deep breath. "I'm gonna die, aren't I?"

I chuckled as I soothingly rubbed my hand up and down her back. "Do you want the good news, the bad news, or the worst news?"

"It's all bad new—" Her words were cut off by another

contraction. This one slammed into her, harder and faster than the last. Beth clawed at the couch cushion, her teeth grinding together like nails on a chalkboard.

Fuck.

I looked up at Missy and communicated through a silent twitch of my brows. Her eyes were wide as she hurried back to the ambulance to get everything we'd need.

As soon as it looked like the contraction was easing up, I caught Beth's attention.

"Good news. You're in labor. Bad news. You're in labor."

A tear slipped down her cheek. "What's the worst news?"

"Austin's on a call right now. I've got dispatch trying to get through to him, but it looks like it's you, me, and Missy for the time being. Is there anyone else I can call for you before we head to the hospital?"

She shook her head. "Layla's stuck in Winston-Salem because of the storm, Caroline's sick, BJ's on her honeymoon, and my mom isn't supposed to be up here for two more weeks." Beth tilted her body, grimacing as she sat on her butt to give her knees a break. "I tried to get my keys to drive myself to the hospital, but the contractions—"

Another one hit. They weren't even two minutes apart.

"I thought these were just Braxton-Hicks! I haven't called my OB yet. I'm supposed to have a C-section!" she cried as soon as her breath came back. "I'm a wimp! I can't push a whole person out of my hoo-hah! I put Orajel on splinters because taking them out hurts too much! I pass out every time I get blood drawn! I need drugs! Please tell me you have drugs!"

I grabbed two throw pillows from the couch and wedged them behind her back for support. Missy returned, hauling in supplies on top of the gurney.

"Not the kind of drugs you were planning on, Dimples." I

caught her gaze. "But what I can tell you is that I'm not leaving your side. Okay? This might not be how you imagined it happening, but you're not going to be alone."

"I just—"

Another contraction.

"What's the plan of action, boss?" Missy asked as she handed me a pair of gloves.

"If we get consent, we'll do a quick pelvic to see how far she is so the hospital can be prepared. Last thing we want is to load up and be going sixty-five when a baby pops out."

"Please get me to the hospital," Beth gasped. "I'm sorry. I know the rescue squad isn't a taxi service, but I literally cannot drive myself and I don't have anyone to—"

"Hey." I cut her off this time and offered a wonky, warped smile. "You did the right thing."

Like I had done for so long, I put all the things I felt for Beth in a box and tucked it away. It was go time.

"If it's okay with you, I'd like one of us to check to see how far along you are so the hospital can get ready for you. Missy is right here and can do the exam if you'd like."

Missy clammed up. "Uh—I've never done that."

Great. *So much for "fake it till you make it."*

"I don't give two flying fucks who does it. At this point, so many people have seen my vagina that—"

While Beth's body went to war, Missy draped a sheet over her bent knees to offer a little modesty. "You're going to feel my hands on your hips. Can I help you get your yoga pants down?"

Beth nodded, but her face was scrunched up in agony.

I looked at my watch again. These weren't slow, methodical early labor contractions. They were hard, fast, and lasting longer and longer.

As soon as the contraction passed, Missy helped Beth

shimmy her stretchy maternity pants down. I rolled up the edge of the sheet as Missy clicked on her pen light.

"I'm going to touch the back of my hand to the inside of your thigh first," I said as I watched her face.

Beth just nodded, her chin tipping back as she slowly took deep breaths and closed her eyes.

"A little to the left, Missy," I said, directing the light to be where I needed to be. I looked back up at Beth. "You doing okay?"

She nodded. "Please tell me I have time to get to the hospital and get an epidural."

But I didn't even have to estimate how dilated her cervix was. Missy's eyes widened in shock, and something akin to horror crossed her face when she saw what I saw.

"Let's play that game again. Good news, bad news, or the worst news?"

Beth cracked open an eye and peered down at me. "Good news."

"Your baby has blonde hair like you."

She arched an eyebrow, groaning as smaller contractions hit her in waves. "You sure that's not just me? I'm just saying. In my case, the carpet does match the drapes. And I haven't shaved down there in—like—two months. I can't even reach it, much less see it. Besides, it's not like I'm getting laid."

I chuckled. "I'm sure."

"What's the bad and worst news?"

"Bad news—no epidural. Worst news—your baby's coming whether you like it or not. On the next contraction, I need you to try to push."

Fear was splashed across her face. "Shane—I... I can't. I need Dr. Benoit. I need drugs." She looked at me with tear-filled eyes. "It—it wasn't supposed to be like this."

"We don't always get to choose our path, but we choose how we walk it."

"That's great, Mr. Fortune Cookie. But I can't—"

Beth grabbed my hand and squeezed the shit out of it as the biggest contraction yet wrung every ounce of energy she had.

Missy and I worked in tandem, getting a mask over her mouth for supplemental oxygen and starting an IV line. While Beth recovered from the contraction, Missy turned the coffee table into a buffet as she unpacked the OB kit.

"Do you want to push like this or do you want to get in a different position?" I asked as I checked her blood pressure. Her vitals were holding strong, and that in itself felt like a damn miracle. We didn't have fetal monitors to know whether or not the baby was in distress. I needed for her to push like hell and for the weather to let up enough for us to make it to the hospital.

I couldn't think about the what ifs. The next contraction was all that mattered.

I knelt between her knees and took another assessment. The baby's head was crowning. "You're going to feel my hand on you. I'm going to put a little pressure on the baby's head to make sure he or she doesn't come too quickly."

I shifted to one bent knee and pressed my other leg to her calf so she had something to brace against.

Beth gave me a weak nod. Blood and bodily fluids were already on the floor beneath her, so I figured an underpad wouldn't make much difference. We'd use it to wrap the baby up right away instead.

"Missy, you got the underpad?"

"Got it."

"Next push, the baby might be yours. Keep it warm. Go through APGAR." I looked up at Beth. "You ready, Dimples?"

Tears streamed down her face as thunder rattled the windows. "No."

"Look at me," I soothed as I grabbed her hand with my free one. "I'm right here. Can't say I've ever been where you've been, so I need you to tell me how much it hurts when it's all over. Commit it to memory. All I want is you pushing and thinking about everything you're feeling." I gave her hand a squeeze. "Got it? Stay with me. Keep your mind engaged."

Her voice was a muffled whisper beneath the oxygen mask. "I'm not strong enough for this."

"Yeah, you are, Mama. You're the toughest one in the room."

I didn't miss the way her eyes shrewdly flicked up and down my sleeves of tattoos.

"Breathe. Get your strength. And when you feel the next contraction coming, I need you to fight like hell."

She barely had time to catch one breath. She jolted forward as her body seized. The baby's head pressed against my palm.

"Push, Beth. Push hard. I need you to work for it."

She cried out in agony, her grip on my hand turning my joints white.

The baby's shoulders turned vertical and pressed against her pelvis. "You're almost there. Big breath and push again. Almost there."

"I can't—I can't—"

I squeezed her hand. "Come on. I need you to fight me."

"I don't have it in me," she whimpered. "I'm not like you or Austin. I'm not fearless."

"It's okay to be scared, Dimples. It's normal to be scared. But you've got me. You've got Missy. And in a little while you're gonna have a whole fucking hospital telling stories about how you did this on your living room floor like a goddamn legend. So let's give 'em one hell of a tale to tell."

Through gasping breaths, she nodded. "I trust you."

Missy readied the placenta bag beside me.

"You're doing great, Beth," Missy said sweetly. "As soon as the baby comes out I'd like to check him or her over real quick and then I'll put the baby on your chest. Is that okay?"

Beth nodded.

"Things might move pretty fast when you deliver. We're gonna get you to the hospital as soon as we can. But we're going to make sure you and baby are safe," she said.

I adjusted my grip on Beth's hand as I cradled the baby's head with my other hand.

Missy smiled. "You've got this, Beth. One big push."

Her usually honey colored hair was plastered to her skin in a damp medium brown. She was spent and, for her sake and the baby's, I needed her to give the next contraction everything she had.

Beth started pushing before the contraction hit. Missy kept a watchful eye on the pulse oximeter as I shifted forward.

We only got the basics of childbirth, but rule number one was the most important. Don't drop the baby.

I watched as the shoulders slid forward. "There you go, Mama. Little more—little more." I wrenched my hand out of Beth's grip as she let out a battle cry.

Holy shit.

My heartbeat was in my ears as I caught the baby and turned *her* upright. I whispered three little words before carefully handing her off to Missy.

Beth slumped against the backrest of pillows. "I can't go anymore."

Missy held the little grub worm, gently rubbing her back

to stimulate her before wrapping her in the underpad as she went through the APGAR assessment.

I wanted to cup her cheek and tell her how fucking incredible that was to watch, but my hands were slimy and covered in fluid. "You did it, Mama."

Her eyes opened weakly. "What?"

As if on cue, Beth's daughter let out an ear-piercing wail.

"Congratulations," I said gently. "It's a girl."

Tears—of happiness or maybe relief—welled up in her eyes. "It's a girl?"

Missy beamed as she used the bulb aspirator to clear the baby's airway. "She's beautiful, Beth. You were awesome."

I looked up at Beth. She was in a tight-fitting tank top that molded to her belly. "We want her to stay warm until we can get her to the hospital and get her checked out. Can I help you get your shirt off so she can lay skin-to-skin?"

She nodded through blubbering tears. "Yeah."

I grabbed the shears and started snipping up the front so it wouldn't get hung on the IV line as Missy laid the baby on Beth's chest.

I looked up at Missy. "Get ready to go. You're driving."

While Missy ran around, packing our supplies and grabbing Beth's things, I continued to monitor Beth's vitals and did another APGAR assessment on the baby. I noted her skin flush, muscle tone, pulse, reflexes, and breathing.

"You did so good," I said with a lopsided smile as I snapped my soiled gloves off and pulled on a fresh pair. I cupped her cheek. "I'm so proud of you."

Maybe I hallucinated it. Maybe I just dreamed it because I wanted to. But I swear, Beth leaned into my hand and closed her eyes.

"Thank you," she whispered before leaning down to press a kiss to the baby's head.

"You got a name picked out?" I asked as her body contracted again and began to expel the placenta.

It was pretty fucking cool when you thought about it—the fact that the human body creates a whole new organ to sustain a baby. It's incredible.

I watched carefully, making sure that the placenta was delivered in its entirety before depositing it into the bag that was earmarked for it. The team at the hospital would probably do a quick check to make sure nothing was left inside Beth's body.

"Katherine," she said as she stared down at the little bundle in awe. "Kat for short."

"Welcome to the world, Kat," I said as I tilted my head and took in Kat's tiny features. Her little button nose was a miniature version of Beth's. "Your mom's a badass."

I grabbed the shears and offered them to Beth. "Do you want to cut the umbilical cord?"

She turned a little green at the thought, and muttered, "God—no." Those pretty bottle green eyes looked up at me the same time Kat opened hers.

Green like the rolling hills around Falls Creek. Like mother, like daughter.

"Will you do it?" she asked timidly.

"Of course," I said as I went to work, snipping the cord and using the sterile clamps that were in the OB bag to stem any remaining blood flow. Her perineum had torn as the baby was delivered, but I couldn't do much about that. When we got to the hospital, the obstetrics team would stitch her up. I tore into the antiseptic towelettes and gently cleaned between her legs as best as I could.

We finished packing up and readied the gurney. Missy held Kat, all swaddled up in a blanket Beth had in the nursery, while I got Beth secured on the gurney and loaded into the back of the ambulance.

Missy laid baby Kat in Beth's arms before hopping behind the wheel and peeling out of the neighborhood.

We bumped and jostled in the back of the ambulance. While Beth cuddled her baby girl, I documented everything and kept an eye on the two of them. Her pulse was strong, but Beth's blood pressure was on the lower side of normal.

Normally it wouldn't have meant much to me as a paramedic, but my "normal" and "normal after bringing a human into the world" were probably a little different.

Lying on that gurney, covered by a sheet with a grubby, wrinkly little newborn in her arms, Beth had never been more radiant.

Watching her give birth… Being a part of it…

It was one of the days I realized I was actually doing what I set out to do all those years ago. I helped bring a life into the world instead of taking one.

It was my atonement.

4

SHANE

"So," I said as I checked Kat's temperature while Beth cradled her. "Is Katherine a family name or something or did you just like it?"

Her smile was weak and tired, but still present. "You'll think it's dumb…"

I chuckled as I stole a peek at the lines around her eyes and allowed myself to momentarily appreciate how regal she looked like this. "I promise you I won't."

Beth cradled her hand over Kat's head. "She's named after Katherine Johnson."

"Who's that? Your grandma?"

She let out a quiet laugh. "She was a mathematician for NASA. She calculated the trajectory for the first American astronaut to go into space. When John Glenn's mission to orbit the earth was ordered, he asked for her—by name—to verify the calculations by hand that had been done with a computer. She was brilliant and that doesn't even scratch the surface of everything she did for the space program during segregation."

"That's fucking awesome," I said with a grin. My interest

was suddenly rerouted when Beth's blood pressure dropped a few more points.

We were five minutes out from the hospital. Even though Missy had called ahead and a team was waiting for Beth and Kat, it would be another few minutes before she could be checked out and an action plan put into place.

I needed her to keep talking.

"I take it Katherine Johnson inspired you to get all your degrees in math?"

Her eyes fluttered shut. I knew she was tired, but that wasn't my worry.

Blood stained the bottom of the gurney.

Bleeding after childbirth was normal, but that was a lot of blood...

"Math is constant. It follows the rules. It's consistent in a world that rarely is. I guess... I guess it makes sense to me when nothing else does."

I laughed softly, trying to keep the tone light as I looked out the back windows.

We were close.

"No surprises." I gently laid my hand over Beth's and cradled Kat's head. "Not like this pretty girl."

"Shane—" her voice was a whisper as we came to a screeching halt beneath the ambulance entrance.

The emergency department doors flew open as doctors and nurses piled out with a bassinet and gurney in tow.

My heart ramped up to a critical crescendo, and my adrenaline roared. Something was wrong, and I didn't know what. "Talk to me, Beth. Stay with me."

A burst of light flooded the back as Missy ripped open the doors. "Shit," she swore when she saw the bright red stain growing bigger and bigger beneath Beth.

"She's hemorrhaging!" I shouted as I released the brakes on the gurney and heaved it out of the back.

"Beth," Missy said, alarmed as she scooped Kat out of Beth's arms and passed her down to a waiting nurse.

Beth's mossy eyes opened a peep and then closed again. "Shane."

"Let's get her to the back," a woman in a white coat snapped. Her ID badge read *Benoit*—Beth's obstetrician.

"I don't feel good," Beth said listlessly.

The bright overhead lights of the hospital seared my eyes, but something about the astringent smell of industrial cleaner and antiseptic steadied my heart.

"We're at the hospital," I said as I pushed the gurney inside. "They're gonna check out what's going on while Kat gets looked over."

The adrenaline from realizing her baby was no longer in her arms was enough to bring her back. Panic filled her voice. "Where—where is she? Where's my baby?"

"There's a team taking care of her right now," I reassured her. "As soon as we know you're good, she'll be with you. I promise."

"I can't—I need her," she cried, looking up at me. "Please don't let her go."

"Beth, they've gotta check her out. We need to know that she's okay. You need help, too."

Tears rolled down her cheeks. "Please stay—" her voice faded as she lulled in and out of consciousness. "Stay with her."

"She's crashing!" one of the nurses called out as the gurney was ripped out of my grip.

I stood in the middle of the busy hall as I watched Beth be whisked away, and felt like a piece of me was going with her.

I FOUND myself walking through the crowded nursery as a nurse slapped a wristband on my arm and a label tag on my chest, partially obscuring the station logo that was stitched on my polo.

Security guards and a very pissed-off looking nurse stood watch at the desk right outside.

"Any news?" I asked the nurse—Lindsay—as she guided me back to a bassinet that held Beth's screaming daughter.

"Not yet, but I'll keep you updated if I hear anything," she said before turning to peer down at the now-clean baby girl. She was wrapped in a white swaddle with blue and pink stripes. A hat in soft pink had been fitted over her head. "Hey there, cutie. Look who's here to see you." She reached in and lifted Kat into her arms. "It's your hero."

"She's okay, though. Right?"

"She's perfect. A little time under the bili lights and she was good to go." Lindsay looked up at me and batted her eyes. "I can't believe you delivered her. You did such a good job." Her words were nice, but the tone indicated some ulterior motives of the romantic variety.

Kat being okay wasn't good enough. Not when there was still no news on Beth's condition.

Lindsay deposited a wailing Kat into my arms. "I'll be right outside if you need anything."

Shit. I shifted awkwardly as Kat screamed her little head off. I'd never actually held a baby for more than a second before. She was small and tried her best to fight her way out of the burrito wrap they'd tucked her in.

Maybe I should just put her down and let the nurses do their thing. They knew how to hold babies, right?

Get your shit together, dude. It's a fucking baby. Not an armed combatant.

Then again, I'd take on a dozen military-aged males over the old bat eyeing me suspiciously from the desk.

She must have sensed my uncertainty. With a huff, she lumbered out from around the nurses' station and plodded in.

"Little one's got a real set'a lungs, don't she?" Patty—as her name badge read—said.

I cracked a slight smile. "Got an attitude like her momma."

If Kat was going to be anything like her mother, Beth was going to have her hands full. Then again, I loved Beth's spunk, so who was I to judge?

Patty held her hands out. "Give 'er to me and git your shirt off, Dad. Skin-to-skin will get her to calm down."

Dad? "Oh—I'm... I'm not..."

But Patty already had Kat in her arms. "Don't be shy. Nothin' I ain't seen before."

Kat's cries only got louder. *If that was even possible.*

What the hell... Might as well.

I unclipped my radio from my shoulder and snapped it on my belt before untucking my polo and pulling it over my head.

Patty let out a whistle. "Whoo—wee." She looked down at Kat. "Your daddy's a looker."

"I'm not her dad," I finally croaked out.

Patty unwrapped the little burrito and put a squirming pink baby back in my arms. "Mom requested for you to be up here, right?"

"Yeah, we are, uh... We're friends. I'm on with the Falls Creek Fire and Rescue. Beth—uh—*the mom*—called 911 when she was in labor."

"Got that much from the gossip going around. Don't matter much to me if you're blood or not. This right here—

this makes you Dad in my book." She unfurled the swaddle. "Get her up on that real nice chest of yours." She cocked her head to a chair that was pushed into the corner before draping the blanket back over my chest and shoulder to keep Kat warm. "Pop a squat if you need to."

Holding Kat against my chest was slightly awkward. I didn't have the cadence of cradling a baby quite right.

"Babies can smell fear," Patty called as she sauntered out.

Kat definitely sensed mine, but after another thirty seconds of screaming her little blonde head off, she quieted down and went right to sleep.

I shifted my weight between my feet, gently bouncing Kat as she snoozed peacefully.

What that kind of blissfully unaware sleep felt like, I would never know.

My phone vibrated in my pocket. Carefully, I sat and shifted little seven-pound Kat into one arm and fished it out of my pocket, quickly reading the text.

It was Missy letting me know that she was taking her sweet time charting and documenting everything. On a normal shift with severe weather, limited resources, and a full moon, we'd try our hardest to get back in service.

But these weren't normal circumstances.

On a normal shift, I wouldn't be doing skin-to-skin with the baby I'd delivered while the mom—the woman I'd been lusting after for a damn year—was receiving critical medical care. I wouldn't have a veteran nurse calling me "dad."

I wouldn't be liking it.

Kat's gentle breathing slowed my heart rate. She made soft suckling noises as she rooted around, but she was out of luck with me. Patty poked her head back in and gave me a thumbs up paired with a frown.

Eh, I'd take it.

I closed my eyes and rocked side-to-side as Beth's baby girl snuggled against my chest. The back of her head fit perfectly in my palm.

My mind slowed, and I lost track of time. The peace was unexpected.

The next thing I knew, Lindsay the nurse crept in. "They're bringing Ms. Hale up if you want to stand by the window. Once they get her settled in her room, I'll check the baby out of the nursery and take her to the room, too."

My heart hung in my throat. A whoosh of air escaped my lungs all at once. I was stunned and grateful and in awe all at once. I'd overthink everything I possibly did wrong later. For right now, Beth was okay and that was all that mattered.

I carefully made my way through the rows of bassinets and moved toward the window, acutely aware of the watchful nursing staff probably judging the way I held Kat. *Or judging whatever the hell this situation was.*

But whatever it was felt right.

I heard the faint rumble of a hospital bed rolling down the hall. As it grew closer and closer, my heart seized.

Beth was pale, but sitting up against the inclined bed. The transport team slowed in front of the nursery, and I stepped up to the window.

As soon as she saw me, Beth's eyes went glassy. I turned so she could get a look at Kat's little face as she snoozed.

Beth pressed her fingertips to her lips as tears rolled down her cheeks. She reached out and touched the glass. I found Kat's little hand curled in a fist and let it peek out of the blanket to return the gesture.

"I'll take her now," Lindsay said as she scooped her up, swaddled her faster than a Taco Bell employee could wrap a burrito, and put her in the bassinet. "You can walk with me if you'd like."

I took my time putting my shirt back on, then waited outside of Beth's room to give her a few minutes alone with Kat.

It had been a hell of a day for both of them.

I barely had the courage to knock. The gentle tap I rapped on the door might as well have been a gunshot as it echoed through the quiet hall.

"Come in."

Beth's summons was enough to get me moving. On smooth, silent feet I slipped inside and closed the door behind me.

A half-smile worked its way up my mouth when I saw her resting with Kat in her arms. Her hair had been neatly braided, and her color was slowly starting to come back.

I shoved my hands in my pockets as I sided up to the bed. "How you feeling, Mama?"

Her lip trembled when she looked up at me.

I carefully lowered onto the edge of the bed and cupped her cheek without a moment of hesitation. "Hey—" I wiped a tear away with my thumb "—today's a good day, Dimples."

"Thank you," she whispered through a trembling breath. "If you hadn't shown up..."

"Just doing my job."

"I mean it, Shane."

And there was the guilt. What could I have done differently? Was I not prepared enough? Was there more training I needed? More knowledge?

"Did they tell you what happened?" she asked softly as she looked down at Kat.

"No. I, uh—I stayed with Kat."

Beth nodded. "I hemorrhaged, but I think you know that part." She let out a tired sigh. "My uterus didn't contract the way it was supposed to after she was born so the bleeding didn't stop. Apparently, it's not uncommon, but most people are at a hospital when it happens." Her voice softened to a near-whisper. "I got lucky that I was with you and not still at home trying to ride it out."

I swallowed the knot in my throat. "I'm sorry I couldn't do more."

"You did everything."

"Are you okay now?"

She tipped her head back against a poor excuse for a pillow and closed her eyes. "A blood transfusion and a cocktail of drugs later, yeah."

I swore under my breath.

"Thank you for staying with her," Beth said solemnly. She swallowed and added, "You didn't have to do that."

"You asked me to."

On a day that should have been filled with joy, there was an incredible sadness in her eyes. "I just wanted her to be safe."

"I'm a man of my word. I told you that you wouldn't have to go through it alone."

"The nurse told me that she wouldn't stop crying until you held her."

I shrugged it off, but Beth didn't let it go.

"You're her hero." She looked up and met my eyes. "You're mine, too."

I leaned in and gave her a half-hug, careful not to crush Kat between us. "I'm so fucking proud of you, Mama."

Beth used her free hand to wipe her eyes as she let out a tired laugh. "Everyone keeps calling me that. I don't think it's sunk in yet." Cautiously, she added, "I don't know how I imagined this moment…" She looked down at Kat. "Or how it would really feel to hold her. I still can't really wrap my head around the fact that I have a daughter. It feels like I'm living outside of my body or something. Maybe I should have found out the gender so I could have had months to mentally bond with her."

"You did exactly the right things. You know why?"

Beth shook her head.

"Because she's here. And you're still here. And that fucking means something. You made the choices that were best for both of you."

A whisper of a smile painted her lips. "Thank you."

There was another knock at the door. Beth didn't even get a chance to acknowledge it before Austin came barreling in, still wearing his turnout gear.

"Beth—"

"Shh!" she snapped.

Austin's eyes went wide when he took in the scene of a sleeping Kat cuddled up against Beth's chest. "Holy shit."

"Don't think you're supposed to swear in front of a kid," I noted.

Beth cut her eyes at me. "You swore in front of her. *A lot.*"

"Holy shit," Austin said again as his heavy boots clomped against the tile floor. "We got called out to a structure fire. Once we had it contained, dispatch got a hold of Chief and said that you were in the hospital." He knelt beside the bed and stared at Kat in awe. "Not that you had—" he choked up at the sight of the pink bonnet "—a baby girl." Austin swore again as he wiped his eyes.

"Technically that happened at the house. This is your niece, Katherine," she said. "We've been calling her Kat."

I liked being a part of that "we" more than I should have.

While Austin hurried to the sink to wash and sanitize his hands, I caught Beth's attention. "Looks like you're in good hands, so I'm gonna go. Gotta get back to the station. Missy may have fallen asleep in the EMS lounge."

She nodded quickly and reached for my hand. "I'm sorry I kept you."

"You can keep me anytime, Dimples."

5

BETH

Everything sucked.

My house was a disaster zone. My front door was constantly opening and closing. Every part of my body hurt. On top of it all, I hadn't slept in three days and my body odor reeked like stale popcorn and pennies.

What I wouldn't give to go back to the hospital where I had nurses to kick people out if I wanted to be alone.

I had been looking forward to a quiet first day home to try and get my footing as a mom. That plan went out the window when Austin pulled up to my townhouse with Kat and me in tow, and the entire parking lot was full.

I cowered in the corner of the couch while Gran Fletcher and a hoard of little old ladies doted on Kat as she slept in the pull-up bassinet next to me.

Baby paraphernalia was strewn about. Something sizzled on the stove, but the smell of it was making me nauseous.

I really needed to pee but that would include spritzing my shredded lady bits with a plastic bottle and reapplying the puppy pad the nurse promised me was totally normal to wear in the sexiest mesh underwear known to man.

Ms. Sepideh—the owner of the bed and breakfast just outside of town and the nicest lady around—reached for Kat and I nearly snapped her arm off her body.

I wanted to scream at everyone to get the fuck out, and I didn't know how much willpower I had left to fight off the intrusive thoughts that made me want to rage like Godzilla.

What the fuck was wrong with me?

I didn't want to hold my baby, but I sure as hell didn't want anyone else to touch her either.

Even my mom—who came up from the coast early to stay with me so I'd have help—risked my wrath every time she picked up Kat to rock her.

"You should be sleeping when the baby sleeps, ya know," Gran Fletcher touted. "It's important that you get your rest."

I could if you left. But instead of saying that out loud, I smiled.

Bea Walker nodded, making the chain dangling from her bifocals rattle against the stack of necklaces around her throat. "And make sure you're eating healthy. Everything you put in your body goes right to this sweet girl. You want to give her only the best, right?"

I'm surviving on chicken salad and tortilla chips because living in three-hour nursing blocks doesn't leave time for things like eating whole meals. But I smiled.

"That's right," Louisa Mae from the salon chimed in. "And make sure she's getting enough tummy time. That's important."

Ah, yes. Tummy time. Or as my newborn probably thought, extraordinary rendition at Guantanamo.

But instead of telling them how hard putting Kat on her belly was, I smiled and nodded.

"Are you tracking her diapers? You need to be recording every time she goes number one and number two. And if it's a number two, write down what the consistency is like. It's important to have that information on hand," Marilyn Dreese chirped.

"And make sure you're taking care of yourself too. You'll always feel better if you shower and fix your hair and make your bed," Estelle Gould clipped. Her silver beehive bobbled back and forth. "You can't pour from an empty cup."

I didn't even have a cup at this point. I had a juice box that got run over by a bulldozer.

But I smiled because it was easier than speaking up.

"And don't come running every time she cries. Let her get it out of her system. That way she can self-soothe," Suzanne Stewart said.

Gran Fletcher hemmed and hawed at that. "Now what's the problem with giving a baby some love when they need it, huh?" She turned to me, as if she were the authority on the topic. "You snuggle this sweet girl as much as you can. Time flies and, before you know it, she won't want to snuggle anymore."

Great. Someday my daughter will hate me. Thanks for that, Gran.

"You're breastfeeding, right?" Tammy Lynn, the jewelry store owner asked. *Why the jewelry store owner needed to know anything about my boobs, I didn't know.* "You know what they say. Breast is—"

"Oh hush," Mavis Taylor snapped, cutting her off. "Formula is just as good. Besides, Kat here will be eating Cheerios off the floor like every other kid in the blink of an eye."

"Beth, honey, what do you think about taking Kat on a walk in the stroller in a little bit?" my mom asked over the melee. "Getting some fresh air will be good for you both."

Spontaneous anger boiled in my gut like a rumbling volcano as the noise level in my small house rose.

The doorbell rang.

That sound alone was enough to push me over the edge.

"I'll get it!" Austin called from the kitchen as he wormed his way through the crowd of old biddies.

"I'm going to go to the bathroom," I announced to everyone and no one. Carefully, I eased out of the junction of the couch and loped off in that direction. But instead of going in and taking care of business, I slipped out the sliding glass door that led to my back deck and let the blazing August sun sear my pale skin.

I looked over my shoulder and watched as the little old ladies cooed over Caroline when she made her way inside. That would give them a distraction for at least ninety seconds. She could dazzle them with the engagement ring my brother had just put on her finger.

I left the chaos behind me and stared at the treeline as I sat on the top step and rested my elbows on my knees.

Birdsongs were accompanied by the rustle of leaves as a gentle breeze whispered across the yard. I had just closed my eyes to rest against the handrail post when a deep male voice startled me.

"Hiding?"

I lurched upright and looked back. Shane stood with his hands in the pockets of his gym shorts. He was wearing a faded United States Navy t-shirt that was so tight I could nearly see his tattoos through the fabric.

I turned back to the trees. "Just needed a breather."

His laugh was low and soft, like he understood it completely. "It's a little intense in there."

"Yeah." I picked at my nail beds. They looked awful. Every single one was broken and brittle.

"I can come back later," Shane said.

I didn't really want him to go... I just wanted a break from the circus.

I scooted over and patted the spot beside me at the top of the stairs. He took the invitation and sat.

"How are you?" he asked.

"Fine, I guess. Kat's been sleeping a lot, so that's good. She had a checkup this morning and everything was fine." Taking a chance, I looked up at him and nearly got lost in his eyes. "Thanks to you."

"That's good," he said. "But I asked how *you* are."

"You don't let anything slip by, do you?" I said as I watched a squirrel bolt up and down the trees like it was on speed.

He grinned down at his Chuck Taylors. "Not much."

"I don't have to see my OBGYN until I'm six weeks postpartum. So, I guess that means I'm fine."

"Seems like a long time to wait to get checked out," he grumbled as he picked up a pine needle and twisted it between his fingers.

I shrugged. There was a long silence, and truthfully, I didn't know what to say.

I was exhausted. I felt like a stranger in my own body. Nothing mattered except getting Kat through her next three-hour cycle. *Suffer through feeding her. Change another diaper. Clean up the spit up. Put her on her belly and try to tolerate the screaming. Pick her up and attempt to settle her. Put her back to sleep.*

Wash. Rinse. Repeat.

"Sorry it's kind of crazy in there... It's been a revolving door since I came home from the hospital. I swear the doorbell's always ringing."

"I can go so you can get some rest," he said. "I picked up Caroline and brought her over. She's still a little skittish about driving after her accident. I don't think she'll give you much grief about hiding."

That was true. If anyone understood how shitty I felt right now, it was Caroline. *Not the hoard of grannies sporting rose-colored glasses.* I was over the moon for my brother and future sister-in-law, but I did not have the energy to express it.

"You and Caroline getting along a little better these days?" I asked.

He snapped the pine needle in half. "I guess."

"Is it weird for you? Now that the whole town knows?"

Secrets didn't stay secret for long in Falls Creek, but Shane had managed to keep a big one for nearly a decade.

When Caroline was a teenager, she was in kidney failure and needed a transplant. She didn't know it, but Shane had been her donor.

Austin had told me bits and pieces as to why he did it, but toed the line of not wanting to tell Shane's story himself.

Shane used to avoid Caroline, almost to the point of being rude. But lately, it seemed as if the two had been making an effort to get to know each other a little more.

It probably helped that Austin and Shane had been roommates for a few months, putting him in proximity of Caroline a little more often.

"I get more weird looks now than I used to," he said. "Still don't know how I feel about it all, but…"

I chanced a look up at him. "But?"

"I'm not the man I was when I went under the knife for her. And I think acknowledging that makes all the difference."

"I don't think I'm the same woman I was three days ago," I admitted to Shane and the trees.

Surprisingly, the weight of his arm wrapping around my shoulders didn't make me want to crawl out of my skin.

I had been poked and prodded in the hospital at all hours

of the night. A lactation consultant woke me up in the middle of the night when she squeezed my boob. *I screamed, and she rolled her eyes and told me I was overreacting because it was her "job."* Nurses and doctors would come in and announce what they were going to do to me, rather than asking.

So much for informed consent.

I thought it would get better when I was discharged, but I was wrong. Breastfeeding was hell, and I was starting to think that the "magical bonding experience" that everyone touted was complete bullshit.

I didn't feel safe in my own body.

But Shane didn't do that... He always asked; always waited as long as was safe to make sure that I was educated and comfortable with proceeding when he and Missy were getting me ready to push.

Maybe that's why I didn't shrink away when he put his arm around me.

"Is this weird?" I blurted out.

Shane looked at me curiously. "Why would it be weird?"

"You've seen a baby come out of my vagina and now we're sitting here like nothing happened."

His crack of laughter startled me. "It's my job, Dimples. When I'm on the clock, I don't think about stuff like that. I'm very, very good at compartmentalizing."

In my heart of hearts, I knew that. Austin often said the same thing when he told me about calls he responded to with the fire department.

But it was Shane... My heart always did something funny when he was near.

"I'm gonna say something and risk you slapping me across the face," Shane said.

I raised an eyebrow. "Fair warning—I don't slap. I punch. Just ask my brother. He's the one who taught me how."

"If I piss you off, I'll sit still and let you get one good swing in."

"Fine." I highly doubted that anything he could possibly say would make me rage more than the cacophony of opinions inside the sliding glass doors.

Shane steadied himself with a deep breath. "You look like shit."

I ... laughed? At least he didn't say I was glowing.

If I was glowing it was because of rage, not some mystical maternal enlightenment.

"Thank you," I said with an exasperated laugh. "I feel like shit."

His fingers were gentle as they grazed up and down my arm. "Be straight with me. How are you really doing?"

I stared down at my slippers and tried to bat away the tears that instantly welled up in my eyes.

"No one's asked me that except for you."

"What do you mean?"

"They ask about Kat. Which is great. But I feel like I'm drowning and instead of throwing me a life preserver, they're shouting at me from the boat about how cute she is."

Instead of treating me with kid gloves, he scooted behind me and wrapped both arms around me, offering his chest as a back rest.

I took it and closed my eyes.

"I've had some horrible thoughts," I admitted in a whisper. "Motherhood ... it's not what I thought it would be. It sucks. All these women are telling me how magical and fulfilling it is and I feel like the victim of false advertising."

He grunted in understanding. "Admitting that something sucks doesn't mean that it's not going to be worth it or that you're not going to want it in the long run. You're just in Hell Week right now."

"What do you mean?"

He took a long pause before his chest rumbled against my back as he spoke. "Hell Week is something you have to go through to become a Navy SEAL. There's no word that really describes it, but 'hell' is pretty damn close. You're sleep deprived. Sore. Sick. Injured. It's a battle against your body and your mind. I went into Hell Week wanting to be a SEAL more than anything. There's a point in the first forty-eight hours where you're wet and cold and depleted and you have to decide how much you really want it. And you know who fails first?"

"Who?"

"The guys who claim it's not that bad."

A small smile twinged at the corner of my mouth.

"Once you admit how shitty everything is and how much you hate it, you start to embrace it. You don't have the expectation of overcoming anymore. You just work through the next five minutes and make it through. Embrace the suck."

"Then what?"

He laughed softly behind the shell of my ear. "And then you chug a gallon of electrolytes, eat a whole pizza, and sleep. And eventually you can look back and be proud of yourself for making it through because it's what's on the other side of the suck that matters."

I let myself relax in his arms and close my eyes. "I knew you were in the military, but I didn't know you were a Navy SEAL. That's really cool."

"I don't talk about it much outside of my therapist's office."

This felt like therapy.

"So you're trained to withstand interrogation and torture, right?"

He nodded, but didn't make a comment about it.

"If I tell you something, will you promise not to tell anyone?"

He hesitated.

I looked up at him. "Shane?"

"I'll keep it to myself as long as—"

"—I'm not a danger to myself or others. I get it."

His voice was tender, yet stalwart. "I care about you."

With a deep breath, I said, "Sometimes I wonder if I kept the pregnancy out of spite—because I'm stubborn and wanted to stick it to Bradley—or because I actually wanted to be a mother. And that maybe this shit fest is the universe's way of punishing me for taking on something I wasn't ready for." I choked on the guilt. "It's a horrible thought, but it's there. I'm overwhelmed, but the minute anyone gets near Kat I want to rip their faces off. I need help, but I can't let myself accept it and I don't know why. Everyone talks about 'mommy brain'—being tired and forgetful—but I don't feel like that. I feel like I'm a completely different person. The intrusive thoughts are getting louder and louder."

"I know how fatal intrusive thoughts can be," he admitted. "So hear me when I say this: calling someone is always better than keeping it to yourself. Even if you don't think it's a big deal or you think it'll pass, tell someone. Get it out there." His hands found mine. "I'm a light sleeper. I will always hear my phone if you call. Day or night."

"Thanks," I said as I sniffed and wiped away a tear on my shoulder. "I just wish people would talk about how unfulfilling this is... Or maybe it's just me."

"The way I see it is that motherhood will never be the source of your value and meaning. You have always been precious and filled with purpose. You're going to be an incredible mom to Kat because you're an exceptional woman."

"Well, there you are!" my mother guffawed as she burst through the sliding door.

Shane jumped back and put some space between us as I quickly dabbed my eyes with my sleeve.

"I almost sent out a search party," she clucked. "Some new guests stopped by to see you, and it's almost time to feed Kat again."

The momentary reprieve was shattered, and it was back to wash, rinse, repeat.

6

SHANE

"Hey, hey, battle boo," I clipped into my phone as I trapped it between my ear and shoulder. I yanked open the cooler at the Falls Creek Filling Station and perused the row of energy drinks.

Cole Crowder's grizzled baritone filled the line. "What'chu doin', Hutch?"

That's how it was with him.

No hellos.

No pleasantries.

Just straight to the point.

It had been that way since day one of boot camp. Just two scrawny ass kids who thought they were going to be G.I fucking Joes.

Seventeen years later, we were no longer pipe hitters. He was the G.I. Joe of the private security sector, and I was the guy who responded to elderly women pretending to have fallen just to get a little male attention.

"Just got off duty." I grabbed a can of blue raspberry and snagged a Snickers bar before heading to the register. *Breakfast of champions.*

"You?" I asked.

"Fuckin' hate paperwork. I miss the sand."

"You and me both," I muttered.

Cole grunted. It was a primitive language that I spoke fluently.

"How's small-town life? You staying busy?"

"You staying busy" was his less-than-subtle code for "are you sober?"

I paid the cashier and headed out. "Yeah. You?"

"Same."

"A-firm."

It hadn't been immediate, but after I finally started therapy to deal with my demons, I called up Cole and told him about the dark place I was in.

It didn't matter that I hadn't talked to him once in the six months between getting discharged from the military and going under the knife for Caroline Tyree. He picked up on the first ring.

That was brotherhood. We were the only two of our brethren left.

"I'm heading out on a new job soon," Cole said. "Don't know how long I'll be downrange."

He worked for an elite executive protection firm out of Rhode Island called Keller & Associates. On more than one occasion, he had tried to recruit me to put my government-funded skills to use, but I couldn't go back to that life.

"You going alone or you got a team?"

"Nah, I got a strap to watch my six. New guy. Too fuckin' chatty for me, but I guess he's alright. I'd say he might require manual sedation, but he was an MMA fighter."

I laughed. "Don't kill him. You'll just have more paperwork."

Cole groaned and muttered something under his breath. "Gotta go. Keller's calling us in for a briefing."

"I look forward to your AAR."

There was a pause on the line, but Cole hadn't hung up yet. I dropped into the front seat of my new-to-me truck and shut the door.

"Anniversary's comin' around again," he said. His tone was almost morose.

Fuck if I didn't know it. "Like clockwork."

"Seven years."

"You goin' up to Virginia Beach?"

"Nah. They always hold it at a bar. Not my kind of place. You?"

"Keller will probably have me on a job."

I didn't blame him. Neither of us wanted to be the two survivors among a group of widows and families who had lost their loved ones in the blink of an eye. The surviving two who had to answer for why we made it out instead of their husbands. Their sons. Their dads.

Survivor's guilt was as deadly as a bullet.

"Holler if you need anything," Cole said. "Got your six, brother."

I ended the call, tossed my phone into the cup holder, and threw the truck into drive. But just as I was about to ease off the brake and hit the gas, a familiar sedan crept into the gas station parking lot.

My heart fucking skipped.

I could make out the silhouette of Kat's car seat wedged in the back. Hopefully, she had been compliant and easy for her mom over the last few days.

I hadn't heard a peep from Beth since the day I stopped by her house and sat with her on the deck.

I closed my eyes as the memory replayed of how good—how peaceful—it had felt to put my arms around her. I could still feel the pressure of her back as she reclined against my chest. She smelled like that shampoo that doesn't make babies cry.

I threw the gear shift back into park and hopped out. Beth had pulled up to a pump, cracked the windows to keep the inside from becoming a slow cooker on a hot August day, and was swiping her card on the pin pad.

"Dr. Hale," I said from a distance since I was pretty sure sneaking up on a momma bear was a bad idea.

Beth looked over her shoulder. There were distinct bags under her eyes and a still-damp spit-up stain on her t-shirt. "Oh—hey."

I peered in the back window at her sleeping baby. "How are my girls doing?"

Beth gave the backseat a quick glance. "Better now that she's not getting shots at the doctor's office."

I grimaced. "Poor thing."

The kiosk beeped, reminding Beth to select which kind of gas she wanted. She punched the pad for unleaded and reached for the pump.

"Let me," I said, wrapping my palm around the black gas pump handle. Our hands brushed. "I wouldn't be much of a gentleman if I let you pump your own gas. How much you want in?"

Beth didn't even argue with me. "Twenty bucks is fine."

I slid the nozzle into her gas tank and started the flow. "We keep meeting like this."

Instead of sitting in the shade of the driver's seat while I filled the tank, Beth leaned her hip against the passenger's side door. "What do you mean?"

"At the Filling Station."

The faintest of tired smiles flickered at the corner of her mouth. "Right... When you judged my coffee choices."

I took her in. The Beaufort Fire Department t-shirt she wore was a little big and had been tied off at the waist to draw it in, but it couldn't hide the seductive curve of her breasts. Her hair was in a knot on top of her head. The denim shorts on her legs were modest, but that didn't stop wicked thoughts from racing through my mind about prying those legs apart.

The stockpile of waning professionalism I had held on to since being called out to her house when she was in labor was nearly depleted.

Beth Hale was a goddamn MILF.

"And you?"

Her nose wrinkled. "What about me?"

"How are *you*?"

"Fine." But she looked away when she said it.

Beth was many things. She was vibrant. She was snarky. She was stubborn. She was brilliant.

But something as mediocre as 'fine,' she was not.

I watched as the digits racked up on the meter. "Bullshit."

Beth scoffed.

$19.81

$19.85

$19.90

I released the handle and gave it quick pulses to get it to twenty.

$19.92

$19.97

$19.98

One more quick pump and she'd be golden.

$20.01

She snorted under her breath. "I swear—it's like they make it impossible to finish filling it up on an even number because they know it'll drive the person crazy and they'll keep going to the next dollar. It's gotta be some kind of industry scam to sell more gas."

I chuckled. "I think you might be onto something, Dimples." I holstered the pump in the cradle and hit the button to print a receipt.

Beth snatched the paper when the machine spat it out, then yawned before anything else could come out of her mouth.

I eyed her cautiously. "You sure you're okay to drive?"

She waved me off dismissively. "I'm fine. I'm heading home right now."

"And I want to make sure you get all the way there and don't end up in a ditch because you fell asleep at the wheel." It came out a little harsher than I intended, but I got my point across.

"Thanks, *Austin*," she said with an eye roll.

I wasn't bothered in the slightest that she was using her brother's name to pick at me. Maybe I didn't really have as good of a reason to be, but I was just as protective of Beth as he was.

Before she gave birth, I wanted her.

After I watched her bring life into the world, there was no way I wasn't going to have her.

However long that took.

I was trained to be a patient man.

"I mean it," I said, my eyes flicking down to her mouth as I stepped closer.

She backed away. "I'm good to drive."

I tipped my head toward the Filling Station. "Need anything inside? I can run in for you or wait here while you go in so you don't have to get Kat out."

She shook her head. "Nah. These days, if it's not in a drive-through, I don't need it."

I nodded and took a step back to give her a little more space. "It was good to see you."

"You too," she clipped as she circled the hood.

"Hey—" I called out before she could get in and drive away. "Will you text me when you get home? Just so I know you made it back."

"I—uh—" she stammered for a moment, blinking at me. "Okay."

I walked around and opened the driver's side door for her.

She eyed me suspiciously like she didn't trust even the smallest of gestures. I waited as she slid in behind the wheel and clicked her seatbelt.

She caught my gaze once more and found me with a smile on my face like a damn fool. I gave her a polite chin tip and backed away. "You look real pretty today, Mama."

I waited for her text to arrive all morning.

By lunch time I was half-tempted to drive over to Beth's just to see with my own eyes that she was inside and safe.

The other half of me was distinctly aware that I couldn't push Beth into anything. Not right now while she was recovering and finding her way as a new mom.

Did she even remember that she was supposed to be recovering?

If I had gone through what I witnessed her soldier through on her living room floor, I'd be laid up for six months and require a round-the-clock butler, maid, chef, and chauffeur.

Instead of bothering her, I headed to the American Legion Post and grabbed the bags of groceries out of the back of my truck.

Electricity buzzed into the fluorescent lights as I flipped the switch. The meeting space was musty, but clean.

What Saves Us

I sure as hell didn't mind.

Some days this place felt more like home than my own house did.

This was the place where family happened. Where demons were exorcized. Where tired combatants could lay their emotional armor down.

Maybe I needed it more than they did.

I went through the motions of pulling out stacks of metal folding chairs and setting them up in a circle. I hauled out six-foot tables and wiped them down with a damp paper towel before plugging in the coffee maker that was decades past its prime.

I didn't run a formal AA group or a veteran's group, per se. It was mostly men and women who, like me, struggled with reintegrating into civilian life after leaving the service.

We had everyone from Vietnam vets all the way up to a kid who couldn't even buy a beer yet, but had lost his leg overseas.

Sometimes my guilt ate at me. I held a job. Owned a house. Had friends. I could still function daily the same way I had when I was in the Teams. I had all of my extremities. I was in fairly good health. I managed the craving for alcohol that still crept up from time to time.

Who was I to complain? My visible scars weren't as bad as his.

Right?

My phone finally buzzed as I unloaded a fruit and veggie tray and unboxed the bakery container of assorted cookies.

BETH

Home.

Just the sight of her name had me forgetting everything.

> **SHANE**
> Thanks for letting me know. Get some rest.

> **BETH**
> My mom is insisting we craft to get me back to doing "normal activities." If I could hot glue gun my eyelids shut, I would.

> **SHANE**
> Aren't you supposed to sleep when the baby sleeps?

> **BETH**
> I am. But I'm not sure it's a possibility since Kat has decided she'll never go to bed again. I swear she's on a sleep strike.

> **SHANE**
> Want me to come give you a break?

> **BETH**
> It's okay. Austin and Caroline are over here too.

Cars pulled into the gravel lot outside, signaling the beginning of the ninety minutes I spent every week making small talk about everything that fucked me up.

I hated it, but it was necessary.

Chasing my darkness with liquor never solved anything. Having a community around me to speak the demons into the light—it actually helped a little.

With the refreshments set, I poured myself a fresh cup of coffee and texted Beth back.

> **SHANE**
> If you need someone to talk to or complain to you can call me.

BETH

I might be all talked out. I swear I'm going to throw myself a party when everyone finally leaves.

SHANE

I mean it, Dimples. Day or night.

BETH

I know.

7

BETH

"Okay, Mom. Undress baby all the way. Use this to wrap her up and then we'll bring her to the scale."

The nurse in cartoon-covered scrubs handed me an infant-size puppy pad and went back to the laptop she was click-clacking on.

"How many wet diapers and solid diapers a day?" she fired off.

I fumbled the snap closure on Kat's onesie. "Uh—" *Shit. I had it written down on my phone, but I couldn't remember the number off the top of my head.* "I can look it up when I'm—"

"How much and how often is she eating?"

"Every three hours," I said as I finally got the onesie off Kat's squirming body. *Every three miserable hours.*

Kat immediately protested the cold pediatrician's office air with a caterwauling scream.

The nurse rolled her eyes. "How much is she eating each time?"

I don't fucking know. My boobs don't come with measuring cup lines. I don't regurgitate it like a bird and measure it before I put it in her mouth.

I blinked back the warm pressure behind my eyes. "Um ... it usually takes about twenty minutes."

The nurse raised a judgmental eyebrow. "That's it?"

Dejected, I said, "That's usually how long it takes before I don't have any milk left."

Something putrid tickled my nose.

Oh no.

Kat looked up at me from the padded exam table, eyes twinkling as rippling explosions belched from her rear. The diaper strained as liquid poop in burnt yellow squeezed out the seams.

Why me? I was already overwhelmed. Why can't just one thing go right?

First it was Kat not sleeping all night. Then it was her not latching when I tried to breastfeed her. My poor nipples would never recover.

Nursing was painful at best. And with my "every moment is magical" mother under the same roof, I cried through twenty excruciating minutes in silence while my heart raced. I didn't want to hear her stories of how wonderful it had been for her. That only made me feel like more of a failure.

Then it was Kat screaming all the way to the pediatrician's office because she thought her car seat was the equivalent of the electric chair. I hadn't showered in over a week, and I could smell myself.

Nurse Ratched's judgmental evil eye for my lack of control over Kat's nuclear bowels and my inability to recall how many diapers I had changed was the cherry on top of the shit sundae.

Everything sucked.

"Well," she clipped, muttering under her breath. "At least we know she got *some* milk in her system."

I tore through my haphazard diaper bag for wipes, a plastic bag, and a fresh diaper while I choked down the inexplicable rage that made me want to throttle the woman for being a complete cunt.

"I'm sorry," I choked out as I snatched up a handful of wipes and cautiously peeled away the toxic diaper.

Oh God—it was everywhere. Up her back. Down her legs. In every skin roll and crevice.

I did the best I could to clean up Kat, but wipes were a far cry from the power washer I needed. After longer than the nurse's sour expression told me was necessary, Kat was finally in a fresh diaper.

The pile of wipes and the radioactive bomb of a soiled diaper were tied up in the little plastic grocery bag I carried around for this exact occasion. With one hand on Kat to keep her from wiggling off the exam table—*even though she literally couldn't turn over on her own*—I eyed the trashcan and grabbed the bag to toss it in.

"Nuh-uh," the nurse snapped and pointed her pen at the laminated sign over the trash can. It had one of those slashy circles with a cartoon dirty diaper in the middle.

Was she fucking kidding me?

I looked around. "Is there another trash can?"

"No," she snapped. "You'll have to dispose of it on your own." With a haughty look at her watch she huffed. "Are you ready to take your daughter to the scale now?"

I was just going to leave the bag on the exam table until I could sneak it into the trash when she wasn't looking, but her searing glare had me plopping it into my diaper bag. I attempted to semi-swaddle Kat with the puppy pad, but it wasn't quite big enough.

She cleared her throat. "Like I said the first time—diaper *off*. We want an accurate weight."

I wondered how much she would weigh, all chopped up and in a garbage bag.

I pulled the diaper off ... *again*... and ended up making the short walk from the exam room to the cradle scale, holding my daughter like she was a midnight snack clutched in a napkin.

Please don't pee. Please don't pee, I chanted mentally as I carefully laid Kat on the baby scale and waited for her weight to register.

As soon as I let her go, she screamed.

I cringed and gave apologetic looks to the other parents and kids milling about and the nurses hustling from room to room.

The scale beeped and Nurse Curmudgeon grunted at the number displayed as she recorded her weight. "Back to the exam room. Doc'll be with you when she gets to you. Leave the diaper off until the appointment is over."

Was she kidding? What was I supposed to do? Hold her in this plastic-backed tissue? It was freezing in here. The AC must've been on overdrive.

With my tail between my legs, I carried Kat back to the exam room and sat on the bench that was made for preschoolers—not grown adults. Thankfully, she had settled down and squirmed in silence.

I fished my nursing cover out of my bag and draped it over her like a blanket.

Shit. Should I be carrying around an extra blanket too? I already felt like a pack mule most days.

My stomach growled. I really should have eaten this morning, but I forgot. Again.

Fifteen minutes passed before I really started getting antsy.

Outside the exam room door, everything hustled and bustled. But inside, I felt like I was waiting for an executioner. Why didn't doctors stock gossip magazines in the rooms for the parents? A storybook about a hungry caterpillar wouldn't do me any good.

I was pretty sure the cardboard books were dripping with the flu and staph infections anyways. Who knew what snot-nosed, plague-stricken kid had been in here before us?

I grabbed my phone and tried to check my messages, but apparently I was in a concrete bunker without a single bar of service.

Checking for guest wifi—and—nothing.

I groaned as I tipped my head back against the wall and closed my eyes.

Ten more minutes passed.

Did they forget I was in here? Should I poke my head out?

I eased off the bench, then decided against it. I didn't want to be the mom who got labeled as "high maintenance."

Kat slept peacefully in my aching arms. For a seven-pound chunk, she tired out my muscles surprisingly fast.

The checkerboard tile floor caught my eye. *If a baby rolled off the exam table they'd—*

If I threw the baby in my arms across the room she'd—

Oh ... Oh God.

I choked down the bile that hung thick in my throat. The demented notion came out of nowhere, lodging in my brain like a fish hook.

I could hurt her.

I could do it.

Panic rushed across my skin like a tidal wave. I clutched Kat to my chest as tightly as I could.

I didn't want to hurt her. I would never—

I had no idea where those thoughts came from. The intrusive urges had been popping up like summer storms, dumping Biblical amounts of rain on an otherwise sunny day.

I felt like a stranger in my own mind.

Eying the carseat wedged in the corner, I contemplated putting her in there to wait for the doctor who seemed to be moving at a snail's pace. I needed Kat out of my arms before I did something irrational.

But she would squall if I put her in there...

I didn't have time to decide. The door opened and Dr. Heath strode in. Her smart slacks were a cheery yellow. The tucked-in blouse beneath her white coat was dotted with bumblebees.

"Good morning, mom," she said with a chipper smile as she secured her long hair with a claw clip.

She dropped down onto the rolling stool that had previously been occupied by the nurse who probably snuggled up at night to the dog that guarded the gates of hell.

"How are we doing this morning?" Her fingers raced across the laptop keys as she skimmed Kat's chart.

Kat went wide-eyed at the addition of a new visitor.

"Um—okay," I said as I shifted her in my arms.

"Good," she clipped as she stood and patted the exam table. "Let's get this sweet girl checked out so you can get her clothes back on."

It wasn't my first time taking Kat to the pediatrician. The first time had been right after I got out of the hospital. Given her birth circumstances, they had wanted to see her right away.

Kat was two weeks old now, and I still didn't know where to stand in the exam room while the doctor pushed on her belly, checked her heart and lungs, and assessed her eyes and ears.

"Everything looks normal, mom," Dr. Heath said as she

pulled off her gloves and tossed them in the forbidden trash can.

I hurried to get Kat back in her diaper before her goodwill ran out. Thankfully, getting the onesie back on was easier than taking it off.

Dr. Heath sat on the stool again and turned her back to me to look at the computer.

Cool. Cool. Okay. Nothing quite like feeling as if I was an inconvenience to a piece of machinery.

Digital charting was probably easier than paper, but a little face-to-face would have been nice.

"I'm looking at her growth chart and I have some concerns. It's totally normal for babies to lose some weight after they're born, but at this point we like to see the baby back at their birth weight. Kat is still shy of that benchmark."

I swallowed. "Okay?"

It would have been nice if she just offered a solution rather than presenting me with the problem. I didn't know what I needed to do differently. Wasn't that her job?

"Are you sure you're draining each breast during every feeding?" she prodded.

I looked down at Kat to keep from having to make eye contact with the doctor. "I think so. I tried to hand express after she was done, but I didn't get anything."

"Try to pump between feedings," she suggested. "It can help stimulate more milk production."

If there was anything I detested more than breastfeeding, it was pumping. The machine that my insurance company covered was awful. It was uncomfortable and anxiety-inducing. Watching pitiful droplets fall into the bottles as my body was literally vacuumed dry sent me into a nervous tailspin each time.

"And make sure you're eating and drinking enough," she said with a smile. "Remember—everything you put into your body goes straight to her." She pointed at Kat with a manicured nail.

No pressure or anything... Now I felt twice as guilty for the pizza rolls I had scarfed down last night. They were fast to make and had been the only thing that sounded good.

Dr. Heath grabbed a sheet of paper the color of khaki pants and scribbled down Kat's growth percentiles.

I loved numbers. They always made sense to me. But for the first time, I was afraid of them. The numbers on that page labeled me as a failure.

Unfit.

"I want to see Kat back in here next week, and I'd like to see if we can put some weight on her before taking drastic measures."

My brows furrowed. "Drastic measures?"

Her smile was probably meant to be comforting, but it was a far cry from it. "Call me old school, but I like to exhaust every *natural* resource before recommending formula feeding. You do want the best for your child, *right?*"

Was nursing really the best thing for her if it put me in physical pain? Was it the best thing if I couldn't breathe every time I neared the nursery to feed her? Was it the best thing if it made me dread picking up my child?

Her thinking seemed more archaic than "old school," but I was too tired to question it.

"One last thing," Dr. Heath said, crushing my dreams of escaping this office with some shred of dignity. "I took a look at the postpartum screening you completed in the waiting room." She plucked a stack of brochures out of a clear caddy.

That *thing*... It had been nearly impossible to juggle a newborn and answer questions about Kat's home situation, my finances, and headspace on a tablet.

I would never have admitted it out loud, but it was the

kind of quiz where I chose the right answers, not the truthful answers.

"Everything seems fine. There were a few flags, but honestly, it's normal to feel out of sorts with all the life changes and your hormonal imbalance. If you have any concerning thoughts, make sure you find someone to talk to."

Her tone very decisively communicated that she was not that someone.

"The transition can be hard and you are a single mom." Her pursed lips dripped with condescension. "And I see that we have a protective order against the father?"

Sperm donor. Calling him anything else was a disservice to fathers everywhere.

Momentarily, I regretted informing the front office about the restraining order.

But what if Bradley showed up and tried to get Kat's medical information? I was the only person authorized to access that information, but I knew him. I knew how persuasive he could be.

"Yes," I said, a little more sure of myself.

There was a list a mile long of all the things I had already done wrong when it came to motherhood, but protecting Kat from my unhinged baby daddy wasn't on the list.

"He threatened me while I was pregnant, and I'm not taking any chances."

Without another word on the subject, she handed over the trio of pamphlets. "If you feel like you need it, here's some information on support groups in the area. It's always good to have a community."

Community. Right. A place where picture-perfect moms sat in a circle and talked about how fucking magical everything was.

No thanks. That was not the place for a mom who just had

just wondered what kind of a sound it would make if she threw her child across the room.

What was wrong with me?

―――――

APPARENTLY BABIES SLEEP incredibly well after blowing up a diaper with a dump as powerful as a nuke. I took advantage of Kat sleeping soundly in the backseat—for once—and treated myself to chicken tenders from a drive-through window on my way home.

At least I was eating something.

But the time I had wolfed down two out of four tenders, I was staring at the façade of my townhouse without a single desire to walk in.

I could just disappear. Kat would be better off.

Austin was total dad material. Caroline was trained to handle children. He and Caroline would make great parents. They could take care of Kat better than I could.

I should just disappear.

I jumped when Stanley opened his front door and Arthur came waddling out. He lifted his hand in a polite wave.

The clock told me that Kat would need to be fed again soon. Time to go back to my prison.

8

SHANE

"Thirty seconds," Austin bellowed as he strode between the lines of battle ropes that were slapping the ground.

Everything burned as I whipped the ropes in time with Callum, who was five feet away.

A few times a week, the three of us met up to work out. For years, it had been just Callum and I. Keeping my body active was the best way to get my mind to stay quiet.

When Beth found out she was pregnant, her brother—Austin—moved from their hometown on the coast to Falls Creek to be with her.

He had taken a job with the fire department, found himself a girl, and fallen in love. In the midst of that, he joined our workout group.

At first I thought it would be great. Before he moved out here, Austin helped run a gym in his free time. He knew his stuff.

Now, I regretted everything.

Sweat dripped from my hair and stung my eyes as I counted down the last thirty seconds.

Yeah, he definitely lied about thirty seconds.

Richard, the asshole tomcat that had adopted me when I moved in, stared at me from the porch steps with haughty judgment in his feline eyes.

Sixty seconds later, Austin called the time. My arms went limp and I dropped my ropes.

Callum slumped over and braced his hands on his knees. "Goddamn—I hate that."

"Nope. Walk it off," Austin said as he pointed to the sidewalk that stretched in front of my house. The hellish temperatures of summer were beginning to dwindle.

It wouldn't last. The heat always came back. This was what I called "fake fall." But I wasn't about to look the gift horse in the mouth.

Callum and I loped toward the cement.

Austin caught up. His bulky frame took up so much of the sidewalk that he ran in front of us.

"Thought we were walking it off," Callum wheezed.

"Come on, Fletcher," Austin said over his shoulder. "You can do better than that."

Callum and I shot daggers out of our eyes at Austin's back. Across the street, lawn chairs lined the road.

Apparently, the three of us provided better entertainment than daytime soaps.

Brenda Brass, Estelle Gould, Marian Boyd, and Martha Mable were passing a bottle of wine between them. They stopped their coffee mug day drinking to wolf whistle as we passed.

The three of us waved before slowing up at the end of the block. Even though it was a breezy eighty degrees today, I regretted taking my shirt off. Rivulets of sweat streamed down my forehead. I needed something to wipe it away.

It was recent that I had started working out without a shirt on.

For years, I had made a point to never be seen without one. Not while working out and not while on duty at the station. I even kept a clean shirt by my front door just in case I had spontaneous visitors. I didn't want to risk anyone seeing my transplant scars and putting two and two together that I was Caroline's kidney donor.

But that cat was out of the bag. Everyone knew.

There were still whispers behind my back and curious looks, but most of the audible gossip died down as soon as the town saw Caroline and I hanging out in public. I was best friends with her fiancé, and I definitely wasn't keeping my feelings for her future sister-in-law a secret.

"Cool down and walk back to the house," Austin ordered.

"I hate you so fuckin' much, dude," I croaked.

Austin was the first to pass the shrubs that bracketed Brenda's single-story ranch. The ladies took last-minute sips from their coffee mugs full of wine before holding up small dry erase boards with—

Were they giving us scores?

Austin got a string of nines as he walked by.

Callum was a few strides behind him.

The grannies quickly erased the scores before scribbling new ones and holding them up.

Nines again. *Fuckin' Creekers...*

Fully expecting the same score, I closed the gap and caught up to Callum.

Ten. Ten. Ten. Ten.

Well, I'll be damned. That put a smile on my face.

"Hold on," Austin said, coming to a halt in front of the cluster of muu-muu wearing mayhem. "Why'd Hutch get a ten, and Fletch and I only got nines?"

Martha was the first to pipe up. "Hutchins has his shirt off." She gave me a coy smile and a gnarled-fingered wave.

I grinned and winked at her.

Not wanting to be left out, Austin grabbed the bottom of his sweat-soaked t-shirt and yanked it off.

The ladies catcalled at him and corrected the scores on their boards, giving him tens.

Callum looked down at his bare chest, then back up. He picked Estelle Gould out of the bunch. "What the hell, Stella? Why'd I get docked a point?"

She snorted. "You pulled me over the other day and gave me a ticket."

He huffed and rested his hands on his hips. "You were doing fifty-five in a school zone."

"That's hearsay."

Callum rolled his eyes. "I clocked you on the Lidar and it's on my body cam and my dash cam."

"Circumstantial evidence," she touted. Someone had been watching too much *Law & Order*.

"You almost hit a crossing guard who was telling you to stop."

That had Estelle coming out of her lawn chair. Wine sloshed out of her coffee mug.

But Callum held his hand up, silently telling her to stay where he was. "I'm off duty. Take it up with the judge and let me have my eighteen hours of peace before I have to deal with you again."

Estelle snatched up her whiteboard and erased the "1" she had written for Austin's updated ten, giving Callum a big, fat zero.

They called out a chorus of boos as he snickered and jogged back to the house.

"Did you just start a feud with a little old lady?" Austin said as we wandered up the driveway.

Callum smirked. "Gotta do something to keep them on their toes. Otherwise they get bored and that's *way* worse."

A phone rang and we looked at each other like the Three Stooges. Realizing it was his, Austin jogged to his truck and plucked it off the hood.

"Hello?" He paused for a moment, his face going from neutral to concerned. "Yeah ... Yeah. I'll be over in a minute. Need me to pick anything up on the way?" Another pause. "Okay. Okay—hey—I got it. I'll be there. I'm leaving Shane's right now."

He pocketed his phone and pulled his shirt back on.

"Is Caroline okay?" Callum asked. The big grump had a soft spot for Austin's fiancé. Hell, I did too. We were all protective of her.

"Not Caroline. That was Beth."

My adrenaline went through the roof. *Was she okay? Was the baby okay?*

"What's wrong?" I asked.

He chuckled. "Our mom is driving her crazy. Beth wants me to get her out of the house for a bit so she can have some peace and quiet." He tossed his phone into his truck. "Her words were—and I quote—'get her out of the house or dig her grave.'"

The hair on the back of my neck stood up. It was the same heightened sense I used to get before my team would spin up for an op.

I was already thinking up every excuse I could get away with to go over there and check on her. "Does she need help?"

Austin sighed as Callum sided up to us. "I dunno. I think it's just been a hard transition for her. Knowing Beth, she's just worried about finishing the classes she's still taking on top of teaching next semester once her maternity leave is over."

I knew Beth loved her job, but my mind went back to the

conversation she and I had on her back deck—when she admitted how hard the transition to motherhood had been.

Austin peeled out to get his mother out of Beth's house, and Callum left to take care of some wedding plans with his fiancé, Layla.

I contemplated going on a run. Maybe I could head over there and use the excuse that I was in the neighborhood. The three of us used to run the length of her winding subdivision. It was shaded and there was little traffic. It wouldn't be out of the ordinary…

But just the thought of another hour of exercise had my muscles singing after the gruesome workout Austin put us through.

Fuck it. I didn't need an excuse. I needed Beth to believe me when I said I'd be there for her.

I took a quick shower, changed, and hopped in my truck with water still dripping from my skin.

The drive to Beth's was quick and, when I arrived, Austin's truck was nowhere to be found.

I jogged up the steps and thought twice about ringing the doorbell. I didn't want to wake Kat or Beth if they were asleep.

But the crying baby on the other side of the door told me that it wasn't likely that either one of them was doing much sleeping.

I took a chance and rang the doorbell.

Thundering footsteps were the immediate answer. The door wasn't even all the way open when Beth shrieked, "Oh my god. *What now?*"

Her face was damp with tears, and her normal glowing skin was red with fury. It matched Kat's as she screamed in Beth's arms.

Beth's eyes went wide when she saw me. "I—I'm sorry. I thought you were my mom coming back again."

I raised my eyebrows. "Again?"

She looked away, blinking back tears. "Austin came and took her out, and just when I thought I had Kat down to nap, she came back because she forgot her sunglasses and it woke her up, and now she won't stop crying, and I can't—"

The nurse's words from the hospital echoed in my mind. Babies could smell fear, and Beth was terrified.

"Can I give you a break?" I asked over Kat's wailing.

She looked completely confused. "What?"

I didn't want to touch Kat yet. It would be weird to reach for someone's child without their expressed consent.

I nodded at her baby and gave Beth a smile. "Is it weird that I miss her? I think she and I bonded while we waited for you at the hospital. I just wanted to check in on my girls." I tried to keep my tone light, but whatever I had said made Beth's lip quiver.

She looked over her shoulder, into the living room. "The house is a mess. I—I'm not really prepared for company."

"I don't care about that."

"I do," she whispered.

I took a step forward and cupped her cheek. "Tell me what you need."

She looked up at me with pools in her eyes. Her lip trembled. "I can't do this." She looked down at Kat. "I'm not made for this. Whatever gene creates capable mothers definitely skipped me."

"I don't believe that for a second. Look at everything you've already done for her. You got a protection order in place. You gave birth in the middle of a storm. Everything changed for you in a matter of minutes and you haven't stopped once to take care of yourself because you *are* being a capable mother to her. Give yourself a little grace, Dimples."

She couldn't put her arms around me with Kat cradled up

against her chest. Instead, Beth leaned forward and rested her forehead on my shoulder. "Thanks. I really needed to hear that."

"I know you're tired. Is it okay with you if I hold Kat for a while so you can catch up on sleep? I'd like to."

Beth eyed her whimpering daughter warily. "She's just going to cry the whole time."

"Will it help convince you if I tell you that I have partial hearing loss so it won't bother me in the slightest?"

"Do you really?"

"You can thank some IEDs in the Middle East for that."

The faintest smile twitched at the corner of her mouth. "I think she's louder than a bomb."

I winked. "I wouldn't be able to make an accurate comparison nowadays."

She leaned into me, but hesitated.

I wanted to hold Beth more than I wanted to hold Kat. Though, truthfully, I wanted to hold them both. But right now I knew that she needed a break more than romance.

Carefully, Beth eased Kat into my arms and stepped back so that I could walk inside.

The house wasn't the disaster Beth described, but baby paraphernalia was everywhere.

Blankets and toys littered the floor. A breast pump and bottles sat on the coffee table. A bassinet was pushed up to the couch that was covered in a pile of tiny clothes and burp rags that needed to be folded. A changing table pad was on the floor beside a package of diapers.

I cradled Kat vertically against my chest as we walked inside. Beth closed and locked the door, then lingered in place. "Don't say I didn't warn you."

"I've got it. Go rest."

"I just need like—five minutes."

Kat's ear-splitting cries began to fade to soft whimpers.

"If you don't rest for at least an hour, I'm sending you back to your room to try again."

Her eyes widened.

"And shower. A hot one. Do all the girly shit women do in there and relax." I glanced at the G-Shock watch on my wrist. "Two hours. If you need something out here, text me and I'll bring it to you."

Reluctantly, Beth retreated to her bedroom and closed the door.

I looked at Kat, who was sizing me up. "Alright, tadpole. How hard are you gonna make this on me?"

9

BETH

Everything was quiet.

I rolled over beneath layers of blankets and nuzzled back into my pillow.

Wait.

Why was it quiet?

I stretched and curled my toes as the faint sound of dishes in the kitchen sink drifted in through my closed bedroom door.

Right. Shane was here.

I wanted to question why he had shown up, but his kind of break was the one I needed. Not my mom's kind of chipper "get back on your feet" break where she wanted me to craft with her while Kat did tummy time.

It was like trying to perform surgery while the patient was screaming from no anesthesia.

Insanity.

I felt around my pillow and found my phone, quickly glancing at the time.

Shit.

Oh fuck.

Shane gave me two hours to rest and shower, and it had been three and a half.

Dammit!

I whipped the bedding back and groaned as soon as I sat up. My boobs felt like concrete, making my entire chest hurt.

I missed Kat's feeding window.

Guilt strangled me as I threw a pair of sweatpants over the hospital-issue mesh underwear I was still in, and hurried out.

I stopped dead in my tracks.

Shane—wearing the backpack baby carrier I hadn't even taken the tags off of yet—was washing a bottle in the sink while Kat slept peacefully against his chest. A soft country tune played from his phone as he rocked between his feet.

He looked over his shoulder and smiled when he spotted me lurking. "Hey, Mama." His voice was a gravelly whisper that sent shivers up my spine.

"I'm sorry I overslept. I usually wake up when I need to feed her and I just ... didn't."

"That's okay," he said as he put the bottles in the dish drainer and grabbed the hand towel. Shane dried his hands before turning the music down on his phone. "I think she likes Chris Stapleton."

"She comes by it honestly."

Shane's smile stretched wide across his face. "My Disney repertoire didn't do it for her, but "Broken Halos" got her right to sleep." His soft gaze focused on me. "How'd you sleep?"

The easy demeanor he carried released some of the tension I was holding in my shoulders.

"Good," I said. "Really ... Really good. I don't think I've slept like that since before I got pregnant."

"I bet," he said as he strode over on smooth feet and turned so that I could get a peek at Kat's sleeping face. She looked so comfortable all snuggled up against Shane's muscular chest.

I was jealous of a baby.

"We hung out for a bit. Talked about life. She gave me some good advice on who to vote for in the next election." Shane smiled down at Kat's tufts of warm blonde hair. "She got fussy about an hour ago so I changed her and warmed up some of the milk you had in those little plastic baggies in the freezer." He looked up. "I hope that was okay. I didn't want to wake you to ask, so I Googled how to prepare it."

I stood, shell-shocked. "You—you what?"

He shrugged. "I just searched how to warm up the milk. She didn't seem to mind. Drank about three ounces, I burped her, and then she looked tired so I put her in this thing." He motioned to the near-tactical baby carrier he had strapped to his chest. "Snug as a bug."

Kat was okay.

My heart started racing the moment I realized I had missed her feeding and only just began to slow.

Shane frowned. "Did you shower?"

"I fell asleep as soon as I touched the bed," I admitted.

He tipped his head toward the bathroom. "Go."

I raised my eyebrows.

He reached out and tucked a lock of hair behind my ear. His palm was warm and comforting as it lingered on my cheek. "Take a hot shower. Not a quick one either. Do all the shit you need to do. I'll hold down the fort."

"Shane..." Every argument was fleeting. I leaned into his touch and closed my eyes. "I can't ask you to do that."

"You're not asking." He looked down at Kat again. "Besides. She's cozy. And what's that rule? Don't wake a sleeping baby?"

Every gland in my breasts screamed at me for going this long without feeding Kat. I didn't understand it. How was she not gaining weight from nursing, but I was in agony after a few hours? The nursing pads stuffed in my bra were adhered to my nipples. It was like peeling dried superglue off my skin. Getting them off would be awful.

Shane would be grossed out.

Then again, he did watch me give birth.

"I need to pump first," I said with a slight tremble of hesitancy in my voice.

That quiver wasn't because I was saying it to Shane. Just the thought of getting everything set up, then sitting down for flange torture made me dizzy.

His features tightened in concern. "What's the matter?"

"Nothing," I choked out.

"Beth—"

I huffed. "I really hate pumping, okay? It's awful."

It was the first time I had ever said it out loud. But instead of feeling lighter by getting it off my chest, I was hit with a lancing stab of guilt.

Shane's voice was a gentle caress. "Will feeding Kat instead of pumping help?"

I shook my head. "If she drank that much from a bottle, she probably won't be hungry and it'll just wake her up. And I'm supposed to be pumping anyway."

He gave me a curious look.

My throat tightened. "Her pediatrician said she's not gaining enough weight and I need to be feeding her more so I'm supposed to start pumping in between so my body makes more milk. I've been doing little bits here and there. What's in the freezer isn't much. It's nowhere close enough to sustain her."

"Do you want privacy or help?"

It wasn't that I was shy about my body. Pregnancy, labor, birth, and breastfeeding had robbed me of any sense of shyness or shame about it. I just didn't want Shane to see how bad I was at it.

But the thought of being stuck to that pump in a room all alone... I hated that too.

I hated all of it.

Where was the bliss?

I studied Kat, all snuggled up in the carrier with Shane.

She was so comfortable with him. I didn't feel anything for her. At least, not the way I thought I would.

I was protective and filled her needs the best I could, but I didn't have that maternal bond everyone talked about.

I swallowed the guilt and let it pool in my stomach with the rest of the shame I felt over being a failure. "I... I don't really need anything, but ... Would you keep me company?"

His smile made my knees wobble like an adolescent schoolgirl who got a little attention from her crush. "I'd love to."

While he meandered around the living room, picking up and putting away all the baby shit I had grown blind to, I put the machine from hell together and warmed up the compresses I used to soften up my breasts. They were so engorged it looked like I had a botched boob job.

I settled on the couch and slowly peeled the breast pads off. My skin stung as I removed each one. I stuffed the warm compress into my nursing bra until it cooled. Shane cautiously kept his back to me. With a deep breath, I swapped the compresses for the pumps and turned on the machine.

The suction made sharp, searing pains shoot straight through my nipples. My eyes screwed shut as I bit down on my lip, but a pathetic whimper escaped anyway.

Shane turned quickly. "What's wrong?"

Panic lingered in my throat like vomit deciding whether it was going to explode or not. Clammy prickles of panic crept up my neck at the rhythmic, mechanical sound from the pump.

It made my skin crawl.

I couldn't even look down at the flanges without anxiety clawing at me. I detested the sound that the stupid machine made. It made me crazy. I tried to speak, but nothing happened.

The couch sank as Shane sat beside me. Fingers slid between mine as he laced ours together and squeezed my hand. "I'm right here. You're doing great."

Goosebumps cropped up on my skin when the AC kicked on. He reached to the back of the couch, pulled the crocheted afghan down, unfurled it, and draped it over me.

I released the air held up in my lungs. Maybe not being able to see the pump helped. It still felt painfully awkward, but at least I didn't have to look at it.

I hated this. I hated all of this. I wanted to turn back time and skip the day I met Bradley. I wanted to disappear and start over. Kat would be better off without me.

Maybe I wanted to disappear completely.

His hand found mine beneath the blanket again as he leaned over and pressed a kiss to the top of my head. "I know what those panic attacks feel like."

How did he—

Shane draped his arm around my shoulders and tucked me into his side. "Trust me. I know."

The whirr and thump of the breast pump was the only sound between us. Not even Kat made a peep.

"Will you keep talking to me?" I peeled my lips apart and gasped. "Please. It—just ... It keeps my mind off ... it."

His breath was warm against the top of my head. "What do you want me to talk about?"

"I dunno," I whispered as I rested my temple on his shoulder. "You make a good pillow. I see why Kat likes lying on you."

Shane kept his laugh soft so he didn't wake the baby on his chest. "I don't mind at all."

"Will you tell me about the Navy?"

He hesitated. It wasn't something he did often, I realized. "What about it?"

"You were a Navy SEAL," I said. "Did you travel a lot?"

His chin bumped my head as he nodded. "Yes, ma'am."

"Where was your favorite place to visit?"

"Chile."

"Least favorite?"

There was a longer pause. "Somalia."

I shifted uncomfortably as my breast milk began to let down. There was a weird sense of disdain mixed with the relief. "What—um—what was your favorite thing to do? You know—as a SEAL?" I looked up, tipping my head back to get a peek at him. "Or is that an 'I'll tell you, but then I'll have to kill you,' kind of thing?"

Shane chuckled. "Uh, I guess HALO jumping was my favorite."

"What's that?"

"Skydiving out of a cargo plane at thirty thousand feet. HALO stands for 'high altitude, low opening.' We would jump high and deploy our parachutes as close to the ground as possible. It allows the jumpers to get on the ground quickly and mostly undetected by radars."

I let out a breath. I couldn't imagine doing that. "That must be terrifying. Why would you jump out of a perfectly good airplane?"

"Let me put it in your language, smarty-pants," he said with a boyish grin. "Let's see if you can calculate my terminal velocity and that'll tell you why it's fun."

I liked math... "How much do you weigh?"

"One-eighty."

I thought for a few minutes, working the problem over in my head. "To calculate your terminal velocity, I'd multiply your mass and the acceleration due to gravity, and then multiply that by two to solve for X." I worked my lip between my teeth. "Then I'd multiply the air density—which would vary depending on your altitude—to the area of the object. Or in this case, your body. How tall are you?"

"Six-two."

I eyed him suspiciously. "Like a real six-two or a dating profile six-two, which is actually five-ten?"

He laughed. "A real six-two. You got a measuring tape? I'll prove it."

I snorted. "Fine. I believe you." I did the math in my head. "Going by the DuBois formula, that means you have 22.37 square feet of body surface if you're spread-eagle."

"Give or take a little. You don't stay spread-eagle the whole jump."

"I'm giving some of this an educated guesstimate."

"Keep going, Einstein."

I worked it over in my head. "I'd multiply that by the drag coefficient to solve for Y, then divide X by Y."

His lips pressed against the top of my head. "Stop showing off. What's your final answer?"

I sighed. "Given the unknown factors of jump style, wind speed, actual air density as you descend—"

"Give it your best shot."

"My guess is about one hundred and thirty miles per hour."

He grinned. "Pretty spot on."

I couldn't imagine doing that. "You're crazy."

"Jumping out of a plane and falling at the speed of a race car? Not opening the chute until I'm eight or nine hundred feet above the ground, immediately descending into chaos? It's a rush."

"It's a death sentence," I countered. My heart was racing just thinking about it.

"Living is a death sentence. We're all terminal. It's how you spend the time you have that makes all of it worth it."

His fingers trailed along my arm, nearly lulling me back to sleep. It felt so good—so comforting. It had been so long since I let myself be this close to a man. The last time was—

I shook the thought out of my head.

"Do you miss it?" I asked.

"I didn't get to leave on my terms, but staying wasn't an option."

"You didn't answer the question," I prodded. "Do you miss it?"

His 'yes' was sincere. "I miss it the way I miss cheap liquor. It was an addiction. When I left the service, I traded one vice for another. Both tried to kill me."

"But you're still here." The comment was meant for him, but it was my heart that took it in.

"Yeah. I am."

I decided not to push any further. Maybe Shane had unpacked his, but I didn't want to know what skeletons I'd find when I started cleaning out my closet.

"I think I'm done," I said, peeking under the blanket at my deflated breasts.

"Need help?"

I tipped my head toward the breast pump machine. "Can you turn it off?" Quickly, I detached the pumps from each breast and slid the cups of my nursing bra back into place.

I did it.

Conversation with Shane got me through pumping without a panic attack.

My heart skipped with pride.

And then I looked at the pump bottles.

There was barely anything in there... Not even three ounces between both bottles.

Anger and defeat burned my eyes, and suddenly seeing Shane with Kat sleeping on him—a feat I could rarely accomplish with her—pissed me the hell off.

10

BETH

"Hey," Shane said as he came up behind me at the sink. "I put her down in the crib and double checked that the baby monitor is on."

I stared at the plastic pump parts swimming in the soapy water. "Thanks."

His chest barely grazed my back, but I could feel the vibration from his words against my shoulders. Thick, tattooed arms gripped the countertop and caged me in. "Thanks for letting me drop in on you."

My jaw ached from grinding my molars together. "Thanks for the nap."

Uninterrupted sleep was incredible, but I was starting to regret it.

Fuck him for being able to get Kat to stop crying. Fuck him for being so fucking good at everything.

A whiff of crisp soap, cologne, and hair gel tickled my senses.

And while I was at it—fuck him for smelling that damn good.

His thumbs caressed my wrists in gentle strokes. I despised the goosebumps that ran up my arms.

"Can I run out and get you dinner or anything?" he asked in that low, sex-filled voice that made me weak in the knees. "Anything in particular sound good?"

"I'm fine," I clipped, pushing away from the sink. "I'm not hungry."

Shane must've had a death wish, because he followed me. "You sure, Dimples?"

"Positive. My fridge and freezer are on overdrive because of how full they are. Besides, Austin and my mom should be back soon."

"Want me to sit and listen out for Kat so you can get that shower? Relax a little more?"

"No!" I shouted.

Shane reared back, but he didn't cower. He approached again, slowly this time. "Tell me where I overstepped." He was calm. Collected. Calculated.

I paused, because I wasn't expecting that.

He pressed his hands together. "Let me try that again. *I'm sorry* I overstepped. Can you tell me what upset you so I don't do it again?"

No, because I'm already acting insane.

"I'll get a shower when my mom gets back. It'll be time for Kat to do tummy time and she's better at it than I am."

"Come here," Shane said as he wrapped his arms around me.

I tripped on the edge of the rug and ended up falling into his chest. Shane caught me, but didn't release.

My skin crawled at the touch. Not because it was him. Somewhere in the depths of my brain, I *wanted* him to hold me. But right now? Right now I hated him for being all the things for Kat that I was failing at.

"You're the best thing for Kat," he murmured into my hair as his arms tightened around me. "No one can replace what you are to her, but it's okay to accept help so that you can be the best version of yourself for her."

For a moment, I closed my eyes and laid my head in the valley between his pectorals. His hand came up and cradled my head, fingers tangling in my hair.

"I'm sorry I lost my shit on you," I whispered against his heartbeat. "I—I don't know what's wrong with me."

The front door opened, the sound of the turning knob shattering the moment.

"The fuck?" Austin said.

I turned to find my brother standing in the doorway. Stepping away from Shane, I wiped my eyes and dropped on a mask of indifference.

It was the one I had been wearing since December when I wrecked a family and my world came crumbling down.

Shane shifted, eyeing Austin, but he didn't back away from me. His hand lingered on my hip. "You sure you don't want me to bring dinner or anything?"

"I'm sure."

Austin loomed beside us, his brows knitting in deep. "What's going on here?" His jaw flexed, eyes narrowed in on his friend.

Shane was a few inches shorter and a third less bulky than my brother, but he didn't flinch. "I stopped by to check on Beth and hung out with the baby for a while."

Austin's tone was flat and unamused. "Then where is the baby?"

Ignoring my ogre of a brother, Shane turned to me. "You've got my number." His voice softened. "Please call me, even if you don't need anything."

"Thanks," I said, my eyes lowering to the ground when my mother walked in the door.

"Well, hey there, Shane," she said with a chipper wave. "What are you up to, sweetie?"

Not once in Shane Hutchins's tall, tattooed life did I think anyone had ever called him 'sweetie.' I was fairly certain he came out of the womb with ink on his arms and challenge in his eyes.

I loved it.

He turned his attention to the other Ms. Hale in the room. "Just came by to check on Beth."

Something warm bloomed inside of me.

To check on Beth.

Not just the baby—though he did that too. Not to pester me about my parenting choices or give cutting looks at the clutter around the house.

Just to check on *me*.

Great. Now I liked him again. *Hello, hormone whiplash.*

The transition from pregnancy to motherhood was startling.

During my pregnancy it was all about me. The attention and care everyone around me showed was what got me through nine months of going at it alone.

But as soon as Kat made her very dramatic entrance into the world, the shift happened.

Everything was about her.

Not that I needed the spotlight on me, but I needed something.

I needed to feel seen. Heard.

For the last two weeks, all I had been was invisible. I was the frame that held the picture.

The thing about a frame is that it's replaceable. Totally inconsequential in the grand scheme of things.

Was that motherhood? Holding her above the waves to bask in the sunlight as I drowned?

Shane turned to my mom. "Nice to see you, Mrs. Hale."

She waved him off. "How many times have I told you to call me Susan?"

"Plenty," he said with that annoyingly charming grin of his. Shane had such an easy presence about him. "But I won't."

I thought back to all the times my mom had been able to visit over the course of my pregnancy. She loved popping in on Austin and Shane when they shared a house. She basically considered Shane her third child.

My mom was the best and it only drove the knife in deeper when I realized that I would never be her.

Shane turned back to me, his gaze lingering. "I'll see you later."

"Bye," I said quietly as he turned and slipped out the door.

"Well, that was sweet of him," my mom said as she hung her purse by the door. "I've gotta say—I love small towns. How great was it to have your brother's friend deliver your baby when you couldn't get to the hospital? You just don't get that kind of community in cities."

The box where I held the memory of Shane and Missy bringing Kat into the world was carefully tucked away in my heart. It was my Pandora's box.

I didn't dare unpack it. I was too scared of what I'd find.

Instead, I opted for my signature sass. "Frankly, I would have preferred the old school method of childbirth where I get drugs and don't feel a thing." I eyed the patch of carpet in front of the couch where Kat had made her grand entrance.

Someone had paid a cleaning company to show up while I was in the hospital and get all of the blood and bodily fluids out of it.

It had probably been Brandie Jean. That was her kind of Robin Hood in pink leggings, pay-it-forward behavior.

Austin grunted like a Neanderthal as he yanked open the fridge door.

I glared at him. "What's your problem?"

"Right now? The fact that he's here sniffing around my sister and my niece."

I rolled my eyes. It didn't matter how old we got or the fact that he was going to get married soon. Austin would always be my annoying older brother.

"Are you forgetting that he helped bring your niece into the world and kept me from bleeding out on my living room floor? Back off."

He nearly strangled the handle to the fridge.

I groaned. "Geez. What? Y'all are practically inseparable. If it weren't for Caroline, I would have thought you two were soulmates. What the hell has he done to piss you off?"

Austin slammed the refrigerator. "He's coming after you."

Oh my god. Did he think I was completely stupid? "I'm aware. It's pretty obvious."

"I mean it," Austin clipped. "The day Shane told me he was Caroline's kidney donor, he wrapped it up by saying that one of these days he would ask you out. He gave me the information I wanted about Caroline, so I wouldn't give him shit about you."

And why was that such a problem?

I marched over to the front door and yanked it wide open.

Austin looked confused.

"First, I'm a grown ass woman and I'm perfectly capable of discerning who gets access to me and my daughter. Shane has been nothing but thoughtful and helpful." *Never mind the insane knee-jerk reaction I had at him being better at calming Kat than me...* "Unlike everyone else who has come in and out of this house. So if you have a problem with Shane being around, then there's the door."

Austin scoffed. "Don't say I didn't warn you."

I was ready to rip his face off. "And what the hell is that supposed to mean?"

"You know," my mom said as she waltzed in carrying Kat.

Hell no. Did she just wake up my baby?

"When we were out, I saw this flyer for a mommy and me group down at the community center," she said. "I took a picture of it so I'd remember to tell you."

That sounded miserable. "When is it?"

She held Kat in one arm and scrolled through her phone. "Well, there's a meeting tomorrow morning."

Was I particularly enthused with the idea of hanging out with a bunch of other babies and their mothers? No. There were probably going to be germs out the wazoo.

But did I want a change of scenery from this insanity?

More than anything.

———

SILENCE.

Not really what I expected from a mommy and me group, but maybe the walls in room 2B of the Falls Creek Community Center were soundproofed.

I steered the tank of a stroller I had strapped Kat into through the narrow hallway and stopped short.

Was I in the right place?

Seriously—where were the sounds of babies and children? I double-checked the photo of the flyer my mom texted to me and confirmed that I was, in fact, in the right place.

"You're kidding!" a woman cackled, her laugh carrying through the half-open door.

A woman with bleach-blonde hair piled on top of her head in an artfully messy bun snickered. "I swear I'm not!"

"Okay, but get this, Miranda," another voice chimed in. "I heard she got him to make her his power of attorney and put her as the sole recipient of his entire estate."

"I believe it," Miranda—aka Pinterest Bun Lady—said. "That knockoff Dolly wannabe isn't a gold digger. She's a tin foil treasure hunter, bless her heart. That man barely has a dime to his name. His son's in jail and is draining him dry from the legal fees and trying to get better attorneys."

Okay. Back out slowly and maybe they won't know I'm here. I can just say I was lost and looking for a bathroom.

"Can I help you?" the first lady asked.

Great. Now she was making direct eye contact with me.

"Um—" I looked down at my rumpled Crystal Coast Kickball Tournament tee and leggings. The postpartum bleeding had begun to slow, so I finally downgraded from wearing mesh underwear lined with puppy pads to super maxi pads—with the wings. Wearing buttery soft leggings rather than week-old sweatpants I couldn't be bothered to change was my celebration.

Could they hear the pad crunch when I walked? Did I have pad panty lines?

I had even washed my hair this morning. Granted, it wasn't styled at all. Not like theirs was. Mine was in a low ponytail that had me halfway to "hello, I'm a founding father."

"Sorry," I finally tacked on. "I was looking for a mommy and me group but I must have the wrong room or ... time."

The ladies shared looks that were weighed down by pursed lips and silent communications. Eyes flicked to and fro. It was like they were having a conversation about me with pointed looks.

At what point in motherhood would I acquire that skill?

Miranda with the messy bun gave me a curt smile. "You're in the right place. This is Mommy's Morning Out. I'm Miranda."

My shoulder ached from the diaper back weighing me down, but it was time for a game face. I could do this. Kat was sleeping in the stroller and, as long as I didn't jostle her too much, she'd stay asleep.

"Nice to meet you. I'm Beth."

"Here's an open seat for you," a lady with short brown hair said, pointing to the folding chair beside her. She sipped from a giant handled tumbler that read, *Moms don't complain. We wine.*

And that's when I realized that they all had matching cups.

"Sorry, it's BYOB," Miranda said as she sipped. Something burgundy darted up the straw. "We don't get newcomers often, so it's not something we advertise."

"Can't exactly put "wine 'o'clock" on the flyer, now can we, ladies?" a redhead in high-end athleisure wear chimed in with a snicker. She offered a pitying smile. "I'm Charis."

"Nice to meet you," I mumbled, feeling all kinds of awkward as I shifted in the folding chair.

"How old's your baby?" Miranda asked, pointing a manicured nail at the stroller.

Not only was I the outsider; I was the only one who had a child with them.

"She's about three weeks old," I said. "I figured it would be good to get out of the house and meet some new people."

Falls Creek was a small, tight-knit community, but I tended to hang out with the same handful of people and didn't venture outside of that.

Charis clasped her hands together. "Aww. I bet she's darling. Does she look like you? You have great features. Have you thought about putting her in the pageant circuit?"

"I—what?" *Was she serious?*

"It's never too early to start. Get her in now. It's easier to get them used to all the prep and primping when they're little and haven't learned 'no' yet."

The women tittered among themselves.

"Oh!" Miranda gushed. "Did I tell you that I got a discount code to that online boutique we were talking about last week? McKinleigh got accepted to their influencer program. My baby's not even on solids yet and she's a brand rep!"

The ladies clinked their decaled wine tumblers together in celebration.

The ruckus was enough to wake Kat.

It was inevitable, I thought as I unlatched her and lifted her out. Thankfully, she only rooted around for my boob for a second before falling back to sleep on my shoulder.

Holy crap on a cracker... I did it! I actually picked her up and got her to go back to sleep!

"What a sweetheart," a lady who was slightly older than the rest said as she tilted her head and studied Kat's face. "She's beautiful. I miss when mine were that little. They were so easy at that age. Soak it up because it's all downhill from here."

...And with that unnecessary comment, my bliss bubble burst.

"Has she been an easy baby?" Miranda asked.

"Not really," I admitted. "But I've never done this before, so it's all pretty new to me. I think the mental load's the worst." I let out a wry laugh to hide the fact that I just word-vomited more than I wanted to share. "I feel like I'm going crazy most days."

"Wine helps," another woman said.

"Oh—I can't drink. I'm trying to breastfeed her."

"Then pump and dump," Miranda giggled. "It's what we all do."

I can barely make enough milk for Kat as it is... If I had to pour a single drop down the drain, I'd break down and drown in a puddle of tears.

The conversation mellowed into sips of wine for them and staring at the scuffed tile floor for me.

This was officially one of the worst decisions in the history of bad decisions.

One of the moms on the far side of the circle sighed dreamily. "I miss the newborn stage. They smell so good. They sleep all the time and you can do everything you need to without a fuss. Now I'm a taxi driver to ungrateful wombats all day long."

"Are you going to have another?" The older lady asked.

I snorted. "Absolutely not."

She looked startled.

I panicked. "I—just—it's been a really hard adjustment." Hesitantly, I added, "My mind's been a scary place lately. Did any of y'all feel like this?"

She huffed. "Don't fall for it. All that new-aged woo-woo mumbo-jumbo about 'baby blues' and postpartum depression that you see on the internet isn't real. It just means your heart isn't right with the good Lord." She pointed a finger at me. "*He* never gives you more than you can handle. So if you're not feeling right, it probably means you've got some sins you need to be confessing. Only Jesus can fix a troubled mind and a sinful heart. You need to pray more."

Oh for the love... Did it make me a bad mom to fake my baby having an emergency so I could leave this nightmare?

"We're made for motherhood," one of the *my baby is an influencer* moms said.

Apparently, I was not. Guilt gnawed at me and I regretted ever opening my mouth.

Actually, I regretted leaving the house this morning.

"Isn't a woman's body miraculous?" one of the ladies riding her morning wine buzz touted. "I mean, we can grow humans and sustain them just with what comes naturally to us. I just don't understand how people don't see how magical that is." She gave me a pitying look. "Well—I'm sure it could be an adjustment for *some*, but I miss those days."

My body was not miraculous. It was betraying me, and my mind was leading the mutiny.

Miranda gave me a quick flick of her eyes. The communication was silent, but the message was deafening. *You're not welcome here.* "Motherhood is the pinnacle of achievement for a woman. If you're not feeling fulfilled by it, perhaps you need to reevaluate your priorities. It's selfish not to put your daughter first."

Selfish?! My eyes burned as tears pricked at them like needles of guilt and turmoil. I was doing everything—*everything*—I could to make it through each day. And I was *selfish* for thoughts and feelings that I couldn't control?

Charis eyed me discerningly. Her exacting gaze raked over me. "I swear I know you from somewhere. What did you say your name was again?"

"Beth. My brother is Austin Hale. He's engaged to Caroline Tyree."

"Beth ... *Hale.*" Her flawlessly landscaped eyebrows winged up. The tone was accusatory.

That's when I noticed the country club keychain dangling from the car keys on her bag. The same country club Bradley —*and his family*—frequented.

"You're *her.*"

11

SHANE

"What crawled up your ass and died?" I asked when Austin came stomping through the station's kitchen. He had been holed up in the gym for the better part of our shift.

I tapped the old wooden spoon that had served generations of first responders on the edge of the steel stock pot.

There was a distinct nip in the air that called for chili in bulk and hoop cheese biscuits. I started chopping vegetables, browning meat, and throwing everything in the pot to simmer as soon as I got through the morning's gear checks and handoff from yesterday's shift.

I knew I was tempting fate with the biscuits. As soon as I put them in the oven, we'd get toned out.

Austin reached around me and pawed through the kitchen cabinet, looking for his industrial-sized tub of protein powder. "Nothing."

Ha. Right.

"Could've fooled me," I said as I stuck a spoon in the chili and gave it a taste. I reached for the cumin and dumped some into my palm before adding it to the pot.

The hand was the middleman. Going straight for the pot was too risky.

Austin grabbed the protein powder canister that had his name scrawled across the front in permanent marker. His back was to me as he started piling scoops into the plastic shaker cup that was permanently fused to his hand. That was, unless he was on a call or texting Caroline.

"Thought you'd be giddy with engaged bliss," I teased. "Or are you in the doghouse with Caroline?"

Austin was generally an easy-going guy. Having him as a housemate for a few months before he moved in with Caroline was great. But this moody asshole wasn't that guy.

I gave the chili another taste before throwing the spoon into the sink. "Seriously, man. The hell is wrong with you?"

Austin jammed his cup under the sink faucet and filled it to the designated line. The little metal ball inside rattled around as he shook it up. "Why were you at Beth's the other day?"

I shouldn't have been surprised that he was up in arms about running into me at his sister's house.

"I told you. I went over to check on her and see Kat. Same as everyone else has been doing."

Except that Beth let her walls down around me. She willingly let me hold Kat when everyone else doing it made her want to lash out. That wasn't lost on me.

His eyes narrowed. "If you have any respect for her, you'll leave her the fuck alone."

Calm. Cool. Collected.

I didn't let his rancor rattle me.

"I respect her. And that's why I'm not going to back off until she tells me to."

In Austin's eyes, I'd always be persona non grata when it

came to his sister. He was protective of her, and I couldn't fault him for that.

I was protective of her.

The moment I knelt between her knees as she fought to bring Kat into the world, I knew I'd never be the same.

I was so far gone for Beth Hale, and she wasn't even mine.

Yet.

"I told you I had every intention of asking her out."

Austin's grip on his protein shake turned lethal. "Then ask her out."

That... wasn't the response I expected.

"And when she shoots you down because she's got Kat to think about, you leave her the fuck alone."

"She also has herself to think about," I countered.

Before he could respond, Elijah Fisher—the fire captain—popped his head in the kitchen. "Hale. You've got visitors."

Austin and I turned. His expression softened when he spotted Caroline in the doorway. Beth, cradling Kat, stood behind her.

My heart leaped.

"Hey, Sweets," Austin said as he left his protein shake on the counter and strolled over to give Caroline a kiss. Straightening, he looked at Beth and reached for Kat. "And my favorite niece." He dropped a brotherly kiss on top of Beth's head as he reached for the baby.

Beth reared back, dodging his approach. Her grip on Kat's swaddled body tightened.

I fought the urge to lurch toward her and get her away from the growing crowd. She needed distance and quiet to feel safe.

Austin frowned at Beth's standoffishness, but paid it mostly no mind. "To what do I owe the pleasure of seeing my three favorite girls?" Gone was the cranky bag of ass from two minutes ago.

Beth's eyes met mine in a silent plea. A menagerie of emotions crossed her features. Hesitant joy. Trepidation. Fear. Worry.

"We made cookies," Caroline said, chipper as could be. "Figured y'all might like something sweet."

I piped up. "We?"

"Beth and me," Caroline said as she handed Austin a massive Tupperware container. "Kat supervised."

Austin cracked into the tub and stole a cookie. "They're good, but you're my favorite sweet," he said as he planted another kiss on Caroline's mouth.

Beth took advantage of her brother being distracted and offered me a wobbly smile. "And they're a thank you. For the other day, I mean." She looked down at Kat. "For helping with her."

I softened. "Anytime." Not wanting to spook a mama bear or encroach on her well-protected territory, I tipped my chin toward Kat. "Is it okay if I hold her or is she comfortable where she is?"

Beth's green eyes shifted with uncertainty. I waited patiently, not pressing her any more than the ask.

"You can hold her if you want."

I didn't hesitate. Weaving through the bodies crowding the kitchen, I made a beeline for Kat.

Beth lifted her off her shoulder and placed her in my arms. Kat let out a little grunt of dissatisfaction at the disturbance, but quickly settled.

"Hey, pretty girl," I said softly as I bounced between my feet, hoping Kat would take kindly to me and not fuss. "I missed you. Long time, no see."

I glanced up and caught Beth smiling. It was a good look on her.

Kat's tiny fist curled around the fabric of my station polo.

"She likes you," Beth said softly as she reached out and smoothed her hand over Kat's sprouts of wispy blonde hair.

"The feeling's mutual."

I wondered if Kat remembered me. I wondered if she recognized the heartbeat that soothed her when she was crying in the hospital.

Part of me wondered what it would be like if I didn't take my shot with Beth. What would it be like in five—ten—fifteen years when I ran into her and Kat at the filling station or the grocery store?

Would I have a place in her life? Would I have to watch her grow up from a distance? Would I have to watch her bond with a step-dad?

I didn't want to be a memory.

Shifting my attention to Beth, I said, "You look real nice today, Dimples."

Beth looked at her feet. "Leggings are my lifesaver right now. They're basically keeping my organs from falling out of my body."

I licked my lips, waiting until her eyes met mine. "What I should have said is that your ass looks fantastic in them."

Her cheeks turned fire engine red.

While Austin was distracted with his fiancé, I let my eyes brazenly roam her cleavage. Her breasts had changed to accommodate the life she sustained. They looked so fucking soft. The tank top she was in criss-crossed in the front—probably giving her easier access if she needed to feed Kat. But in my depraved, sex-starved mind, all I could think about were the things I would do with that access.

I shifted Kat to one arm, keeping her snug against my shoulder as I took a step toward Beth, flicking my eyes to her breasts once again. "Your ass ... and everything else." A wickedly amused smile worked its way up my mouth at her surprise.

"*Shane*." My name was a whisper on her lips.

"I'm just telling you the truth, Mama."

Her smile was coy, but present. And that felt like a fucking win.

"How're you feeling?" I asked. "I haven't heard from you in a while."

Beth looked at the toe of her sneakers. "Alright, I guess. Just pushing through Hell Week, right?" She looked up. "Embracing the suck?"

The way she was so casual about it stabbed at my gut.

"What are you up to today?"

She sighed. "Feeding my diva every three hours. Pumping in between. I tried to help my mom plan a bridal shower for Caroline—" her voice lowered to a mumble "—counting down the hours until my mom leaves to go back to Beaufort."

I chuckled.

Beth continued. "Caroline came over and we baked. My mom's leaving town this afternoon. Kat has a doctor's appointment in a little bit, and then Layla's bringing dinner by."

Kat roused from her sleep and wailed in protest.

Across the kitchen, Austin snapped to attention, then froze when he saw her in my arms.

Beth tensed at the screech, her body on high alert.

But I wasn't fazed. "I can walk Kat around the station and show her the sights to help her settle down or I can give her back. Up to you."

Beth immediately reached out. "I'll take her."

I didn't argue. I simply placed Kat back in Beth's waiting

arms. The relief flooding Beth was instant as she held Kat to her chest.

I wasn't mad or jealous of Beth taking Kat from me. Quite the opposite. I loved seeing Beth hold her.

And I wanted to be the one holding Beth.

With the imaginary threat to his niece gone, Austin retreated and went back to discussing a wedding venue with Caroline. I tipped my head toward the future Mr. and Mrs. Hale. "I know you tagged along with Caroline, but I'm glad I was working today and got to see you."

"I didn't tag along," Beth blurted out. "It was my idea."

My eyebrows lifted.

She looked sheepish for a moment. "I really did want to say thank you for the other day." Sighing, she added, "I'm not good at accepting help, but you knew I needed it. So, thank you."

I allowed myself the pleasure of putting my hand on her arm. "Anytime. My phone's always on."

Tones rang out across the station.

"Station Two. Vehicle-versus-vehicle. Requesting fire and medical. Possible entrapment. Stand by for cross-streets."

"We gotta go," Austin said as he cut the stovetop burner off for me and gave Caroline a searing goodbye kiss.

I looked at Beth. "I'm off in the morning, but call me anytime. Even if it's just to talk."

Her lips were pursed, but she nodded.

Austin jumped between us and hugged his sister and niece. "Thanks for coming by, kiddo."

I lifted a hand and waved to Caroline. "Good to see you."

"Don't do anything stupid. You gotta keep your kidney safe," she said as she snapped the lid on the cookie tub and left it on the counter for us. "If you mess that one up, you're outta luck. No take backs."

I laughed, and jogged down the stairs.

———

THE HOUSE WAS dark when I let myself inside. I hadn't bothered opening the curtains yesterday before I left for my shift.

Usually I did.

It was one of those habits that was first to get skipped over when I was sliding into the abyss.

The calendar tacked onto the fridge told me why.

Cole was right.

It was coming up again. Once a year. Like clockwork.

I lumbered into the kitchen, wearing the stench of a wellness check that turned into a call to the coroner.

My partner had showered off at the station, but I just went through the shift change routine and came home.

The *tick, tick, tick* of the clock on the wall was the only sound in the dead air.

I think the cat's out. If he was inside, he would have been clawing at my leg for food.

I dropped my shift bag and noticed that the vinyl flooring was peeling up at the seam again. I should fix that.

Tick, tick, tick.

The clock echoed louder and louder.

Tick, tick, tick.

Each jolt of the pin moving every second sounded like a gunshot.

My vision tunneled as screams of agony began to fill the quietness.

Hails of bullets rained down from every corner. The bone-chilling sound of grown men wailing and crying out for God or for their mothers. Screams for even the devil himself to end the torment.

Explosion after explosion.
The smell of searing flesh.
Flashes of heat warped my skin and strangled my lungs.
Make it stop. Drown it out. Make it stop.
Each thump of my station shoes on the kitchen floor turned to the doomed *whump, whump* of the spiraling helicopter.
Make it stop. Drown it out.
One thing was a sure fix. A tried-and-true way to stop reliving that mission like it was fucking Groundhog Day.
I craved the burn of whiskey coating my tongue. I salivated like Pavlov's dog at the thought.
I had seen death. Tasted it. I had walked up to its door. I had stepped on the threshold.
But I was never welcomed inside no matter how much I begged to be let in.
Sweat slicked my palms as I grabbed the handle of the refrigerator door.
I yanked, the bright light stabbing my vision like a spear. I welcomed the bite of artificial light.
Should have opened the damn curtains.
That's the thing about the tip of the spear—it goes where the master throws it. It has no choice in the matter. No way to change the trajectory.
The one causing the most pain is the one pointing the spear.
Once upon a time, I was the arrowhead. Sharp. Useful.
Now, I was dull, dented, and damaged.
I braced against the frame of the refrigerator, basking in the cold air that wafted out like a caress.
Week-old takeout, wilted lettuce, condiments, and eggs were the only things on the shelves.
I really needed to get to the grocery store.

I left the refrigerator door open as I opted for the leftover takeout that was ten minutes from sprouting mold, and grabbed a fork from the dishwasher.

Just go to bed. Take the food with you. Keep it dark and go to sleep. It's the closest thing to being dead.

My stride hitched, and I reached out to close the fridge.

No.

I needed the light.

Just open the fucking curtains, Hutch.

The living room was one big shadow. I knew when I pulled the curtains back, I'd see the jar that held my chips and keychains from years of AA meetings.

Usually seeing that jar would get the taste of whiskey out of my mouth, but it was strong today.

Before I could think about grabbing my keys and going to the liquor store, I crossed the living room and threw open the curtains.

Bright morning light flooded inside. I abandoned the takeout and resided to the fact that it would probably grow legs and walk away.

That was fine. Going to the store would be good for me.

The couch groaned as I sank down and grabbed the old mason jar that was piled high with sobriety chips.

The commitment coin.

Twenty-four hours sober.

Thirty days sober.

Sixty days sober.

Ninety days sober.

Four months sober.

Five months sober.

Six months.

Seven months.

Eight.

Nine.
Ten.
Eleven.
One year.
A black keychain for two years.

There were handmade coins and keychains for milestones that the recovery program didn't recognize. Those were Brandie Jean's doing. Seven years of having Dolly Parton 2.0 as my unofficial sponsor meant that most of those tokens covered in body glitter or some shit.

2,190 days sober.

Six years of fighting the addiction that promised relief.

I knew it could deliver that promise.

It would make the nightmares go away.

I would sleep.

I would be numb.

I used to think addicts had a choice in the matter. That they had a hand in their own downfall.

Not anymore.

Being one myself made it easier to administer Narcan. It made it a little easier to give the frequent flyers grace. It made me sympathetic to the drug seekers.

We were the same.

Just people trying to get through the next twenty-four hours.

My phone rang and, for a moment, I hoped that it was Beth.

I squashed that hope like a bug under my shoe. She didn't need to see me like this. She didn't need another burden.

But it wasn't Beth.

"Crowder," I said by way of a hello when I swiped across the screen.

Road noise mingled with Cole's voice. He must have been traveling for a job. "What'chu doin', Hutch?"

"Just got off duty. You?"

"On a job."

"Then why are you calling?" My voice had a bite to it; an edge of annoyance. I knew damn well why he was calling.

"Had a feeling."

"I'm good. Charlie Mike."

His laugh was low and wry. "Bullshit. You left the curtains closed, didn't you?"

"They're open now," I countered as I leaned back on the couch and closed my eyes.

"Good. Keep 'em open."

12

BETH

"Alright, Mom. Get baby undressed all the way and we'll take her to the scale."

I went through the motions of getting Kat out of her onesie and diaper. At least there was no radioactive bowel movement to thwart this appointment.

... Knock on wood.

The nurse—thankfully not the judgmental bitch from last time—lingered in the doorway as I wrapped Kat in the puppy pad. I followed her down the hall to the communal scale and height measure.

Kat—utterly displeased with the air conditioning on her skin—screeched like a banshee.

"Sorry, kiddo," I whispered in an attempt to sooth her as I placed her in the cradle scale.

Kat squirmed like a wiggle worm, clenching her fists.

The nurse kept a shrewd eye on the ticking numbers until they stalled.

It had been such a good day. Well—maybe, not a *good* day. But it had been a neutral day.

I hung out with my future sister-in-law, my mom finally

packed up and vacated my house after three weeks, and I saw Shane.

But more than that, Shane saw me.

When everyone else saw Kat, Shane saw me.

I had butterflies every time I became the center of his attention.

But all those good things were crushed by the number on the scale.

Still under birth weight.

The nurse's pursed lips told me everything I needed to know.

Lazy.

Disappointment.

Failure.

Inadequate.

Unfit to be a mother.

"You can head back to the exam room and get her dressed. Dr. Heath will be with you in a minute."

I retreated with my tail between my legs. Kat's eyes pierced my heart as she stared up at me.

She was the last person I wanted to fail, but I was failing her.

There wasn't a minute in the day that I wasn't worrying. There wasn't a single second where I felt like I could do this. Not one moment that the intrusive thoughts were at bay.

She'd be better off without you.

You should just disappear. Pretend this never happened. Someone else can take better care of her than you.

Pack a bag and just drive until you find a small town where no one knows you. She's better off thinking you're dead.

I tried to chase away the thoughts by—as my mother would say—focusing on the positive things that had happened today.

But suddenly, they were gone.

The knock at the door startled me. Dr. Heath, in green pants and a coordinating frog shirt today, poked her head in. "Good afternoon, Beth."

Her tone was formal and uneasy.

I finished fastening the snaps on Kat's onesie and scooped her off the table. Apparently being held by her mother was the last thing she wanted, because Kat let out an ear-piercing scream.

I swear Dr. Heath's eye twitched at the sound.

"Sorry," I muttered as I perched Kat against my shoulder and rocked between my feet.

"She's probably hungry," she said without any amusement. "Babies cry when they're hungry."

My heart sank.

"I—I know. I fed her right before we came."

"Are you feeding on demand?"

I stammered. "Uh—no. I was ... Everything I read said to feed on a schedule."

"Well, you should be doing both."

On demand and on a timed schedule? How the hell did that make a lick of sense?

Her eyes were shrewd and judgmental. "Feed on your schedule, but if she's giving hunger cues, feed her then, too."

I swallowed. "It's just ... breastfeeding is really hard. It hurts and I get really—you know—anxious about it. And I've been trying to pump more, but I'm not getting anything in between. I just—I don't feel right. I feel like there's something wrong, and I'm having all these crazy thoughts. It's scary. I feel like a stranger in my body and in my head and it gets so much worse when I try to feed her."

Her response was placating. "It's very common to experience some baby blues, and it usually goes away when you get some sleep. Are you sleeping when the baby sleeps?"

Like sleeping when the baby sleeps was actually a reasonable thing to do. My house would be a garbage dump, my life would be in shambles, my doctorate would go out the window, and I would lose all sense of existing as a human.

I gritted my teeth. "I've experienced the baby blues. I've experienced the baby pinks, reds, yellows, greens, and oranges. I have experienced the full spectrum of feelings about having a baby and where I'm at now, and I'm telling you that something doesn't feel right and I'm scared. I'm looking for help."

Her annoyed huff wasn't at all encouraging. "If you're experiencing anxiety, perhaps chat with your obstetrician at your next appointment."

"That's three weeks away."

"Feelings are no excuse to let it impact your ability to feed her. Lots of women go through it and they manage to care for their children just fine."

So much for trying to confide in someone who was supposed to help...

"Are you eating and drinking enough?" Her words were sharp and accusatory.

Probably not, but I was trying. "Yes."

Her pinched face silently said that she didn't believe me.

Her fingers stabbed the keys on her laptop. "How long are you feeding her each time?"

"Um. About thirty minutes."

Dr. Heath turned away from her laptop and crossed her arms. She gave Kat a silent, distant assessment as I held her.

After a long, hostile standoff, she finally spoke again. "Kat doesn't have a tongue tie, so she should have no trouble latching. And at this point, we don't have time to spare for you to see a lactation consultant. Your baby needs to be putting on weight and what you're doing isn't enough."

My heart sank.

Failure.

Unfit.

Inadequate.

Her face conveyed the utter dismay she felt toward my capability to be a mother as she punched in a few commands on her laptop. A printer below the desk spat out a sheet of paper.

"Formula on your *schedule*." Her slight sarcasm was an insult. "Breast on demand." She offered the paper with instructions on how to prepare bottles. "Pump as much as you can. Emergency methods are no excuse to not give your child your best."

"It hurts."

The flick of her cool irises was a barely restrained eye roll. "If you're doing it right, it shouldn't. Did you not listen to the lactation consultants in the hospital?"

It had been kind of hard to do that when I was barely human and half asleep when they would stomp in the room, flip on all the lights, and grab my boobs without permission.

No one warned me about how violated I would feel after childbirth.

"I did ... But it's—It's hard."

She blew a breath out of her nose. "No one said motherhood was easy."

At this point I didn't care about it being easy. I just wanted it to be possible.

I left the pediatrician's office with tears in my eyes and a small sample bottle of premixed formula that Dr. Heath had begrudgingly given me.

The moment I sank into the driver's seat, I cried.

Kat screamed from her car seat, reminding me just how badly I sucked at this. How much I was failing her.

Layla was already at my house when I pulled in. She stood on the doorstep with a stack of aluminum baking dishes in hand. I grabbed a wad of fast food napkins out of the console and dabbed my eyes.

Kat hadn't stopped wailing yet.

Layla was one of my best friends, but the last thing I wanted was company.

"Hey," she said when I finally eased out of the car and circled to grab Kat's car seat.

"Hey."

"I hope you're hungry."

I wasn't. Guilt and shame had a way of diminishing my appetite.

The food in her arms smelled amazing, which only insulted me further. I'd choke down a few polite bites and then take the leftovers to the fire station.

It was better that way anyways. I was just one person. I couldn't finish the buffet that Layla brought. It would go bad before I ate it all.

I shifted the car seat into the crook of my elbow and unlocked the door, letting Layla in first.

"Okay, spill," she said as she dumped the load of dishes on the kitchen counters. "You look like you're about to explode."

"I'm fine. Just tired," I lied as I set the car seat on the floor and started to unbuckle Kat. If she was going to scream anyway, I might as well get some tummy time out of it.

She snorted. "Bullshit. What's going on?"

Layla Mousavi. Human lie detector.

She helped herself to my kitchen, preheating the oven and playing casserole dish Tetris to make space in the fridge while I eyed the bottle of premixed formula that had been handed to me like an insult.

Was I a bad mom if I used it? I was just following what Dr.

Heath said to do... But the disappointment and disdain was evident. Should I just try to nurse Kat again?

"Nothing. Like I said—I'm just tired."

"I haven't given birth, but I know what tired looks like." She pointed at my face. "That's not tired. That's the face Cal has when he's seen something so horrific that he can't talk about it."

Worn out from screaming, Kat fell asleep the moment I laid her in the pop-up crib I kept in the living room. *Thank God.*

The kettle whistled from the stovetop, and Layla pulled it off. "Tea?"

"Uh, no thanks." I had been drinking a tea blend that was supposed to boost lactation for a week straight, but all it had done was make me hate hot tea and have to pee every ten minutes. Top it off with the homemade lactation cookies that tasted like cardboard and grass, and my appetite was gone.

Layla carried a tray of tea cups, *nabat*—Iranian rock candy that I fancied—and a teapot into the living room and set it on the coffee table.

"Chai," I said in relief.

"I know it's still warm outside, but chai is comforting."

I sank onto the couch. "Sorry. When you said tea, I figured it would be the tea bags I had on the counter."

She snorted and poured me a cup. "You should know me better than that." She paused, eyeing me before pouring herself a cup. "So, are we going to have this standoff where we pretend everything is fine until you eventually crack, or are you just going to get it over with and tell me what's going on?"

I groaned and closed my eyes. "You're like Shane. And my brother."

"It's a first responder thing. We see too much shit to beat

around the bush. Nothing fazes us. Callum's the same way. But speaking of Shane—"

"I'm not speaking of Shane," I said definitively. *No matter how much I wanted to be with Shane right now. He didn't need me as a burden. Besides, I was a package deal. Sure, he was smitten with Kat now. She was cute. But a few hours with her didn't compare to the 504 hours I had survived. It was too much.*

Layla grinned like the cat that had just eaten the canary. "Fine, then. If you don't want to speak of Shane, then speak of whatever's going on with you. How'd the doctor's appointment go?"

I couldn't even fake the dread that consumed me. I stared down into the mug of chai as my warped reflection stared back. "She's still underweight." A tear slid down my cheek. *Thanks, hormones.* "I failed."

Layla didn't argue with me like I thought she would. Instead, she studied me with a cool assessment. "Why?"

I dabbed my eyes. "Why what?"

"Why do you think you've failed?"

The floodgates burst. "I can't make enough milk to feed her. Using that fucking breast pump makes me want to crawl out of my skin. I can't breathe and my mind starts racing. I hate breastfeeding. *Hate* it. It's painful. And—" my voice choked off, turning to a whisper "—*God... It sounds awful...* I—I have these thoughts. They come out of nowhere. These little thoughts that slide in my mind when I look at her... About how easy it would be to hurt her. What it would be like if I—I j-just threw her across t-the room."

I was full-on sobbing. Tea sloshed onto the saucer as my hand trembled.

I couldn't catch my breath. Couldn't get the words out.

"I don't want to hurt her," I whispered through gritted teeth. "I don't know what's wrong with me. I don't know why I thought I could do this. Someone needs to take her away from me. I shouldn't be a mother. I—I should just ... I shouldn't be here anymore. She's better off without me."

I couldn't see her through the tears blurring my vision, but I could feel her arms around me as she leaped out of her chair and wrapped me into a hug.

For the longest time, I sat there with her holding me and cried. The oven timer beeped, but Layla didn't move.

"Honey, how long have you felt like this?" she soothed.

I used the edge of a throw blanket to wipe my eyes. "I don't know."

She waited.

"I just ... It crept up on me. I've never had thoughts like this. I've never been depressed before. And it's terrifying. I feel like Jekyll and Hyde, and I can't control it. It's like I'm a puppet on a string, but something else is controlling the strings. I'm scared of myself."

"Have you talked to your doctor?" she prodded.

I shook my head and reached for the tea that Layla had plucked out of my shaking hands and set on the coffee table. The heat stung my lips as I took a fortifying sip. "No. My appointment is three weeks away."

"Didn't you try out that mommy support group? How was that?"

I stared into my tea. "They told me I needed to pray more, drink wine, and then treated me like the whore of Babylon when one of them recognized me. Apparently, she's friends with Brad—*his*—wife."

I didn't dare utter the sperm donor's name.

"Okay," Layla said, turning on the couch to face me. "First off. You probably have postpartum depression. It's not uncommon." She paused in thought, then continued. "Actually, it's pretty common. But no one talks about it, so it stays taboo.

Second—you couldn't pray it away even if you wanted to. The chemicals in your brain are going haywire because you literally created a new person. It's going to take your brain a while to get back to normal. I'll forward you the medical journals I was reading about it."

"Why were you reading medical journals about post—" saying it would confirm it. If I didn't say it, I didn't have it. Right? "—about *it*?"

She shrugged. "Had a feeling. But since you seem like you don't want to talk about it, do you want to rant about the wino mommies or tell me about the pediatrician."

"God, I hate that woman," I muttered under my breath.

Then the guilt set in.

She was just looking out for her patient, which was more than I could say for myself.

"So, she's still under her birth weight?" Layla said, peering into the pop-up crib.

I nodded as tears flooded my vision again.

"Will she take formula?"

"I don't know," I admitted. "I haven't tried. I—I want to give her my best. I wanted the magic so badly. I wanted what everyone else has. And then Dr. Heath... And that nurse..." I set the cup down and dropped my head into my hands. "I'm doing everything I can and it's not enough. I'm not enough."

Layla didn't hesitate to butt in. "Giving your daughter your best means giving her you." She reached out and squeezed my hand. "Kat needs you to be here. Do what you have to do to stay. If that means giving her formula, then fuck the magical tit juice. Give her formula. No one's gonna be asking if she was breastfed or formula fed on a college application."

"That's easy for you to say," I countered. "You're not a mom. You don't have a judgmental shrew of a pediatrician looking at you. You don't have Mommy and me groups judging you because you had the audacity to open your mouth and say that you're struggling."

"Beth, listen to me. Breastfeeding—formula... There's no moral high ground. You're feeding your kid." Her voice softened. "There will be magic. It doesn't have to come from this moment. But I need you to be around to experience that magic. Do you hear me?"

I gave her a blubbering nod.

"Good. Now get the formula bottle ready and I'll fix you a plate for supper."

———

KAT'S CRIES filled the house. It was the witching hour.

The warm aroma of the leftovers that Layla packed away after she made sure I ate an entire plate of food still wafted around me. The glow of the oven clock told me it was after three in the morning.

Earlier, Layla had sat with me while I fed Kat the little sample bottle of formula. Kat chugged it down like a champ, which only served to pour more salt in my invisible wounds.

Your body failed you.

But Layla was gone, and I was on my own again.

Nights were always the worst.

Kat's cries grew louder as I padded into the kitchen to grab a little baggie of milk that I had popped in the fridge after a miserable and fruitless pumping session.

Condiment bottles clinked in the fridge door as I opened it. Light bounced across the kitchen.

Where was it?

I pawed around Tupperware containers and takeout boxes for the bag I had put in there.

Shit.

I had given it to Kat in a bottle before I went to bed.

There had to be one more in the freezer. I could thaw it and warm it quickly. Where was it?

But there wasn't any more.

I had given her the only sample of formula the doctor gave me, and I was out of my stock of frozen milk.

I glanced at the time.

3:08 AM.

Every store in Falls Creek was closed, and driving to Chapel Hill in the middle of the night when I was delirious was out of the question.

Okay, Beth. Make it to seven AM and go to the store for formula.

Kat's screams intensified, and it made my pulse skyrocket.

She couldn't wait until seven AM.

I resided to another grueling nursing session. It was the only way to get her to go back to sleep.

But with each step toward the nursery, my heart rose higher and higher into my throat.

Cold sweats and hot flashes burst across my skin like fireworks. An elephant sat on my chest as invisible zip ties cinched around my stomach.

My vision tunneled and I went limp.

Everything went sideways as my knees buckled.

I couldn't even bring myself to walk in there to sooth her.

I couldn't breathe. The roaring in my ears was as loud as a freight train. I fumbled in the pocket of my sweatpants and found my phone. I curled up on the floor with my knees to my chest as tremors shook through me.

His name glowed like a beacon on my screen. I pressed it, then dropped the phone on the floor as I fought to breathe.

It only took one ring.

"Hello?"

I couldn't get the words out. I couldn't speak.

"Beth? Did you butt dial me?"

I closed my eyes and tried to make a sound. "S-Shane—"

"Beth—" he was more alert now. "Where are you, Mama?"

"Home," I choked out. "I—I need h-help."

13

SHANE

I lingered in the twilight zone; asleep but still aware of the sounds around me. It was how I slept most nights.

I had just descended into a light doze when my phone rang.

If that was the station calling me to cover for someone, the answer was no.

I felt around for my phone and peered bleary-eyed at the screen.

What the fuck? It was Beth, and it was just after three in the morning.

I swiped across the screen. "Hello?"

There was muffled static and a distant cry from the baby.

I rubbed my eyes again. "Beth. Did you butt dial me?"

I heard breaths. It was shoddy and quick like she was gasping. My feet hit the floor.

"S-Shane—"

"Beth—" I said as I jumped into a discarded pair of sweatpants and a t-shirt, grabbed my keys, and slid into my sneakers on the way out the door. "Where are you, Mama?"

The hair on the back of my neck stood on end as I bolted out to my truck and gunned it out of the driveway.

Lights turned on in the surrounding houses at the ruckus as I peeled down the street.

"Home." Her whimper broke my heart. Before I could get anything out, she said, "I—I need h-help."

I didn't remember the drive to Beth's townhouse. I blew every red light and went double the speed limit.

I pulled into the space beside her car and hopped out. Kat's faint crying echoed in the air. The call was still connected, so I pressed the phone to my ear and knocked on the door. "Beth. I'm here. Open up."

No response.

"*Beth.*"

Nothing. Not a peep from her. No sound except Kat's cries and the explosive pounding in my heart.

Fuck it.

I ran back to the truck and rifled around until I found the spare Swiss Army Knife that I kept in the console. I flipped open the lock picking mechanism and started working my way inside. It felt like hours went by as I adjusted the tension wrench bit by bit to get the lock to release. My lungs burned from holding my breath.

The tumbler released and the door opened.

"Beth!" I called out as I hurried through the living room. It was dark and I didn't have time to find the light switch.

Whatever made her call me in the middle of the night ... It wasn't good.

There were two sets of cries, I realized as I neared Kat's nursery.

Beth was lying in a huddled heap in the narrow hallway between her room and Kat's. I dropped to my knees. "Beth, I'm right here. What's going on? Are you hurt? Sick?"

She was lying in the fetal position, pinned up against the wall. Her body shook, fueled by the tears rolling down her cheeks. She was barely able to catch a breath. It was then that I realized her phone was trapped under her body.

"I c-can't," she whimpered.

"Can't what?" I pushed as I brushed her hair out of her face. "Is Kat okay?"

No response. Just more tears.

I didn't know what I was expecting to find when I showed up, but I would have been lying if I didn't admit to assuming the worst.

I slid my hand into hers. "Squeeze my fingers. Once for yes. Twice for no." I paused a beat until I felt her grip flex around my hand. "Are you hurt?"

Two squeezes.

"Okay. Is Kat hurt?"

Two squeezes.

"Okay. Is she safe?"

No answer.

"Is Kat in her crib?"

One squeeze.

"Okay. She's safe, then. Is it alright if I pick you up?"

She hesitated. Then, one squeeze.

I didn't wait. I scooped her off the floor and carried her into her bedroom, keeping her snug against my chest. She was still shaking.

I sat on the bed and shifted so she was upright in my arms. "Can you breathe?"

She shook her head.

"Close your eyes for me." I tightened my arms around her. "Block it all out and listen to me."

Beth settled between my legs. Every muscle in her body was wound tight like a coiled spring.

I found her hands and held them, lacing our fingers together as I crossed her arms and mine over her body.

Her hair was piled high on top of her head, and my breath clouded against her neck. "Do you feel my heartbeat against your back?"

I felt her lean into me.

"Focus on that. It's the only thing I want you to think about right now."

The tremors slowed, and I finally felt like I wasn't restraining her. I was holding her.

I was holding Beth Hale.

"I want you to try to breathe with me."

"I can't," she whispered.

"Try for me. Just try." I inhaled deeply, held it, then slowly exhaled. "Just like that. You don't have to do it on your own. You're gonna do it with me."

Instead of waiting for her to agree, I resumed the breathing pattern that used to help me steady my trigger finger.

Fire as soon as you start exhaling, and reload on the inhale.

But this wasn't a sniper's nest in Fallujah. I was in Beth's bed.

Beth sucked in a shoddy breath and let it out all too quickly, but it was a start.

"There you go," I murmured against her skin. "Try again. Deep breath."

It was surer the second time.

And then Beth crumbled into me. She buried her face in my chest and sobbed. "I can't do this," she cried. "I can't feed her. I can't. I can't—"

"Hey—" I murmured as I buried my nose in the mess of hair on top of her head. "You don't have to do anything right now. Just breathe for me. Kat is safe, and she'll be okay for a few minutes."

She collapsed into me and cried. I didn't say anything; just let her get it out.

A purge was necessary when emotions were too bottled up.

I wanted to kiss her so fucking bad, and I deserved to go to hell for it.

I tightened my arms around her. If this was the only time I ever got to hold her, I'd remember the way she felt in my arms until my dying day.

"It's gonna be okay," I said when her tears slowed. "I promise you. Tomorrow will be better."

"It's not," she whimpered as she sucked in a threadbare breath.

I brushed my thumb across her cheek. "I know it doesn't feel like it. You're in the tunnel, and it's pitch black. I've been there. I know how fucking dark it is. But I'm standing at the other side and I promise you—*I promise*—there's light."

"I can't feed her, Shane." Beth looked up at me. Her eyes were pools of emerald filled with torment. "I—I can't."

"Hey—" I said before she spiraled again. "I'm glad you called." Pressing a kiss to her forehead, I murmured, "Can you tell me what happened?"

I sat quietly, gently rubbing her back while Beth word-vomited the last twelve hours at me. She started with her mom finally going home, then moved to the bitch of a pediatrician. She told me about the way the medical staff gave her shit about Kat's weight, then about running out of the small sample of formula and her freezer stash of breastmilk. Beth was more guarded when she told me about the panic attack in the hall when Kat needed to be fed, but she bared it all in her own time.

Her breathing was stronger and the tears had slowed, but Beth hadn't moved from her place curled up against my chest. I didn't want her to.

"I'm sorry I called you and scared you and dragged you out of your bed," she said as her eyes fluttered closed. "I shouldn't have."

"Bullshit. I wanted you to. I'm glad you did."

On that sentiment, Kat started her next round of crying. Beth flinched.

"What's your game plan? I'm gonna stay, and I'm gonna help. Just tell me what you want to happen."

Beth was quiet, but I could see her mulling it over. I could feel the worry, the fear radiating off her. She was nuclear, verging on meltdown.

"I have to feed her."

"How do you want to do it? I can drive the three of us to Chapel Hill so you don't have to be alone."

"Going all the way out there will take too long." She sniffed. "I gave her a bottle right before I went to sleep. I was trying to wait until the morning to go to the store in town."

"Okay. Tell me how I can support you while you nurse her right now."

She looked at me. "Why do you always say the right thing?"

But it wasn't curiosity. It was blatant mistrust.

"Words matter." I cupped her cheek. "I won't always say or do the right thing, but when I fuck up, I'll apologize and do better. It's really not that complicated."

She seemed to relax a little, and let her guard down again.

Kat's pitiful cries ramped up again.

"Take the way it makes your body feel out of the equation. What goes through your mind when you're feeding Kat?"

Her eyes darted across the room like she was planning an

escape. But, to my surprise, she didn't jolt out of my arms. "I ... I can't explain it. I just feel ... *rage*. I've never felt like that before. And it comes out of nowhere and it scares the living hell out of me."

"And you feel like that when you hold her?"

Beth nodded. "I'm scared of hurting her. I'm scared of myself. I'm scared of my mind." Her confession was a sacred whisper. "And whenever I try to tell someone, it gets downplayed or dismissed. I feel like I'm screaming into the void."

I tilted her chin up. "I hear you."

There was sincerity in the way she looked at me. "I know. That's why I called."

I assessed the way I was holding her right now. Her between my legs, sitting up and resting against my chest, with my arms around her. She was still understandably upset, but little by little she was relaxing.

I pressed my cheek to her temple. "Could you feed her if I held you like this? Or would you rather have some privacy?"

"I really don't want to be alone with her." There was so much more she didn't say, but it was written in the tired lines on her face.

"How about you go get a snack and something to drink. I'll get Kat changed and bring her in here for you."

She hesitated, but slowly eased off the bed and padded into the kitchen.

Kat was beet red from crying. Her tiny fists were balled up as she screamed from the crib. The few times I had held her, she settled pretty quickly.

Not this time.

She fought me every step of the way as I tried to change her diaper. Getting the onesie closed was a fucking battle.

"Come on, tadpole," I soothed as I tried to fasten the last snap. "Work with me, kid."

Finally, she was dry and dressed. *Still wailing, but one problem at a time.*

I propped her up against my chest and hoped by some shred of magic that my heartbeat would calm her down the way it had in the hospital.

Nope.

Beth was getting back into bed when I carried the baby into the room. She had a sports drink on the bedside table and a cookie wrapped in a napkin.

"What kind is that?" I asked, nodding to it.

Beth sighed. "It's supposed to boost my milk production. It tastes like what I imagine the cabin floor on *Little House on the Prairie* tasted like."

I laughed. "That's unfortunate. We'll get Oreos tomorrow."

She lifted an eyebrow.

"When we go to the store for formula," I clarified. "You're gonna make it through the night, grab a cat nap, and I'll take you as soon as they open."

"Shane," she sighed. "You don't have to. I—"

"I want to," I said as I sat on the bed and scooted up against the headboard.

Kat, seemingly aware of the change of scenery and her mom in the room, temporarily settled down.

Beth looked downright terrified as she looked at the spot where she was supposed to sit.

"I've got you," I promised.

She nodded timidly and reached for a thick, U-shaped pillow before settling between my knees.

I kept Kat against me while Beth shucked off her tank top and exposed her nursing bra.

Huh. Popcorn ceilings. I hadn't noticed that before.

The ends of the U-pillow bumped me as Beth fitted it around her waist, then turned and silently reached for Kat.

I lowered the baby into Beth's arms. She was stoic, like she was trying to keep every emotion on lock just to get through this.

"Breathe with me," I said as I pulled my girls back against my chest.

My palms skated down Beth's arms as she positioned Kat on the pillow. She was tense and rigid.

The corner of my mouth brushed the tip of her ear. "Focus on me."

I closed my eyes at the unsnap of her nursing bra.

I was in emergency medicine. Bodies were bodies to me. I had watched Beth give birth and, apart from the miracle of life, didn't give her physique another thought. She had been my patient. She was my friend. She was my former roommate and best friend's little sister.

Not once had I struggled with compartmentalizing.

Until now.

So, I closed my eyes.

Beth's sharp intake of breath and failure to release jarred my attention.

I wrapped my arms around her, beneath the pillow. "Let it out. Exhale."

I peeked when she didn't.

Kat's face was squished against the curve of Beth's breast, and Beth was frozen in fear.

"It hurts," she gritted out on the exhale. Her fingers barely grazed Kat's head. *Beth really was terrified of hurting her.*

I braced her hand against Kat with my own, giving her more support as she held her daughter. I'd keep her safe. I'd keep them *both* safe. "I wish I could fix that. Just focus on me. Don't look at the clock."

Her head tipped back on to my collarbone and she closed

her eyes. "I hate this." The words were crushing, but her hold on Kat tightened protectively.

"I know, Mama. But hear me. You remember when I came over and hung out with Kat for a few hours while you caught up on sleep?"

She nodded.

"Remember when you told me you weren't made for this and that the motherhood gene skipped you?"

She nodded again.

"I said that you were wrong then, and I'm gonna say it to you now. You're wrong, and you're incredible. I know how much you hate this, and how much it hurts you, but the fact that you're choosing to do it because it's what your child needs in this moment makes you a good mom. And in the morning when we go to the store and get whatever shit you need to feed her with a bottle? That makes you a good mom, because you're taking care of your child. I admire the fuck out of you, Dimples."

A tear slipped down her cheek, and I was quick to wipe it away.

"And asking for help—" I squeezed her between my biceps and dotted her temple with a chaste kiss. "That makes you a good mom."

"You have a really good bedside manner."

This was the farthest thing from my job and I felt guilty as fuck about it. She was trusting me to keep myself in check.

"This isn't bedside manner, Beth."

"Oh…" Her voice trailed off. "It's because you've been here. You know—with the panic attacks and everything."

"No. It's because I *want* to be here."

14

BETH

I wanted to believe him, but fear was a wraith, slow dancing with my anxiety. I could feel the wisps of its pernicious garment grazing my wounded heart.

But Shane's arms were stronger. Safer.

I adjusted Kat and gave in, fully reclining against him. "Will you tell me about the Navy again?"

His scruff grazed my temple. "What do you want to hear about tonight?"

"Tell me about Chile."

His laugh was soft, rumbling from deep in his chest like a distant landslide. "Why Chile?"

"You told me it was your favorite place." I closed my eyes and tried to distract myself from nursing Kat by memorizing the plateaus and valleys of his muscular chest against my back. "Tell me something happy. A good memory."

"This is a good memory," he whispered under his breath. "But settle in. There was this one op that we got spun up for." He chuckled. "Everything that could go wrong, did go wrong. It was Murphy's law 101."

"Sounds like my life right now."

The corner of his mouth drew up in a half smile. "Then let me tell you where it got good."

―――――

"I THINK SHE'S DONE," I said as I lifted the back of my head off Shane's chest.

The muscles in my shoulders were tight and strained from the tension of sitting still and trying to keep the internal urge to run away at bay.

I managed to get Kat to latch for twenty minutes on one side and twenty minutes on the other.

Shane's arms around my middle loosened as I sat up and peered over my shoulder.

Nerves zipped up my spine. What did he think about my post-baby body?

I used to have the kind of body that I didn't mind showing off. I had a great rack and, thanks to hours in the gym, an ass to match.

But all of it was gone.

My boobs were lopsided and covered in stretch marks. They used to look great during my pregnancy and when they were actually making milk, but my body had given up before my mind did. Now, they were deflated and wonky. My stomach had tiger marks, extra skin, and a pooch that hadn't gone away yet. My navel was misshapen and weirdly stretched out. One of the town's busybodies had brought me a belly binder so I could get back to "feeling and *looking* like myself."

I didn't have the brain cells to spare worrying about that at the time.

But now I *was* worrying about it.

Shane's hands slid up and down my hips in a soothing

motion. "Do you want me to burp her so you can have your hands free?"

Yes. Please take her away from me. You're so much better at this than I am. She's safe with you.

"Yes, please," I said instead of all the things that raced through my mind.

Shane reached around me, carefully cradling Kat. I dipped under his arm so he could pull her around without lifting her over my head.

"I just need a minute to go to the bathroom," I said as I eased off the bed.

"Take your time."

As I stepped through the doorway, I peered back over my shoulder. Shane was staring at Kat like she hung the moon and stars. She snuggled right up to him and fell asleep.

He was smiling as he spoke softly to her.

The taste of guilt and shame on my tongue was familiar.

I disappeared into the bathroom and took care of business, changing my diaper-like pad and hiding the bloody one at the bottom of the trash can just in case Shane dipped in here.

I didn't know why I cared. It wasn't like the crush I had on him could go anywhere. And was it really a crush if I couldn't trust my thoughts?

When I came out of the bathroom, Kat's nursery door was open and music filtered through.

Curious, I peeked inside.

Chris Stapleton's "Broken Halos" played from his phone. In the glow of the night light, Shane slow danced with my daughter against his chest.

"Come on, tadpole," he soothed. "Go back to sleep. Give your mom some rest. She needs a break, so I need you to work with me."

My heart clenched as Kat whined, fighting sleep.

"There you go," he cooed in as manly a coo as one could. "Go to sleep." He turned as the chorus ramped up again, and gave Kat a supported dip. "Shit—" Shane realized I was watching. He cleared his throat and tucked Kat into the crook of his arm. "She got fussy. I was just trying to get her to fall back asleep."

"Thank you." I stepped in the nursery, busying myself with refolding a blanket that didn't need folding. "I think she'll sleep if you put her in the crib."

Shane leaned over the edge and lowered her in. Kat didn't even stir. She was out like a light.

I sided up to him and peered in at her serene face. She had most of my features, but some of Bradley's mixed in.

Before my mind could fall into the pit of how Kat came into existence and the ruin left in the wake of my choices, Shane wrapped his arm around my shoulder, pulling me into his side.

"You did good, Mama."

I shook my head. "I didn't. I should have picked up formula before I came home from the pediatrician, but I was flustered and upset and couldn't think straight. I should have checked the freezer to make sure I had enough milk stashed away to make it through the night. I should have just gone in there and fed her and not made such a big deal out of it."

"Beth, listen to me," he said as he turned me away from the crib and walked me out of the nursery. "You wanna know why you weren't able to do those things?"

I stared at the floor.

"Because you were worried about a million other things. You're carrying a big load, and it doesn't help when your judgment and ability are constantly being called into question. You're beating yourself up because Plan A didn't work, and your medical support staff—the people who should be supporting you in Plan B—are being self-righteous, archaic pricks." He hooked a finger beneath my chin and tipped it up until I was looking at him. "Hear me. You did the right thing. You called me."

"But I should have been able to do it on my own. You can't breastfeed. I don't know why I needed someone to sit with me."

He laughed. "I'm sorry my nipples are useless." Then, cupping my cheek, he added, "It's okay to need someone to sit with you. There have been plenty of times I've needed someone to sit with me. I still do sometimes." His thumb stroked my cheek. "It's okay to let yourself need people. I know you got burned by your baby daddy, but I promise I'm not him."

I rested my forehead on his chest and closed my eyes. "I know."

Instead of saying anything else, he wrapped an arm around me and cradled the back of my head against his chest.

So this is why Kat falls asleep so easily.

"Go get some sleep, Mama. I'll keep watch."

"You don't have to stay."

"I'm going to stay, Beth. So don't argue with me." His fingers tangled in the hair at the nape of my neck. "Sleep, and I'll take you to the store as soon as they open."

"I can't ask you to do that. I can drive myself. It's ten minutes away."

"What did I tell you about arguing with me?"

A vaguely familiar feeling of excitement zipped down my spine.

"Go to bed. I'll sit out here and listen out in case Kat wakes up."

I looked up and caught him staring at my mouth.

Was he—

Did I want him to—

I stepped out of his arms. "Okay. I'll set an alarm."

"Sleep as long as you need to. It's my day off. I've got a few things to do later, but I'm yours."

I closed my bedroom door behind me and made sure the volume on the baby monitor was turned up.

My pulse ramped up as every side-eyed look and passive-yet-mostly aggressive comment I got at the doctor's office played in my mind on a loop. But as soon as I laid my head on the pillow, the thoughts went away.

My pillow smelled like him. It was woodsy and masculine without being overpowering. Quickly, I grabbed another pillow to rest my head on and turned the one I was intoxicated with sideways so I could cuddle up to it as I closed my eyes. While I slipped into the sleep I had been craving, it was Shane's chest I imagined myself resting on.

"No, ma'am," Shane said when I reached for the car seat handle. His hand wrapped around mine as he peeled it off. "I've got it."

Fine. I wasn't going to argue with him. The car seat was a beast. I had a bruise on my hip from the side always bumping against me. I made a move for the diaper bag instead.

"Let me get that," Shane said.

"You're getting the car seat."

"I have two hands. I'll get both."

"I feel weird with you being my pack mule."

He just gave me that stupid smile that made my insides turn to warm, melted chocolate. "I know you can get both, but I want to."

"Stupid southern men and their damn manners," I grumbled dramatically, earning a smirk from Shane as he carefully loaded Kat into the back of my car. He double-checked that her car seat was secure, and then opened my door for me.

I winced, bracing against the doorframe as a sharp cramp fueled by nerves ricocheted through my gut.

"What's the matter?" he asked, his face full of concern.

"Nothing." I breathed through it. "I'm fine."

He arched an eyebrow. "You sure? You'd tell me if it was something more, right?"

I nodded and dropped down into the seat as soon as it passed. "Promise."

He shut my door, jogged around, and hopped behind the wheel, taking a moment to adjust the mirrors and push the seat back.

Falls Creek didn't have all the bells and whistles of the larger cities in the county, but it had a respectable grocery store with a medium-sized baby department. Cars filtered in and out as Creekers slipped in for their early morning grocery runs.

Shane circled the lot until a space beside a cart return opened up. Even though the majority of the patrons were busy running errands before they dispersed to their jobs and schools, it felt like every eye was on the three of us.

Watching Shane pull Kat's car seat out and secure it into a buggy was oddly domestic. His attention to detail was bar none. He was so much like my brother. Always safety first.

"Lead the way, Dimples," he said as he pushed the cart across the blacktop.

I looked down at my sneakers and tried to hide my smile. I got schoolgirl giddy when he called me Dimples. Ever since that day at the gas station, I had harbored the tiniest of crushes on the guy who let me in on the secret of Falls Creek coffee.

Every time I stopped there on my way to campus, I still got the light roast even though it was the same as the other percolators.

We made it off the uneven asphalt and glided onto the slick tile floor. I pulled back the stretchy nursing cover that doubled as a car seat cover and peeked in to make sure Kat was still sleeping.

Swatting hands away got tiring. I had learned early on it was best to keep Kat hidden from shoppers unless I wanted their germ-riddled paws on my baby.

My palms began to sweat as we rounded the produce section and cut through the pet supply aisle.

Why did this make me so nervous?

"You're a good mom, Beth. You're doing right by your kid."

"Thanks."

His dark eyes pierced my heart as he looked down at me. "Breathe for me."

"I am."

"No, you're not." He stopped the cart and took my hand, giving it a squeeze. "I'm right here. No one's judging you. There's no running commentary. And I have a hunch that you'll feel better once Kat has a full belly and your body is a little more yours again."

My heart was racing, but I managed a series of deep breaths that made me a little less frantic.

I stayed glued to his side as we traipsed the diaper aisle. I needed wipes, so I snagged a package and tossed it in the buggy.

Rows of formula canisters and boxes loomed in front of me, all painted in cheery colors.

Even Shane looked surprised. "I didn't know there were this many different kinds."

I spotted the same brand and type of formula as the sample. Kat chugged it down, so I figured that was a safe start.

"Can you grab that one for me?" I asked in a whisper, discreetly pointing to the package on the very top shelf.

Shane reached up and snagged it with no problem. "Anything else?"

"I should probably get a few more bottles since I'm going to be using them all the time now."

Shane led the way, a man on a mission.

By the time we were done, I had enough bottles to last me through Kat's entire childhood, a brush to wash them, and a handy little container that let me pre-measure scoops of formula for making bottles on the go.

I had gotten distracted by the display of household child-proofing supplies when I realized I had lost Shane.

I poked my head around to the next aisle. *Nope.*

I turned the cart and went two aisles down. *Still no sign of him.*

"Shane?" I called out.

"Right here," he said, appearing behind me and tossing something into the cart.

I pulled it out. "What's that?"

"Mine."

I looked at the onesie and raised an eyebrow. "Really. You fit in newborn clothes?"

He grinned. "I'm getting it. It's for my tadpole."

I unfurled the folded onesie and inspected it. A little baby frog was on the chest, surrounded by letters that read, "Toad-ally Adorable."

It *was* totally adorable, and Shane looked so fucking pleased with himself.

"Come on, Mama," he said, taking control of the buggy.

"Let's get checked out and get you two pretty girls home. I have a feeling today's a 'naps all around' kind of day."

He was right. It was the kind of fall day that had a clean crispness to the air. It made me want to throw open the windows, wash my sheets, and sleep with the cool afternoon breeze on my skin.

I followed Shane toward the checkout line, reaching into the diaper bag for my wallet.

The cart stopped abruptly.

"What—" I looked up and froze.

Bradley Childers stood in the aisle holding a hand basket full of microwave dinners.

His face went to anger in the blink of an eye. *And then his gaze turned to the car seat in the buggy.*

"Bethany." My name slipped out of his mouth like a muttered profanity. I felt violated and disgusting as he assessed my stomach. "You had our baby."

"*My* baby," I shot back. The momentary shock was replaced by a tidal wave of adrenaline.

Was this how mothers lifted cars off their trapped children? Because right now I felt like I could rip him limb from limb without breaking a sweat.

Shane stepped between me and Bradley, completely blocking my view of the other half of Kat's DNA. "Beth has a protective order against you. Let's not make a scene. Take your things, check out, and leave." His tone was calm, but there was a lethality woven into it.

Bradley scoffed. "I'm not doing anything wrong. It's a fucking grocery store. How was I supposed to know she'd be here? It's *incidental contact.*"

I don't know why I was surprised. He was the type to read everything and find even the smallest of loopholes.

I peered around Shane. Bradley was transfixed on the car seat. Thankfully, Kat hadn't made a peep.

Please stay asleep. Please stay asleep. Please stay asleep.

"Had my baby and didn't even have the fucking nerve to tell me," he spat.

Shane yanked on the cart handle and rolled the buggy backward into my care. He stepped forward, completely blocking him from looking at me or Kat.

"You will lower your eyes to the goddamn floor. You do not have the privilege of looking at either of them." Shane grinned like a comic-book villain. "And I swear to God, I will rip your eyeballs out of your skull if you are so much as tempted to open them in the direction of *her* town when you wake up every pathetic day of your sorry life. Do you hear me?" Shane said in a menacing growl. "Now *get out.*"

15

BETH

I was shaking as Bradley backed away from Shane. Malice lingered in his eyes. I wanted nothing more than to grab Kat out of her car seat and hold her tight against my chest.

But I wouldn't expose her to him.

Never.

Not after he showed up back at Christmastime, drunk, and threatened me. Not after he kept blowing up my phone with endless texts full of accusations and thinly veiled promises of revenge. Not after he kept showing up at my house, out of the blue.

Austin had been living with me at the time, but Bradley always managed to show up when I was alone.

Eventually, I filed for a restraining order. Up until now, that piece of paper had done its job.

He had been put on leave from the university, giving me a reprieve from chance encounters.

Chance encounters like this. Run-ins that didn't feel very spontaneous.

Shane kept his place between Bradley and me. His stance

was wide, and his shoulders were tense. Everything about him screamed "high alert."

"Shane," I said as Bradley disappeared, heading toward the front of the store.

He didn't turn. "Yes?"

"Are... Are you okay?"

That caught his attention, and he finally looked over his shoulder. "What? Of course." His exhale was heavy. "I should be asking you that."

"Thank you," I said as I slid my hand into his and gave it a squeeze. "A confrontation with him is literally the last thing I could handle right now. Thanks for stepping in."

"You sure I didn't overstep?" His eyes, framed in thick lashes, searched my face. "I know you hate when Austin—"

"No. That's *nothing* like what my brother does," I interjected. "For starters, Austin steamrolls me because he always thinks he knows best. You listen to me."

"And second?" Shane prodded.

I paused. *Second, I didn't want to cuddle up to my brother and sleep on his chest.*

Having a crush on your brother's best friend while also in the early days of being a new mom was baffling. My heart wanted him in every way possible, but my body was seemingly frozen in time. My libido was so deep in hibernation, I wondered if it would ever thaw.

And sex after giving birth? That was laughable.

I felt like a squatter in my life. My mind and emotions weren't my own, but neither was my body. Everything had changed and I didn't recognize the house that my spirit lived in.

Shane was hotter than a summer day, but maybe I wasn't actually falling for him. After a volatile end to my accidental affair with a married man and ten months of celibacy, maybe I was just craving Shane's attention. I couldn't toy with him. Shifting the precarious stability that I had managed to give Kat was out of the question.

She had to be my first and only priority. And right now, I was barely managing my maternal responsibilities.

So, I put my uncertain feelings about Shane in a box and stored it in a mental vault.

"That's all," I said as I retreated into my shell.

Shane cupped my cheek and studied my face. "I'm gonna give him a few minutes to get out of the store before we check out, and if he's still here I'm going to need you to call Callum."

My brows pinched together. "Why?"

"Because I'll need to be arrested for killing him."

"No three-strike system in your book?" I teased, though I had the distinct feeling from his lethal tone that Shane wasn't kidding.

Shane shook his head. "Not when it comes to you."

He took control of the cart and escorted Kat and I to the front of the store to check out.

"Well, good morning, Beth," Patty Wu, the checkout lady, said as she lifted her pearl-chained bifocals and perched them on the tip of her nose. She looked up. "And Shane Hutchins. What are you two doing out and about this early?"

But Shane didn't have time to answer.

Patty craned over the credit card reader and clasped her hands together. "Oh, and is that sweet little Katherine?" She eyed the car seat cover. "Why's she all covered up like that? Let me see that pretty girl."

"No ma'am," Shane said with a sharp edge to his voice. He was teetering on the edge of protector and friend.

Patty seemed taken aback, but shook it off by looking down the conveyor belt at the haul of bottles and baby formula.

I held my breath and waited for the judgmental comment, but it never came.

One by one, she scanned each item and dropped them into a bag. She fiddled with the tag on the onesie Shane picked out until it finally registered in the system.

"Well, isn't this darling," Patty said as she admired it.

Shane grinned from ear-to-ear. "I thought so too, Mrs. Wu." He winked, and she blushed crimson.

I reached out to swipe my card through the card reader, but Shane beat me to it. With lightning fast hands, he plucked my debit card out of my grip, tucked it in my pocket, and then swiped his card instead.

That devious motherfucker.

I smirked to myself. Maybe I didn't mind him being a devious motherfucker if I was the mother he was fucking.

Jesus, Beth. Hello hormones. Where the hell did that come from?

I was still bleeding like a Biblical plague. No way was anyone getting close to my shredded lady garden anytime soon.

Shane's palm was warm against my lower back as he punched in his PIN. His thumb stroked back and forth across my spine.

Did he even know how much every touch made me crave him? Made me crave things I couldn't have?

"You didn't have to do that," I said as I took the bags from Patty and dropped them into my cart.

"My treat," he said as he grabbed the receipt.

I arched an eyebrow as the automatic doors slid back and we stepped into the parking lot. I took a moment and studied the rows of cars. I didn't see Bradley's car, and let out a sigh of relief.

"Baby bottles and formula are a treat to you?"

His smile was kind, crinkling his eyes at the corners as he

guided me back to the car. "No," he said as he loaded Kat's car seat into the back, then tossed the grocery bags in. "The treat was spending the morning with my two favorite girls. And if formula and bottles are the cost for entry, then I'll show up with truckloads."

I melted right then and there.

"Come on, Mama," Shane said as he opened my door and waited until I lowered myself in. "Let's get this little tadpole fed."

"How's she doing with it?" Shane asked as he poked his head into the nursery.

I was sitting in the rocking chair, cradling Kat as she sucked down her first bottle of the morning.

I sighed while I studied her scrunched little face as she ate. "She was hungry."

On silent feet, he crept across the carpet and knelt beside the rocking chair. "How are you doing with it?"

Fuck. I was not going to cry again. A guilt-laden tear slipped down my cheek. *Dammit—yes I was.* "I could have really hurt her," I admitted. "I was so set on doing the thing I thought moms *had* to do rather than what was best for her. I ... I was selfish."

"Hey—" his voice was calm and sure "—you were doing the best you could. You were trying. And it didn't help that you had people judging you rather than helping you. And I know my two cents isn't worth much, but I think you should find a different pediatrician."

"One mountain at a time." I closed my eyes and rested the back of my head against the blanket draped over the back of the chair. "Layla sent me a bunch of medical journals that made me feel a little better. I—I really did try. I wanted the magic."

Kat had nearly drained the bottle. Her tiny lips were parted with droplets of milk still clinging to them.

"Out like a light," Shane said as he smoothed his hand over her blonde tufts.

"I guess full bellies help with that," I said as I set the bottle on the little table beside me.

"Don't beat yourself up." Shane stood behind me, caging me in against the crib with arms braced on either side of me. "Life is hard enough as it is." His chest was warm against my back. "You'll find the magic, but looking for it in the way you give your baby food is like looking for magic in changing diapers. All you'll ever find is shit."

I laughed, then quickly stifled it. Thankfully, Kat didn't stir.

We slipped out of the nursery, pulling the door behind us. It was an oddly domestic scene.

"How are you feeling?" he prodded.

I dropped my shoulders. "A little relieved. A little guilty. A lot tired. My boobs hurt, so I'll probably have to suck it up and pump a little just to take the edge off." I poked at my cleavage. "My milk supply was already dying off. It shouldn't take long for it to dry up completely. Gotta say. I might actually miss these girls."

He chuckled. "I wouldn't worry about it. You were a bombshell before, and that hasn't changed."

I blushed and looked at my feet.

"Do you want me to sit with you while you pump?" He looked at his watch. "I've got twenty minutes before I need to get going."

"I mean, I know you're a paramedic and all that, but it doesn't gross you out?"

Shane's eyebrows winged up like he was genuinely surprised. "Gross me out?"

His hands skated down my arms, lingering dangerously close to the side of my breast. I stepped closer, entering his bubble. The strong musk of his cologne, even after being with me all night, was intoxicating.

Shane wrapped his palms around my ribs. His eyes bore into mine as he slowly slid them up. His thumbs pressed into the side of my cleavage, gently stroking back and forth, but never going further.

"Trust me, Mama," his voice was raspy and full of lust. "You never have to worry about me being grossed out."

That should have made me shoot off like a rocket. My heart skipped, but my libido fizzled. I was waiting for the sparks, but they never came.

Come on, sex drive. Get out of hibernation, already. There's a very attractive man who isn't scared off by your crazy or the fact that you vacuum your breasts like they're at a car wash.

Shane stepped back, putting a foot between us as he reached down and adjusted the growing erection that was clearly visible through his sweatpants.

My cheeks flamed as hot as the surface of the sun. Gone was the professional compartmentalization that he touted. Shane wasn't standing in front of me as the paramedic who delivered my baby.

His intentions were very clear. *As was the outline in his gray sweatpants.*

Did I want that?

Bradley burned me, but I wasn't calloused enough to think that all men were like that. He was a special kind of narcissist.

But I had Kat to think about…

But it was Shane…

"I—um..." I hooked my thumb over my shoulder. "I'm just gonna... get my stuff."

I kept a curious eye on Shane as I collected the pump parts from the dish drainer. He took a seat on the couch and stretched out those long legs of his.

Fucking gray sweatpants...

I snagged a throw blanket on my way to the couch. Shane had already seen all of me, and I never felt weird about it. But in the last seven hours, the rules had changed.

He didn't hesitate to drape his arm around my shoulders when I sat down, scrolling through his phone with his other hand. His relaxed posture made me relax a little more.

When I had the dreaded torture device put together, I sat back, covered myself with the blanket, and turned it on.

The whirr and click of the pump made my hair stand on end. Fear prickled up my spine. I despised the sucking feeling on my nipples. It was awful. Seeing them distended and deformed made me feel ill.

Then I felt Shane's fingers drawing abstract shapes on my arm. I closed my eyes and tipped my head to the side, resting it on his shoulder.

"Thank you," I said, focusing on his touch instead of the blasted machine.

He leaned over and pressed a kiss into the top of my hair. "Any time."

"I mean it. Thank you for showing up for me. I ... I don't know what would have happened if you didn't pick up the phone."

"I told you—I'll always pick up if you call."

"I know, but—"

"No buts."

"You're a good friend."

His pregnant pause and the grinding of his teeth told me

just how unhappy he was at that statement. "No, I'm not." His lips grazed my ear. "A good friend wouldn't be thinking the thoughts about you that I am."

"What thoughts?" The question escaped before I could stop it.

He chuckled. "I'm not sure I should tell you, Dimples. Maybe someday I will. But I'm not a good friend."

Now I really wanted to know.

I looked up at him. "Then you're a good man." When he checked the time on his watch, I asked, "Where is it that you have to go?"

He tucked me further into his side. "I run a veteran's support group. There's a meeting at lunchtime. I just have to go a little early and make sure the coffee's made and the chairs are set up." He looked down at me. "You're welcome to come. It might be good for you."

After the experience with the Bible-thumping wine moms, I was done with support groups. "You do know I was never in the military, right?"

He laughed. "I know, Dimples. But I don't think the group will mind." He tucked an escaped strand of hair behind my ear. "I bet they'd make an exception for a beautiful woman."

I blushed.

"I'm serious, though. You probably have more in common with them than you realize. And if you're not ready to talk to a therapist yet—which, if opinions are welcome, I think you should—the group might be a good stepping stone."

I definitely was not ready to see a therapist yet. Why wasn't there an option between judgmental influencer moms and a professional who could have you put on an involuntary seventy-two hour psychiatric hold?

"Why would you think I have things in common with

people who have been in combat?" I asked almost sarcastically.

Shane scrubbed his hand down the dark stubble on his jaw. "They know the mental battle you're going through. They know the physical battle you're going through. They know what it feels like to have your life change in the blink of an eye. What it feels like to be out in the world, feeling like a ghost." He smiled. "There's no marketing. No one's trying to brand themselves. They show up to support each other. Not to share discount codes and brag about their social media following and brand deals."

I let it roll around in my mind as I peeked under the blanket. The ache in my breasts was gone. There was a dribble of milk in the collection bottles, but nothing more was being expressed. I reached forward and turned the machine off.

"I don't know that I'm ready to try the whole 'group thing' again," I admitted as I detached the pump and pulled my bra back into place.

"I get that." His palm was warm on my back. The pressure soothed me. "But the offer stands."

"Thanks," I said as I set the bottles on the coffee table.

As soon as my hands were free, Shane pulled me into his arms. "Come here." The hug was everything I needed.

It was safe.

"I'm proud of you. You're doing a great job. And Kat is in good hands. You're the mom that she needs. I want you to keep fighting."

A knot tightened in my throat, and my eyes were watery. I tucked my head into the corner between his chest and bicep. "Thank you."

"Is it okay if I swing by later? I'll bring dinner."

For some reason, that request threw me for a loop. *He*

wanted to come back? Even after experiencing the full spectrum of my crazy?

I backed away, wiping my eyes from the spontaneous tears. "I'd like that."

With one last squeeze, he backed away. "Text me if you think of something that sounds good—or doesn't sound good."

"Okay."

"Have a good rest of your day," he said as he strode to the door, then paused. A playboy smirk swiped across his mouth. "And Beth?"

"Yeah?"

He looked me up and down, pearly-white teeth working over his bottom lip. "Your ass—and everything else—looks pretty fucking fantastic today."

And with that, he disappeared, pulling the door behind him.

I went lightheaded.

Bradley had always been generous with compliments. He was a manipulative sweet-talker. But not even at his best had he *ever* made me feel like that.

Shane stole my breath with one cocky compliment. Damn him.

Footsteps shuffled outside, and a body bumped against my door.

Probably Shane having forgotten something or Stanley taking Arthur on a walk. The dog loved sniffing my doormat.

I opened the door and didn't even have time to react before Bradley came barreling inside.

I screamed as he shoved me into the wall. Without even thinking, I grabbed my phone out of my pocket and pressed the emergency SOS buttons that would connect me with 911.

"Where is my fucking child?" he roared, ignoring me as he stormed through the entryway.

I prayed to God that the 911 dispatcher was listening. "Get out of my house, Bradley. I have a restraining order against you and the cops are on their way."

I hoped that was true.

He was getting too close to the nursery.

"Leave!" I screamed. Maybe a neighbor would hear me and come over to investigate the ruckus.

The manic look in his eye chilled me to the bone. He was unhinged and uncontested. I could only slow him, but I couldn't take him down.

"I want to see that baby," he hissed.

"No!" I shouted. "Get out of my house or get arrested."

He lunged toward the closed nursery door, but I jumped in front of him and shoved. Bradley teetered backward before rushing toward me again.

Sirens wailed in the distance, and I could hear the dispatcher desperately trying to get me to answer her questions.

I couldn't let myself get distracted. All it would take was one moment of me looking at my phone for Bradley to get into Kat's room.

The wail of cop cars grew closer. *Thank goodness for small towns.*

Bradley realized he was shit out of luck. He backed away and stabbed a finger at me. "I told you this wasn't over. It's not. It's not fucking over. That child is *mine*. You're done taking things from me."

16

SHANE

"Oooh, you got the good stuff today," Kelsea said as she made a move for the danishes I picked up from the Falls Creek Filling Station after I left Beth's. They were dropped off daily by one of the local grannies.

"Gotta keep you coming back," I teased as I nudged her with my elbow.

Kelsea was in the Navy for a decade, though we had never crossed paths. Fluent in two languages and a wizard at cryptology, she had done her time with Naval Intelligence and was quite possibly one of the smartest women I had ever met.

"That's me. Just here for the pastries," she joked.

The door to the American Legion Post opened, and Daniel strode in. His new running blade gleamed in the morning sun. I tipped my chin to him. "Hey, man."

"Sup," he said as he made his way to the coffee maker.

"Did you get a run in this morning?" I asked. I was always trying to get Daniel to join Austin, Callum, and I for our workouts, but he was a tough nut to crack.

Daniel graduated from rehab about a year ago, but was

still learning the ins and outs of his prosthesis. I had been hoping that getting the running blade would help him take some of his life back, but he was still struggling.

We all were in our own ways.

I had nightmares. Sound triggers. Alcohol addiction. Though she tried not to show it, Kels was grieving the loss of her husband—another Navy vet—who took his own life two years ago.

Daniel was a Marine. During his first and only deployment, he lost his leg. His twenty-first birthday was next month.

Visions of grandeur crushed by a calling.

The door swung open again and Beverly, one of the Ladies Auxiliary menaces, rolled in on her power chair. She was a nurse who had served during Vietnam.

A few more old timers made their way inside and descended on the refreshments like a hoard of locusts.

When the spread was reduced to crumbs and stray carrot sticks, we migrated to the circle of folding chairs.

I was just about to open my mouth when my phone rang. I looked at the screen just to make sure it wasn't Beth.

Callum Fletcher.

I silenced it and put it back in my pocket. He knew I ran the support group today. I'd call him back later.

My phone vibrated again. *Motherfucker...* I pulled it back out of my pocket and silenced it again.

"My, my," Beverly said as she slurped from her paper cup of coffee. "Someone's popular today. You finally get yourself a lady friend?"

Sure, I'd tell them about my nightmares. About the cravings to self-medicate with liquor. About the survivor's guilt. No way in hell would I tell them about Beth and Kat.

Lord only knows what a Ladies Auxiliary member would do with that kind of information.

Then again, maybe if I talked about a little of it, Daniel might think of putting himself out there.

I chuckled. "Actually, I'm—" I paused. I wasn't actually dating Beth. I hadn't even tried to broach that topic yet. I was more concerned with her trusting me. With her feeling like I was a safe person for her daughter to be around. We'd get to dating later. "I, uh... We're not seeing each other yet. But yeah, I was making sure it wasn't her."

Beverly raised a drawn-on eyebrow. "Well, don't be so coy about the name of the young lady. Sharing is caring, Hutch."

Quiet laughter rose up from the group.

"Yeah, I'm not telling you, Bev."

She flipped me the bird, and I flipped it right back.

"How is everyone—" My fucking phone went off again. "Sorry," I muttered as I looked at it again, fully expecting it to be Callum. Didn't he know texting was a thing?

Layla Mousavi.

That was a little strange. Not that Layla and I weren't friends, but we definitely weren't the "call out of the blue and chat" type. Right as I sent the call to voicemail, a text came through.

> LAYLA
>
> Stop ignoring Cal and answer your fucking phone. If you see this, go to Beth's house.

"Everything okay, Hutch?" Kelsea asked.

I blinked as everything came back into focus. "What? Uh—"

"Go check on your woman," Beverly croaked. "I'll run this lemonade stand."

We had the space for two hours. By the time I went to Beth's, checked on whatever the fuck was going on, and made it back, our allotted time would be up.

My chair scraped across the floor. "I'll be back to clean up. Just lock the doors when you leave and don't burn the place down."

"Stop worrying," Beverly guffawed, dismissing me with a wave of her hand. Turning back to the group, she said, "Alright. Who has a nightmare they'd like to share and have the group interpret it?"

"No, Bev," I called over my shoulder. "Kels, you're in charge."

"Fucking kill joy," Beverly grumbled.

My truck revved as I careened around a turn, heading to Beth's. I tried to call Callum over and over again, but it went to voicemail each time.

Now was not the time for phone tag.

I tried calling Beth next, but there was no answer.

I almost called Austin, but there was the slightest chance he'd be ready to snap my neck since I hadn't backed off when it came to Beth.

When I pulled into Beth's neighborhood, my heart dropped. A trio of cop cars were parked around her townhouse unit. Austin's truck was alongside them. Blue lights flashed in strobes. I came to a screeching stop and jumped out.

If something had happened because I left...

My heart was in my throat as I jogged up the steps and yanked open the door.

"Beth—"

My pulse stopped as I took the scene. Beth was sitting on the couch. Austin, holding the baby, sat beside her. Callum and Lauren, another cop from the FCPD sat across from them, scribbling down notes.

Beth looked up, red-rimmed eyes meeting mine, then

bolted off the couch. She nearly knocked me off my feet as she collapsed into my arms.

If Austin hadn't been holding Kat, he probably would have killed me on the spot.

"Are you okay?" I whispered.

Beth shook her head. "No."

She was shaking. I tucked her head beneath my chin and closed my eyes, reminding myself that she was here. I hadn't lost her the way I seemed to lose everyone else I cared about. There were some fears that would never go away.

"Can you tell me what happened?"

"H—He showed up."

I paused. "He—Bradley showed up?"

She nodded, and I looked over her head at Callum. He did nothing but flick his gaze between Austin and me, but it spoke volumes. It was a silent communication that the situation was serious.

Beth tucked her head back in my chest as she hiccuped with silent sobs.

I held her closer. "I'm right here," I murmured, rubbing her back. "I'm right here. I'm not going anywhere."

Callum stood, and Lauren followed. "Beth called 911. Most of their conversation was caught on the recorded line, which is helpful when it comes to building a court case." He tipped his chin to Beth. "You did great."

I looked around. There was no stodgy professor in handcuffs, which was unfortunate for him. If I got to him before the law did, he wouldn't have hands left to cuff.

"He ran," Beth rasped.

"We have officers canvassing the neighborhood and additional units looking around town. A BOLO has been issued. We'll bring him in. And we'll have a unit parked here until we do."

Beth looked up at me with fear in her eyes. She didn't have to say it. I knew what she was thinking. No badge would make her feel safe. Not with her hidden struggles battling for residence in her mind.

"Thanks for calling me," I told Callum. "Pass on my thanks to Layla, too."

I figured he had told his fiancé to keep trying my phone while he helped Beth and took her statement.

Callum nodded. "Will do." He signaled for Lauren to follow him out. "Beth, I'll give you a call as soon as we hear something or bring him in."

She nodded, peeling away from me long enough to wipe her eyes and whisper, "Thank you."

Callum and Lauren showed themselves out, leaving me alone with Beth and her brother.

Austin rose to his feet. I couldn't tell if his murderous expression was meant entirely for me or split between me and the current situation.

"I don't want you staying alone. I'll call Caroline and tell her I'm sleeping over here tonight," Austin declared.

Beth raised an eyebrow. "Do you realize how ridiculous that sounds? I'm not taking you away from your fiancé."

"Then come stay at our place," he said.

"You don't have room for me and a baby. And I'll be up every three hours feeding her. Isn't Caroline going through a flare right now? She needs rest and low stress. Not a screaming baby and me rattling around at all hours of the night."

"Stay with me," I said out of the blue.

Both of them went silent and stared at me. Even Kat blinked her pretty green eyes my way.

I shrugged. "I have plenty of space and that chucklefuck doesn't know where I live."

"Okay," Beth said at the same time Austin said, "Absolutely

not."

I ignored him. He didn't make decisions for Beth. "I'll go on shift in the morning, but I'll be there tonight."

Beth nodded. "Okay. You sure it's not encroaching too much?"

Austin looked like he was five seconds from combusting. "What the fuck is going on?"

Again, I ignored him. "Not at all. Do you want help packing up what you need for Kat?"

"Holy shit," Austin swore. "One of you better start talking or I'm gonna punch someone while I'm holding a baby. And spoiler alert—it's not going to be my sister."

I kept my focus on Beth even though Austin was stomping all over my last nerve. "Tell me where I can help you, or I can just wait."

Beth thought for a minute. "How good are you at disarming bombs?"

"EOD wasn't my specialty, Dimples."

She pointed to the pop-up crib that was shoved against the living room wall. "Think you can break it down and get it back in the carrying bag? It's a pain in the ass. There are instructions in a little pouch under the crib mat."

"I'll do my best."

While Beth disappeared into the nursery, I got to work on the portable crib.

Austin's shadow loomed over my shoulder as I studied the godforsaken contraption. *Maybe disarming a bomb would have been easier.*

"I told you to let her shoot you down and then get lost," Austin clipped between gritted teeth.

"And she hasn't shot me down," I said casually as I pulled the mattress pad out and tried the release button on the top rails. Nothing happened.

I tried the release button on the opposite side and the whole thing collapsed in a heap of metal, mesh, and waterproof fabric. When I attempted to close it up, the sides locked again like a frozen dead spider.

Fuck me. I eyed the instructions, then decided against it. I could do this. I didn't need fucking instructions.

"Need help?" Beth called from the nursery.

"Nope," I lied. "I got it, Mama."

"You're a good man, Hutch," Austin said as he switched Kat to his other shoulder.

"Then there shouldn't be a problem," I countered.

"A good man wouldn't subject her to all your baggage." He huffed. "I'll level with you. I appreciate you helping, but you should know when it's not your place to get involved. She's got enough on her plate. Don't make her deal with your shit too."

For the first time, I didn't blow him off or pretend like I had my shit together. "I won't wake her up tonight."

On more than one occasion when we lived together, I had accidentally woken him up when I was having a night terror. Austin never made me feel bad about it. He'd check in with me and make sure I was good and that I had my meds, and then give me space.

Putting his mind at ease, I said, "Look. Doc changed the dosage on one of my 'scripts. It's helped a lot." *Somewhat.*

"Stress can exacerbate PTSD," he reminded me. "Stress like having a baby under your roof."

"I'm thoroughly aware," I said as I reached for a loop of fabric that looked like a pull handle and yanked. The whole crib folded up nice and neat. The tote bag was on the floor beneath it. I unzipped it and started shimmying the crib inside. "But I slept on the couch here last night and I was fine."

Maybe it ended the conversation. Maybe it pissed him off so much that he was silent. Either way, I was fine with Austin not pushing the topic. As soon as I got the crib into the carrying bag, Beth came out, shouldering three giant duffle bags. The diaper bag was in one hand, and her purse was in the other.

"Jesus, you're gonna give me an aneurysm, kid," Austin muttered, depositing Kat into an infant rocker and unloading Beth's arms before carting it out to her vehicle.

"Need anything else?" I asked.

She shook her head. "I think this is everything. I probably overpacked. I know it's only one night, but I didn't want to run out of anything."

"If there's anything you don't have, I can come back and get it for you or we can slip out to a store."

Beth cut her eyes to the open front door. Austin was manhandling her things into the trunk of her car. Police officers still strolled about, talking to neighbors and looking through the wooded area at the back of the subdivision. "Thank you," she said softly, leaning into my side as she stared at Kat. "I didn't know they called you, but…"

I tipped her chin up. "But?"

"I'm so glad they did."

Tick. Tick. Tick.

Bullets ricocheted in my mind as I stared at the ceiling fan.

I couldn't close my eyes. Maybe Austin was right. I had to work in the morning and I was too afraid of waking up screaming and scaring Beth to close my eyes at all.

Tick. Tick. Tick.

The baubles at the end of the fan's pull chain tapped together with each rotation of the blade.

As soon as I tried to sleep, I knew what I'd see. *The helo going down. Explosions ringing out. Barked orders to secure the HVT while my brothers were consumed by the flames.*

Fuck it.

I tripped over Richard. The asshole cat let out a yowl as he retreated into his corner. I moved on silent feet through the house, navigating the creaky floorboards so I didn't wake Beth.

We had spent the rest of the day in companionable silence. I slipped out and made sure that the American Legion building had been cleaned and locked up. Beth buried herself in research for her Ph.D. while Kat hung out on the living room rug, alternating between tummy time, chewing on her own feet, and staring suspiciously at the cat.

We made small talk over grilled chicken and vegetables. When it was time for her to sleep, Beth took Austin's old room. The pop-up crib had been erected in the living room, against the wall it shared with Beth's room. The baby monitor was on, and it was close enough for Beth to be there in a split second if Kat woke up.

Midnight. The time on the oven clock taunted me as I snuck into the kitchen for a drink of water. I wasn't even able to sleep through the witching hour

Kat stirred in the crib and let out a quick cry like a warning shot.

The notebook Beth used to track Kat's feedings was on the counter. I flipped it open and went to the most recent entry. Beth had fed her around nine before she went to bed.

If I was going to be awake, I might as well be useful.

After a minute of checking and double-checking that I had mixed and warmed the formula properly, I settled on the couch with Kat on my chest and the bottle in hand.

"Hey, tadpole." I cradled her in the crook of my arm. "What'cha wanna talk about tonight?"

17

BETH

"Fucking asshole cat." Shane's voice echoed through the house.

So this is what actual sleep felt like, I mused as I stretched, curling my toes beneath the layers of quilts on the bed. I hadn't felt this rested in weeks. I wiped the sleep from my eyes and rolled over to look at the time. It was just after six in the morning.

Shit! Shane probably thought I was the worst mom on the planet. I slept through not one, but two feedings. And I set alarms for them! I had no idea why Kat wasn't screaming for me.

Oh my god. She was so quiet. What if something was wrong!

My heart raced as I jumped out of bed and hurried out, only to come to a screeching halt.

Kat, sporting the tiny frog onesie Shane bought her at the grocery store, was nestled in the crook of his thick, tattooed arm, chugging down her bottle.

Shane, casually reclining in the chair, looked up from Kat. A slow smile worked across his face. "Morning, beautiful."

I didn't even blush when he said it. My heart was pounding so fast, I thought it was going to explode.

"She's okay." It was the only thing I could muster as I stood in Shane's living room, gaping like a fish.

His brows knitted together. "Did you think something was wrong?"

"I—I... I didn't wake up. She was supposed to get bottles twice last night and I must have slept through my alarms."

"I turned them off."

"I—" I blinked, dumbfounded. "You what?"

He eased out of the chair, keeping Kat safely reclined in his hold. "I turned your alarms off."

"Why would you do that?" I blurted out.

He shrugged. "I couldn't sleep. You needed sleep. Kat kept me company. Win-win. She and I discussed my fantasy football options during her midnight feeding, and then we tackled the age-old debate of the Backstreet Boys versus NSYNC during her three AM feeding."

For some reason, I couldn't fathom why he would stay up all night with her when he had to work this morning.

Shane's easy-going expression darkened. "Talk to me. Tell me what's going through your head."

Even when my mom had been staying with me, I got up for every feeding. Granted, I was still attempting to breastfeed then, but realizing I had slept through the night had terrified me.

Shane was right. I needed to sleep. I was one exhausted outburst away from completely losing it. But not knowing he turned my alarms off frightened me.

"Sit down," Shane said, nudging me to the couch.

I stared aimlessly at the coffee table as I sank into the cushions.

"Take her. It'll make you feel better," he said as he shifted Kat into my arms.

She squalled when he took the bottle away just long

enough to get her situated, but quickly settled as soon as it was back in her mouth.

Having her close was exactly what I needed. *She was okay. She was fed. She was safe.* I love the feeling of her curled up against me.

All of my fear rushed out as quickly as it had rushed in.

This... This was a new feeling.

And it felt good.

"I'm sorry," Shane said. "I was just trying to help, but I shouldn't have made that decision for you."

I closed my eyes, resting my head on the back of the couch. "I was just scared. I woke up in a panic, worrying that I neglected her."

Shane cradled the back of my head with his palm, his fingers tangling in my hair. "I'm really sorry."

I let out a heady breath and felt the anxiety release with it.

"How'd you sleep?" he asked.

"Really good. You know—until I woke up. It'll take a few minutes for my heart to stop racing."

"I'm sorry I scared you, but I'm glad you slept."

"It felt good," I said as I tilted the bottle to see how much Kat had left to drink.

"I never really thought about it before now, but I have no idea how they expect moms to be able to have a baby—even under the best circumstances—and go home to immediately give 'round-the-clock care to an infant. It's insane. I don't know how you do it."

I looked up at him. "I have you." I set the bottle aside and lifted Kat so she could burp against my shoulder. "And as much as she drove me crazy, my mom did help a lot with the housework and cooking while she was here. But it's an adjustment. And it scares me to realize that I'll always feel like I'm drowning. But hopefully I'll just be drowning in laundry and not uncontrollable thoughts."

He let a wry chuckle slip.

"Why couldn't you sleep?" I asked. "Don't you have to go to work in a little bit?"

"Yeah." He looked at the time. "Tell you what. Come have breakfast at the Copper Mule with me, and I'll give you the whole spiel."

"Well, hey, Beth!" Tiffany said as she made her rounds on the patio, distributing plates piled high with waffles and hash browns to a table of hungover college kids before beelining for Shane and me.

Kat was in her stroller, enamored with her ability to curl and uncurl her fingers. I reached in and adjusted the sunshade. Even though the temperatures had begun to cool off just the slightest bit, I was still careful.

"You look nervous," Shane said, just quiet enough to keep the comment between us.

I looked at Kat again. "This is the first time I've been out to eat since she was born. And she's been way too relaxed today."

"Ah."

"I'm waiting for the other shoe to drop. She'll have a diaper blowout or start crying or want something that I forgot to bring."

Shane eyed the overflowing diaper bag. "I don't think you forgot anything."

"I'm just saying."

He reached across the wrought-iron table and laid his hand over mine. "And I'm just saying, what if it's great? What if we have a nice breakfast together before I have to go on duty? What if nothing goes wrong?"

"What if everything goes wrong?" I countered.

"Then we regroup, adjust, and proceed."

"Sorry about that, y'all," Tiffany said as she pushed her long braids over her shoulder and clicked her pen. "Crazy morning. But I'm so glad to see you." She beamed in Kat's direction. "And look at that pretty girl. What a sweetheart. I'll tell ya—I love my kids but I'm so glad they're not that little anymore. Heaven knows it took having babies of my own to understand why some wild animals eat their young. I'll admire yours from a distance and thank the good Lord that mine can wipe their own asses and make their own lunches now."

I laughed, and Shane squeezed my hand. We put our orders in and almost got back to our conversation when a shadow fell over the table.

"Hey," I said when Callum appeared in front of us, wearing his FCPD uniform. His hands rested on his heavy-duty belt.

He tipped his chin toward me. "Morning. I was gonna give you a call, but I heard y'all were here."

Shane's hand tightened around mine and I didn't pull away.

"Chapel Hill police helped us locate Mr. Childers and bring him in last night. Thanks to your doorbell camera and the 911 call, we pressed him with some beefy charges."

There was something uneasy in his tone. "Why do I feel like there's a 'but' coming?"

Callum sighed and rubbed the back of his neck. "He made bail."

My stomach tightened into a knot and I couldn't breathe. I knew Bradley better than I wanted to admit. All those things I thought were admirable—tenacity and drive—were anything but. He was vindictive and persistent.

Shane swore and pushed away from the table. His chair scraped against the patio, but I yanked him back, keeping a tight hold on his hand.

"Your protection order stands, but a piece of paper can only do so much. I don't want you to think you're being a bother if something feels off. Call 911. Call the precinct. Call me. I don't care who it is. If something seems fishy, call right away."

"Thanks," I said, though it was barely audible.

Shane laced our fingers together and squeezed my hand when Callum left. "It's taking everything in me to not come over there and hold you right now. The only reason I'm not is because we're in public and I want to give you the time you need to wrap your head around this."

Wait ... What was he getting at?

"Tell me what's going through your mind."

Well, thanks to that little truth nugget, a whole fucking lot, Shane.

I wasn't blind. Shane and I had enjoyed a flirtationship when I first moved here. Things were never serious with Bradley. I was always monogamous, but I didn't see any harm in flirting. Shane reciprocated, but never crossed the line.

But the rules were changing. Shane was moving the unspoken goalpost, and I didn't have a game plan for that.

I sighed and pulled the stroller as close as possible. "Honestly? I'd rather not talk about him."

There was a distinct flex in his jaw, but Shane nodded and sat back in his seat, leaving only his fingertips against mine.

Tiffany reappeared and slid standard beige dinner plates in front of us. After she topped off our drinks—coffee for both of us—Shane didn't hesitate to dive into his pancakes.

I picked at my biscuits and gravy. "So..." Awkward air hung between us. *Or maybe that was just the humidity.* "Why couldn't you sleep last night? I'm sorry if I made noise or you heard me snoring or something. I know I never sleep when I have people staying at my house."

He chuckled and shoveled a bite into his mouth. "It wasn't you." His fork clinked against the ceramic plate with slight aggression. "I don't sleep a lot as it is. Short bursts here and there. I'll get power naps in, but I don't sleep for long stretches at a time. Works out pretty well since I'm a paramedic. I can handle the busy nights. I caught some shuteye in between Kat's feedings. Honestly, it was nice having something to do when I couldn't sleep."

"What do you usually do when you can't sleep?"

He speared a sausage link. "Scroll my phone. Read. Caroline got me into reading this author—Whitney West. Sometimes I'll just get up and start my day."

"But why?" I prodded. "That can't be healthy."

His jaw flexed. "I have PTSD. Sometimes episodes get triggered by sounds. Smells. Things like that. I'm on medication for it, but there's no curing it. Just managing it."

I stared at my gray-matter covered biscuits.

"You can ask, Beth," he said softly. "I said I'd tell you."

"What happened?"

"My last op with the teams. 2015. We were on a six-month deployment in Djibouti. Camp Lemonnier. Shelby—a, uh... CIA targeting officer we worked with a lot—had a target package on an HVT named Anton Yassin. He was what we called a private terrorist. No political affiliation. No loyalty to a nation. He wasn't ideologically or religiously driven. He simply dealt in power and money. Whatever could make him more money, he did without qualms. Yassin was funded by anti-American governments and radical groups. Shelby wanted him brought in alive so she could find out where weapons were being trafficked and stashed. Rumor had it this guy was dabbling in the sale and transport of radioactive materials. He was a big fish and, if he got his hands on materials for dirty bombs, he'd be a shark."

"Did you capture him?"

"We did." His teeth ran over his bottom lip as he stared at his plate. "We were running through exercises for the capture, but an American paramilitary contractor went missing in Khartoum. It was rumored that Yassin took her hostage and was planning to move her out of the area before either using her as leverage or putting her on the open market. We dubbed it 'Operation Archangel.' We were saviors and judges that night."

My stomach churned at the thought.

"The op wasn't ready, but with the hostage in play, we were put on a clock. Yassin was moving the hostage out of Sudan onto a cargo ship in the Red Sea. We were going to intercept the ship when it passed through a narrow strait between Djibouti and Yemen. Since we needed Yassin and the hostage alive, we couldn't go in guns blazing. We were supposed to do an amphibious insertion, climb up the side of the ship, and sneak our way in. A storm made the currents and conditions too risky to use the Zodiac boats, so we had to let the cargo ship keep going."

I hadn't realized how much I was hunching over the table, hanging on his every word.

"We loaded up on helos and did the raid the next night while they were in the Gulf of Aden between Yemen and Somalia. We fast-roped down, infiltrated the cargo ship, and bagged Yassin and the hostage."

"Mission success?"

The weight on his shoulders conveyed the opposite. "We

were en route back to base when we started taking fire from a smaller vessel in the Gulf. We returned fire, and our pilots evaded and pushed closer to the Somali coast. But remember when I said this guy had no country affiliation or loyalty?"

I nodded.

"Well, money talks and it can buy a lot of loyalty. Word got out as soon as he was taken. The first helo carrying half of my SEAL team was hit by an RPG and went down on the beach in Somalia. Then our helo started taking fire."

Shane had dropped his fork, so I reached over and squeezed his hand.

"Our pilot rerouted again and called in for a QRF. Command scrambled two F-18s. We took more fire and the on-board weapons system went down. We crash-landed a quarter mile from the first helo. Fighter jets are fast, but this happened in the time it would take the pilot to run from the hangar to the tarmac. Our team leader—my buddy, Cole—was on board with me, one other SEAL, a translator, and our two targets. I had been treating the hostage for some injuries when we went down. Two big-ass helicopters crashing on the beach in Somalia in the middle of the night was a fucking wake-up call for anyone and everyone who wanted a piece of us, but especially Yassin's people. They lit up the beach. We held out as long as we could."

He clenched his eyes shut as painful memories flooded through him.

He took a shoddy breath. "The F-18s stomped down the insurgents long enough to get another helicopter over the border to get us out. Cole and I made it onto the new helo with the HVT and the hostage, but..."

Shane looked down at his plate and I realized that silent tears had pooled in his eyes. A single one streaked down his cheek.

"Shane..." I laced our fingers together.

He reached for his coffee and took a sip, steadying himself. "Six SEALs. Two pilots. A translator." He shook his head. "All dead. And for what? So a terrorist can rot away in a blacksite cell for the rest of his life?"

He swallowed. "There are some sounds you never forget. The alarms when a chopper is going down. The way the rhythm of the rotors changes. Grown men screaming for their lives. We had been on more ops than we could count where we faced certain death moments, but none of those compared to that night. Then there's the quiet that sets in when you realize that there aren't that many people screaming and shouting anymore. That it's just bullets, because your brothers are dead. There was the sound of the pilots coming over our comms, identifying themselves as 'Casper' and 'Bugs' and asking us to throw smoke to mark our position. There was the eerie quiet when we arrived back to base. The squeak of the wheels as the line of caskets with the bodies of my brothers were positioned together to be taken back to the States.

"Cole and I were both injured, but he was able to return to active duty for a few years before he called it quits. He does private security and executive protection now. I was medically discharged after a long stay in the hospital."

How badly had he been injured?

"Can I ask what your injuries were?"

"I was shot three times," he said without an inkling of emotion. "It's not like it is in the movies. You don't get the bullet extracted, get taped up, and are good to go. It rips through muscle. Breaks bones. Tears tendons and ligaments. And that's if it doesn't hit a vital organ. I took a round in my arm, in the ribs, and in my hip."

He pushed his plate away, his appetite clearly gone. "We completed the mission. We made the world a safer place. Cole and I were hailed as heroes, until we returned to Virginia Beach and had to face the families of the rest of our team, wondering why we were the two who God deemed worthy to survive. My dad was a deadbeat. My mom was an addict. I'm an only child. The military was my way out. The Navy was my family. My team was my family. Their families were mine, too.

"I had months of physical therapy to regain use of my arm and had to wait out my ribs healing. I had to learn to walk again. Then I was turned out into the civilian world. I left Virginia Beach as soon as I could. I drove without a map and landed in Chapel Hill. Slept in my car. It was too loud. There was too much going on. So, I moved to Falls Creek. I needed the quiet. There hasn't been a night since that op where I haven't replayed every second of it in my mind. Liquor used to help the noise, but it made the survivor's guilt so much worse."

My thumb stroked the back of his hand. "So, that's how you ended up donating a kidney to Caroline."

He nodded. "I'm sure you've heard a thousand versions of the story by now."

I nodded, not making him explain it again. Even though it initially stayed between Shane and Brandie Jean, it widened to Austin and Caroline. Eventually the story of how Shane planned to donate a kidney to Caroline before he killed himself had gotten out. Now, everyone in town knew.

"I'm not saying there's some greater meaning and purpose behind losing your team in that mission," I said. "But I think what you're doing with your life now honors them."

He nodded. "I went from taking lives to saving them. Caroline was my first. And each one after that is my atonement."

18

BETH

"This is my treat," I said as I reached into the diaper bag for my wallet. It was nearing the start of Shane's shift, and he had to head over to the fire station. "It's the least I can do after everything you've done for me."

Shane wiped his mouth with his napkin before balling it up. "Absolutely not."

I huffed, but there was a smile on my face. "Shane..."

"Breakfast was my idea. I'm paying."

"Shane." I was more serious the second time around.

He flagged Tiffany down and handed her his debit card. "Don't argue with me, Mama. Let me treat you."

I caught his free hand in mine. It felt so natural to hold his hand.

Bradley and I never held hands. There were no casual breakfasts where we shared our pasts. No quiet nights on couches where we just talked. There was just sex and eating and sleeping between sex.

I liked these little touches with Shane. Maybe this thing between us would never grow into anything, but stolen moments with him were the thing reminding me that I was a woman, not just a mom.

"I'm not trying to argue," I said in a rather defensive tone.

He lifted an amused eyebrow like he didn't quite believe me.

I tempered my tone. "I promise."

He rested his elbows on the table and leaned forward. Turning my hand up, he traced circles in the middle of my palm with his finger.

I sighed and focused on his fingertip against my skin. "I'm sorry if me asking about everything brought up bad memories."

His eyes never left our joined hands, but a sad smile crept up his mouth. "Those memories are in my mind always. They'll always be a part of me. There's no bringing them up. Only speaking them into the world and acknowledging them."

"Yeah," I croaked, remembering that he had told me something similar once. That it was better to acknowledge my feelings by speaking about them rather than keeping it bottled up and hoping it would pass. "Then thank you for telling me."

His thumb pressed against the inside of my wrist. I could feel my pulse rushing faster and faster at the contact. My heart beat wildly in my chest, and my breath came in quick bursts.

"I'm not a good man, Beth."

There was no playfulness in his tone. He didn't call me Mama or Dimples. His eyes were downcast still as he made the admission.

"Then you're in good company. Because I'm not a good woman."

Here we were—the home-wrecking mistress and the former special operator. But for some strange reason, it felt like the place we were supposed to be.

"Thanks for listening," he said, coming out of his daze to look at me.

"Thanks for telling me."

Shane looked at the time and sighed. It was clear as day that he didn't want to leave this moment, and I didn't want him to. It was intimate and sacred. Something that, if I was being honest, I didn't know if I had ever felt before.

"I gotta get to work," he said morosely before stealing one last sip of his coffee and pushing away from the table.

I dabbed my lips and stood, peeking in on Kat. She had fallen back asleep and looked rather content in the stroller. *She felt safe with him, and it made my heart flutter.*

"Be safe driving back to my place. Keep the doors locked. If you see anything suspicious, call 911 first and then call me."

I nodded. Since he was heading to work, we had driven separately.

"I'll get off work tomorrow morning, so you'll have the house to yourself tonight."

If I was being honest, spending the night at Shane's house after Bradley showed up at mine had been a knee-jerk reaction to a terrifying intrusion. Shane always made me feel safe. It was an easy yes when he offered it up.

But two nights?

When did I make the call to go back to my house?

And what if I didn't want to?

But instead of deep-diving into all those necessary questions, I nodded. "Okay."

He tipped his head toward the stroller. "Alright with you if I say goodbye?"

My heart did a flip-flop, and I nodded.

Shane hunched over, his biceps flexing and straining against his uniform polo shirt as he braced against the frame of the stroller. "Be good for your Mama." He smoothed his hand over her soft blonde hair and smiled before pressing a quick kiss to the top of her head. "Sleep tight, tadpole."

I melted. My heart was a puddle and I was drowning in it.

His gaze landed on me and that puddle bubbled up in anticipation. "You gonna stay out of trouble for me, dimples?"

I snickered. "Probably not."

"Fine by me," he grinned. "I like your trouble." He cupped my cheek, his jovial attitude turning soft. "I'll be thinking of you." His thumb swept across my skin. "Call me before you go to sleep tonight. And you can text me when you get up to feed her if you need help staying awake. I'll be up, and I'll answer as long as I'm not driving the ambulance."

"I'll be okay," I said, trying to reassure him even though my voice was unsteady. I loved that he was trying to stall. It made me feel wanted, not just needed. "Be safe out there."

He dipped his chin. "Yes, ma'am."

"Yooohooo!" Knuckles pounded on the front door.

I panicked, thinking one of the old biddies that lived beside Shane had finally spotted my car and were coming over to pester Kat and me.

Richard, the oversized asshole cat, glared at me from his perch on a chair as if to say, *"You gonna get that?"*

Kat immediately opened her eyes when the knocking started again.

No.

Her lips turned upside down in a fierce frown.

No, no, no, no.

Her mouth parted, but nothing came out.

Okay. Good. Maybe we avoided a meltdown.

Bang! Bang! Bang! "Open up or I'm coming in!" the pest on the other side of the door sing-songed.

"*Waaaaaaahhhhhh!*"

And there it was.

I closed my laptop and eased off the kitchen chair. Kat thrashed in the pop-up crib, screaming her little head off. Little bursts of fear and rage bubbled up like lava inside of me, but I tamped them down. I reminded myself that it wasn't Kat's fault that she got woken up. She was just doing what babies do.

I had just gotten Kat out of the crib when the front door creaked open.

"I'm *baaaaaack*!"

I smelled her before I saw her. Love Spell perfume filled the house like tear gas. I shrieked as Brandie Jean skipped into Shane's house, jewelry clinking from the rows and rows of bangles on her arms.

Brandie Jean screamed right back at me, her drawn-on eyebrows nearly darting off her forehead. She teetered on her silver stilettos and careened backward into the armchair.

The cat went flying, leaping through the air and landing, claws out, on the closed drapes.

The curtain rod ripped from the wall. The cat yowled. The baby screamed. Brandie Jean was spread-eagle on the chair.

Okay. So she was a commando, landing strip kinda woman. I could have died happily, never having known that. Or having seen that.

I clapped a hand over my eyes. "Geez, BJ," I said over Kat's wailing. "You scared the crap out of me."

Instead of closing her legs, she screeched so loud I was sure the lightbulbs were going to have cracks. "OH. MY. GOD."

I covered Kat's ears in preparation for the scream.

Brandie Jean opened her bubblegum-pink lips and let out a happy sound so high-pitched that all of the neighborhood dogs started to bark. She collected her splayed limbs and bolted out of the chair. "There she is!" There were tears in her eyes as she let out a tempered gasp. "She's *perfect*," BJ whispered. "I'm so proud of you, Beth."

Before I could get a word out, she cupped my cheeks between her inch-long acrylic nails.

This was oddly intimate for friends.

"You're *glowing*, my precious MoonPie. You were a caterpillar and now you're a butterfly. She looks so much like you. How are you? Are you sleeping? Do you need a spa weekend? What do you need help with? Cooking? Cleaning? Sleeping? Ooh! I know! We should do a spa weekend. Facials. Massages. Yoga. Hair and nails. I'll start looking for a spa with childcare. Do they have spas with childcare?" She dismissed the question with a flit of her hand. "If I can't find one, I'll hire a nanny. I feel *awful* that I missed your immaculate birth, but the honeymoon couldn't wait. Hubby's at that age where you gotta strike while the iron's hot. Anywho. Tell me about you. Tell me what you need. Say it and it's yours."

There wasn't a doubt in my mind that Brandie Jean and her mysterious wealth could make *a lot* of things happen.

Kat's little nails were digging into my throat, but at least she had stopped crying.

"Is it okay if I hold her?" Brandie Jean whispered. Tears glimmered beneath her false eyelashes.

I hesitated.

Brandie Jean took a step back. "Totally okay if you say no."

It was because of that statement that I said, "Yeah. It's okay."

She let a stifled squeal slip before blurting out, "Let me wash my hands."

She darted to Shane's kitchen sink and unloaded the bracelets and rings from her arms and hands before soaping up like she was about to go into surgery. When her spray tan was thoroughly scrubbed off, she dried her hands with a paper towel and reached for Kat.

"Well, hey, beautiful. It's nice to meet you. I'm your Auntie BJ."

I let the unofficial title slide. Brandie Jean was a lot, but she was good. She had the greatest heart.

BJ kicked her heels off and curled up on the couch with Kat nestled in her arms.

Sensing it was safe, Richard the cat peeked out from beneath the downed drapes and hopped up on the couch, settling beside Brandie Jean's hip.

That was weird. The cat hated everyone. It only tolerated Shane because he fed it.

Brandie Jean seemed awfully at home in Shane's house and it raised my hackles. Unchecked jealousy flared through me.

"How did you get in, by the way?" I pointed to the front door. "Everything was locked up."

"I have a key," she said with a gleeful smile.

Hold the fuck up. She had a key to Shane's house?

I filed that information away for later. "How'd you know I was over here?"

"I didn't," she said, innocent as a newborn lamb. "Not until I saw your car in the driveway. I was coming over to see Shane."

The jealousy was back and I wasn't so sure I could keep a lid on it.

"Why?"

"Well, it's what I do, silly!"

Thanks to what I heard from Austin and Caroline, I knew about the part of Shane's story that BJ had been involved in. Back when he was struggling, she caught him at the liquor store, buying enough booze to get wasted for the day he would come home from the hospital after donating his kidney to Caroline. The day he planned to kill himself. Apparently, he confessed everything to her.

Bile filled my mouth every time I thought about the darkness Shane must have felt to be in that place. To make that decision.

Torture and hopeless.

Brandie Jean, working her bedazzled magic, wormed her way into his hospital room and refused to leave his side.

"Do you check on him often?" I asked as I picked at my nails. I was curious for information, but I didn't want to show my cards. I didn't want her to pry into how I felt about Shane, and then call my bluff.

"Not so much anymore," she said, smiling as Kat's hand wrapped around her finger. "But I make sure to keep an eye on him around this time of year."

"Why's that?" I asked before I could think better of it.

Brandie Jean eyed me curiously. "What are you doing here, Beth?"

Gone was the small town Barbie. She was assessing me like a CIA interrogator, sizing me up to see how much information she could wring out of me and how little she would have to provide in return. She held the posture of a protector.

"Bradley showed up at my place yesterday. I didn't feel safe, so Shane let me stay here last night since he had room." It was the simplest explanation I could come up with.

Brandie Jean and I had been friends since I moved to Falls Creek, but things didn't feel friendly right now.

"Oh, I know that," she said with a giggle. "Shane told me."

The hair on the back of my neck stood up. I had been with Shane almost every waking moment over the last few days, and Brandie Jean had been sunning herself on an island.

"He checks in with me from time to time when he's feeling stressed, just to make sure someone knows." Her eyes drifted to a mason jar full of AA chips. "Alcohol addiction never goes away. The journey to sobriety has no destination. Every day he has to choose to keep his back to the bottle."

I swallowed, retreating into a chair. Shane told me every detail of the mission that ended his career as a Navy SEAL. I knew the details of his depression and his decision to donate an organ to Caroline before taking his own life. But for some reason, hearing it in the present tense—the choices he would have to make today, tomorrow, and the next day, weighed more heavily than the past.

"He's miles past where he was when I drove him home from the hospital. Shane wasn't just haunted. He was an *angry* man. Therapy helped. The support group he runs helps. Getting a job and joining the rescue squad gave him a purpose. But he still has hard days. That's why I have a key. Sometimes he gets into pits of despair and can't climb out. He won't open the curtains for days. Won't take care of himself. He'll shut the world out and hide. I got tired of climbing through windows when he wouldn't answer the door, so I had him make me a key."

"Oh..."

"The anniversary of Archangel is coming up soon. The families always get together for dinner or something, but Shane and Cole never go. It's too hard for them to be the only survivors."

"He didn't..." I sighed. "He didn't tell me that."

"Has he been sleeping?"

I shook my head. "I don't think so. He's been helping me a lot."

She smiled at Kat. "I know. He loves this little sugar cube. He sent me pictures of her last night."

Something warm bubbled up in my heart at the thought of Shane loving my daughter. He had been there for her since her very first breath. He had been there when I couldn't be.

"Have you and Shane ever..." My voice trailed off. It was an awkward topic to broach. I had no claim on Shane. He was my brother's friend. His former roommate. He was my friend. But he wasn't mine.

"Oh heavens no," BJ said. "I love him like a brother, but he's not my type."

Brandie Jean's type came with a senior discount.

"But just so we understand each other," she continued. "I've been involved in his health and sobriety for a long time. I'm protective of him. He talks to me a lot, so I know exactly how he feels about you. Maybe more than he's told you."

Heat flooded my cheeks.

"So let me be clear." She was deadly serious. "You can hurt him. He might seem invincible, but he's not. He might tell you not to worry about him, but you should. He might say he's fine and he's got it all together, but he doesn't." She looked at Kat. "You're not the only one with more than your heart on the line."

I nodded. "I understand."

"He's already in love with you," Brandie Jean said.

"But we've never—"

"I know, Cupcake," she said with a wink. "But the heart wants what it wants. So if your heart doesn't want him, do me a favor and cut him loose sooner rather than later."

I looked down at my hands. "I'm ... I'm not ready to get back out there. I'm still trying to figure out how to function."

"I know you, Beth. You're a tough little glitter bomb. You'll be alright with or without a man in your life. But decide if your heart will be okay without him." Dismissing the topic without a second thought, she beamed. "Now, let's plan this spa weekend. I'm thinking we bring this sweet little sugar plum with us. Let me grab my credit card."

19

SHANE

"Morning," I said as I strolled through the station kitchen and beelined for the coffee maker.

I was running on a steep sleep deficit and needed another hit of liquid caffeine even after my breakfast at the Mule with Beth. Austin was at the kitchen counter, measuring out a protein shake.

"How's Caroline? Doing okay after that last flare?"

Austin just lifted an eyebrow and went back to measuring out edible chalk.

He didn't trust me anymore.

So much for being friends.

So much for being coworkers.

So much for being former roommates.

But I thought of Beth and that little girl who already had me wrapped around her finger, and there wasn't a doubt in my mind that they were what I wanted.

"You got a minute?" I asked, since it was apparent that Austin wasn't too keen on speaking to me. "There's something I want to talk to you about."

He screwed the lid onto the tub of protein power and

threw it back in the cabinet, slamming the door. Austin straightened, crossing his arms over his fire department t-shirt. "Did something happen with my sister last night?"

"No," I clipped. It wasn't entirely true, but it was true in the way that he was getting at. I hadn't made a move on Beth. I hadn't even neared her door last night.

Not that I wasn't tempted to.

"But Fletcher caught up with us at the Mule this morning and said they arrested Professor Twat Goblin, but he made bail."

"Fuck," Austin muttered. He ran his hands through his hair in frustration.

Finally, it seemed like we were on the same page.

"She's still at my place. Figured it was safer for her and Kat to be there just in case he gets another hit of audacity and comes back for round two."

"Probably smart," he grumbled begrudgingly as he leaned against the countertop.

"Look—there's something I want to talk to you about."

"No," he clipped, stomping out of the kitchen before I could get another word out. Austin jogged down the stairs, heading to the garage bays where the rigs were parked, gleaming in the sun from the bath they got during yesterday's shift.

Great. I was hoping to make this as quick and painless as possible. *And private.*

But we were going to have this conversation whether he liked it or not.

Austin didn't have jack shit to do in the bays right now. Gear checks had been done as soon as we all got in. A rep from a company that installed safe surrender baby boxes would be here in an hour for a demonstration about the installation they were going to do at the station next month.

Barring that we didn't get toned out for a call, the entire shift —fire and EMS—were to be in attendance.

But if he thought going to the bays where most of the guys were getting morning workouts in before the training session would deter me, he was wrong. If Austin wanted an audience, then we'd have a damn audience.

"Hale," I barked. I didn't raise my voice often, but it made everyone freeze when I did.

Austin stopped in his tracks, his back to me.

"You're thirty-five fucking years old. Grow the fuck up."

Elijah Fisher, the fire captain, rose from the weight bench.

Slowly, Austin turned. The bay went silent.

"I'm not asking for your permission. I've been clear as goddamn day about my intentions with Beth."

Austin opened his mouth to retort, but I cut him off.

"I'm having this conversation with you as a fucking *courtesy*. So *she* knows how serious I am about her. About *both* of them."

His eyes narrowed. "If you were serious about her, then you'd—"

"I told her everything," I snapped. "All of it. Every fucking detail. She knows."

That stumped him. Austin went silent, and no one else dared make a peep.

"What do you want me to tell you?"

"Tell me you won't hurt her," Austin said.

"I treat relationships the way I treat my patients. I don't make promises I can't keep."

"Exactly."

"Like I said—I'm not looking for your permission. She's a grown woman and a mother. She doesn't need your permission either. This was a courtesy call. You can take it or leave it.

Doesn't matter to me, but I know it matters to her. I'm doing this for *her*."

And with that, the tones rang out.

FIRE AND EMS tag-teamed an MVC that resulted in a crushed sedan with an entrapment. When the scene was clear, the engine headed back to the station for the baby surrender box training session while Missy and I headed to the nursing home to take a cardiac patient to the hospital.

I shot Beth a text while we waited for the transfer of care to be complete, and offered well wishes to the patient as she was admitted to the emergency department.

SHANE

> Thinking about you. How's your day going?

BETH

> It was going well until an intruder broke in.

My blood pressure skyrocketed. There was a break in? And she was telling me over a text message? What the fuck?

My phone pinged again.

BETH

> You didn't tell me Brandie Jean had a key to your house...

Was that ... was that jealousy?

A smile curved my lips. For some reason I liked that. Not that I would weaponize it, but it was nice to know that maybe this wasn't completely one-sided. Beth probably had that irritated frown on her face that I couldn't resist—the one that made her look like an angry puppy.

BETH

She was lucky that I was getting some work done and not naked.

Shit. The thought of Beth naked in my house had things happening beneath my uniform pants.

SHANE

Sorry. Should've warned you. Didn't know she was back in town.

BETH

I smell like Love Spell now.

SHANE

You might need a decontamination shower.

There was a break in the messages. Three dots intermittently popped up and disappeared. Missy and I traded off, her taking the wheel as we pulled away from the hospital and headed back to Falls Creek.

BETH

Don't you need someone else to help you with a decontamination shower?

Fuck. Me.

"You alright over there?" Missy asked, arching an eyebrow at me as she pulled on a two-lane highway. "You look like you're having a stroke."

She wasn't far off. I was definitely having a blood flow issue to my brain. All of it went straight to my dick the moment that text came through.

"I'm fine," I grunted.

"So," she said, settling into her seat. "Wanna tell me what that hissy fit between you and Hale was about this morning?"

Missy was—for lack of a better term—my work wife. Granted, she was somewhere around a nickel and a dime younger than me, but we got along great. Some shifts we didn't talk about anything too serious, and other times we got philosophical.

She knew part of my history in the military and why I was discharged, but she didn't know all of the intimate details. It wasn't out of the ordinary for her to ask about the temper tantrum Austin threw this morning when I was just trying to be the good guy.

"I'm gonna date his sister."

"Congrats," Missy said, not at all surprised, without taking her eyes off the road. "Why was that a surprise to him? We've all seen it coming from a mile away."

I shrugged and looked to see if Beth had sent anything else. "He likes to stick his head in the sand when it comes to her. Likes to think she's still a kid. Likes to think she'll never not need him. He probably likes to think that her baby was immaculately conceived."

Missy snorted. "Sounds like my brother."

"I told him a long time ago that I was going to ask her out. I've just been waiting for the right time."

"When's the right time?" she asked. "Because I have the feeling that it's going to be an easy yes for Beth."

"Why do you say that?"

Missy slowed to a halt at a three-way stop and looked at me. "Because you're the one she calls when she needs help." She hit the gas and headed into downtown Falls Creek. "And you've got the tattooed, broody, military thing going for you. Women like that."

I raised an eyebrow. "You think I'm broody?"

She grinned. "Broody with a jawline that she won't be able to resist."

"How was your night?" Tommy asked as he climbed out of the back of the ambulance. He was the EMS shift lead taking over for me.

Missy finished restocking the jump bag and tossed it to him. "Not bad."

"Estelle Gould's been minding her business the last few shifts, so you might hear from her."

"Nice," Tommy said with a grin. "I've been craving muffins." He pressed his hand to his gut. "The wife's got me on this low-carb diet."

Missy cringed.

"Morning, Hale," Tommy said, tipping his chin at Austin as he finished the last of the gear checks on the ladder truck and handed things over to the next shift.

Austin looked up. "Hey." His attention turned to me, but he didn't say anything. The grumpy ass had been moping for the entire twenty-four hours we spent on duty. Even Caroline dropping by when she finished her workday at the school didn't brighten his sour mood.

"You got plans today?" I asked Missy.

"I have a hot date with my bed and a practice test to get ready to sit for the paramedic NREMT."

I fist bumped her. "You've got it. Holler if you have questions."

"Thanks, Hutch." She lifted a hand and waved at Austin. "See you, Hale."

"Bye."

"What crawled up his ass and died?" Tommy said, tipping his head toward Austin.

Me, apparently.

Beth's car was still in my driveway when I got home. I

pulled my truck up, leaving her very little space to back out without me having to move my vehicle.

As far as I was concerned, she and Kat could stay at my house as long as they wanted.

Hell—she could stay forever.

But even if she wanted to leave and go back to her place, we were going to have this conversation. No matter the outcome.

I grabbed the flowers and groceries I had picked up on my way home from work and hopped out. My heart was a grenade, and I had just pulled the pin.

The screen door squeaked as I pulled it open, holding it with my hip as I unlocked the door.

I paused, peering through the crack.

Beth was at the sink, using it as a makeshift tub. Her hair was tied up in a ponytail. Tendrils like dripping honey framed her face. Her melodic laughter filled the air as she used a cup to carefully rinse bubbles off Kat. It was accompanied by Martina McBride belting out "This One's for the Girls" from Beth's phone.

The baby let out a piercing squeal, and Beth laughed some more.

The strike lever on my heart released, and it exploded.

She was happy.

I couldn't take my eyes off her. Beth—she was radiant.

Goddamn. I lingered in the door, sweat beading on my palm as I clutched the stems of the cellophane-wrapped bouquet.

Kat kicked her little legs in the water, sending a tidal wave splashing on Beth's shirt. But instead of freezing up and panicking, she threw her head back and laughed some more.

When Beth turned her head to wipe her cheek on her shoulder, her eyes met mine.

"Morning, Dimples," I said with a grin, letting the door close behind me.

Like I had conjured it, those dimples puckered her cheeks. Kat squealed again, showing off a set of dimples of her own.

If that kid didn't already have my heart, she did now.

Beth kept a safe hold on Kat as she finished rinsing her off. "Sorry I hijacked your sink. She decided to blow up her diaper, and then when I went to change her, she followed it up by spitting up all over herself. Bathing and starting from scratch was easier than trying to wipe her off."

I unloaded the groceries onto the counter and took advantage of the position, standing behind Beth. I rested my hands on her hips and peered over her head.

"Morning, tadpole. Mama's getting you started in the water early, huh? That's always been my favorite place."

Beth's teeth sunk into her lip as she fought a smile.

My chest pressed into her back as I tilted my head, keeping my mouth close to her ear without actually touching it. "How's your morning been? Barring the weapon of mass diaper destruction."

"It's been good," she said as she lifted Kat out of the water and bundled her up in a towel.

"How was last night? Were you able to sleep at all?"

She shrugged. "Up every three hours as usual, but it was a little easier fixing a bottle and knowing for sure that she ate. It's nice knowing exactly when she's done and how much she's had."

"You and your numbers. I'm glad it went okay."

"Numbers are safe," she said thoughtfully.

"No arguments here."

I liked the way Beth felt against me, so I kept one hand on her side while I peeled back the top edges of the towel Beth had wrapped around the baby. I wanted to see Kat's face. "I missed you two yesterday."

Beth rolled away from the sink and headed for the crib and the stash of Kat's bags.

"I asked Austin how things were when he called last night and this morning. He said you and Missy were running all over creation."

She had already talked to Austin? *Shit*. I had planned this out to a T. I even had a backup plan if flowers and breakfast didn't seem like the right move.

Stifling the panic, I followed her. "You, uh... You talked to Austin?"

"Yeah, he called to make sure Bradley hadn't tried to contact me."

Dammit. I should have done that.

"I checked the feed from my doorbell camera and didn't see him, so hopefully I'll be able to get out of your hair today," she continued as she pulled a onesie dotted with bumblebees out of the bag. "I'm sorry we're still here and cramping your bachelor style."

A portable changing station clipped into the top of the pop-up crib. Beth unwrapped Kat and had her in a fresh diaper before I could blink. In the pause when she reached for the onesie again, I caught her wrists and spun her to face me.

"Wha—" she squeaked.

"I'm not sorry," I said with morning gravel in my voice. I loosened my grip on her wrists and gently brushed my thumb across her veins.

Her breath hitched, and everything went silent.

"I'm not sorry, so you shouldn't be either."

Beth's eyes never left mine. She stared at me like I was something to behold.

"I like you being here," I said finally. Speaking was better than silence. If we had another split second of silence, I'd kiss her.

"Why?" she whispered.

Why? I could have written a dissertation on it, but four words were easier. "Because I like you."

'Like' didn't quite encompass the entirety of what I felt for Beth, but anything more probably would have scared her off.

Kat let out a cry of dissatisfaction at not being the center of attention. Beth blinked, like she was coming out of a stupor, and turned back around to finish getting her dressed.

Exhausted from the bath, Kat fell asleep almost immediately when Beth laid her in the crib.

I didn't waste a second. "These are for you," I said as I took Beth's hand, giving it a tug until she finally followed me into the kitchen.

My offering of grocery store wildflowers was grossly inadequate, but part of me wondered if Beth would enjoy the simple things.

Professor Plum wined and dined her as a sort of payment before he got what he wanted.

But had she ever been courted? Had anyone ever pursued her?

Beth's gaze fell to the flowers, and her lips parted. "You... You got me flowers?"

"I brought breakfast too. Have you eaten?"

Her eyes hadn't left the cheery mix of daisies, dahlias, and sunflowers. "You got me flowers."

I swallowed. "Sorry they're from the grocery store. It was impulsive."

She trailed the tip of her finger around the soft petals. "Thank you."

"I brought breakfast too."

Her lashes glimmered with tears like raindrops hung in the night sky by God himself. "Why?"

"Because there's something I want to talk to you about."

Beth looked up.

Now or never. "I'd like to take you out sometime. And by sometime, I mean the sooner the better. This isn't some indefinite, abstract ask. I want to take you out on a date. Romantically."

I expected an easy yes. Maybe a hesitant yes. But definitely not her stepping back and eyeing me suspiciously.

"Why?"

"Why?" I tried to laugh the nerves away. "Because I like spending time with you. Because I think you're incredible. Because I like hearing you talk. I like talking to you. Because I'm attracted to you so much it fucking hurts sometimes. Because I think we could have something real special, Dimples. And it's worth pursuing. *You're* worth pursuing."

There it was. I laid everything out for her. Heart on the fucking line.

"No."

The word was so simple and it was a point-blank shot to the heart.

"No?"

Missy must've been right about that stroke...

What the hell happened to *you're the one she calls for help?* What happened to *broody military guy with a jawline?* I scrubbed my hand down the side of my face just to make sure Missy hadn't been fucking with me.

When I looked up, Beth's eyes were downcast. "I can't."

I gritted my teeth together, because this is not how I saw the morning going. Where had the bubbly woman who laughed as she bathed her baby gone?

"Why not? Look—if I misread this and you don't feel the same way..."

"No." Beth slumped down into a kitchen chair. "It's ... It's not that at all. I do feel the same way. I just ... I can't trust myself, Shane. So if I feel like I want to take you up on it, then I probably shouldn't do it."

"Give me a chance. That's all I'm asking." She was retreating, but that didn't stop my advance. "Your terms. Your rules. Your boundaries."

"I can't, Shane," she said, her voice cracking with forlorn regret. "I have Kat to think about. I have to give her stability. I have to give her one hundred percent of my attention."

"I agree. But who's taking care of you?"

I cupped her cheeks, tangling my fingers in the loose bulb of her ponytail as I gently scratched her scalp. She relaxed immediately.

"You've let me in so many times," I murmured against her forehead. "Please don't push me out."

"One good day doesn't mean I won't have a hundred more bad days," she croaked. "I still have *those* thoughts. I'm a wreck. I'm a mess, and I can't ask you to wait until I have my shit together."

"I want your shit." I pressed a kiss to the crown of her head. "All I'm asking for is a chance."

"Shane..." she sighed, leaning into me.

I wrapped my arms around her. Everything was right. This was the way it should be. It was natural and comfortable. How did she not see that?

"Go on a date with me. And if something indefinite scares you, then give me ten." I pressed a kiss to her temple. "That whole list thing worked out pretty well for Austin and Caroline. Maybe we should try it. Give me ten dates and if you never want to see me again, then you'll never have to see me again. I'm a man of my word."

She was quiet, but only because her cheek was pressed to my chest and her eyes were closed. "How about three dates?"

"Skipping straight to negotiation, huh?" I chuckled. "I knew you were a shark."

"Ten is too many."

"Three's too few. Give me seven dates."

"With our schedules, seven dates could take months."

"Give me six, then."

"Four."

"Not good enough. You deserve all kinds of dates."

I felt the tug of her cheek lifting in a smile against my chest.

"Come on, Mama. Meet me in the middle."

Beth sighed, but it was in amusement and not despair. "Five dates."

"Deal."

20

BETH

"This looks awful," I groaned, staring at my reflection in the mirror. Where was the body I had ten months ago?

That body was great. I loved flaunting that body.

My stomach still had a bump, which just made me look like I was a bloated whale rather than adorably pregnant. My boobs had deflated. Thanks to my attempt at breastfeeding, the right one was smaller than the left.

I had stopped hitting the gym like I used to and my thighs showed it. Everything was softer. Lumpier. Paler. Gone was the luscious pregnancy hair. Handfuls fell out every time I got in the shower.

"You look great," Layla said from her perch on my bed. She was overseeing Kat's tummy time while I attempted to get dressed for my first date with Shane.

Which, given the current state of affairs, I was beginning to dread.

"I don't," I said with a huff as I pulled off the clingy wrap dress I used to love. It joined the growing pile of rejected wardrobe options on the floor.

"What did he say y'all are doing?" Layla asked.

"I have no clue," I grumbled as I went back to square one and pawed through my closet.

It was like returning to the fridge every five minutes to see if the contents magically changed.

"And I'm still wearing a diaper. I should not be going on any kind of romantic excursion while I'm bleeding out. Like seriously—I've been bleeding for weeks. How am I not dead yet?"

Layla laughed. "You downgraded to a pad. That's progress."

"A maxi pad," I clarified. "For a *super* flow. With the wings."

"Still not a diaper," Layla countered.

"Feels like one."

Maybe separates would work better... It was warm out. I could do shorts.

Granted, the only shorts I had that still fit had the stretchy spandex top for pregnancy.

I couldn't wear maternity shorts on a date.

Dates were for being impressive and sexy.

"Are you sure you don't need a babysitter?" Layla asked as she picked Kat up and cradled her. "You know Cal and I don't mind."

I shook my head, recalling Shane's instructions.

I'll pick you up at noon. Wear something comfortable you can walk in. Bring Kat, but don't worry about the diaper bag.

That last part didn't make any sense. I had the diaper bag packed and ready just in case.

"Shane said to bring Kat." I eyed the belly binder that had been given to me. The tags were still on it.

I could probably make the dress work...

I slapped the wrap around my stomach and cinched it tight. My trusty Spanx were next. I needed to smooth everything out. I swapped the soft nursing bra I still hadn't stopped wearing for one with padding and lift, then dropped the dress over my head and did a little turn in the mirror.

I felt like a stuffed sausage. It was a little hard to breathe, but at least I wasn't so self-conscious about how much my body had changed so quickly.

"He's really going all-out," she said with a grin. "I knew it was only a matter of time. He was head over heels the first time you two met."

"Things changed. Everything is more complicated now."

"Life gets complicated, but feelings don't. You either want to see where this goes or you don't."

"I want to see where it goes," I said defensively. Since Shane said to wear something I could walk in, I opted for a pair of sneakers with the dress. "But I can't expect him to deal with my ... situation ... forever."

"Yeah, you can," she said. "If he's saying he's good with it, then trust him to know what he can handle. Don't make that decision for him."

"How's wedding planning going?" I asked, ready to be done with the topic of me and Shane. "I'm sorry I've been MIA."

She waved it off. "My mom, Aunt Sepideh, and Gran Fletcher are taking care of most of the details. Callum and I get the fun stuff like food tastings."

"Do you wish you had planned for a shorter engagement?"

She laughed. "No. Even if we hadn't pretended to be engaged for the town and fell in love the old-fashioned way, we still fell fast. Taking the engagement slow was good for both of us." Smirking, she added, "And it helps that we live together because the sex is awesome. As far as I'm concerned, the wedding is just a party. The commitment to stay is made in private. It's a daily choice."

I didn't have long to chew on that. The doorbell rang, and my heart leaped.

Layla cocked her head. "Go kiss your man. I'll take a few more minutes of snuggles with *azizam* and then hand her over. I get why Shane wants her to come along, but mark my words, one day I'm gonna send you on a proper date without your baby. Cal and I will be great babysitters." Her smile was nefarious. "There's something about a ripped, tattooed man snuggling a baby that gets me every damn time."

I laughed. "You're not using my baby as a wingwoman!"

"I don't need a wingwoman." She wiggled her hand, flashing the ring that had once belonged to Callum's grandma. "I already have the ring. I just want to see what he'd be like as a daddy."

Layla promised to change Kat's diaper while I answered the door. Nerves boiled up in my stomach as I smoothed down the dress. I had done my hair as best as I could and put on a little makeup to hide the tired circles around my eyes. I even spritzed on some perfume.

When I opened the door, I paused.

Shane, in a t-shirt, slate-colored chino shorts, and Converse sneakers, filled the doorframe.

The first four words out of his mouth made my knees wobble.

"Goddamn, you look beautiful." The backpack slung over his shoulder shifted as he leaned in.

My breath caught. His eyes lowered to mine and he licked his lips. My gaze locked on his mouth.

Shane had kissed my cheek. My head. My forehead. But never my lips.

My heart fluttered as he stepped closer. Those strong, capable hands wrapped around my hips. His fingers edged the curve of my ass, but never went further.

I tipped my chin up to meet his lips.

Only silence except our breath.

His fingers dug into my hip, pulling me close until his lips met—my cheek.

I looked down at my feet, feeling a little foolish for thinking he'd...

It was best just to forget about it.

If I thought about how stupid I felt, I'd spiral and not climb out of it for the rest of the day. My hormones were already out of control and it only magnified my insecurities.

I stepped back, giving myself a little breathing room.

But I underestimated Shane's perceptiveness. "What's the matter?" He cupped my jaw and stroked his thumb over my cheek, as if a simple assessment gave him clues.

"Nothing," I said, trying to brush it off. "Layla's got Kat in my room. Give me a sec to get her and then we can go."

"Beth." Shane's firm command rooted me in place. "What went through your head just now?"

"It's nothing," I said dismissively.

"It's not. Tell me."

"It's—"

"It's something. Don't keep it in."

My cheeks burned. "I... I just misread that hello is all."

Concern turned to amusement. In one swift movement, Shane dropped his backpack and had me pinned. Picture frames rattled as my back hit the wall. His hands shackled my wrists.

"You thought I didn't want to kiss you as soon as you opened that door?"

I looked at the floor until his nose bumped against mine.

"I want to kiss you, Mama. And I'm going to—mark my words." Our lips brushed. "But it's our first date and I've only got five to make a good impression. I'm gonna be a gentleman today and keep my hands mostly to myself."

"What if I don't want you to be a gentleman?" I whispered against his mouth.

His smile widened. "Behave yourself and I'll kiss you goodnight."

"Is that a promise?"

Shane nodded as he let go of my wrists and stepped back. "Yes, ma'am. And it's not gonna be a hard one to keep."

"Are you sure I don't need to bring the diaper bag?" I asked when I caught my breath. Being close to Shane always made it feel like my heart was a runaway train. "Because I don't even go check the mail without the diaper bag."

He picked up his military-style backpack and unzipped it. "I'm sure. Let me take care of all the worrying for the day."

I peered inside. There were bottles and diapers. A formula container with pre-portioned scoops just the way I did it. Bottled water. Wipes. Backup onesies. A pacifier—and that was just the top layer.

"See anything I forgot?" he asked.

I shook my head. "I... I don't think so."

"Good. We can keep yours in the truck if it'll make you feel better, but you're not carrying a thing or pushing a stroller today."

"What are we doing?" I asked as he zipped it up and put it on his back. "You never told me."

"It's a surprise, but I think you'll like it." He grabbed my car keys off the hook on the wall and hitched his thumb over his shoulder. "Give me just a minute to put her car seat in my truck."

———

HOLY CRAP. This was a bad idea.

My stomach hurt like I was being stabbed, and my feet began to tingle. It felt like there was a zip tie around my thighs, cinching tighter and tighter with each breath.

"You're quiet," Shane said over the rumble of the truck. His hand was wrapped around mine, his thumb gently stroking my skin.

It should have been nice. It should have been sweet.

It would have made me swoon, had the layers of suffocating spandex not been acting like a tourniquet.

"Just thinking is all," I managed to squeak out.

Shane raised an eyebrow, then turned his attention back to the road. "I can tell when you're lying."

I just needed to stand up. I had been just fine getting dressed. It must have been sitting down that caused the edges of the belly band and Spanx to cut into my limbs.

The truck bobbled and it made everything cinch tighter. I hissed when he took a sharp turn.

"Seriously. What's the matter? You feeling okay?"

This is why I hated surprises. I needed more information to make a solid wardrobe plan. Had he told me where we were going, I would have tried to track down a better outfit.

"How far away is wherever we're going?" I wheezed.

He looked at the clock. "Twenty minutes?"

Cheese and crackers. I was going to explode. I couldn't go without oxygen for twenty minutes.

"Where are we going?" I squeaked as I looked in the side mirror and prayed that my face wasn't as purple as it felt.

"I told you. It's a surprise."

Another cramp. Shit.

I doubled over and groaned as the belly binder nearly bisected my abdomen.

The truck jerked. Brakes squealed. The driver in the car

behind us laid on their horn. We jolted, dropping onto the shoulder that was a few inches lower than the asphalt road.

"Warn a girl," I clipped.

Shane threw the gear shift into park. "Tell me what's going on. We can sit on the side of the damn road all day. You want to be stubborn? Two can play that game, Dimples."

I leaned back against the seat and closed my eyes, trying to straighten my posture and suck in my stomach enough to take a breath.

His hand wrapped around the back of my neck. It was sweet until his finger pressed against my carotid artery and he looked at his watch. *That fucker was checking my pulse.*

"Breathe," he soothed. "Your pulse is elevated. Just close your eyes and relax."

"Can't... Breathe."

Through lowered lids, I watched his brow furrow and his face morph with concern. "Talk to me."

Oh God. My face burned with embarrassment, and my mouth went dry. I couldn't tell him! Being strangled with compression wear didn't make for a great first date.

"It's ... um ..." I bit my lip. *I didn't want to cry, but the hormones had other ideas.* "The dress."

"What's wrong with it?"

I shook my head. "I, um... I tried to use this belly band and now I... I can't breathe."

"Okay. Take it off."

"And there's Spanx on top of it."

He went quiet like he was trying to decipher how the Spanx came into the equation.

"You know, to smooth it all out."

His eyes were kind, and his voice softened. "Just take it off, Beth."

I looked around the truck. "It's not that easy."

"What do you mean?"

I waved my hand around my upper half. "It's a whole ... full-body situation. And I can't get naked in your truck."

Shane smirked as he reached into his pocket. "I'll take that as a challenge." The silver pocket knife glinted in the sun. A swift click, and then he was reaching for the hem of my dress.

"Shane!"

"What? You said you couldn't get it off, so I'll do it for you." He grabbed my thigh, but instead of pulling my dress up, he yanked my legs across the bench seat and into his lap. "Lay down on the seat and stay still."

"These are expensive!"

"You can't breathe, and you don't need them anyway. They're coming off." His tone left no room for argument as he pushed my dress up, exposing the bottom half of the skin-colored Spanx.

It was the type of contraption that looked like a tank top with shorts on the bottom, but it was all one piece. I couldn't have gotten it off without taking my dress off. I would have been stuck scrambling in my push-up bra and granny panties in the front seat of his truck.

One flick of the blade along the bottom edge, and the stretchy fabric tore in two. Shane set the knife aside, grabbed each half of the leg, and pulled as thread after thread burst apart.

He repeated it on the other side, slicing then tearing the shorts away. Skin popped out like a busted can of whack-em biscuits as he moved up, carefully slicing up the middle.

He pushed my dress all the way up to my neck. The tip of the knife grazed my sternum, scratching my skin as he cut the compression garment in half. He went for the shoulder straps next, a quick flick of his wrist breaking each one apart.

Blood rushed back into my extremities as he tugged the

scraps out from under my dress and tossed it into the floorboard.

"That's so embarrassing," I muttered as I went to sit up and pull my dress down.

But Shane stopped me. "One more thing." He tapped the edge of the knife against the belly band still strapped around my middle. "Do you have to wear this?"

"I—"

He raised an eyebrow.

"No."

"Do you want to wear it?"

I shook my head.

"Then why'd you put it on? I told you to be comfortable. Not suffocating in the passenger's seat."

I huffed. "Because I want you to be attracted to me!"

"I am attracted to you!" he countered in a decibel that was a step louder than mine.

I jerked, looking into the backseat to make sure Kat wasn't about to cry.

Shane pocketed the Swiss Army Knife, pressed his hands together, and took a breath. "Beth, I think about your body day and night. I think about what you looked like when you were in labor. In the seconds and minutes after Kat was born. I think about what you looked like the first time I got to watch you pump and breastfeed. Because yeah—I fucking watched." His voice softened like he was exasperated and tired. "Sometimes I think about your body professionally. I think about everything that happened in labor. Things I should have been more aware of. Things to look out for if I'm ever in that situation with a patient again. Sometimes I think about the way you created and sustained another life, and how fucking incredible that is. And sometimes I think of the way your body looks and moves when you don't think I see you. When you're around the house or working on your computer or taking care of Kat." He slid his fingers around the band, looking for the closures. "And sometimes I think about what it would be like to touch you the way I want to. I want to kiss every square inch of your body. I want to make you feel as good as you look. I want to worship you. I've had dreams about your body. It's what I think about when I can't sleep. So don't waste your energy wondering if I'm attracted to you, Beth. I am."

Now I actually couldn't breathe.

Shane found the Velcro tabs and pulled. Air flooded my lungs and the tightness around my gut released as he pulled the binder away.

I went to drop my dress back down, but Shane caught my wrists. "Not yet," he whispered and leaned across my legs. His breath clouded against my stomach, and I fought the urge to suck it all in and tell him to back off.

"I'm sorry you can't have the version of me you wanted ten months ago."

His lips pressed against the loose skin that was slashed with silvery stretch marks. "This is the exact version of you that I want."

I tipped my head back against the juncture of the seat and the door. Shane's hands smoothed across my belly the way I used to when I was pregnant.

"I wanted to touch you like this when you were carrying her," he said with a rasp. "I thought about it every time I saw you. Remember that time at The Copper Mule right before Austin and Caroline's engagement party?"

I nodded, nearly gasping when he kissed my stomach again.

"You almost passed out and I caught you. I put my hand on your belly and felt her kick."

"I remember."

"I didn't want to let go, Beth."

I opened my eyes and looked down at him. His forehead was just below my ribcage, hands holding my waist.

"I swear to you I didn't want to let go. And every day since I finally got to hold you, I've been trying not to let go."

"Shane—" I reached down and ran my fingers through his hair, letting them tangle in the strands at the nape of his neck.

"You know what makes a painting valuable?" he asked.

I shook my head.

"Texture." He pressed a kiss to a cluster of stretch marks. "It's beautiful. It's a work of art."

A horn blared as a semi-truck blasted by. From the outside looking in, the driver definitely thought we pulled over for a quick fuck.

But this was so much more than that.

Shane retreated to his seat and fastened his seatbelt as I righted my dress, thankful for the ability to take a full breath, but still self-conscious about the way the fabric hung on my frame.

It had taken nine months for me to get used to seeing my pregnant body, and then I had been handed a different one. It was constant self-esteem whiplash.

"Listen to me," Shane said as he cautiously pulled back onto the road and took my hand in his, lacing out fingers together. "Don't hide from me. I've seen nearly every inch of you and I'm telling you—I want it all. Badly."

"Thank you," I whispered as I dabbed my eyes.

It was something I had lost sleep over in the early days of my pregnancy. Wondering if I'd ever find someone who was willing to take a chance on a hot mess of a single mother who had some serious issues and a psychotic baby daddy.

But Shane had been there ever since day one. I never realized how much I treasured those text messages where he'd check in on me just because. The insistence that I wouldn't be a bother if I needed to talk. He and my brother were living together at the time, so I never took him up on it. Sometimes I wouldn't even respond.

Maybe that was my way of trying to mitigate the hurt if he decided I was too much trouble.

But there was something I had misjudged about Shane Hutchins. It made sense now that I knew his military record.

Shane wasn't the type to run away from the fight. He'd sprint through the hail of bullets with a smile on his face.

21

BETH

The sweet, oily aroma of funnel cake wafted through the crisp air. It was almost as delicious as the smug smile on Shane's face.

He absolutely crushed planning our first date. A street festival one county over was the perfect place for us to have a day together without the prying eyes and loose lips of Falls Creek.

Live music from a bluegrass band echoed over the loudspeakers, but the noise didn't faze Kat in the slightest. She was cuddled up against Shane's chest, snoozing away in the baby carrier he had worn more than I had. The tactical diaper bag he had made for himself was strapped to his back.

True to his word, I wasn't holding anything but his hand as we perused vendor tents selling handmade goods and food. Not a bag. Not a bottle. Not a stroller.

It felt good to be able to walk around and talk without nosey Nellies and chatty Cathys snickering about us.

My daughter was safe with Shane. I was safe with Shane. My heart was safe with Shane.

The savory smell of smoked meat enticed us both and, before we knew it, we were on our way to a shady spot with massive turkey legs and fresh squeezed lemonade.

While Shane held the food away from the ants, I pulled out a blanket he had put in the backpack and spread it on the ground. Kat was next. I lifted her out of the baby carrier on his chest and let her stretch out on the blanket under the towering oak tree. Shane and I sat shoulder to shoulder, snacking away on more meat than either of us could stomach and sipping on cavity-inducing lemonade.

But it was bliss.

The breeze took my worries away, letting them float on the air to the sounds of fiddles and lyrics about simpler times.

Once we were full, we cracked into the package of baby wipes to clean our hands. We divided and conquered—Shane grabbing a lemonade refill and me changing Kat's diaper.

Everything was so easy with him. Well, except for me nearly passing out in his truck or potentially losing a limb.

He was so good to me.

Too good to me.

Bradley was good too. Until he lied to you. Until he made you his mistress. Until he threatened you. Until he came at—

"You ready to go or do you wanna sit here a little longer?" Shane asked as he strolled up, holding a cheery yellow cup that sported a lemon mascot.

Why did those intrusive thoughts always ruin everything? I was having the best day I'd had in a long time!

"I think so," I said. "Kat's been easy today and I don't want to push my luck."

Shane laughed. "I understand."

We loaded up and began the meandering walk back to the truck—my daughter on his chest and my hand in his.

The ride back to Falls Creek was significantly less eventful than the one to the fair. My torn compression garments were a lump in the floorboard. I felt so stupid for trying to look like the old me...

Maybe once life settled down I'd be able to go to the gym again...

But then my maternity leave would be up and I'd be back to teaching...

There weren't enough hours in the day.

"What's on your mind?" Shane asked as he laced our hands together, then lifted mine to his lips and pressed a kiss to the back of it.

"Nothing," I lied. "Just enjoying the quiet."

"I don't believe you," he said. "But if you don't want to talk about it, I won't pry this time."

I didn't want to talk about it, because I knew there wasn't a solution. I'd never be the woman I wanted to be for him.

I used to be what every girl dreamed of—almost thirty, recklessly flirty, and thriving in my career.

Now, I hated my body. I hated everything it put me through. It gave me Kat and that was a kind of love that I couldn't even begin to describe, but it betrayed me in every other way.

I didn't want Shane to lie to me and pretend he loved it.

By the time he pulled into my neighborhood, Kat had begun to chirp in anticipation of her next bottle.

"Stay right there," Shane said as he unbuckled his seatbelt. "I'll come around."

I gathered the remnants of the Spanx and belly band while he got Kat's car seat out and opened my door.

While I prepared a bottle and fed her, he battled the engineering nightmare of switching her car seat back to my vehicle.

Shane was an anomaly. He was so comfortable in every situation that was thrown at him.

Being a paramedic and going into people's homes to treat them? Check.

Talking my psychotic, hormonal self off a ledge in the middle of the night? Check.

Taking care of a baby? Check.

Looking that positively edible in those shorts? *Fucking check.*

He shut the door and locked it, thoughtfully toeing off his shoes before casually strolling into the living room as if dealing with car seats and packing a diaper bag was an everyday occurrence for him.

Kat had reduced her bottle to bubbles. I set it aside and dabbed her tiny Cupid's bow lips with the hem of her bib before propping her up against my shoulder. She let out a body-vibrating belch as Shane snagged the empty bottle from the end table.

"I'll wash it up."

"Oh—" His back was already to me. "Shane, you don't have to—"

"I'll take care of it," he said as he started the kitchen tap.

Was I taking advantage of his kindness? Shouldn't I be the one to do all that? Surely it had to be okay for a bottle to sit unwashed long enough for me to burp the baby.

Gratitude turned to resentment in the blink of an eye.

Kat's eyelids turned heavy as I tucked her in the crook of my arm. Green irises disappeared behind delicate eyelashes. *She was so beautiful. So perfect.*

The water turned off, and I looked up in time to see Shane lingering with his shoulder against the wall that separated the kitchen from the living room. His arms were crossed over his chest, and a smile painted on his face.

"You gonna put her down for a nap?" he asked as he dried his hands with a tea towel, then slung it over his shoulder.

Why was that the sexiest move on the planet?

"Yeah," I said as I carefully eased off the couch. "She's had a big day. Hopefully, that means she'll sleep like a rock."

Her diaper was still dry, so I didn't bother changing it. Shane lingered at my back as I laid her in the crib and double-checked the baby monitor. When I turned around, he was hunched over the crib railing.

"Sleep tight, Tadpole." He dotted her forehead with a light kiss. "Be good for your Mama."

My heart combusted.

"Come on," Shane whispered as he wrapped his arm around my waist, guiding me out of the nursery. I pulled the door behind me as he whisked me back to the living room. "I want a few minutes with just you before I have to go."

Earlier, Shane told me that he had an evening meeting tonight for the support group he ran, then he'd go on shift at the station bright and early. Since Bradley hadn't attempted to show up or contact me, I felt okay sleeping at my place. All of Kat's things were here, and I couldn't stay at Shane's forever. Still, I'd miss being close to him.

"Thanks for today," I said as he led me to the couch. "I had a lot of fun."

But we never made it to the couch. Oxygen left my lungs in a gust as my spine hit the wall. His hands were both firm and gentle as they roamed my sides.

"Now," he rasped, breathless. "Where were we?"

I tipped my chin up, but he didn't kiss me.

Shane pinned my hips down with his. His scent was all-consuming. The slope of his nose grazed my temple as he peppered my forehead with kisses.

But these weren't the same kisses he gave my daughter.

Far from it.

When he kissed Kat's head, it was pure affection and adoration. But these were exploratory. He was learning. Memorizing.

Shane wedged his knee between my legs. Something thick and rock hard pressed against my body.

His chest flattened my breasts as he edged closer and closer. "I can't get enough of you, and even when I do get all of you, it still won't be everything I want."

My breath caught as one of his hands circled my throat. His thumb stroked the taut tendons as I stretched higher to meet his mouth.

Eyes, sharp and assessing, studied my face as his hands roamed my body. My arms. My hands. My hips. My waist. My stomach. My neck. My back. Few things were off-limits to him. And those limits were temporary.

"Shane," I whispered when his palm smoothed over my stomach again. I tried to suck it in, but it was impossible.

"I need you to trust me."

"I do, but—"

"Trust that I know what I want. I'm not lying to you. I'm not blowing smoke up your very fine ass." He grabbed my hand, opened my palm, and pressed it against his erection. "Do you feel that, Mama? I want you."

I swallowed, because I could feel it. I could feel his thickness. His length. The flex each time a new rush of blood flooded his cock.

Shane didn't let go of my hand. Keeping it pressed firmly against his dick, he raked his fingers up the back of my neck and grabbed a fistful of my hair.

The anchor keeping my head in place sent a ripple of sparks down my back.

My heart stopped.

His lips were soft as suede. The first kiss was tender. Warm. I melted in his hands, following his lead. He tipped his head to the side to explore a new angle. Everything was delicious and new. It was effervescent, like the first sip of champagne.

My hand fell away from his bulge the second he let go of it. Then both of his hands were in my hair, cradling my cheeks, kneading my hips, sliding up and down my waist and arms. He was everywhere, consuming every part of me. The kiss started as a Sunday drive, but now, he was flooring it.

I opened for him, parting my lips in anticipation of his tongue. But instead of giving me more, he pulled my lower lip between his teeth. The gasp he eked out of me made him smile in satisfaction. Shane dotted the corner of my mouth with a kiss, then rested his forehead on mine.

"Yeah," he said with a boyish grin on his stubbled face. "That was worth waiting for."

We stood chest-to-chest, lingering in the cataclysmic glow. Shane's smile stole my breath. I wished I had that kind of excitement. I wished I had even an ounce of his giddiness.

This felt big.

But it also felt too good to be true.

BRANDIE JEAN

Are you coming?

BRANDIE JEAN

I'll come pick you up.

BRANDIE JEAN

Please come.

BRANDIE JEAN

If I drive by your house and see your car still there, I'm going to drag you out whether you're dressed or not.

BETH

That's kidnapping.

BRANDIE JEAN

I've done far worse than kidnapping, my sweet little angel. I have plenty of money. I can pay my own bail, pay off the judge, and not even touch my savings account.

BETH

Fine. I'm putting pants on.

BRANDIE JEAN

Yay! This is going to be so fun! 10 AM sharp!

I ROLLED OVER AND GROANED. I was officially five weeks postpartum, but it had yet to get any easier.

Sure, I wasn't popping stool softeners like TicTacs and worrying about busting my stitches, but I still hadn't gotten the hang of being a mom.

Some days were better than others. I didn't actively hate myself quite as much, but the self-loathing still lingered in the back of my mind.

Being near Shane helped.

Shane always helped.

Our second date was on my calendar, but he had been working back-to-back shifts that made his appearances sparse. Still, he found time to swing by every other day to give me a kiss and see how I was doing.

Thanks to Layla, I fired my pediatrician and her bitch of a nursing staff. She went with me to Kat's first appointment at the new practice and celebrated Kat making progress in her growth charts with mani pedis. We spent the appointment passing Kat back and forth and gushing over her and Callum's wedding plans.

The next day, I was a zombie. I could barely get out of bed. I would lope from my room, to the kitchen, to the nursery, and then back to my room.

I still didn't understand depression. I didn't understand why I couldn't just be happy. Or at least neutral. The highs were high, but the lows gutted me and brought me to my knees.

Yesterday had been one of those low days, and I could still feel the dreary clouds looming in my mind.

Brandie Jean had been on my case about joining her for some get-together with the Ladies Auxiliary, but I didn't have the energy.

My phone chimed again with another text from Brandie Jean, telling me to get my ass out of bed.

She wouldn't know that I grumbled while I did it.

Dread filled my stomach as I pulled into the Community Center parking lot at exactly 9:45 AM. Kat had been surprisingly cooperative when it came time to leave home. It's like she knew I was dreading being social with the people who had done nothing but nitpick my parenting choices and give unsolicited and nasty opinions disguised as advice.

The smell of stale air and mildewy ceiling tiles doubled the dread. That god-awful odor took me back to the last time I was here when I attempted to join a mean girls meeting that was touted as a support group for moms.

A shrill southern twang echoed down the hall.

"How in your existence in my pink sparkly world did you think that scaring her half to death with your rose-colored memories is what I told you to do?"

I stopped in my tracks.

There was hemming and hawing, but BJ wasn't having any of it.

"I swear to Dolly Parton's 36-E boobs, I can't leave for my own flippin' honeymoon without you people going batshit crazy. Well, guess what—" her sweet as cotton candy tone turned lethal "—I'm back and it's about damn time y'all remember who runs this town. Are we forgetting why we started the Ladies Auxiliary? What's our motto?"

Damn. BJ had the "mom voice" down to a science. I needed her to teach me.

A chorus of properly scolded geriatric women chimed in. "Left to our own devices we are a collective menace to society. We will dedicate our days to helping the citizens of Falls Creek. We will provide financial, moral, and tangible support to those in need. We will seek out and assist those who may not ask for help. This is our duty as the Ladies Auxiliary."

I peered around the doorframe, and caught a glimpse of BJ standing behind a pink painted podium. She wore bejeweled reading glasses and had a gem-encrusted pointer stick in her hand.

I felt like Dorothy peeking behind the wizard's curtain. *So this was the Ladies Auxiliary.*

"Excellent!" BJ said. "Don't make me remind you again. Now—" she turned to the cork board behind her. Names and photos were connected with pink string like she was a detective hunting down a murderer.

Wait. Why the hell was my photo up there? And Shane's. And Austin's. And Caroline's. And Layla's. And Callum's.

There were more photos, but they all had bright green checkmarks plastered on top of them.

Two more of the uncovered photos were Ms. Sepideh and Henry Calhoun from the Ballentine House Bed and Breakfast. There was a photo of Layla's brother, Karim, on the other side with a question mark on top of it. Missy, Shane's EMS partner, was on the board, as was Lauren—the rookie with the police department.

What was this?

I eased away from the doorframe, wanting to eavesdrop a little longer. BJ set the pointer stick on the podium and clapped her hands. "Now, who has updates on our long-term projects?"

"I do," Gran Fletcher said from somewhere in the room. "We kept this meeting a secret like you asked, but Sepideh will be at the next one. She and Henry have been spending more time together, but he's still not making any moves on her."

Wait. They were trying to set up Henry and Sepideh?

"I propose we destroy Henry's cabin and make him move into the B&B," Estelle Gould chimed in. "I have access to an excavator."

"No," Brandie Jean clipped. "What's rule number three?"

The ladies huffed. "We do not destroy, only tamper."

"*And*," Brandie Jean prodded.

"Only as a last resort," they grumbled.

"That's right," BJ said. "The cabin situation we concocted to get Austin Hale and Caroline Tyree together was effective and didn't harm anyone. It was also a one-and-done. If we repeat our methods, people get suspicious. Come up with a better plan for making Sepideh and Henry spend time together. Next?"

"We tried to get Shane Hutchins and Beth Hale together, but she's a stubborn one."

Brandie Jean turned candy apple red. "Beth and Shane are now my responsibility since you lot deemed it appropriate to spout off all kinds of bullshit glory-days rhetoric while she was drowning! Did you invite her to the salon for a hair wash? Did you offer to do her laundry? Did you give her a hand? Did you ask what *she* needed or did you just tell her what worked for you without considering that her situation might be different?"

"Well, we just thought—"

Brandie Jean bared her teeth and growled. "I realize it's been a long, long time since some of you had babies. But the next time you see fit to overwhelm my sweet little momma bear, I'm gonna need y'all to dig deep into your memories to put yourself in her shoes."

"But—"

"Did you sit with her in the dark and help her open the curtains or did you walk away and wonder why she wasn't turning on the lights?"

Someone must have been dumb enough to open their mouth because Brandie Jean hunched over the podium. "Hush." One word shut up whoever dared question her. "I will bury you, marry your husband, and have a rock on my finger before the funeral. You won't even have dirt on your casket yet and I'll be looking for wedding dresses. Wanna test me?"

No one made a peep.

"Well," Maribel Gonzalez said cautiously. "Louisa Mae and Christy Spellman said they saw them together at the grocery store."

Another voice chimed in. "And I saw all three of them together at that street festival when I was there with my prize-winning quilts. You know I got a blue rib—"

"Shut up about the quilts. You're all in the doghouse. Leave Shane and Beth to me. And think before you speak next time. Updates on John Prosser? He lost his wife. Do we have a meal train scheduled?"

"Yep!" Marilyn Dreese piped up. "He's got breakfast, lunch, and dinner for the next month. And we found enough in the budget to hire a cleaner to drop by to help him twice a week.

He loves golf, so I'm thinking we come up with a charity golf tournament to get him out of the house. Maybe he can even help us plan it."

"Excellent," Brandie Jean said, rather pleased with her charge. "You went above and beyond. You're out of the doghouse, Mare."

The heavy car seat hanging from my arm ached from sneaking, but I was too fascinated to care.

Brandie Jean played me. She played us all.

The checkmarks on Callum and Layla's faces proved it. I knew from Layla that Gran Fletcher had 'fessed up to scheming with the Ladies Auxiliary to come up with the charity date auction to get him to break out of his bachelor ways. But Brandie Jean pretending to be obsessed with him was the kick in the pants that got him to pretend to be engaged to Layla. Of course, it wasn't quite so pretend anymore. Not with the *actual* wedding date on the calendar.

...That glittery, evil, wonderful mastermind.

The car seat bumped against the wall, and Kat let a cry escape. *Shit.*

Brandie Jean turned and caught me lurking. She squeaked and lunged for the corkboard, flipping it over so the whiteboard on the opposite side that read, *First Responders Charity Calendar Project,* was visible instead of her matchmaking plans.

"Beth!" she exclaimed, flustered. "You're early!"

I crept into the doorway and spotted the army of silver beehives staring at me.

"Sorry."

She batted it away with a flick of her wrist. "No worries, hot stuff. Come on in and set that sweet girl down. We've got snacks and a whole to-do list to plan this calendar shoot."

"Calendar shoot?" I asked as I took a seat next to Gran Fletcher.

"That's right!" Mavis Taylor said. "Our next fundraiser! All the first responders are gonna strip down, get oiled up, and pose for a calendar."

"That we'll sell at a hefty premium," Bea Walker added. "Have you seen those boys at the police and fire department? We'll sell out the first day."

22

SHANE

My heart was in my throat as I jogged up the handful of steps to Beth's front door. *I shouldn't be this nervous to take her out again.*

The first date I planned was done with precision and intention. The street fair was a great icebreaker. Kat came with us, it gave me a chance to show off my baby-wearing capabilities, and it was casual. Beth and I were able to hold hands and share flirtatious touches while we walked without her worrying about me pushing it any farther.

Even though moving at a snail's pace meant my dick was becoming calloused from all the jerking off, I would take things as slow as she needed.

But tonight was just her and me. Maybe that's why I was nervous. I hadn't gotten Beth all to myself ... ever.

Austin's truck was parked beside Beth's car. I peeked inside and saw that he had already taken care of getting the car seat switched over to his backseat. Briefly, I contemplated trying to find one on sale to keep in my vehicle. It'd make going out a lot easier if we didn't always have to cram into Beth's little sedan or put that child safety puzzle into my truck.

The future Mr. and Mrs. Hale were going to babysit Kat tonight. When I made the ask, I went to Caroline instead of the idiot brute she fell in love with.

Austin still wasn't my biggest fan, but he had gone from being an ass about it to just giving me the cold shoulder. Yesterday we had even worked our way back up to two-syllable words. Maybe by the time things really got serious with Beth, he'd say a whole sentence to me.

I pressed the doorbell and waited. Heavy, masculine footsteps echoed through the townhouse.

Shit.

A breeze carrying the scent of lemon candles hit me in the face as the door swung open.

Austin loomed in the doorway. I tipped my chin to him. "Hey."

He looked me up and down, eying the bouquet and stuffed animal I had in my hands. "Beth's almost ready."

"I'm ready," Beth called from inside as she hustled out of her room, still fastening an earring.

She shoved Austin aside, sending him tumbling into a coat rack, and gave me an out of breath smile. "Hey."

I didn't care that her brother wanted to snap me like a toothpick. I shifted my gifts to one hand, pulled her in by the small of her back, and planted a kiss square on her mouth. She let out a little squeak when I slid my tongue along the seal of her lips, but I didn't take it any farther.

"Damn, Mama." I raked my gaze over her body. "You look good enough to eat."

She was wearing a black dress that stopped just above her knees and highlighted all those delicious curves that I ached to get my hands on.

Beth's body was written in cursive. Elegant, flowing lines that curved and dipped as they went from commonality to art.

She was abstract poetry; prose that I'd never forget. Structured, yet fluid. The meandering form that created life was a lyric I wanted to be stuck in my head all day.

Beth's palms smoothed down the front of my shirt, resting squarely on my chest. "Likewise."

"Hi, Shane!" Caroline chirped as she popped out from the kitchen. Kat was up against her shoulder, enamored with her blonde ringlets.

My heart softened as I looked over Beth's shoulder. "Hey, kid. How you feeling?"

Caroline wasn't the kid I donated a kidney to anymore. In fact, if I had anything to say about it, she'd be my future sister-in-law.

I knew what my target was. Now, it was all about getting there.

But even if things went my way and Caroline and I became legal family, I'd probably always call her 'kid.'

"Better today," she said.

"Good. That's good." My heart clenched as I saw Kat all snuggled up in a swaddle. It was crazy to me that she was a little over a month old. It felt like it had been so much longer than that. I had been there for her first breath. I saw her, at the least, every few days. I fucking loved that kid.

Loved her Mama, too. But I'd have to temper those expectations for the time being.

"Is it alright if I hold her before we go?" I asked Beth softly.

She looked somewhat surprised. "You want to?"

"I want to hold her as much as you let me." I handed Beth the fuzzy green frog. "Even brought her a friend."

Beth's eyes went misty as she clutched it to her chest.

"These are for you," I said as I handed her the bouquet of flowers. Yellow and white blooms as usual. A little makeshift sunshine never hurt.

I took Kat from Caroline and cradled her against my chest while Beth found an ornate white pitcher to put the flowers in. She and Caroline gushed in hushed tones while I soaked up the snuggles with one of my girls.

"Where are y'all going?" Austin clipped. It was reluctant, but neutral. At least he didn't attempt to take the baby from me or make a cutting comment.

"I made reservations in Chapel Hill. Figured Beth was due for a nice dinner somewhere without a drive-through."

Austin looked at his feet. "Look. I'll be straight with you. The way Beth is about Kat? That's how I always felt about Beth. She's always been mine to protect." He hesitated, then added, "Don't make me regret trusting you."

"I respect that," I said. "And I won't."

"Then we won't have a problem."

"Okay," Beth said. "I think I'm ready."

I made the handoff, giving the baby to Austin. Beth oversaw the transfer and ran through a laundry list of things for them to be aware of and what constituted an emergency in her mind. *Which was pretty much everything, but I wasn't going to diminish her protective maternal instincts.*

"I know this is a big step for you," I said as I opened her door. "I'm proud of you."

Beth climbed into my truck and dabbed at her eyes. "I haven't been away from her since they separated us at the hospital."

"I know, Mama." I kissed her forehead, letting my lips linger on her skin simply because I could. "And you trusted me with her since Austin couldn't be there. And I'm so fucking honored. But Austin's got her. I know that doesn't make you stop worrying, but I trust him. And I haven't trusted anyone but you with my baby girl."

Beth stopped breathing. I counted the seconds until she

took another one. It was softer this time, but steadier. "Okay," she whispered.

THE RESTAURANT WAS cozy with dimly lit bulbs hanging over each table. I kept my hand on Beth's lower back as we followed the host to our table. I went through the dance of pulling out Beth's chair and pushing it in before taking my own seat. When the waiter dropped by with the wine list, Beth dismissed him immediately.

"It won't bother me at all if you want to drink," I said, reaching over the table to drape my hand over hers. "Trust me. I'm good. I hang out for breakfast at the Mule all the time while everyone gets Bloody Marys and screwdrivers."

"Nope," she said, going straight for the main menu.

A smile tugged at the corner of my mouth, and a little knot of stress eased from my shoulders.

"What's good here?" she asked, eyes roaming the entrees.

It had been a long time since I had been to a restaurant this nice. I didn't date, and the last short-lived fling I indulged in had been years ago.

I unfolded the leather-bound menu and scanned the options. "No idea. Guess we'll have to try everything out together."

She peered over the edge of her menu, eyes assessing me with shrewd curiosity. "You brought me to a restaurant you've never tried before?"

"If I took you to a restaurant I've tried before, it would be the Copper Mule, and that's not special enough for a date."

"I like going to the Copper Mule."

"I do too. But if I only have four more dates to win you over, we're not sitting on the patio with my coworkers."

The waiter came back and took our orders. Beth went with a steak—rare—and I went for the pork chop.

"So," she said as she trailed her fingertip around the rim of her sweet tea. "How'd you hear about this place if you haven't been here before?"

She wasn't getting away with being that coy. I knew what Beth was poking around at.

"Ask what you really want to know, Dr. Hale. I'm an open book."

Her cheeks turned crimson. It had been a while since I threw in a 'Dr. Hale' for good measure.

"You don't talk about yourself a lot. Or you use personal information like a lure to distract from the hook."

I raised an eyebrow. "Rather astute. Are you saying I get what I want by tempting you with things about myself?"

She smiled. "Yes."

I laced my hands together, feeling a little stiff in the dress shirt I pulled out of the back of my closet, and rested my elbows on the table like a proper Neanderthal.

"Then how about this? Brandie Jean recommended this place. She said the food is great. It's nice enough to impress without being so stuffy that we can't have a normal conversation. It's far enough away from Falls Creek that we won't have to end the night as soon as the check comes. And since I think you're baiting me, I'll bite. No, I haven't brought dates here before. I have had two very brief, very consensual, and very casual hookups since I moved to Falls Creek. I learned pretty quick that it's awkward when the call you're responding to is a former fling—"

Beth laughed under her breath.

"—and the patient is her new partner who decided using a cucumber would be better for trying out anal play on himself, rather than being a man and ordering a toy online or going to a sex shop to pick out something with a flared base. I had a couple of girlfriends while I was in the Navy, but the divorce rate among special operators is over ninety percent. Most of my brothers were paying alimony, child support, or both, so I never pursued anything serious."

Beth hunched over the breadbasket between us. "I don't think gentlemen say 'anal play' in fancy restaurants."

I mirrored her posture, leaning in even more. Our lips touched. "I never said I was a gentleman."

The fire in her eyes was the desired response.

Her lips curved as she sat back in her seat. I was thankful for the pressed linen tablecloth hiding the tent in my slacks.

"What else do you wanna know, Mama?"

"Tell me about you and BJ."

"If the question is if she was one of my two flings, I already told you that she and I—"

"I believe you," Beth said. "I want to know how it all came to be. And I want to hear it from you. Not second-hand information from my brother or Caroline." Hesitantly, she added, "And I want to know how she fits in your life now."

"Why does this feel more like an interrogation than a date?" I asked just as the waiter appeared with our meals.

My irritation reached critical when the waiter wouldn't fucking leave and lingered like a statue while we cut into our dinners to make sure the temperature of the meat was to our liking. I would have downed a piece of jerky instead of the thick-cut pork chop I was salivating over if it meant he would just walk away.

Finally, after Beth and I offered polite nods of approval, he disappeared.

She sliced into her steak right away, the stream of juices turning the base of her mashed potatoes pink. "Oh my god," she mumbled around the bite. "This is incredible."

"Yeah?" I started cutting into mine.

Beth closed her eyes and moaned. "It's like butter."

Why was everything about her a turn-on? I couldn't even watch her eat without my flag flying.

"I'm glad," I said, taking a fortifying sip of my water.

"Eat up, but you're not getting out of this," she said. "I want your side of the story."

I could wait to eat. If the price of moving on with Beth was giving her the dirty details, she'd get them and we'd live happily ever after.

"The first time Brandie Jean meddled in my life was the night before Caroline's kidney transplant. I was leaving the liquor store with the haul of booze I wanted to drown myself in after I got sliced open and sent home. I was gonna get drunk off my ass, put my gun to my head, and end it all."

Her fork stalled, and her eyes softened. "Looking at you now, I never would have guessed you were struggling back then."

"People walk around, pretending like they're not falling apart every single day. Death is easy on the dead and hard on the living. The entire time I was in the Teams, I lived with plenty to die for and little to live for. I looked death in the eye more times than I could count. Sometimes, it was a tease. By the time I was out of the Navy, I was excited for it."

Beth stopped chewing and looked down at her plate.

I gave her a reassuring smile and continued. "Brandie Jean was in the parking lot, handing out takeout containers from the Mule to some folks who were taking shelter under the awning. It was like she was undercover. No pink. No makeup. She was wearing an old hat and had her hair up. Normal jeans, sneakers, and a plain sweatshirt. She was driving this little gray clunker—not the Brandie-mobile with the eyelashes. The perfume was the same, though.

"She caught sight of me and offered a meal, but I was fasting for the surgery. Clear liquids only. Unfortunately, vodka didn't count. Up until then, I hadn't told a soul that I was Caroline's donor. But she chased me around that fucking parking lot like she already knew."

"What'd she do?" Beth asked.

"I told her I couldn't eat because I was going under in the morning, got in my car, and drove home. Never gave it another thought. Well, until I woke up after the surgery. She was sitting in the chair beside my hospital bed. She lied to the hospital staff—or paid them off. That wouldn't surprise me either. But she didn't leave my side the entire time I was recovering. When I was discharged, she drove me home. I thought I'd have the chance to pull the trigger when she went to the pharmacy to pick up my prescriptions, but she managed to have them delivered. For an entire month, she slept on my couch."

"That must've been awkward. She was basically a stranger to you."

I shrugged. "Blame it on the military, but being in close quarters with strangers never bothered me. But she did get me talking. She saw all my shit from the Navy stuffed in the closet and started asking questions. Not big ones—she didn't get into the big stuff right away. Just little questions here and there. When I stopped taking the painkillers after the transplant, my nightmares came back. That's when she started making me talk about the big stuff.

"She spent hours on the phone fighting the VA for me. When they didn't come through the way they should have, she marched my ass to a therapist, a psychologist, and a psychiatrist. Paid out of pocket for me. She took me to AA meetings and helped me stay sober. One day a package showed up on the porch. She had ordered the textbooks I needed to start studying to be an EMT. I had a little experience in combat medicine, so it made sense.

"Slowly but surely, she backed off. It was like a parent teaching their kid how to ride a bike. You know as soon as you let go, they're going to fall over and skin their knees. But BJ never let go long enough for me to fall. She'd let me wobble a little and remind me how to get back up. She was Falls Creek's bedazzled Robin Hood. But instead of stealing from the rich to give to the poor, she uses her own wealth to get people back on their feet. That's why she started the Ladies Auxiliary."

Beth's eyes bugged out of her head. "Hold on. I knew she was involved and led it now or whatever, but she started it? I thought Gran Fletcher started it."

I chuckled. "Nope. It was BJ. She used to sneak around doing her good deeds in the dark, but it was too hard to be effective when she was trying to stay incognito. So she built an army of puppets and now she just pulls the strings."

Her fork hit the plate with a clatter. "That lying, scheming —" She clammed up when the table adjacent to ours stopped chatting and stared. "How does she do it?" she whispered. "Get the grannies to do her bidding, I mean. They're some stubborn old bats and she plays them like a damn fiddle."

"It gives them a purpose," I said. "Gran Fletcher lost her husband years ago. Callum lived with her as a teenager, but when he moved out she was a little lost. Same with Estelle Gould. She needed a place to belong after her husband passed. Some of them are retired. Some of them just like being a part of it. BJ doesn't have to tone down her sparkle to get her work done. She mobilizes her granny gang and hides off to the side, letting them take all the credit. It's easy for people to tell her 'no' if she offers help. But no one says no to a little old lady who just wants something to do."

23

BETH

"I'm dreading going home, and it makes me feel like a shit mom for saying that."

Shane reached across the cab of the truck and found my hand as he pulled out of the restaurant parking lot. "It doesn't make you a shit mom. You're allowed to want and enjoy a break. It's good for you."

I stared out the window as Chapel Hill nightlife flew by. College kids and young professionals milled about, hitting up bars and coffee shops. They were just getting their nights started and I could barely keep my eyes open.

It was a peculiar dichotomy; the desire to turn back time and be that carefree, while wanting to hold on to Kat for dear life. Guilt ate at me both ways.

"So," Shane said, tugging me across the bench seat. "I'll go out on a limb and say that you had a good time?"

I rested my temple on his shoulder. "The best time. I haven't been out like that in so long. It was just what I needed."

He drew our clasped hands to his mouth and kissed the back of mine. "Good."

We made the drive in silence, simply soaking up the time we had alone. These moments would be few and far between.

Guilt flared again. Was I being selfish, going out on dates and pawning my kid off on her uncle? Was I creating a home environment that was volatile? Or even just unstable at best? Would Shane be the first in a revolving door of attempts to salvage what I thought I had with Bradley?

"You're a good mom."

Four words uttered in the dark stopped my train of thought on a dime.

Shane glanced at me, grinning. "You have a shitty poker face, Beth. Everything that goes through your head is written across your face." He squeezed my hand a little tighter. "Listen to me. I know you're worried about this. I know you want a guarantee that it's going to work, and I'm sorry that I can't give you that guarantee. But I can promise you that I'm going to try my best. I need the same from you. And if your best is giving ten percent, that's fine. I'll give 190%. Fifty-fifty is for divorce settlements. I just need to know that you're in this."

I exhaled the uncertainty. "I'll do my best."

"That's all I want, Mama."

Everything about him eased my mind and warmed my heart.

Street lamps sporadically dotted the road as we cruised back into town. I reached into the floorboard for my purse when Shane took a sharp turn. I yelped as I jerked to the side and peered out the window. "What—my house is the other way."

"Yep."

"Austin and Caroline are bringing Kat back to the house. We don't have to go to them."

"Yep."

"Then what are you—" I was cut off by the truck bouncing

in and out of a pothole, then coming to a skidding stop behind a grove of trees.

"Just a few more minutes," Shane growled as he unlatched my seatbelt and yanked me into his lap.

Strong hands kneaded my hips as his mouth crashed on mine. A gasp slipped from my lips the second he pulled my hair, yanking my head back. The path of sloppy kisses he left down my throat lit me up like I was covered in gunpowder and he was a flame.

"Shane," I whimpered.

He groaned, deep and resonate. "Say my name again."

It wasn't difficult to do, I prayed his name as his hands roamed my body. Every scrape of his fingers over my breasts was electrifying.

Aha! My libido was finally beginning to emerge from hibernation. Thank God.

"Shane..."

He laid me down across the bench seat, straddling my legs with one knee on the vinyl and one foot on the floorboard. Sparks skittered down my spine as his body pressed against mine. His teeth sunk into the juncture of my neck and shoulder. My toes curled as he skated his hands up my thighs and under my dress.

He buried his face into my throat, kissing across my collarbone. Down, down, down, until—

"Goddamn," he groaned as he kissed around the swell of my cleavage. "You are heaven."

I ached for him. Every part of me wanted to belong to Shane Hutchins.

Those capable hands slid around my hips to my ass. His fingers curled around the edge of my sensible briefs, not quite tugging them down, but definitely letting me know that's where he wanted things to go.

"Shane, I can't have sex yet," I whispered as I grabbed his biceps. The muscles flexed underneath my palms.

Shane dropped his forehead on mine and nodded regretfully. His thumbs gently stroked my skin. "There's no pressure. I just want a few minutes with you. No distractions. No chores. No to-do list. Just us." He dropped a kiss behind my ear. "And for the record, our first time isn't going to be in my fucking truck."

"What's it going to be like?" I stammered as I tilted my head back, giving him more access to my throat.

The scrape of his sandpaper jaw was exhilarating.

"Our first time will be whenever you say it is. Whenever your mind and your body are ready for that step." His words were sincere, but his smile was Cheshire. "I want to strip you down. I want to lay you out on the bed without a stitch of fabric covering this perfect body. I think I'd start by kissing your tits."

Just to make his point, he cupped one of my breasts and squeezed gently, making me writhe beneath him.

"I'd kiss down your stomach, then move to your thighs. I'd kiss them too. Open them up wide. I'd tease you. Make you tremble with anticipation. Maybe I'd put you on your hands and knees and kiss down your spine. I want to fuck you from behind. I want to see you throw your head back. I want to see your tits swing. But not for our first time. Our first time I want to see your face. I want to see everything you're feeling. I want all of it. I'll take my time with you. We'll have an eternity to get creative, but that first time—it's not about sex. It's about you and me."

He kissed my forehead. "So I need you to let me know when you're ready." His grin was guilty. "But that doesn't mean I won't pull this truck over for a little making out any chance I get."

We shared casual kisses, hands exploring and tongues tasting until we called it quits and righted our clothes. Shane drove back to my place with me tucked against his side.

Being with him felt right. I wasn't worried about being picture perfect for him the way I had always been with Bradley.

Being with Kat's father ... It always felt like a test. Like there were invisible hoops I had to jump through to please him. It was like he kept score to see how well I measured up, but when I'd meet the benchmark he would change it up. There was never any pleasing him, only holding onto little bits of approval that made me insatiable for more.

But not Shane. He met me right where I was. Being with him wasn't a test.

"When can I see you again?" I asked when he pulled back into my townhouse complex.

He swung into a space and threw the truck into park. "I don't have to go home."

As much as I liked this, I wasn't used to it. Bradley always led our rendezvous. Everything was on his terms all the time.

"I can spend the night," he murmured as he wrapped me up in his arms and started kissing up my neck again. "Split the night feedings with you." He nipped at my earlobe. "Help you get going in the morning before I have to go to work."

I laughed as he buried his face into my neck.

"Don't send me home," he murmured.

I wrapped my arms around his neck. "I don't have a guest room anymore."

He sucked my bottom lip between his teeth and bit down. "Good."

"Shane..." It was somewhere between a plea and a moan.

"Let me in." His fingers twined with mine. "Please. I'll

sleep on the fucking floor if I have to. If that's what makes you feel safe."

I curled up against his chest. "You need a good night of sleep before you work tomorrow. Kat will be up every three hours."

"If you're trying to say no by making up an excuse, just tell me no. I'll respect that. But if you're actually worried about how I'll sleep, I promise you, I'll sleep better near you. Every day I've felt like a piece of me was missing. And then Kat was born and that piece split into two. It's fucking painful to know you're right here and I'm still on the other side of the door."

My lip wobbled. "Are you sure?"

He kissed me and nodded. "Yeah."

My words were a ghost of a whisper against his lips. "Then come inside."

We shared a handful of latent kisses before Shane hopped out and opened my door. My phone was in my hand as I texted Austin and let him know that we were back and he could bring Kat home.

"Ms. Hale." I froze with one foot on the asphalt and one on the sidewalk.

I hadn't heard that voice since December.

Shane felt the tension in my spine and stopped. He spotted Julie Childers before I did, positioning himself so that I was shrouded by his frame. "Can I help you, ma'am?"

I peered around him and nearly fell over. It wasn't just Bradley's wife. It was his daughter, too. They lingered by a shiny black SUV parked beneath a tree.

"That's Bradley's wife," I whispered to Shane.

His back stiffened, and his demeanor changed on a dime. Shane went from being cautious to going on the offensive.

"Leave," he barked, not caring that it was a woman and her child. All he saw was an enemy.

I stayed glued to his back, trying to make myself small and invisible. Guilt ate away at me like acid every time I thought about the family I had been complicit in wrecking. I had no idea Bradley was a married man, but if the accidental confrontation in December was anything to go by, his wife didn't care that I was clueless.

I peeked through the space between Shane's elbow and ribs.

Julie held her hands out in a gesture of surrender. "I'm here on behalf of my daughter."

My breath caught.

What was that phrase some of my freshmen always said? Game recognizes game?

If the game was motherhood, I recognized it. The moment she mentioned her daughter, my protective instincts toward mine flared to life.

"Send an email next time," Shane snapped. "Or your husband won't be the only one with a restraining order."

"I'm divorcing him," she called from across the parking lot.

That caught my attention. It didn't seem like the kind of thing she'd lie about in front of her daughter. Cautiously, I stepped out from behind Shane, but still kept him in front of me like a protective shield.

"Why are you here?" I asked.

Julie swallowed. There was pain in her face. "My daughter, Olivia, wants to meet her sibling." She paused, then added, "Well—her *half*-sibling."

"Absolutely not," Shane growled under his breath.

"Can I be frank?" Julie said, a little more softly.

For the love of God, yes. I hated these mind games. "Please."

"You weren't the only one." She twisted her fingers. "After ... after you showed up I started going through everything.

Our bank accounts. His phone. His computer. There was another woman... besides you. One of his students, apparently."

My stomach dropped. Not just for her. Not just for her family. But for me too.

It really was just a game to him. We were *all* a game to him. Prizes to be kept, as my brother once said. Wins and losses.

There was a reason I had a restraining order against him. I wasn't about to let my child be a pawn.

"I'm very sorry to hear that, but like I told you back in December, I had no idea you existed."

"I know that now."

"How did you find where I lived?"

She looked guilty. "I found an email confirmation for some flowers he had sent you. The delivery address was listed."

"Restraining order," Shane hissed through clenched teeth.

I was done with this conversation. "I'm sorry, but you can't see my daughter."

Olivia's face lightened. "I have a sister?"

Shit. I shouldn't have let that slip.

Julie's eyes softened. "Can I ask how you're doing? Those first few months were always hell for me."

Shane nearly lunged for her, but I grabbed his jeans and kept him beside me.

Oh. I grabbed his ass. I wasn't mad at that.

"I'm figuring it out."

Her attention flicked to Shane, attempting to silently dissect who he was to me. "Josh and Luke ... they're having a harder time coming to terms with what their father did."

It was me. I was the thing their father did.

"But Olivia would really like to meet your daughter."

I looked at the gangly-legged teenager and addressed her

instead of her mom. "I wasn't lying when I said you can't see her."

Olivia's face fell.

"She isn't here. Her uncle and aunt babysat her tonight." I looked up at Shane and tried to read his expression, but it was blank. I guess the decision-making was on me. "But maybe we can find some time in the future."

Olivia's eyebrows lifted. "Really?"

I dipped my head. "Yes."

Shane clenched his fist.

I rummaged around in my purse and found a scrap of paper and a pen. I scribbled my number down and handed it to Olivia. "Text me if you have a free afternoon and I'll see what we can do."

"Thanks—um—"

"You can just call me Beth." I glanced at Julie. "If that's alright with your mom."

Julie nodded, then backed toward the SUV. "We'll leave you to your evening. Have a good night."

Shane stood sentry on the sidewalk and watched as Julie and Olivia Childers pulled away. He never slouched, but stood at the ready until he was sure they were gone.

"Austin should be here in a few minutes," I said, trying to break the tension.

Shane took my keys and unlocked the door without a word.

"I'd offer you a drink, but I haven't had to buy alcohol in almost a year and you don't drink anyway. Do you want some coffee or something? Then again, it's late and you have to work tomorrow..."

"Do you trust her?"

I paused in the entryway. "Do I what?"

"Do you trust his wife and his kid?"

I didn't owe either of the Childers women anything, but my daughter was also included in the category of "his kid."

"She asked how I was doing," I said.

"So?" Shane was agitated, and I'd never really seen him like this before.

"She didn't ask how Kat was. She asked how I was doing. Only a handful of other people have asked me that and one of them is standing in front of me. So yes. In some weird, fucked-up way, I trust her."

He pressed his palms together and let out a steadying breath. "I'm trying very hard not to overreact right now."

"Why would you—"

"I held her, Beth," he snapped. "I held her the moment she entered the world." Pain and anguish flooded his eyes. "I held her skin-to-skin while no one knew whether you were going to make it or not. I held her while she was screaming in the hospital because she didn't have you." His voice broke. "I've lost every good thing I've ever had, so I'll be damned if you or my baby girl are on that list too. So, no. I don't trust her. Not one fucking bit."

It was the second time he had called Kat "his baby girl." The first time was a fluke, but the second time…

"Do you love my daughter?" The words echoed in the empty house. I heard nothing but my heartbeat.

Shane hesitated, then nodded. "Yeah, Mama. I do." Tension leached from his hands as he slid them around my waist. "It was the first thing I said to her when she was born. Missy was talking to you, but I wanted the first words your daughter got to hear on this side of heaven to be 'I love you.' I would do anything for her, Beth. I swear to you. I would die for her. But I'd live for her too, and sometimes that's a lot harder."

Tears rolled down my cheeks. I babbled, surprised when a coherent thought came through. "A-and me?"

Shane cupped my cheeks. "I would live for you, too." His kiss was sweet and heartfelt. "I love you, Beth."

I fused myself to his chest, wrapping my arms around him and holding on for dear life. "I love you too."

24

BETH

"Alright, Beth. Feet up and scoot down to the edge for me." Dr. Benoit clicked on a light and pointed it right at my lady temple. The exam room was uncomfortably cold. I busied my mind with contemplating why they would position the end of the exam table toward a window—even if the window blinds were closed.

"You might feel some pressure," she said as she slid the speculum inside of me.

Pressure my ass. That was bullshit.

Whoever coined the term "pinch and pressure" and decided that's how every gynecological procedure should be described should be tried for war crimes.

The tune to "Gaslighter" by The Chicks floated through my mind.

I stared at the ceiling tiles. *Why didn't they paint these? Or put posters on them?* The OBGYN would be a far better experience if I got to stare at a 90s boy-band poster or something.

I closed my eyes instead.

"Everything looks normal," she said from down under. "Your stitches are completely dissolved and your tear is healed." There was a long pause as she poked and prodded around down there. The wheels of her stool creaked as she rolled backward and removed the speculum, dropping it on the tool tray. "You can go ahead and sit up."

Getting up from being spread-eagle on an exam table was almost as awkward as getting into the position in the first place. My feet dangled over the edge like a child. I crossed my arms over my midsection, trying to keep the paper gown closed. Dots of moisture bloomed through the thin pink paper.

"Lay back for me and we'll do a quick breast exam."

I shifted back on the table, worried that the gown would rip up the back if it got caught under my ass.

"Sorry," I said as she peeled the damp paper gown back. "I still have a little milk left."

"That's okay," she said. "It's normal. Doesn't faze me at all. Are you breastfeeding?"

I bent my right arm behind my head while she palpated my breast. "Not anymore. I couldn't make enough to feed her."

She nodded and lowered my arm, then repeated the process on the other side. "Any tenderness? Swelling? Redness? Have your breasts felt warm to the touch?"

I shook my head.

"Alright. You can go ahead and sit up and we'll talk about a few things." She rolled over to her laptop and made a few notes as I got situated. "Let's chat about your birth control options. You were on the pill before you got pregnant. Is that something you want to return to or would you like to discuss some different options?"

"The pill is fine." *I'd just keep that 93% efficacy rate in mind and condoms on hand.*

"Excellent," she said. "I'll get the prescription in. Same pharmacy that we have on file?"

I nodded.

Her voice softened. "I know your daughter was a bit of a surprise, but are future children something you want to discuss? You could try sooner, but just as a rule of thumb, we recommend waiting at least eighteen months to try to conceive again. It gives your body time to recover."

"I'm not having more children," I blurted out.

My stomach sank like an anvil in a pond. *What if Shane wanted kids? Kids of his own. I was adamant that I was done, but was I shortchanging him? If this thing between us lasted long-term, would he resent me?*

Dr. Benoit gave me a placid smile. "Very normal reaction, but that might change."

It wouldn't.

"And how have you been feeling? How were your post-partum screenings with your pediatrician? Anything you want to discuss?"

The stone of dread in my gut turned into a wrecking ball. "No."

What was the point? She'd tell me to "suck it up, buttercup" just like everyone else had.

Why did people treat motherhood like it had to be trial by fire? Why couldn't someone just be like, "Yeah. There's fire. Here's a map. You don't have to get burned."

Dr. Benoit tilted her head. "You sure?"

I huffed and decided to go for broke. "I don't feel like myself at all. I have these really scary intrusive thoughts. There are days where I can barely get out of bed. There are days where I want to pack up and start over somewhere where no one knows me. My daughter would be better off with literally anyone but me. I love her, but I don't have that bond that everyone talks about."

Her smile was probably supposed to be reassuring but she

kept looking at the clock. "Baby blues are fairly common. Continue to monitor those feelings for a few weeks and if they escalate, give us a call and we'll have you come back in. I can give you a referral to a provider who specializes in postpartum depression, but she's booked out for about six months and insurance doesn't always cover it."

More problems and no solutions. Just great.

I hadn't mentioned the suicidal ideation that liked to creep in the back of my mind from time to time. She'd probably tell me she'd be right back and then make a call to CPS for Kat and a psych facility for me, then wash her hands of the situation.

Wait a few more weeks? Go to an expensive ass specialist who wouldn't see me for months?

Fuck that bullshit.

Dr. Benoit was a great OBGYN, but I was sick and tired of getting the runaround when it came to my brain.

"So," she said, pivoting to a cheery tone with a clap of her hands. "You're healing up great which means you can resume sexual activity. Any concerns there?"

I hated talking about sex with doctors. Sure, they were supposed to be safe people to discuss it with, but it always felt like trying to talk about sex with your mom.

"Is it weird that I want to have sex, but my sex drive is like trying to start a really old lawnmower with a pull-string? It sputters."

Dr. Benoit actually laughed. "Not weird at all. Your hormones are still trying to figure themselves out. Take it slow with your partner. Have him or her focus on foreplay. Get used to your body being yours again. Use lots of lubricant. Usually I don't say keep your expectations low, but in this instance, keep your expectations low. Your body won't immediately go back to reacting the way it did before you had your baby, but you'll get there eventually. Ease back into it. Be patient. Slow and steady wins the race."

Dr. Benoit submitted my birth control prescription and gave me the green light to leave. I dressed, checked out at the desk, then found Caroline waiting with Kat in the lobby. She had wrapped up her school day then helped me out by coming with me to the appointment so I didn't have to take Kat into the exam room with me.

"How'd it go?" she asked as she lifted the visor on the stroller so I could get a peek at Kat.

"I'm officially licensed to bang and have some anti-baby pills waiting for me at the pharmacy."

She laughed. "I'll keep that just between us. Austin thinking that you and Shane aren't getting busy is probably for the best."

Caroline wasn't wrong.

We loaded up and headed back to Falls Creek. After a pit stop at the pharmacy where I got my birth control, popped the first pill and dry-swallowed it, then set a daily alarm on my phone, we headed back to my house.

I put Kat on her play mat for tummy time while Caroline settled on the couch. "How are things with Shane?"

"They're going," I said evasively.

The night we said I love you to each other changed everything. I couldn't deny the existence of a relationship anymore, nor did I want to.

But this wasn't how relationships usually went for me.

I always fell for the carnal side of things first. Emotions came after that. But it was the opposite with Shane.

He showed up for me every time, without fail.

Trusting someone with my body was always easier than trusting them with my emotions. When someone did damage to a body, it was easy to point it out. But when they did damage to a heart, recovery was harder.

Shane had always kept my emotions safe. He treasured and protected them. Now, my body was the thing I was worried about sharing with him.

He said he wanted me as-is, but that was easy for him to say when I was mostly covered up.

"Are you guys going out again soon?" she asked.

"Tonight actually." I checked the time. I really needed to start getting ready. "Well—we're staying in. He's cooking at his house."

"Oooh—that'll be fun. Sleepover after?" She waggled her eyebrows.

Shane had spent a few nights at my place. We'd fall asleep together, but I'd always wake up to an empty bed and him hanging out on the couch.

I didn't tell him how much that stung.

"I think so. He told me to pack a bag for me and Kat. He worked last night and got off this morning. Since he's off tomorrow, we'll probably just hang out."

"And will things be ... progressing?"

I shot her a look. "You can just ask if we're going to have sex. It's fine."

"I still feel weird about asking stuff like that," Caroline said with a bashful smile.

I raised an eyebrow. "Weirder than me knowing you get it on with my brother?"

"I can't help that Brandie Jean got us snowed in a cabin and I asked him to take my virginity!" Her voice lowered to a mumble. "Or that he wanted to teach me more things after that..."

"Caroline!" I shrieked. "I definitely didn't know *that* part of it."

She blushed. "Then I certainly shouldn't tell you that he was the best possible person I could have lost it to."

I shrugged. "You're probably not wrong—he's got that whole 'gentle giant' thing going on. I know how women react to him."

"Anywho—back to you and Shane. Are you worried about sleeping with him? And I don't mean *actually* sleeping."

I stood in the bathroom with the door open and rummaged around for my curling iron. I was about to say no, but Caroline was my future sister-in-law.

I never had a sister—only my ogre of a brother who liked to think I was still a child.

I was so happy for the two of them, and I couldn't think of two better people to be partners.

"Yeah." I sighed. "My body's changed so much since I had Kat."

"And you're nervous about Shane seeing you?"

I nodded as I jammed the plug into the outlet by the mirror.

Caroline stood up and walked over, untucking her thick sweater from her flowy skirt. My girl always looked like a fairy princess who belonged in a storybook cottage. She stood in the bathroom door and lifted her shirt, tucking it up into her bra. She shimmied her skirt until it was low on her hips, revealing a swooping surgical scar from her kidney transplant. There were smaller scars, too—remnants of rashes from lupus flares.

"Austin doesn't care," she said with the conviction of a tent-revival preacher. "I do, but it's never once changed the way he looks at me." She lowered her shirt and tucked it back into her skirt. "Maybe it's just because I have one of Shane's organs and sometimes I think we have extrasensory perception, but he's not going to care. He'll make you feel the way he feels about you."

I hoped she was right.

"Enough about me," I said as I started sectioning my hair into pieces. "Let's talk about your wedding plans."

———

KAT CHIRPED HAPPILY in the backseat as I pulled into Shane's driveway. It's like she knew we were going to see him. She gravitated toward him whenever he was in the room, reaching and cooing until he picked her up.

The two of them shared a bond that I couldn't really explain.

I eyed the haul of overnight bags I'd thrown in the backseat and debated carrying them in now or later.

I didn't know what Shane's plans were, especially when it came to the two of us in the bedroom. Cuddling—being wrapped up in his arms—it was heaven. But he made it clear that I was going to have to make the first move when I was ready to take things further.

Was I ever going to be ready?

Maybe that's why I still hadn't told him I got the green light at my six-week checkup today...

I unlatched Kat's car seat and hooked it in the crook of my elbow. I'd send Shane out for the rest of my stuff later.

It was weird that he hadn't answered the door yet. Usually he met me in the driveway and got Kat out himself.

I would have been alarmed had I not heard thundering feet inside. *Was he running?*

The doorbell let out a high-pitched chime, and I stepped back and waited.

Something clattered. The cat yowled. There was a crash as he yelled, "Shit!"

The door whipped open and Shane grinned, trying to catch his breath and look casual.

I raised an eyebrow. "Everything okay in there?"

Richard, the cat, darted out and hissed at Shane as he leaped into the bushes. His charcoal colored tail stuck out like a middle finger.

"Better now," he said as he lifted his ball cap, pushed his fingers through his thick, inky hair, and then fitted it on his head backward.

Hello, Mr. Backward Cap Bad Boy.

To top it off, he was wearing one of those dual-colored baseball tees with the three-quarter length sleeves and gray sweatpants.

Oh, this man had something up his sleeve... And in his pants.

The casual nature of our dates was something I loved about Shane. Sure, I liked to be wined and dined. Who didn't? But more than that, I loved just being with him. I liked his domestic side.

It also meant I could show up in leggings, and a soft sweatshirt and not be at all out of place.

"Hey, gorgeous." He leaned in and gave me a quick kiss before relieving my arm of the car seat. "Hey, tadpole," he whispered as he set the seat on the floor and unbuckled her. In a flash she was up against his chest.

"It smells good in here." Something fragrant was baking in the oven and it made my mouth water. It smelled like fall—buttery with warm herbs. Something sweet and savory.

"I hope you're hungry." He closed and locked the door behind me, then took my hand. "But there's something I wanna show you first."

Shane led me into the living room and waved his arm like Vanna White.

A play mat was spread on the floor. Little toys and rattles were scattered on it. Every outlet had a socket cover. The edges of the coffee table had some kind of foam on it to protect little heads from getting whacked. The entertainment center had a child safety lock keeping the lower cabinet doors closed.

A small stack of cardboard books with the likes of *The Very Hungry Caterpillar, Guess How Much I Love You,* and *The Frog Prince* sat in a little woven basket.

My throat felt like someone had shoved a rock covered in tissue paper down it. "Shane..." I turned to look at him but ended up looking around him and into the kitchen.

Everything was baby-proofed.

He pressed a kiss to the top of my head. "One more thing I want to show you. Then we can eat."

My body felt like it was radioactive, verging on nuclear meltdown as I followed him down the hall. I clasped his hand like a lifeline, not trusting myself to stay afloat if he let go.

He opened the door to the second bedroom and turned on the lights.

I gasped.

Austin's few remaining belongings and the spare bed that had been in here were gone. A crib was pushed to one wall. A fitted sheet in pale pink was around the mattress.

An old-school rocking chair with a quilt draped over the back sat in the corner. A dresser had been turned into a changing table with all the bells and whistles in a little cart beside it. A baby monitor—the same model I owned—had the green light already going.

But it was a teddy bear placed on the seat of the rocking chair that made me pause. That knot in my throat grew tighter, wringing tears from my eyes.

Carefully, I picked it up and ran my finger down the tight stitching that held the dark blue fabric together.

Shane's shadow loomed behind me. The warmth from his chest radiated against my back. "It's made out of the shirt I was wearing the day she was born."

25

SHANE

Beth whipped around, clutching the bear to her chest. Eyes that matched her daughter's looked up at me, stunned. "You... But... How?"

Kat squirmed in my arms, kicking her little legs like a frog until I laid her in the crib. Beth's gaze never left me.

"I made it," I said simply, sliding my hands onto her hips. I tugged until her body collided with mine.

"When?" she blurted out.

I smiled softly as she ran her finger over the embroidered star of life that had once been stitched onto the left breast of the shirt. Above and below the star, it read, *FALLS CREEK EMS.*

"I got the pattern from a website while the shirt was in the wash the day after she was born."

Beth was speechless as she used the edge of her sleeve to dab her eyes. She just kept shaking her head as she stared at the bear.

"Is it alright?" I asked, moving in to cup her cheek and wipe her tears away with my thumb. I tasted salt when I kissed her temple. "If I overstepped—"

"No," she blurted out. "Oh my god, no. It's... I'm floored." She held it to her chest. "I can't believe you'd do that. And you know how to sew? I think I'm more surprised that you can sew!"

I laughed. "Most people are surprised, yes."

"Thank you," she whispered. "This is..." Beth looked around the nursery I had been working on since she agreed to five dates. "So much more than I could have ever asked for. I don't know how to repay you for this."

Beth was playing checkers, but I was playing chess. And I was thinking ten moves ahead.

I tipped her chin up and pecked her lips. "You'll never have to beg me to love you. And stuff like this—it's how I express it. Let me help you. Let me ease your burden. You letting me be your partner and a part of Kat's life is payment enough." Gently, I wiggled the bear out of her hands and set it aside. "Come on, Mama. Supper's ready."

While I finished plating the dinner I'd made for the two of us, Beth fixed Kat a bottle and curled up in the corner of the couch to feed her. Richard had screeched at the door until I let him back in. He immediately hopped up beside Beth and fell asleep.

Furry asshole.

This scene was so right. For the first time since I'd moved into this house, it felt like there was life in it.

It wasn't just the curtains that were open. It was the sound of Kat's soft grunts as she chugged her dinner. It was Beth rambling about the work on her doctorate she was trying to accomplish before her maternity leave was up.

The Archangel anniversary was right around the corner, but there were no clouds in my head. No survivor's guilt.

If surviving against all odds meant I had more time on this

earth, then dammit—I was going to fucking *live*. And I hadn't felt this alive in years.

When Kat's eyes had drifted lower and lower and she was in a happy milk coma, Beth took her back and laid her in the crib.

I had dinner on the table as soon as she was back.

"This is so good," Beth mumbled around a mouthful of apple and sausage stuffing. "It's like the best parts of breakfast and dinner all at once."

"Estelle Gould gave me the recipe," I said. "We all take turns going over there at least once a week. It keeps her from calling 911 to report bogus emergencies. She's just lonely." I sliced into my golden apple that had been hollowed out and filled with a sausage, cornbread, and sage stuffing.

Beth raised an eyebrow. "So is she the one who taught you how to sew?"

I chuckled as I speared a green bean. "No, ma'am. That would be the US government."

She nearly spat out her sweet tea. "What?"

"I learned how to sew in the Teams. Most guys like to customize their ghillie suits depending on the fit or the type of camouflage you need. So, you learn how to follow a pattern, thread a bobbin, and sew some shit."

Beth took another bite and pointed her fork at me. "What's a ghillie suit?"

I swallowed and paused. "It, uh... It's camouflage." I forced a smile. "Kinda makes you look like Chewbacca if he was covered in leaves and grass."

"And you made your own?"

"Quite a few. Some to blend in with snow. Some to blend in with the desert. Some to blend in with the jungle. Sometimes I had to remake one if we had to haul ass out of the AO and it got left behind."

Her brow furrowed, and I could see the wheels spinning in her head. "You were a sniper."

They were words I had heard for decades, but they sounded so foreign coming from Beth's lips.

"Yeah."

Her fork stilled. "That must have been a lot of pressure."

I nodded. "It was."

I hated talking about this shit. Some guys liked to relive the glory days in shitty hole-in-the-wall dive bars in Virginia Beach, Coronado, or Annapolis, but I didn't. I never talked about it. Most of the guys I worked with knew I was in the military, but they didn't know much more than that. Beth's brother was the exception. He knew all my shit. Maybe that was why he was so adamant about me leaving his sister alone.

I couldn't blame him either.

But for some reason, I didn't mind talking about it with Beth.

"My team leader, Cole, and I went through BUD/s together. Did SQT together. We were both selected for three months of sniper training. We were inseparable. We made it into DEVGRU."

"But he became your team leader," she recalled. "Did that make it weird?"

I shook my head. "We were never competitive with each other. Maybe a little, but it was always friendly. Iron sharpens iron, you know? When our old team lead retired, Cole was moved up."

"What was it like for you? Having to report to your best friend?"

I laughed as I finished off the sausage stuffing. "The team lead takes care of the team and his number two takes care of him. We were yin and yang."

"What a bromance." Her smile was flirtatious. "Should I be jealous?"

"Maybe a little. He's real snuggly."

Beth snickered. "I'm snuggly."

She stood to clear her plate, but I beat her to it. "Sit."

"You cooked. Let me help you clean."

"Nope. This is a date, which means you don't do a damn thing except sit there and relax."

"Shane..." Beth stood behind me, put her hands on my hips, and peered around me at the sink. "Let me do something."

"Fine." I dropped the dishes in the sink, turned, picked her up, and set her on the counter. "Keep me company and tell me about your day." I cut the water on and started rinsing the dishes before loading them into the dishwasher.

She crossed her legs at her ankles and twiddled her thumbs. "Well..."

I lifted an eyebrow but didn't say anything else.

"I, um... I saw my OBGYN today."

That could mean a million different things. Was she sick? Was something wrong? Did her postpartum depression take a turn? Why didn't she tell me she had a doctor's appointment today? I could have taken her there.

Endless possibilities were on my mind, but I didn't want to freak her out. It could have very well been something routine, and nothing was wrong.

"How are you feeling after the visit?"

"Okay, I guess." Her tone didn't give anything away.

I dried my hands on a towel before parting her knees and standing between them. I kept her anchored to the counter with my hands on her hips. "Was it just a checkup or was there a concern?"

"It was my six week postpartum appointment," she said,

completely neutral yet again.

It was as if she wanted to offer up the information, but she was waiting for my full attention to be sure I was interested in what she had to say.

Even though I was 99.9% certain that was the case, I still wasn't going to pry.

"If there's something you want to talk about, I'm all ears because I care. Deeply. But I'll respect your boundaries if that's all you want to share."

She picked at her nail bed again. *So, she wanted to share, but she was nervous about whatever it was.* I rolled my thumbs back and forth over her hips until she spoke up.

"Dr. Benoit gave me the go-ahead to have sex again if I want to, and I went back on birth control today."

Holy shit. My brain—and my dick—went straight to DEFCON 1.

I cleared my throat as my gaze slowly crept down the column of her throat. "That uh... That's good. It means you're healing. So that's good. Good. Really good." My hands worked up her sides, grazing the lower swell of her breasts. "That's..."

"Good," she said with heavy eyes watching every flick of mine.

Fuck me... I couldn't think straight. Everything was a jumbled mess. I had waited for her for so long. And as much as I wanted to reassure her that I'd wait forever, I was only human.

Sure, this was only our third official date, but this thing between us had started a long time ago, and we both knew it.

"Shane..." My name was warbled on her lips.

I needed her to say it. I needed her to tell me—verbatim—that she wanted to take this next step.

I slid both hands deep into her hair, holding her head in place so I could kiss up beneath her jawline. "Yeah, Mama?"

Her gasp was sharp. "Tell me again."

I felt her pulse and nibbled on the spot. "Tell you what?"

She arched toward me, pushing into my chest. "Tell me what it'll be like."

I smiled against her skin. "I'll start right here." I opened her hand and kissed the center of her palm, then the inside of her wrist. "I want to kiss every inch of your perfect body. I want to take your clothes off as I go." I pushed her knees open farther and pulled her ass to the edge of the counter. "I'll take my time with you. Worshiping you. I want to taste every part of you. And once I have—" I cupped her pussy on the outside of her leggings "—I'll bow between your knees until you see heaven."

Her head tipped back and a soft "yes" escaped her mouth.

"Tell me what you need," I said as I traced her lips with the tip of my tongue before diving in for a kiss.

Her whimper of desperation had my blood running hot. "I need you to be patient with me. It..." She rested her forehead on mine. "It might not be great the first time and I might bleed and it's still hard for me to—you know—get wet."

Just to remind her how much her life had changed since the last time she had sex, Kat started crying.

Beth sighed. "And now the mood has been murdered."

I shook my head. "Here's what I want you to do. Go get a shower. Forty-five minutes minimum. Relax. I'll see what Kat needs and get her settled and bring your things in from your car."

She chewed on her lip. "And after?"

I kissed her slow and deep, sliding my tongue along the length of hers. I kissed her until she was melting in my hands.

"I'll be in charge of that, too."

THE SHOWER SQUEAKED and the water shut off as I carried the last of Beth's things into my bedroom. I double-checked the baby monitor and made sure Kat was sound asleep. It only took one bottle, tummy time, some rocking and bouncing, and two diaper changes to get her there.

I turned down the bed and placed Beth's overnight bags on her side.

How long would it take before overnight bags turned to leaving a toothbrush here? When would the toothbrush turn into a dresser drawer and then half of the closet?

Even in my younger years I always focused on the next place in life. Maybe that was just the training that had been ingrained in me.

Evolve or die.

Adjust your heading and pivot.

Beth hadn't been meant for me when we first met, so I evolved. I stayed on the perimeter of her mind while she was treading water with Professor Dumbfuck. But now that she was mine, I had to evolve again.

I made it out of the friend zone and I wasn't going back.

"Hey," Beth said from behind me. I spun and found her with one towel wrapped around her torso and one around her hair. "Sorry. I didn't think to bring a robe."

My dick went hard so fast it was almost painful.

Her eyes trailed south and she bit back a smile.

I stood at the edge of the bed and crooked my finger, beckoning her to come to me.

Beth raised her eyebrows.

"Right here, Mama."

With a bashful smile, Beth tiptoed to me, clutching the towel around her body.

"Well," I said as I took her in, damp and glowing. "I can't undress you piece by piece, now, can I?"

Her cheeks were flushed. I reached up and undid the knotted towel that was soaking up the moisture from her hair. Honey colored locks darkened from the shower spilled down her shoulders. I pitched the towel into the hamper then combed my fingers through her hair until it was parted the way she usually did.

Emerald eyes were locked on mine. Her knuckles were white, holding the towel around her body with a death grip.

"Why are you nervous?" I asked gently as I tipped her chin up and kissed her.

Beth's eyes lowered to the floor.

My tone was more stern this time. "Beth."

She sighed. "I just haven't gotten used to this body."

Her cosmetics pouch was sitting at the top of her duffle bag, and a thought popped into my head.

A full-length mirror was mounted on the back of my door, so I closed it and moved Beth until she was standing in front of it.

Leaving her clothed in the towel, for now, I grabbed her makeup bag and unzipped it, rummaging around until I found the two things I was looking for.

"Tell me what you don't like about your body," I said as I tied her hair up with an elastic. I trailed my knuckle down her spine. Immediately, there was something on the tip of her tongue. Before she could speak, I stripped off my shirt and added a caveat. "But you're going to look at me in the mirror and say it about *my* body."

Beth stammered. "But—"

"What's the problem?" I kissed her bare shoulder. "If you're going to talk shit about something I love, you might as well be saying it about me. So, go ahead. Tell me what you don't like."

She didn't say a peep.

I reached in my pocket and pulled out the tube of lipstick I'd lifted from her makeup.

"That's what I thought." I uncapped it, trapped the tube between my teeth, then spun Beth to face me. Her back hit the mirror with a *thud*. I pinched the tube between my fingers like a pencil and wrote, *MINE* across her collarbone.

I peeled one of her hands away from holding the towel and wrote *MINE* down her arm. Scared eyes met mine as I repeated it on her other arm. The towel stayed tucked in around her breasts, but not for long.

I pulled one side away, exposing half of her body. Beth closed her eyes, resting her head against the mirror. The towel crumpled around her feet as I claimed her body with lipstick graffiti.

Her breasts. *MINE*.

Her stomach. *MINE*.

Her hips. Her thighs. Her ribs. *MINE. MINE. MINE*.

I grabbed her by the waist and spun her naked body away from me, plastering her front against the mirror.

Down her spine, I wrote those four letters.

Her shoulders. *MINE*.

Her ass. *MINE*.

Her legs. Her feet. Her palms. *ALL MINE*.

I tossed the now-blunt tube of lipstick on the floor. Scraping my nails up the back of her scalp, I firmly gripped a handful of the bun I'd fashioned and tugged her back into my chest.

When she peeled off the mirror, my proclamations had been stamped onto the glass.

MINE.

We stared at our reflections through the words. "You're mine. And whenever you look in this mirror, you will be reminded of who you belong to."

I spun her, dropped to my knees, and pressed her back against the mirror. "This body is mine to worship. To pleasure. To protect. To love. And the soul inside of it is mine to love. To cherish. Don't speak ill of what's mine."

I hooked my hand around the back of her knee and threw her leg over my shoulder. Her pussy peeked at me, flushed pink with arousal. I sealed my mouth around her clit and sucked, lapping at it until her body loosened and her fingers tightened in my hair.

"Atta girl," I mumbled into her sex as soft moans of delight filled the air. Her hips pushed forward, seeking more as her knees trembled. "You're the most delicious thing I've ever tasted." I pressed my face into her cunt, lapping at each edge and curve of skin, teasing those nerves until her abstract sighs of wanton delight turned to profane cries for more.

I grabbed the inside of her thighs and pushed them out farther. Her sex opened for me and I dipped my tongue inside, testing her responsiveness.

Beth's cry was a shot of adrenaline straight to my dick.

"You look so beautiful like this. So depraved. I think you're gonna like getting fucked. Imagine what everyone would think if they knew that the quiet new mom liked getting her pussy eaten out like this." I gave myself time to look up at her by sliding two fingers into her heated cunt. "You dirty girl."

"Shane," she whimpered as her walls fluttered and contracted. "Please—more—"

I nibbled at her clit, eliciting a piercing cry.

"Come for me, beautiful."

It only took a few strokes before she was shattering around me. I stood and caught her before her knees gave out, but I didn't give her a chance to catch her breath. I grabbed her around the waist and threw her on the bed.

26

BETH

I screeched, then clapped my hands over my mouth as I bounced across the mattress. How thin were these walls? Would we wake Kat up? What would happen if she woke up and started crying when we were mid-coitus?

The train of thought was derailed by Shane grabbing my ankles and yanking me to the edge of the bed. "Come here, Mama." He flipped me to my stomach and jerked my hips up. "Get that ass up for me."

The mattress sank beneath my elbows and I spat a strand of damp hair out of my mouth. He could see me, but I couldn't see him.

Shane let out a deep, groan of pleasure as he gripped the back of my thighs and parted them. "Nuh-uh. Arch your back for me. Get that ass nice and high again."

I leaned forward on my forearms, letting my hair spill around my face like a curtain. Losing my sight heightened every other sense. I was acutely aware of the creak of the floor under his footsteps. The texture of rough skin on the pads of his fingers. The warmth from his body.

Shane swore under his breath as he smoothed his hands all over my skin. It felt so good to be touched like this.

There came a point each day where I was touched-out after having Kat clinging to me for hours. It started with the endless loop of doctors' appointments for nine months, labor and delivery, and the hospital stay where I was poked and prodded at all hours of the night, but I hit a breaking point trying to breastfeed. It had been a long time since my body was used for pleasure rather than for function.

"You're still wet," he murmured as he trailed a single finger up and down my slit. Shane slid that finger inside of me and crooked it, stroking my inner muscles. "Is this all for me?" Something warm touched my spine, and I realized that Shane was hunched over me, kissing down my back. I shivered when he left a trail of kisses down the curve of my ass.

The glittery afterglow of the orgasm had passed, and my fears about not being able to be aroused were unfounded. My body ramped back up immediately.

"Um—Shane?" I whispered when I realized what was happening.

He peeled away from kissing the back of my thighs long enough to say, "Talk to me."

"You might wanna grab a towel or something."

He peered around to see what concerned me.

I looked through the strands of hair shrouding my face and caught his grin.

Shane disappeared from my line of sight, presumably to grab a towel. But instead of coming back with one, he shucked off his sweatpants and eased onto the bed.

I didn't have time to think. He sat against the stack of neatly arranged pillows against the headboard and manhandled me into his lap.

Lipstick was starting to smear all over my body. A pink

stain was on the lower end of the sheets from my hands and knees.

Shane's cock pressed into my ass as he set me between his legs. "Tell me something," he said gently as he cupped one of my breasts.

I nearly jumped out of my skin when his thumb rolled across my nipple. A bead of milk dotted his thumb.

"Are they sore?" he asked before bringing his thumb to his lips and licking that droplet off.

"A little," I whispered, wide-eyed.

"Then I'll be gentle," he said before cradling me in his arms high enough to bring my breast to his mouth. He tugged my nipple between his teeth and flicked it with his tongue. "I want to taste you. No way am I wasting it on a fucking towel."

My head tipped back as he held me between his arms and feasted on my body. The dread at the thought of his mouth being on my breasts evaporated. He groaned like I was the best thing he had ever eaten.

"So fucking sweet." He squeezed the swell of my breast and sucked harder. I tipped my head back, crying out in relief as he drank from my body.

There was something different about the way he touched me. It didn't make my skin crawl the way it always had when I tried to nurse or pump.

Shane was warm and gentle. Every touch, every lick, every pull from his mouth was for my pleasure.

Through heavy lids, I watched his throat constrict as he swallowed.

I wasn't sure how much he was actually tasting since my milk supply had withered. But every time he would catch my eye as he switched back and forth between my breasts, I felt like I was getting part of myself back.

"I love this body." Four words from his lips that vibrated

against my skin were the opposite of everything I had been feeling, but it was the shift of the rudder that I needed to start changing my mental heading.

His cock bumped against my ass, and I could feel the wetness leaking from his tip in a steady stream.

"If this is the only time I get to taste you like this, then I'm still one lucky son of a bitch. Do you know how long I've been wanting to do this?" he growled as he swirled his tongue around my nipple before pulling away from my breast and laying me out on the bed. "Having you just like this; all to myself?" He tangled his fingers with mine and stretched our joined hands over my head as he settled his legs on either side of my hips.

Being on my hands and knees was fine. It hid my stomach. Being in his arms with his focus on my boobs was fine. He wasn't looking at the stretch marks that striped my skin in angry purples and reds.

But laid out beneath him with his eyes all over me, I felt exposed.

"Mine," he whispered against my lips, bringing my attention back to him.

I looked up and took him in. Tattoos covered both arms and most of his chest and abdomen. A surgical scar warped one of the designs.

That's when I really noticed it.

Not his monster cock that jutted out from between his legs.

No—it was the smaller scars that speckled his skin. The tattoos did a pretty good job of hiding them, but the ridged skin glinted from the light.

I ran my hands up and down his chest as he hunched over and braced his arms on either side of my head.

"What are these from?"

He captured my lips in a searing kiss as his cock nestled against my pussy. "Depends which one you're talking about."

"All of them."

He remained stock-still as I explored his chest with my fingers. "Mostly shrapnel. A few from getting shot. Some minor surgeries from other injuries."

"And the tattoos? Before or after the scars?"

"Both," he admitted. His fingers found my stomach, and stroked my stretch marks as I touched his transplant incision. "Scars are evidence that what saves us is found in the margin where hurt and healing collide."

I moved my hand lower and wrapped my fingers around his cock.

His face knitted in a tight expression, like he was trying to stave off any kind of pleasure for himself as long as possible.

"Shane," I whispered as I arched toward him, offering my body. I pumped my hand up and down his shaft. The skin was silken in my grip, and the pressure made him swear.

He nibbled on my earlobe, but it was sporadic, his focus waning as I teased the head of his cock with my thumb. He let out a shaky breath. "Tell me exactly what you want."

I smiled because his restraint was on the verge of snapping. "I want you to stop being so fucking nice."

He chuckled. "I'll stop being nice another night."

"Fine." I grinned against the side of his neck. "Then just put on a condom and fuck me like you want me." I hesitated and added. "Fuck me like you love me."

Condoms had been conveniently placed on the bedside table. He grabbed one and rolled it on. Gently, he ran a knuckle through my pussy, then reached for a little bottle beside the spare condoms.

He... He thought of everything *before* I ever told him I was ready.

I watched through heavy lids as he slicked up the condom with a little extra lube.

I didn't even have to ask.

"Tell me what feels good," he murmured against my lips. I nodded into the kiss as he notched his cock at my entrance. His fingers dug into my hip as he hitched my leg around his hip and pushed in slowly. "Tell me if something doesn't."

I hissed at the first push of pressure, and Shane stopped.

"Breathe for me." He tilted his hips as he pulled out and changed the angle, coating the outside of my pussy and making the next thrust smoother. "Atta girl. There you go. Breathe and relax. Let me do the work tonight. I want to hear all those little sounds you make when you're on top of the world. Let me have them."

His cock was obnoxiously thick, and since it had been so long for me, everything felt tighter. It was like losing my virginity all over again.

Shane pushed all the way in and stalled, giving me time to adjust around him. "You feel so fucking good, Mama." He peppered my chest with kisses as he rocked inside of me. The lipstick painting my body coated his face as he buried his head between my breasts.

A light twinge of pain danced across my pelvis as he pulled out, and Shane froze.

"I didn't say anything," I whispered.

"No, but your face did." He kissed me gently—once, then twice. "I promise you, it'll get better. I'm not in a rush."

"But I want this to be good for you."

"Listen to me, Beth." He pinched my chin between his fingers and forced me to look him in the eye. "Having you like this is the best I've ever felt. I know it's not how either of us probably imagined this moment, but that just makes it different. It doesn't make it bad."

Tears welled up in my eyes, and I blamed the hormones. "I told you to stop being nice."

He laughed. "I could come on command right now. The only reason I haven't is because I don't want it to be over yet."

A devilish smile worked its way across my mouth. "Then come."

Shane laughed, using the distraction to thrust into my relaxed body. "No."

I gasped as he held deep and ground against my clit.

His chuckle was sinister. "And that's why."

A familiar sensation of desperate need built inside of me as Shane found a steady rhythm.

I wrapped my legs around his hips, deepening the connection and savoring the feeling of being wholly and completely his.

This wasn't my first time by a long shot, but it was my first time making love.

Because that's what this was. There was safety in his love. There was healing in it. Maybe he was a broken savior, but he was mine.

Shane's breath hitched as he tapped into every ounce of restraint he had to keep from blowing his load.

I pressed into him and whispered, "Come inside of me."

Shane shook his head. "Not until you come again."

"Shane—"

"Not—" he ground the base of his shaft against my clit "—until you come again." His mouth found my breasts and he lapped at each nipple, tasting and teasing until I was trembling beneath him. "You're doing so good. Just give me a little more."

The orgasm washed me away on swells of bliss. It was steady and powerful like a riptide, sweeping me up without warning in currents of ecstasy. I shuddered beneath him as he finally let his control slip.

There were days I didn't want to keep going, and there wasn't a doubt in my mind that Shane knew exactly what that felt like.

But this... This felt like living.

———

"You seem tense." Shane stood in my living room and bounced Kat in his arms as I rearranged the throw pillows on the couch for the fifth time.

He was keeping her entertained while I neurotically picked at my living room and second-guessed the snacks I put on the coffee table.

"I'm fine," I clipped as I assessed the pillows again. I grabbed the beaded one and put it on the armchair and then grouped the plain ones in a cascade on the left side of the couch. Asymmetry was good, right?

It still didn't look right.

I grabbed the pillows again when Shane yanked them out of my hand and threw them back on the couch.

"What the fu—"

"I need you to take a minute and breathe."

"I'm fine. I just need to make sure everything looks good before—"

Shane laid Kat on her play mat, pulled my back flush to his chest, and crossed my arms over my stomach in a submission hold. "The house is fine. But you need to take a minute because you're not." He pressed a kiss to the top of my head. "Tell me what's going through your mind."

That wasn't happening.

It was one thing to tell him all the ways I made myself crazy, but now that he was my…

I hadn't uttered that word yet.

Labels scared me.

"Come on, Mama," he murmured in my ear, peppering my temple with kisses as he rocked me side to side. "Talk to me."

"I just didn't sleep well last night and I'm stressed about Julie and Olivia coming over."

Bradley's soon-to-be ex-wife and his daughter would be at my house in ten minutes. What seemed like an olive branch at the time felt like the worst peace offering I could have possibly started with.

"Why didn't you sleep?" He nibbled on my ear, turning me into pudding. "You were out like a light as soon as we laid down."

Because you got up after two hours and I couldn't sleep after that.

"I just couldn't," I said, jerking away.

But Shane didn't let me go. "Try again."

Why couldn't he let anything go? If I said what was on my mind, I'd piss him off or make him feel bad or make him think I was being too needy.

"Beth. Tell me."

I rested the back of my head on his chest. "You always get up after I fall asleep."

He nodded in understanding. "I never sleep through the night, and I don't wanna keep you up."

I turned and wrapped my arms around his neck. "You don't have to get up with Kat every time she makes a sound. Just wake me up if I don't hear the monitor." I combed through the back of his hair with my fingers. "You've been a godsend, but I know that she's my responsibility."

Something akin to frustration flashed over his face. "Your daughter isn't my blood, but as far as I'm concerned, she's mine in every way that matters. I respect your position as her mother, so if you're not okay with that or you have boundaries that I need to be aware of, I need you to tell me. But believe me when I say that I want *both* of you. I don't do things halfway. So if I'm in her life, then I'm in it. I'm not gonna be some random guy who plays with her sometimes and brings a birthday gift once a year. I'm here for the mess. I'm here for the middle of the nights. I'm here for the diaper changes and the doctor's appointments and helping you pack up clothes she's outgrown so we can put new stuff in her closet. I know this is new, but I'm all in, Beth. All in. And if you're on the fence—even a little—then I need to know."

My heartbeat roared in my ears. Those were all good things, right? Why did it scare me so much?

The doorbell rang, shattering the moment.

Shane didn't flinch. He cupped my chin and looked me in the eye. "Do I need to get your lipstick and let all these people know who you belong to? Or do I need to keep proving to you that you're not a burden?"

I broke his gaze and looked at Kat.

"I'm not him," Shane murmured gently. "I'm not going to use you for some twisted game like he did. I'm not going to hide you away. I'm not going to run."

His touch leeched the tension from my shoulders. Ignoring the second ring of the doorbell, I rested against his chest. "I think I have commitment issues."

He smirked. "You and me, Mama. More issues than a magazine."

Shane scooped Kat up again and stood behind me as I answered the door.

Julie and Olivia Childers were spitting images of each

other. Olivia, at fourteen, still held on to some of her childish features that had an eerie resemblance to Kat's.

"Hi, Miss Beth," Olivia said nervously as she gripped a small gift bag. Our interactions leading up to this had been brief, sticking to curt text messages to find a time for her to come over.

I lifted my chin and gave her a polite smile. "Hi, Olivia." I nodded toward her mom. "Julie."

Mrs. Childers was distracted. She looked back at her vehicle at the boy in the passenger's seat.

Josh Childers, my former student and Bradley's oldest, sat stoically in the front.

Julie turned back to me. "I'm sorry. He was on the fence about coming, and decided to join us at the last minute, then decided he wanted to wait in the car instead."

"That's alright. I understand it's a weird situation, to say the least." I raised my hand and gave Josh an acknowledging wave before stepping aside so the ladies could come in.

Shane's posture was defensive. One hand cradled Kat's body. The other cradled the back of her head. Olivia's eyes went wide when she spotted the baby in his arms.

I didn't know if she was more enamored with Kat or Shane, and I honestly couldn't blame her either way.

"Ma'am," Shane said, tipping his chin toward Julie.

She pursed her lips and smiled politely.

"This is my..." I looked at Shane, wondering how I should introduce him. Boyfriend was accurate, but it just didn't sound right. "This is my partner."

The tiniest of smiles flickered at the corner of Julie's mouth. "I see you've upgraded."

Did she just make a joke about... A quiet snort slipped out of me. "Yes. Quite a lot."

Shane handed Kat over and I positioned her in my arms so that the Childers women could see her face. "And this is my daughter."

Olivia gasped. "She's beautiful."

Julie's face softened, but it flickered with discomfort. "What's her name?"

"Katherine. Kat for short."

Olivia beamed. "Hi, Kat." She looked up at me, "Does she have a middle name?"

I chewed on my lip. That was something I had kept quite private, but if Shane needed to know where I stood with him, it was a surefire way to tell him that I was all-in, even if I was scared.

I nodded. "Katherine Shane Hale."

27

SHANE

It was definitely the hearing damage.

That had to be it.

One too many close-range blasts that made the ringing in my ear intensify the moment Beth said the baby's full name.

Katherine Shane Hale.

I was too stunned to speak.

I wasn't sure why I hadn't asked about Kat's middle name before, but it had never been important to me. She was Beth's, so she was mine. The details were inconsequential to me in the grand scheme of things.

Beth had settled on the couch with Kat. Olivia Childers sat beside her, and I watched like a hawk as Beth carefully placed the baby in Olivia's arms. Olivia gave Beth a small gift bag with some clothes and a stuffed animal.

"Oh wow," Olivia said, beaming from ear-to-ear. "She's so small. I always wanted a sister, but I just have Josh and Luke."

Julie was sitting ramrod straight in the arm chair. This had to be one of the most uncomfortable days of her life, but part of me was impressed that she was here at all.

I half-expected her to drop Olivia at the door and wait outside like her oldest son was doing. Not that I blamed him.

Beth wasn't a bad person, but all of them—Beth included—were put in a bad situation by one narcissist's selfish, egocentric choices.

Julie Childers and Beth shared a few similar features. Blonde hair, though Julie's was mostly gray now. Beth's eyes were green, but Julie's were hazel with green flecks. Their skin was a similar shade of ivory. Maybe it was why Olivia and Kat looked like more than half-sisters.

The door opened and I whipped around, ready to tackle whoever dared set foot in Beth's house.

But it was just Austin and Caroline.

"Hey," Beth said as she eased off the couch and gave Austin a quick hug. "This is my brother, Austin, and his fiancé, Caroline."

Caroline waved. "Hi. It's nice to meet you both.

Austin said a polite hello and took up the space beside me, mimicking my posture by crossing his arms over his chest. Caroline joined the ladies on the couch.

"What are you doing here?" I said under my breath.

Austin didn't tear his gaze away from Beth. He kept his comment quiet, just between us. "The other day when we were on duty you told me the wife and the daughter were coming over. Figured a big-ass buffer would be a good idea. Just in case."

I nodded in gratitude.

The doorbell rang, but I didn't move. Beth and Kat were mine to protect. Austin relented and answered it. Two more bodies joined. Callum and Layla.

Callum was still in uniform, his hand resting comfortably on his service weapon. That definitely wasn't a coincidence.

Layla said a quick hello, then found a spot on the floor and struck up a conversation with Julie.

"Buffer, party of two," Callum said as he took the position on the opposite side of me. "Anything to report?"

"Negative," I said.

My attention never strayed from Beth. Her eyes cut back and forth, and her breathing picked up. She licked her lips; her body wound tight like a coil.

She was about to have a panic attack.

Beth sprang off the couch, muttering a quick, "Excuse me," before beelining through the kitchen and out to the back deck.

"Go," Austin said. "We've got eyes on Kat."

I was already catching up to her. The sliding door whipped back as Beth bolted outside. I caught it, closing it behind me. "You're doing great. You can breathe. I've got you."

Her hair hung on either side of her face like a curtain as she hunched over the railing and gasped. "I can't. I can't do this."

Standing behind her, I pushed the rest of her hair off the back of her neck and blew cool breaths on her skin.

"No one says you have to. Close your eyes and take your time."

The slide of the glass door caught my attention. I turned to tell whoever it was to get lost, but Julie Childers was already at the railing with Beth.

"This really sucks, doesn't it?" she said as she rested her elbows on the stained wood next to a flower box that was filled with the skeletons of a dead summer attempt at an herb garden.

Beth's laugh was carried on a heavy exhale. "You can say that again."

"I needed a little air too," Julie said before peering over at me. "I hope that's okay."

Beth stared at the ground. "Be my guest."

I kept one hand on Beth's back, gently rubbing up and down to keep her grounded while she caught her breath.

Tension hung heavy like humidity after a hurricane. Energy pulsed between the two women who should, by all counts, be enemies.

"I owe you an apology," Julie said after a long stretch of silence.

Beth shook her head, keeping her eyes trained on the ground. "You don't owe me anything."

"Maybe," Julie said. "But I'm sorry anyway. December... that wasn't my greatest moment. I can only imagine what it felt like for you."

Beth straightened and rested her hip on the railing, looking Julie in the eye. "It probably felt a lot like trying to tell your boss that you're pregnant with his baby and finding out he hid a wife and family from you."

Julie looked at her feet. "My world came crumbling down that day."

"Mine too." Beth didn't cower, and she didn't apologize.

The laugh Julie let slip was unexpected. "My therapist is going to have a field day when she finds out about the two of us out here like this."

Beth didn't latch onto the joke. Instead, she went for the kill. "Have you spoken to him recently?"

"My husb—Bradley?"

Beth nodded.

"No." Julie sighed. "Not since I kicked him out and had him served with divorce papers."

Beth glanced up at me like she was looking for reassurance that she was doing the right thing. I gave her a little squeeze.

"Then you should know that he violated the restraining order I have against him. He found Kat and me at the grocery store and then showed up here at the house, insisting on seeing her. He was arrested, but made bail. You might want to be cautious. I'd hate for him to take out that anger on you or your children."

Julie looked stunned, but quickly blinked away the surprise. "Um. Thank you… for letting me know. I'll have a chat with Olivia and the boys."

Leaves danced through the air as a light autumn breeze eased the strain between them.

Laugher carried from inside, and the three of us turned to see what was going on. Olivia was sandwiched on the couch between Callum and Austin. Kat was cradled in her arms.

Beth sank into me. I loved when she did that. It made me breathe a little easier when she clicked into place with me like a missing puzzle piece.

"Thank you for doing this for Olivia," Julie said. Before Beth could respond, she kept going. "I don't expect us to be friends, but I don't hate you anymore."

It was the first time I saw the exhaustion around her eyes. She was probably having her fair share of sleepless nights and worries of the unknown.

"I used to hate you," she said. "I blamed you for everything that Bradley did. I made up these stories in my head about you." She sighed. "But it changed when I made the decision to find a lawyer. I had to sort through Bradley's role in all of this and I realized that it wasn't just me who was his victim. You were too."

Beth didn't speak. She didn't move. Didn't breathe. Until finally, she extended her hand to shake Julie's. "Then here's to not being friends."

Julie shared a coy smile with Beth as they shook hands.

"Whenever you're drinking again, your first glass of wine is on me."

———

"So," Beth said as I eased on the brake to take one of the hairpin turns. "This is date number four?"

I chuckled and reached across the darkened cab for her hand. "What kind of a Creeker would I be if we didn't have at least one date where we go up to The Lookout?"

After making it through the most awkward afternoon of our collective lives, Beth and I decided that we'd celebrate surviving it with a date night.

"Really pulling out all the stops, aren't you?" she teased.

I kissed the back of her hand and peeked into the rearview mirror. "Only the best for my girls."

Kat was snoozing soundly in her car seat, lulled into relaxation by the gentle jostle of the truck.

The shoulder with the best view of the mountains was, thankfully, completely vacant. I pulled into the space beside the faded sign that read, "Scenic Overlook - Mile Marker 23 - Falls Creek, NC," and cut the engine.

We had picked up takeout from the Mule for dinner. The styrofoam boxes squeaked as Beth pulled them out of the to-go bag and separated our orders.

"Not gonna lie," she said as she popped her straw out of the paper wrapper. "This is the perfect night. A nice drive, windows down, and food. I'm easy like that."

But I wasn't in the mood for small talk. Not after the bombshell Beth dropped without so much as another word about it.

"I need to know something," I said as I stared out at the valley painted in brilliant oranges and yellows.

Beth stabbed her straw into her cup and took a sip. "Yeah? What's that?"

How was she so casual about this?

I scrubbed my palm over the stubble around my mouth. "Is her name really... Did you actually—"

Beth paused, raising an eyebrow as she opened her to-go box. "Did I actually name her Katherine Shane?" She separated the triangle halves of her turkey melt and sucked the melted butter dripping from the bread off her thumb. "Yes."

The world spun like a chopper in an autorotative descent. "How are you so casual about it?"

She smiled as she grabbed a sweet potato fry and popped it in her mouth. "Because it was never a question in my mind. You have always been a constant." Beth reached over and laid her hand on my thigh. "You showed up for me when I needed you most. You showed up for my baby when I couldn't. And you stayed for both of us." Adoration swam in her mossy eyes. "If she's even the smallest bit like you, she's going to do amazing things."

"You gave her my name," I said in complete disbelief.

Beth looked down at her food. "When she was born there may have been a part of me that still held out hope that I might get your last name someday. I wanted her to have your name, too. Even if it wasn't your last name." She swallowed. "I shut you out after I got pregnant. I didn't believe that someone would want a baby *and* me. And even if they said they did, words are easy. I fell for slick words once and I promised myself that I'd never do it again. But you didn't just tell me that you wanted Kat and me. You showed me, and you continue to show me every single day. I have commitment issues. I can't always promise that I'll be good at accepting your love, but I feel it. Not just in my head, I feel it in my bones."

Fuck it. I grabbed her dinner and mine and threw them onto the dashboard before hauling her into my lap. "Get your ass over here, Mama."

Warm thighs slid on either side of mine as she straddled my lap. I fisted the front of her sweater, yanking her against me as her mouth crashed on mine. I bit down on her pillowy lower lip, devouring her like she was forbidden fruit.

She was putty in my hands, pliable and willing.

"Are we really having car sex at The Lookout?" she whispered as she tore off my shirt in a hurry. "With my baby asleep in the backseat?"

I grinned and latched onto the side of her neck, leaving a rather prominent bite mark. "Why are you asking me? You're the one taking my clothes off."

"Yeah—well—you're taking too long to get me naked. One of us had to get things rolling."

I caught her wrists in mine and gave her gentle directions. "Lay down on the seat."

Beth was obedient. She slid off me, stretched across the bench seat, and kicked her shoes off.

For once, I was glad to have an old-as-dirt truck. She hooked her fingers in the waist of her leggings, but I caught her wrists.

Laughing, I said, "Slow down. We're not in a hurry."

"I am," she countered with that sharp tongue of hers.

I loved seeing her sass come back. I was worried I'd never get it after everything she had been through.

I grabbed her wrists and pinned them to the vinyl seat. "Mine." I leaned over and pecked her nose. "Don't touch."

Her nails dug into my hands. "Then hurry up."

I scolded her with a *tsk-tsk* as I peeled her leggings off. "I think you're forgetting who calls the shots here." I smirked. "I'd be very careful with what you wish for."

Beth grinned like a gorgeous lunatic. "Put up or shut up, Hutch."

I grabbed the inside of her thighs and parted them. "Open these up for me, Mama. I'd rather have you for dinner."

Beth squealed at the first swipe of my tongue through her sex.

"So fucking sweet," I growled before teasing her clit with the tip of my tongue. "On second thought, I've always been a believer in dessert first."

Headlights flashed through the windows, shadows dancing over our bodies.

"Get your shirt off," I said in a low rumble.

"There's a car coming!" she whispered.

"Then you better stay lying down." I pulled back and used my fingertip to trace the lines of her pussy. "So pretty. I like seeing you opened up for me. I like looking between us when I'm fucking you and seeing my cock stretch you wide." I looked up and caught a glimpse of her parted lips. I trailed my knuckle through her wetness. "Better get that shirt off or I'll hold you open like this all night and not let you come until the sun rises."

She arched her back, pushing her hips toward me. "Please."

"I told you what to do. Now do it."

She scrambled, abs straining as she ripped her shirt over her head and tossed it onto the floor.

I pinched her clit and rubbed it between my fingers. "You're still wearing a bra. Not very obedient, are you?"

The smile on her face gave away that she was loving this. "You said my shirt. If you want my bra off, you'll have to be more specific."

This fucking woman...

I grinned. "You mouthy little brat."

"You knew what you were getting into with me. Don't act surprised."

I softened, sliding my hand under the cup of her bra to caress her breast. "I'm not surprised, Dimples. Just grateful."

She contorted and unfastened the band of her bra and let it fall away. "Then show me how grateful you are."

I kissed her stomach. "Yes, ma'am."

Beth laid still for me, trusting me with all the parts of herself that she was still self-conscious about.

"Beautiful," I murmured against the marks just above her hips as I slid my fingers into her sex.

She whimpered, letting go of the control she held so dearly as she submitted to me. I thumbed her rosy nipples until they hardened into diamond-tipped points. Latent droplets of milk formed, and I licked them up.

She released a breath, and her strained muscles loosened. "Shane," she whispered as I crooked my fingers and steadily stroked the inside of her pussy, slowly dragging my fingertips over the roughness of her G-spot with each flex. Her toes curled. "Please."

"Atta girl," I said as I used one hand to pop the dashboard console and grab a condom. "Much more polite now, are we?" I unzipped my fly, pulled my rock-hard dick out, and tore into the packet with my teeth. Multitasking was a talent of mine. I kept her on edge, never changing the speed or pressure of my strokes as I rolled the condom on.

Her head lolled to the side, and I took a minute to admire the stunning body laid out for me to pleasure.

"Please fuck me."

I eased over her, suspending my body weight by bracing my hands on the dash and the seat. One foot was on the floorboard. The other knee was wedged into the crevice of the seat.

She was more than wet enough to take me without lube. I

nudged the head of my dick into her pussy and paused. "Do you want me to fuck you or make love to you?"

Beth looked up at me. Trust was suspended in her gaze like stars in the night sky. "With you it's always both."

Slowly, I slid into her and gave her a moment to adjust, waiting for her to breathe again. "There you go," I whispered, brushing her hair away from her ear. "How's that feel?"

She shifted her hips. "A little more."

I grabbed the back of her knee and pushed it up so I could slide in further. "Good girl. Talk to me and tell me what you need."

"Right there," she gasped. "Oh my god, yes. Right there."

Blood rushed straight to my cock, making it throb inside of her. "Your cunt is strangling me," I lightheartedly groused into her neck before tasting the salt on her skin.

"Please fuck me," she begged.

"We gotta go slow or someone'll see this truck rocking."

She smirked and thrust her hips up. "You might need to replace your shocks and get some bail money because I want it hard and fast."

"Fuck," I grunted as I braced myself, pulled out, and slammed inside of her. I nearly came on the spot.

Beth hissed, her fingers digging into my ass as she pushed me back.

"Too hard?"

She nodded, biting her lip.

"Tell me when you're ready again."

"Maybe I'm not quite ready for hard-and-fast," she admitted with bashful embarrassment.

I pushed in slower and rocked my hips, feeling every glorious inch of her. "Your mind is there. Your body will catch up soon enough."

The position was precarious, but I managed to reach between our bodies to massage her clit as I slowly fucked her.

I was enamored with every piece of her. The bounce of her breasts. Each slight gasp of excitement and exhale of pleasure. She was an intoxicating addiction that I'd never kick.

"Shane," she whimpered, holding on to me like a life preserver. "Don't stop. Just like that."

I snagged her nipple in my mouth and murmured around it. "Yes, ma'am."

Her lithe body went rigid, pulse racing as she chased her climax. Beth went silent.

"There you go, Mama. Come for me."

She doubled over, rocketing up and burying her forehead into my shoulder, breathing deeply before slowly lowering onto the bench seat.

Two more thrusts and I was done for. The residual tremors from her climax squeezed my own release from my body.

We lay chest-to-chest, catching our breath in the humid cab.

"Oh my god," Beth laughed as we separated and scrambled to get our clothes back on. "I haven't done that since I was a teenager."

I snickered as I tied off the condom and stashed it in an empty grocery bag. "I forgot how fucking hot it gets. I'm surprised the windows didn't steam up."

She grinned. "I'm surprised we didn't set the truck on fire."

I craned around and checked on Kat in the backseat. She was sleeping soundly in her car seat, completely unaware of what her mom and I had been up to.

"Come on," I said, grabbing our takeout and opening the door.

Beth and I climbed out of the truck, leaving the windows down so we could hear even the smallest peep Kat made.

We climbed into the bed of the truck, then up to the roof. Beth settled between my legs, reclining against my chest as we devoured our dinners.

"Can I ask you something?" Beth said as she popped a fry in her mouth and gazed at the galaxies above us.

"Of course."

"Have you ever been in love before?"

"You mean before this?"

She nodded.

"No."

"Me either," she said softly. "If I'm being honest, it makes me doubt if I know what love is."

"I've never felt it before and I think that's how I know this is it," I said as I set my food aside and wrapped my arms around her. "I've never loved or been loved by anyone the way that I am with you. So I'm gonna do everything I can to fight for us and keep this safe." I pressed my lips to her temple. "You with me?"

She smiled, closing her eyes. "I'm with you."

28

BETH

"I'll get it," I said, hopping down from Shane's kitchen counter when the doorbell rang.

Bacon sizzled in the skillet on the stove as Shane flipped each strip.

The first batch had burned to a crisp when Shane decided he was going to eat my pussy as an appetizer while he made breakfast. Every window was open and the ceiling fans were on high speed, but the smoky haze still lingered.

"You're not wearing pants," he called out.

"That'll teach whoever's interrupting us before nine AM to mind their own business."

Shane just shook his head, laughing as he turned back to the stovetop.

The doorbell rang again. I looked down at the dress shirt I had stolen from Shane's closet this morning. It was held together by a single button under my breasts. *At least I had underwear on.*

The person on the other side knocked impatiently, and I yanked the door open.

"It's about time. You ready to—"

Oh great. My brother looked up at the sky and swore. "Put some fucking clothes on before you answer the damn door."

I just grinned and propped myself up against the door frame. "Morning."

Austin scrubbed his hands down his face like he was trying to erase the sight from his memory. "I fucking hate this."

"Get used to it," I chirped as I turned, leaving the door open for him to enter if he so dared.

Shane looked over his shoulder as he placed strips of perfectly crispy bacon onto a paper towel-covered plate. "Hey, man."

"Don't 'hey man' me," Austin grumbled as he made a beeline for Kat as she lifted her little head like a champ. "My sister's in your fucking shirt."

I snorted as I took a seat at the table. "Your friend was in me last night."

Austin scooped up Kat and placed her on his chest. "Come on, squirt. Let's get you away from these heathens."

"Put the baby down," Shane ordered as he set a plate in front of me. "You want some food?"

Austin sat on the couch with Kat and directed a judgmental eye at Shane as he kissed up my neck. "Nah. I don't feel like throwing up this morning."

"Right," I said as I crunched on a piece of bacon. "You guys and your little workout crew."

"Gotta get ready for that fucking charity calendar," Shane said with a sigh.

Shane had nothing to worry about. He was all kinds of ripped.

The doorbell rang again, and I raised an eyebrow. "Seriously? Are you running some underground gym I don't know about?"

Callum let himself in.

Shit. I actually wasn't wearing pants.

I squeaked as I bolted out of the kitchen to throw on some clothes.

"Oh, so you put on pants for him," Austin called out.

I heard Callum snicker. "She torturing you?"

"It's the fucking worst."

Shane snuck into his bedroom as I was pawing around for some leggings, grabbed me by the waist, and pinned me to the wall. "Don't leave. We'll only be outside for an hour or so."

I kissed him, tasting maple syrup on his lips. "I wasn't planning on going anywhere."

"I like the indefinite nature of that."

"You built my daughter a nursery."

He shackled my jaw in his grip and tilted my head to the side, kissing the sensitive spot right behind my earlobe. "What do I have to build to get you to stay forever?"

"Y'all better not be hooking up in there," Austin shouted.

Shane and I shared hushed snickers.

"Go easy on him," Shane said. "He just stopped giving me the silent treatment."

"I will do no such thing." I pecked his lips. "Go invest some time in your bromance."

Shane chuckled and changed into a pair of gym shorts and a t-shirt that was more like a loose tank top after the sleeves and sides had been cut down to the bottom hem.

I studied the tattoos that wrapped around his shoulder. I tilted my head, studying them a little closer. Frog skeletons were worked into his sleeves. It was odd, to say the least.

"Speak up, Mama. You're thinking really loud over there."

I touched one of the skeleton tattoos. "What's this for?"

He peered over his shoulder. "The Bonefrog?"

"Yeah."

He sighed as he sat on the edge of the bed and laced up his sneakers. "The Bonefrog honors SEALs who died."

I smoothed my palm over his arm, realizing the weight and sheer number of his tattoos. "It's your team."

"It *was* my team."

The skeletons were connected with waves and clouds, a tapestry of his time as a special operator.

"Navy SEALs are called Frogmen. When you're just starting out in BUD/s, you're a tadpole and you work your way up."

I froze. "You call Kat your tadpole."

He cracked a smile. "Yeah. She's just starting out. And I'll protect her with my life."

I choked down the knot of gratitude and adoration that hung in my throat. "What about Cole?"

Shane reached backwards and lifted the back of his shirt. In a haze of black clouds, a shrewd bullfrog, not a skeleton, peered through. "He's still watching my six."

I had seen Shane naked or shirtless more times than I could count, but looking at his story painted on his skin, I saw him in a whole new light.

Down his spine was a shattered whiskey bottle, honoring his choice to save himself and turn his back on what hurt him.

To the right side of his spine, a tattoo of a kidney was inked into his skin. It was mirrored on the left side, but that was done in lighter ink—a ghost of the one he gave to save Caroline.

Geographic coordinates were drawn on his ribcage. The numbers fascinated me.

"What are these?" I asked as I trailed my finger down the stack of locations.

"The places where each of my brothers died."

"And this one?" The last set of coordinates had a line through it.

His eyes met mine. "That's my old house. The place where I was going to die, and I chose to live." He laced our fingers together. "Hardest choice I ever made. It was a fucking uphill climb, but I'm so damn glad you were waiting for me at the top."

I slid onto his lap and wrapped my arms around him. "Thank you for holding out for me."

We shared lazy kisses for a few minutes, simply enjoying the quiet together. When Shane finally went out to the yard to join the guys for a pre-photoshoot workout, I put Kat in an infant swing and got started on cleaning up from breakfast.

I cracked open the window over the sink to let the crisp morning air drift into the house. Callum's favorite four-letter words aimed at my brother blew in on the breeze.

"Ten!" someone shouted from down the street.

It was followed by a very decisive, "In what world was that a ten? Eight and a half."

Then, laughter.

What in the world?

I dried my hands on a dishcloth before poking my head out the door.

Across the street, lawn chairs were lined up in a row. A gaggle of old women, mostly from the Ladies Auxiliary, sat with small whiteboards with scores written on them.

And to the left of the row were Layla, Brandie Jean, and my future sister-in-law, Caroline.

"Beth!" Brandie Jean screeched, rocketing out of her hot pink lawn chair. "It's about time!"

I looked to the side of the yard where the men were doing squats. They weren't fazed at all by the silver-haired commotion.

I gave BJ a "one-minute" finger and went back in to grab Kat and my cup of coffee.

When I made it out to the judging line, someone had pulled out a soccer-mom camping chair and set it up between Caroline and Gran Fletcher. Someone else produced a throw pillow and shoved it behind my back. Gran Fletcher draped the bulk of the blanket she was working on over my lap and kept the row she was knitting in hers.

Liking the coziness and not caring much for the socialization, Kat curled up against my chest and closed her eyes.

"So," I said, peering down the line as I sipped my coffee. "What's going on here?"

"Just our Saturday morning entertainment," Estelle Gould said as she watched the boys do mountain climbers. She scribbled a perfect score on her whiteboard and held it up.

"Uh-huh." I raised an eyebrow at Caroline. "And why have you never told me about this little get-together?"

She giggled. "Because then you'd have to see me ogle your brother."

"The man has an ass like a pair of melons and thighs like logs," Gran Fletcher noted before lifting her chin and hollering, "Ten for the firefighter!"

Austin turned and winked at her.

I pretended to hurl. "I guess turnabout's fair play. I greeted him at the door this morning in Shane's shirt."

Layla cackled and took a swig from a thermos. "I bet he had an aneurysm."

"That's an understatement."

"How's that little nugget doing?" Gran Fletcher asked.

I looked down at Kat. "Okay, I guess." Frankly, after the day one inquisition of unsolicited and unhelpful advice, I was a little wary to volunteer any information to the old biddies.

That's when I noticed Brandie Jean shooting daggers out of her eyes at the back of the blue-haired heads.

"How is Shane with the baby?" Estelle asked as if she were a robot, regurgitating whatever Brandie Jean communicated telepathically.

Layla pursed her lips and hid a laugh behind her travel mug.

"He's great with her." I shifted Kat in my arm and attempted to drink my coffee without spilling it.

Brandie Jean's gaze turned to Martha Mable. Martha reached over Caroline. "Would you like me to hold her so you can finish your coffee? Lord knows you probably need the caffeine between those middle of the night feedings and—well—keeping up with that hunk." She gave Shane a ten on her whiteboard as soon as he finished his burpees and looked over.

I laughed. "Actually, that'd be really nice."

Caroline held my mug while I gently transferred Kat into Martha's arms.

Martha held her with the confidence of a veteran grandma. "She's a doll. Looks just like you, honey. Just precious."

"You're doing a good job," Gran chimed in. "Motherhood is hard."

"That's right," Estelle agreed. "It's two full-time jobs with the pay of a volunteer internship. If you need help, *you* just let us know what we can do to support you."

Brandie Jean sat back in her throne like a proud ruler, watching her subjects tout the party line.

I leaned over to Caroline and whispered, "Does Brandie Jean have mind control powers?"

Caroline tipped her head toward me. "I wouldn't put it past her. After that snowstorm that trapped Austin and me at the B&B, I think she controls the weather. Mind control is child's play compared to that."

When I caught BJ doing her telepathic glare at Brenda Bass, I had to speak up.

"Alright. Someone spill. What the hell is going on?"

BJ's face was neutral. Gran looked guilty. Estelle and Martha averted their gaze. Layla just sat back, ready to watch it all unfold.

"I mean, seriously? You all pile into my house the hour after I get home from the hospital and nitpick and contradict each other on every possible child-rearing choice, and now you're out here being considerate and reasonable?"

Estelle laid her hands in her lap. "We may have realized the error of our ways."

Brandie Jean raised an exacting eyebrow that had Estelle stammering.

"We were thinking of ourselves," she went on. "I think us older mamas like to relive the glory days and act like we did it all right. When really, if something went right, we were just lucky."

"I want to be a good mom so bad and you all made me feel like I was terrible at it," I clipped.

They hung their heads in shame.

"You're a good mom, Bethany Hale." Brandie Jean sat forward and crossed her legs one over the other. "You can want something with every fiber of your being and, at the same time, admit that it's hard and it sucks. Both things can be true."

My eyes welled up.

"We got carried away. I, for one, am really sorry," Estelle said.

The rest of the ladies nodded in agreement.

"It's easy to forget how hard it is. Decision-making is easy when it's not your decision to make." Gran Fletcher sighed as she set her knitting needles down and put her hand over mine. "At the end of the day, parenthood is like playing blackjack. You can have all the strategy and game play in your head, but there will always be a wild card in the mix. We were treating ourselves like the dealers rather than the players."

I raised an eyebrow. "Blink twice if BJ held a bedazzled gun to your head and made you memorize that line."

BJ giggled. "I'd never do that, you silly little pumpkin."

"Bullshit!" I laughed. "You have everyone out here thinking Gran Fletcher and Ms. Sepideh run the Ladies Auxiliary while you stand over to the side and work the concession stand at the events, but you run the whole damn thing!"

BJ shrugged, completely nonplussed. "Leaders lead from the trenches. Besides—they're like herding cats," she said, pointing at the row of grannies.

I took a fortifying gulp of coffee, draining the mug. "Start from the beginning. How the hell did this start?"

"Well," Brandie Jean began. "Let me tell you a tale. Once upon a time I was a social worker."

What?

She nodded, acknowledging my surprise. "The system burns out its workers. It's hard to keep being restrained by red tape and bad policies when the solution is easy if people just pitched in. I couldn't handle how ineffective the system made its caseworkers. I tried to change things, but changing things from that position was like trying to fill a dam with a water dropper. So I took some classes and became a home health aide." She giggled. "It was a little taboo at the time, but that's how I fell in love with my first husband. He hired me to help him around the house, and we ended up enjoying each other's company. I know everyone thinks I'm a gold digger, but they can say what they want. Love is love. I cared for him and he cared for me. When he passed, I was the sole beneficiary of his estate. His kids were all up in arms that I got everything, but he was in his right mind when he had his final wishes tended to by his lawyer. He never even spoke to me about it. But he explained it all in a letter that the lawyer handed me after his will was read."

Everyone was on pins and needles, and I wondered if the grannies had ever heard the lore of Brandie Jean Palmer before.

"For years, he had listened to me tell him about the people who fell through the cracks by a system made to fail them. Kids. Old folks. People on disability. People needing medical care they couldn't afford. Our homeless Creekers—" she eyed me "—our veterans."

I looked across the street at Shane. He and the guys had taken a break, and were sitting on the front porch and guzzling water bottles. Callum said something that made Shane laugh. His smile reached the corner of his eyes.

"He left me his fortune for the purpose of helping people who need it, however I see fit. I started trying to be Robin Hood. That's how Shane met me. I'd sneak around in dreadful gray clothes and jeans and take meals to people or make anonymous donations, but it was hard to do it all myself and keep it secret. On top of that, people don't like handouts. I was surprised at how many times I was told, 'no.' So, I regrouped and decided to put these troublemakers to good use. They needed something to do and I needed people to do my bidding."

Gran grinned. "It's easy for people to say no to BJ, but it's a hell of a lot harder for them to say no to a lonely little old lady."

And that's when I saw it. They weren't lonely at all. It was an act. Thanks to BJ, they had found a new purpose in life after their kids left the house or their spouses had passed.

"They raised enough money to cover the cost of Shane's and my medical bills from the transplant and enough for my mom to be able to stay home to care for me for a while after the surgery," Caroline said.

"We've di-ver-si-fied," Estelle said, enunciating every syllable. "Any need big or small. We keep an ear pointed at the rumor mill so we can get to planning as soon as possible."

"Gossip can be a good thing," Martha said as she rocked Kat.

I raised an eyebrow. "And the money hasn't run out?"

"Lotta us were born right after the Depression," Gran said. "We know how to stretch a dollar."

"And how to make a buck with a good fundraiser," Estelle chimed in. "Why do you think those boys are giving us prime entertainment? We're gonna sell enough calendars to harvest a forest."

"What are the proceeds going to? I asked. When I sat through the Ladies Auxiliary meeting that BJ demanded I attend, they had discussed the logistics of the shoot, but not the cause.

BJ shared nefarious grins with the ladies. "You wanna know?"

"Um? Yes?"

She sat back in her chair, "Then welcome to the Ladies Auxiliary."

29

SHANE

Silence hung in the cab of the ambulance.

It had been one of *those nights*. The tones never stopped dropping, and they were brutal.

The last one was a man—forty-two-year-old father of three—who was DOA from a self-inflicted gunshot wound.

Some first responders were calloused from those types of calls. They treated them as if they were any other scene.

Those never got easier for me. They only grew heavier and heavier, like concrete blocks tied to my ankles. I could swim with one or even two. But after a while, there was no fighting the pull from those interactions.

Missy stared out the window at the passing fields as we made our way back to the station after waiting for the coroner.

"You did good," I mustered, shifting my hand on the wheel to dodge a pothole.

Missy didn't say anything in response, and I was fine with that.

Everyone coped in their own ways. Returning from one of those calls was a sacred time.

To each their own.

Downtown Falls Creek was teeming and bright as Creekers sped off to work.

The firefighters had the engines pulled out of the bay as they went through the shift change gear checks and the new shift prepared to give the rigs a wash.

Austin was out front, getting ready to head home to sleep off his equally busy night. They had started the shift with back-to-back car crashes. They spent the rest of the night battling a residential fire that started from a bonfire that the family thought had died off, but flared up when the wind changed.

Missy and I went through the motions of shift change with the incoming crew. I gave her a fist bump and left her with the reminder to call me if she needed to talk.

"You heading home?" Austin asked as he sauntered into the bunk room and grabbed his station bag.

As much as I wanted to get home and crawl in bed beside Beth before she got up and going for the day, I knew myself. I knew what seeing that suicide victim would do to my brain, and I needed to get myself right before I saw her and Kat.

"I've got some errands to run," I lied.

"Oh yeah?" Austin zipped his bag and threw it over his shoulder. "What errands."

That fucker didn't believe me.

I couldn't blame him either.

"Come on," he said as he lumbered down the stairs. "Get in the truck."

———

"Are you taking me out in the woods to shoot me?" I asked from the passenger's seat of Austin's truck. "Because I don't own a gun anymore, so if you're planning to lie and say it was self-defense, you probably won't get away with it."

"I'm not going to shoot you," he said without peeling his eyes off the road. "Yet."

"You can kill me, but just know, Beth will probably kill you."

He chuckled. "That's true."

Austin pulled into the parking lot of the county community college and hopped out. Reluctantly, I followed.

"Walk it off," Austin said as he stuffed his hands in his pockets and headed for the paved walking trail that looped through a few miles of woods.

I almost caught up to him when—*pop!*

Everything went black.

"Hey—" Austin grabbed my arm and jerked me onto a bench. My ears were ringing and the fight or flight instinct pulsing through my veins was intense and unshakeable. "You're good, man. Breathe through it."

He sounded like he was shouting into a canyon.

Helpless. Hopeless. A million miles away.

"You're at the walking trail. It's you and me. You just got off work."

"Fuck," I muttered as the tunnel vision faded. I hunched forward and scrubbed my hands over my face. "What the fuck was that?"

"A car backfiring in the parking lot."

I hunched forward and took a deep breath, trying to shake it off.

"Take your time," Austin said.

I waited until a cluster of power walkers passed before I tried to get up. As soon as I was back on my feet, Austin started walking.

"Sorry about that. It hasn't happened in a while."

"How've you been sleeping?"

"Like I always sleep."

"So, you're on Kat's sleep schedule, then," he clipped.

I shrugged. "Makes it a little easier on Beth. I can help her out at night since I'm up anyway."

He just grunted.

We did the first mile in silence, letting the cool morning air clear the fog of the previous twenty-four hours. When we hit the bend in the loop that would take us back to the parking lot, Austin spoke up.

"Heard Fletcher's babysitting for y'all tonight."

I chuckled. "Yeah. Apparently, Layla called Beth and asked if she could borrow Kat. Sounds like she's got baby fever and she's trying to get Fletcher on board."

Austin grinned. "Yeah. Kat's got Caroline wrapped around her finger, too."

"She's a good kid."

"You sure you're ready for a two-for-one?"

I kicked a piece of gravel. "If you had asked me a few months ago, I probably would have said no."

"And now?"

I paused, waiting for a duo of college kids to pass. "Kat was mine the second she was born. A moment like that—it sticks with you. Walking out of the hospital to get the ambulance back in service after doing skin-to-skin with Kat in the nursery and leaving Beth in her hospital room—that's the hardest walk I've ever made." I cracked a smile. "And trust me. I've made some hard walks. This one evolution in BUD/s, one of the candidates pissed off a whole crew of higher-ups and they made us walk the beach from Coronado to the Mexico border carrying telephone poles."

Austin cracked a smile. "No shit?"

I laughed. "No shit. I swear to you—leaving Beth and Kat

was the hardest walk. Give me a telephone pole and make me walk in the sand. I'd rather do that every time."

Austin stared at the pavement under our feet. "So, this shit is real for you, huh?"

I rubbed the back of my neck. "I don't know what to tell you to make you believe that I love her, but I do. I love them both. I know I'm not perfect. I've still got a lot of work to do to stay clean. And she knows that. But I'm not going anywhere. You're just gonna have to deal with it."

We walked in silence back to the truck. I had said my piece, and he could take it or leave it.

"She's always needed me," Austin said out of nowhere as he fished his keys out of his pocket. "I know she's grown, but I guess some part of me thought she'd always need me.

I didn't say anything. Didn't even move. I just gave him space to say what was on his mind.

"But if she needs anyone now, she could've done worse than you."

I slapped him on the shoulder. "That was almost a compliment. But I'll take it."

He raised his hands in surrender. "Treat her right and make her stop answering the fucking door without pants on, and you have my blessing."

I laughed as I hopped in the truck. "I can only promise one of those things."

"Hey, handsome." Beth jumped, wrapping her arms around my neck and her legs around my waist.

I hadn't even closed the door behind me before I had Beth pinned against the wall of my living room with her mouth on mine. "There's my girl." I drank her in, tasting the coffee lingering on her lips.

When we pulled away for air, mischief danced in her eyes. "What are you up to?"

"Well," she said, dropping down to her feet. "I had a good day yesterday."

"Yeah?" I grabbed her hand and dragged her into my kitchen to see what was left in the coffee maker. "That's great, Dimples."

And on cue, those puckers in her cheeks popped out.

"Kat's finally falling into a routine, so it's a little easier to keep up with my course load so I don't get behind. I turned a bunch of stuff in yesterday and I cleaned my house. So this morning I broke in here and cleaned your house, then took some two-month pictures of Kat with your cat and sent them to my mom. She thought they were hilarious, by the way. And then Layla showed up early and stole my child, so we have the whole day together."

I picked up the empty coffee pot out of the maker and held it up. "How many cups of coffee have you had today?"

She pursed her lips and looked guilty. "A cup."

I leaned in, my mouth grazing her ear. "Just because you put a straw in it and drink it straight from the pot doesn't mean it's just one cup."

Beth's smile pressed against my cheek. "You asked for the quantity of the vessel. Not the volume."

"You're about to be asking for the quantity of times my hand is on your ass."

Beth smirked. "Promises, promises."

I lunged for her. "Come here, hot Mama."

Beth squealed, dodging out of reach. "No!"

I charged at her, sending her shrieking through the house. She plastered herself against the wall, chest heaving with excited breaths. As soon as I reached out, she darted under my arms and scurried back down the hall.

I spun on a dime, snagging her around the waist just before she got into the living room, and threw her ass-up over my shoulder.

Her laughter was uncontrollable.

I hauled her fine ass into the bathroom and promptly tossed her, fully clothed, into the shower.

"Shane!"

I cut the water on, making her screech as I stripped my shirt off. "I'm tired. I need a shower, and you have too much goddamn energy. So—" I stepped out of my pants and boxers, then pulled her soggy body out of the tub and made her stand "—I'm going to fuck that energy right out of you, and then we're gonna take a nap."

She plastered her hand to my chest. "Shower sex is a really terrible idea. Everyone knows that. You should definitely know that. How many calls have you responded to where people had dislocated shoulders or broken bones from trying to recreate carefully choreographed TV-show shower sex scenes?"

I laughed. "Quite a lot." I stepped under the spray and had her naked in the blink of an eye. "But I also haven't had breakfast, and you know what they say—" I dropped to my knees in front of her and threw one of her long legs over my shoulder "—most important meal of the day."

"Babe!" she squealed, and damn did I like hearing her call me that.

Her foot slid an inch, jolting her body toward me. I caught her ass cheeks, cradling soft skin as I lapped at her pussy like a fucking dog.

"Careful, Dimples," I warned as I circled her clit with my tongue. Her toes curled on the shower floor. Rivulets of water streamed down her stomach and into my mouth as I dug my fingers into her skin and sapped the mischievousness out of her.

"Shane," she whispered as she tangled her fingers in my hair.

I used my thumbs to spread her open and teased her entrance with my tongue.

"More. Please more," she begged in reverence.

"You'll get more on the bed." I bit her clit and made her scream. "Come for me first."

Beth was on her tiptoes, and I wasn't having that. I grabbed her ass and yanked her down onto my face like she was on a saddle. Her knees buckled, and she grappled at the slick shower wall for purchase.

"Ride my face."

"Shane, I—"

"Use those sexy hips, Mama." I ran my hands over her curves, staring up at perfection as I memorized the feel of her cunt over my mouth. "I can't stop watching you."

I smoothed my hands over her ass, sliding my fingers between her cheeks. She let out a little gasp and bucked her hips forward.

"That's my girl," I murmured. Hot water beat at my back. Frankly, if this was how I was starting my morning, I wouldn't be mad if I had to rinse off in ice water. "Give me some more."

Her hips rocked, grinding her pussy on my face. I had a morning shadow, and the rough texture made her gasp.

Water stung my eyes, but I wasn't looking away. She was captivating.

"God, that feels so good," she moaned, her body tensing as she started to crest the wave of an orgasm.

I pulled away and stood, my vision going starry as I pinned her against the shower wall and slammed my lips against hers.

"I was so close," she gasped, as I shoved my dick between her legs, grinding the base of my shaft against her clit.

Our naked bodies were plastered together, skin-to-skin. Connected. Not quite sure where she began and I ended.

I palmed her soft breasts and brought each one to my lips, kissing them. Marking them as mine until bright purple spots bloomed on her alabaster skin.

Mine.

"Make me come and I'll suck your cock," she said, her head knocking back when I sucked on her throat.

I chuckled and backed away, stepping under the spray. "This isn't a negotiation."

"Everything's a negotiation," she said with a sultry smile. "I just have to figure out what you want." She drew closer and walked two fingers up my chest. "I can be very persuasive."

I leaned in and pecked her lips as I soaped up. "And I have extremely strong willpower."

Her smile fell and a hint of bratty annoyance crossed her face.

Fuck—it was cute.

I grabbed her loofah, squirted on some of the fru-fru coconut scented body wash she had started leaving in my shower, and worked it into a lather.

Beth raised an eyebrow as I slowly backed her against the wall.

Her gasp echoed when I shackled her throat with my free hand and slowly started working the loofah over her breasts, taking my time teasing her nipples before I moved it between her legs.

"Shane," she whined, her body writhing as it got close to climax again.

I squeezed her throat. "Ask me nicely."

"You already got me close once!"

I squeezed a little harder. "That wasn't nice."

She gasped, and I let off the pressure. "Please make me come." Beth batted her lashes to give me the full effect.

I chuckled and let go of her throat. Her excitement was adorable, and so was that sarcasm.

"Try again without being a sassy ass." I slid my hand down her back, keeping the loofah between her legs while I teased her tight ring of muscle between her cheeks with my fingers, dipping inside ever so slightly.

She gasped. "Yes."

"Not so snarky now, are you?" I nipped at her bottom lip. "Ask me for what you want, and I'll give it to you."

She slumped forward, trusting me to catch her, and whispered, "Please make me come."

I dragged her into the spray of the shower, rinsing away the bubbles before cutting the water and hurrying out.

Beth argued when I scooped her up and carried her to the bed, but I wasn't having it. She was mine to have and to hold.

Exhaustion was creeping up on me. I laid us down on the bed, pulling her on top of me.

Droplets of water still clung to her like diamonds.

I grabbed a condom and rolled it on. "Ride me, beautiful." I reached up and pushed her hair over her shoulder. "Let me watch you this time."

Beth was magnificent. She threw her head back as she dropped down on my cock. The morning light made her look angelic.

I pressed my thumb to her clit, teasing it each time she took me inside of her. It didn't take long before she was trembling.

"Shane," she whispered as she tucked her head in the crook of my shoulder, grinding her cunt until it was leaking wetness. "Let me come."

I pressed my lips to her head as I gave her shallow thrusts. It was just enough to tip her over the edge.

Beth shattered on top of me, crumbling into pieces. She was detonated by ecstasy, riding each tide of pleasure.

"That's right, Mama." I tipped her chin up and kissed her. My dick was still inside of her as she settled on my chest and closed her eyes.

30

BETH

"We were supposed to go on a date," I snickered into Shane's chest.

He laughed, stretching out his sinuous arms and legs. The flex of each muscle and tendon was riveting.

His comforter was dumped off the foot of the bed after round three of sex, leaving him with a crisp white sheet draped between his legs. Half of it covered my ass and not much more.

Shane slid his hand into my hair, and stole my breath with a slow, bed-incinerating kiss.

Little whimpers and moans floated between us as I arched into him—wanting, *needing* more.

Hands wandered over warm skin. We learned each other like explorers crafting a map of new terrain.

"To be fair, I had really good plans for us today." He smoothed his hand up and down the back of my thigh, drawing it over his hip. "And then I came home to you in my kitchen and all those plans went out the window."

I combed my fingers through his mess of midnight hair, bumping my nose against his. "You were doing so well, too. You came in strong with those first four dates. I was almost ready to agree to date you."

"Smartass," he teased with a grin as he flipped us, pinning me to the mattress. "I don't want to be presumptuous, but considering I have you in my bed, you stole the spare key to my house, and I've told you I love you, I think that means we're an item. Arguably, it's been a long time since I've done the relationship thing, but I think I remember it going something like this."

I gasped when he started teasing my clit again. "I can't go again," I mewled. "I'm already sore. You put me through one hell of a workout."

Shane cupped my sex, holding tightly between my legs. "Tell me you're mine."

I smiled against his lips. "Yours."

"That's what I want to hear, Dr. Hale."

I opened my mouth to argue with him, even though I secretly *loved* when he called me that, but Shane cut me off.

"Save it," he murmured as he draped the sheet over our bodies and pulled me chest-to-chest with him. "I'm gonna be in the crowd when you graduate as Dr. Hale. You'll get your degree with *your* name on it. Because that honor is yours and yours alone. But mark my words, pretty girl. The next fucking day I'm gonna marry you and change your name."

That presumptuous, wonderful, audacious man... "That's quite the plan."

"None of this is chance, Mama." He kissed me again. "I wanted you from the day I met you. I may have played the long game, but I was ready to do whatever it took to make you mine."

I closed my eyes and soaked in his strength. "I love you."

He pressed a kiss to my forehead. "I love you too."

"What time are Cal and Layla bringing my baby girl back?" he asked as he kissed up my neck. "I miss her."

And I was melting all over again.

"Actually, I'm meeting them over at my house."

"Are we sleeping over there tonight?"

Shane and I had fallen into somewhat of a routine. On nights that he worked, I stayed at my house. On nights he was off, Kat and I stayed at his. If Kat was having a bad night or there were things I needed to get done, he'd crash at my place.

Slowly but surely our bathroom sinks had been cross-contaminated with extra toothbrushes that never seemed to migrate back to their original homes.

"If you want to."

He pressed a kiss into my hair. "I never want to rest my head without yours on my chest."

"As much as I would love to pull a sexcapade all-nighter, I should probably put some clothes on and head to the house."

"Fine." He pecked my lips. "But I will get you naked again tonight."

I laughed as I peeled myself away from him and started pawing through the dresser for the spare outfit I kept here just in case. "You're insatiable."

He came up behind me, hands groping me in an instant. "Yes, I am."

"Shane!" I squealed. "I have to get dressed."

He reached into the drawer for a t-shirt. "Fine. I'll keep my hands to myself, even though I don't want to."

I rolled my eyes on the outside, but inside, I was giddy and squealing. "I love you, you know." I tipped my head backward onto his chest. "Thank you."

He craned his neck and kissed my forehead. "For what?"

"Just ... being there for me."

Shane chuckled as he pulled his shirt over his head. "I'm always here if you need a shoulder to put your pretty thighs on."

"Shane!"

We made a hurried attempt at getting back to my place, and ended up pulling into the parking space at the same time as Callum and Layla.

I reached for my purse, but Shane didn't move.

"Did you give them a key?"

Car doors slammed as Callum and Layla got out of the car. Both of them stared at the house.

Shane's spine stiffened, and I saw what he was looking at.

My front door was wide open, and the fall wreath my mom had made for me was askew.

"Shane—"

A haze fell over his face as he got out without another word.

"Y'all ain't been over here?" Callum asked, keeping his eyes on the house and his hands on the gear-packed belt on his hips. He was getting ready to go in for a night shift.

"No, we were at my place."

"No one else has a key?" Layla asked, standing guard by the back door of the sedan that separated us from Kat's car seat.

"Austin does," I said, easing out. "But he was going with Caroline to a doctor's appointment today."

Callum shared a look with Shane. He spoke into his radio, reporting a possible burglary in progress.

"Do you carry?" he asked Shane.

"Not anymore."

Callum popped the dashboard console and retrieved a

handgun, handing it over to Shane. "Now you do. I'm not technically on duty. That's my personal firearm."

My heart was pounding in my ears. Layla must've seen the panic on my face. She pulled me over to stand with her as Shane released the magazine, checked the number of bullets that were available, clicked it back in place, then pulled the slide back and chambered a round.

The ease with which he handled the gun was almost intimidating. His stance was confident and practiced.

It had been years since he was in the military. But, from what I knew about his time as a sniper, he could probably outshoot the entire Falls Creek police force, blindfolded with one hand tied behind his back.

"It's probably empty," Layla said as the boys disappeared inside. "You know Callum. He's never not a cop, and Shane's protective of you."

"What if it's not nothing, though," I whispered.

Doors opened and shut as they went room to room, clearing the house.

"Kat didn't nap for me, but she wasn't fussy," Layla said. "She's such a cutie."

I couldn't peel my eyes from the house. What if a robber came running out or something?

Everything was unnervingly quiet for a few minutes, then Shane appeared. The gun was tucked in the waistband of his jeans.

"What happened?" Layla asked.

Shane jogged down the steps. "Open the doorbell app on your phone. Start when you left the house this morning."

"Shane—"

Worry lingered in his eyes. "Just look through the app, Beth."

Beth.

Not Mama. Not Dimples. Just Beth.

With shaking hands, I pulled out my phone and looked through the footage. I watched myself leave and lock the door this morning.

A little while later, Stanley took Arthur on a walk.

Cars emptied out of the spaces as most of my neighbors went off to work.

As the timestamp approached midafternoon, a shadow appeared. Bradley's face was partially obscured, but I knew it was him.

He wedged a metal bar between the door and the frame, splintering the wood enough for the lock to pull away from the plate.

Shane swore as we watched the scene play through. Bradley disappeared into the house, then came out ten minutes later with two grocery bags and disappeared from the camera's view.

What the hell?

"I had the notifications silenced," I admitted.

"It's not your fault," Layla said, reassuring me. "It's a good thing you weren't home."

"Lay, can you wait out here with Kat for a minute?" Shane asked.

"Of course. You guys go do what you have to do."

Shane nodded and took my hand. "Cal needs you to look at a few things and then we're gonna pack up and go back home."

"But I need to—"

Shane spun on the sidewalk. "This is not a discussion, Beth. You're coming back to my house."

I reared back. "Excuse me?"

"You can be mad at me later. Let's go."

I ripped my arm away from him. "I don't think so. Now,

you can either talk to me like an equal or you can leave and I'll wait for the cops to show up."

He pinched the bridge of his nose and growled.

Growled. Like a wild animal.

"I don't know why you're being so difficult about this." He pointed at the busted lock. "Are you actually planning to sleep here tonight with your child?"

"No, but I'm sure as hell not sleeping with you if that's the tone you're taking with me."

"Don't mind me," Layla called out, her back turned to us. "Just pretend like I'm not here."

I cocked my hip and crossed my arms, hitting him with the raised maternal eyebrow.

Shane huffed and pressed his palms together. Just when I thought he was going to speak, he took a deep breath.

And then another.

And another.

"Bethany Hale. Light of my life and pain in my ass. Will you *please* come inside with me and take a look at the damage? I would feel better if you slept at my place until someone can handcuff your psycho baby daddy."

I held my thumb and index finger apart. "You were so close."

Something inside had set him off, and the version of Shane in front of me now was holding on by a thread.

I softened and laid my hand on his chest. His heartbeat was a drum roll. "Treat me like an equal. You did it while I was in labor. You did it when I was on the floor and couldn't bring myself to feed my baby. Just treat me like a partner who may have input into the situation. Don't run roughshod over me."

Shane tipped his chin in agreement and took my hand, leading me inside.

"Try not to touch anything," Callum said. "I've got a unit

coming over to take pictures, document, and fingerprint everything."

"What did you want me to see?"

Shane pressed his hand to my lower back. "The nursery."

I followed Shane and Callum into Kat's room and clapped my hands over my mouth.

Everything had been ransacked. The drawers of neatly folded onesies had been tossed. Diapers were strewn about. A bottle of baby power lay in a cloud on the carpet. The closet doors were open, and the storage bins were open and tossed.

Shane wrapped his arm around me.

"What else?" I whispered.

He steered me out of the nursery and down the hall to my room.

It wasn't tossed the way the nursery was. Instead, it was a single drawer at the top of my dresser that was open.

My underwear drawer.

"What a creep," I whispered. I felt violated, but more than that, Kat's space had been violated.

I tried my best to remember everything that I kept in Kat's room, but I wasn't much help to the detective who came in with a laundry list of questions. So many of my baby things were split between my house and Shane's. On top of that, I could never remember what was clean and what was in the never-ending pile of laundry.

What would have happened if Kat and I had been home?

What would Bradley have done?

"I'm gonna get a few things to take back to your place," I said softly to Shane.

He nodded as he handed the gun back to Callum. "I'm gonna get Kat from Layla and put her in the car."

I caught his hand before he could slip out the door. "Thank you."

"For what, Mama?"

I paused, because I didn't really have an answer. I hoped that the gratitude could drown out the voices in my head telling me once again that I was insufficient. Unfit. Unworthy. Unprepared. "Just... For everything."

31

SHANE

"Winchester! Winchester!" Fear struck my core as I plastered my back against the shell of the helo that was still smoking from the crash landing. Bullets whizzed by, clipping the metal and ricocheting wide.

"How much left?" I shouted at Cole.

"Two rounds!" He had one hand on his gun, and the other gripping the collar of Anton Yassin.

Another explosion lit up the beach in a hellish orange.

The hostage whimpered, clinging to my leg in a crumpled heap. She was sick, injured, dehydrated, malnourished, and ten minutes from expiring.

I grabbed my last magazine and threw it to Cole, hoping the five rounds left in my gun would keep us alive long enough.

Long enough for what, I didn't know.

"Blue Team One, this is Command. What is your sitrep?" Our commander came across our comms in a burst of static.

Cole grabbed a grenade, pulled the pin, and pitched it at a surge of enemy combatants. The blast showered sand, dirt, and shrapnel like rain from Hades.

"Command, this is One," Cole shouted. "We need that QRF immediately!"

"Copy. QRF inbound. Two mikes."

"I don't know if we have two minutes of ammo left!" I shouted.

"Hundred and twenty seconds!" Cole shouted as he jammed the new magazine into his gun. "No wasted shots. Make 'em count." He fired off a few rounds, buying us moments, not minutes.

One hundred and twenty seconds.

I moved on muscle memory, counting each shot. We were pinned down, the two of us hunkered down by the skeleton of the helo with our HVTs. Dead bodies all around.

Blood pooled, staining the sand in a sick crimson tide.

Five rounds.

Pain slammed into my side, only to be dulled out by a rush of adrenaline.

"You good?" Cole hollered.

"Charlie Mike."

Cole turned. "You're hit!"

"I said I'm fucking good!" I shouted. It wasn't the first shot to hit me, it was just the first one he noticed. "Mind your fucking business!"

"Command! This is Blue Team actual. Two is hit. I repeat, two is hit! Where the fuck is my QRF?"

My head was starting to swim, but I managed to get two more shots off.

"Blue team, this is your captain speaking." The pilot of one of the F-18s came over our comms, chipper as ever. "My name is Casper and I'll be flying overhead shortly. For today's flight, I'm requesting that you mark your position with colored smoke so I can clear the way for the helo to come pick you boys up."

"Smoke out!" I shouted, ripping the tab and throwing it to the left of the downed helo. Cole did the same, then returned fire.

"Casper, this is Blue Team Two." I gritted out. *"Our position is marked with orange and blue smoke."*

"Orange and blue smoke confirmed. I see you Blue Team. Stand by. Bugs and I are coming in hot. Exfil helo on our tail."

The floor creaked, and I jolted upright, sweat coating the back of my neck. A shadow darted across the room, then disappeared.

I was hallucinating. Had to be.

I was sleep deprived. That's what I was imagining.

I hadn't gotten more than a half hour of sleep at a time since Beth's house had been ransacked. On top of that, I'd worked two shifts that had us criss-crossing the county more times than I could count.

Something dropped, echoing through the dark room like a gunshot. I hissed, still feeling the phantom pains ripping through me.

"Shane—"

I jumped, jolting the bed as I scrambled in the sheets.

Beth turned on the bedside lamp, bathing the bedroom in light as she crawled in beside me. "Baby, what's wrong?"

Shit.

I peeled back the covers, immediately shivering as my sweat-soaked body turned to ice.

Beth looked up as I got up and tugged on a pair of sweats.

She yawned. "Shane?"

"I'm fine. Just gonna get some water."

Beth caught my hand and I recoiled, ripping it from her grasp.

"Babe..." Hurt and offense were slashed across her face, but I couldn't face her right now. Not after she saw me like that.

I was supposed to be her strength. I was supposed to be the one she leaned on. I was supposed to be *her* rock.

What would she think if she saw me crumbling?

I braced against the dresser, taking breaths measured in counts of four before I spoke. "Get some sleep."

"I'm not tired," she sassed.

I scrubbed my hands down my face. "Beth, it's three in the morning."

Her response was to pat the spot I had just vacated.

"Beth—"

"Get your water," she said. "I'll stay up until you come back in."

Why wouldn't she leave this alone? At least I didn't wake up screaming. I didn't know if Beth would be able to see me the same way if she heard that.

"I can't sleep. I'll get Kat up for her next bottle, so you can get some shut-eye."

"I just fed her and put her down," Beth said.

Shit. There went my usual excuse.

"Shane?" Her tone softened. It was hesitant and pleading.

"What'cha need, Mama?"

Beth looked up through her lashes. "Will you hold me?" She was sitting cross-legged on top of the bed, her silk nightie shoved up her thighs, pooling around her hips.

She knew I couldn't say no to that.

I sighed, relenting. "Lay down."

Beth curled up with her head on the edge of her pillow and mine. I didn't take my sweatpants back off. As soon as she drifted off, I'd get up and go to the couch.

It was the kind of night where—if I had some nearby—I'd be finding peace at the bottom of a bottle.

I climbed in behind Beth, spooning her as I pulled her curled body into my chest.

Being still made my heart beat faster. I needed to pace.

Needed to move. If I was still, it felt like I was trapped. Wounded. Defeated.

Then Beth's ass wiggled against my dick.

I sighed and focused on the curve of her body in my arms.

"I needed this," she whispered.

I pressed a kiss to the back of her head. "Why's that?"

Beth was silent for a moment as she collected her thoughts. "Ever since ... Ever since he broke in... All those thoughts..."

"They're back?"

She nodded.

I pulled her closer. "I've got you."

"I know."

If I was going to be lying down, I might as well close my eyes. I shifted, getting comfortable on the pillow. "Have you thought anymore about going to talk to someone?"

"Someone like..."

"A therapist. A counselor. A psychiatrist. Something like that."

She was silent. After a long stretch, she whispered, "Who do you see?"

"A psychiatrist in Chapel Hill who specializes in PTSD. I take medication to manage it, so BJ helped me find someone who could prescribe it."

Beth rolled in my arms, burying her face in my chest. "It had gone away for a while. I was hoping that ... I don't know. I guess I was hoping that being with you distracted me enough to forget about it."

"That's not how it works, Mama." I pressed a kiss to the top of her head. "I'm not a Band-Aid."

I wished I was. I wanted to take away her pain. Her fears. I wanted to carry them for her. I didn't want to ease her burden. I wanted to take it away.

"You feel like it," she admitted. "I feel better when you hold me."

I nuzzled into her hair, focusing on the smell of coconut and flowers rather than the whirr of the ceiling fan.

"What's it like?" she asked.

"What's what like?"

"Therapy."

I thought about it for a moment. "I dunno. I guess it's nice to go somewhere and talk about yourself. I think we're taught to be selfless to a fault. It's healthy to be able to talk out your problems without someone thinking you're selfish or vain. It helps you make sense of the way your brain works and why it works the way it does. You're not sitting there and getting judged. It's more like working as a team to put the puzzle pieces together so you can figure out what's missing or what's in the wrong spot."

Her cheek was burrowed between my pecs. Her silken threads of gold hair tickled my skin. "It's scary to be a mom, because it's not just me. There's another factor in the equation," she said. "Every time I think I'm brave enough to make an appointment and talk about everything going on in my head, I get scared. What if they freak out and call CPS? What if Kat gets taken away from me because I tried to get help? I'm scared to get help, but I'm also scared about what might happen if I don't."

I understood that more than she knew.

"Your baby deserves the best version of you. But more than that, you deserve the best version of yourself."

"Was it scary to go for the first time?"

I chuckled softly. "It wasn't scary so much as infuriating. But I also had Brandie Jean dragging me into the office by my ear. I'll keep her away from you."

Beth nuzzled into me. "If it counts for anything, I'm glad you went. I'm glad you stuck around and waited for me."

"You were worth waiting for." I tipped her chin up and kissed her softly. "You both were."

Somehow, I managed to drift off to sleep and stayed that way until the sun rose.

Maybe it was Beth's warmth as she slept curled up in my arms. Maybe it was her gentle breaths grounding me. All I knew is that I slept for more consecutive hours than I had in years.

I crept out of the bedroom, leaving Beth to catch a little more sleep while I made coffee and fixed Kat's bottle.

After nearly two and a half months of helping Beth, I had my routine down to a science.

I carried my mug and Kat's bottle in the nursery for my favorite time of day. I loved the quiet mornings I got to spend with her when I didn't have to work.

"Hey, tadpole," I said in a hushed tone as I set everything on the little end table I had found at a thrift store and refinished for the nursery. "How'd you sleep, pretty girl?"

She blinked those emerald eyes at me and let out a babble of delight.

"Were you nice to your mom last night?" I asked as I scooped her up, letting her rest against my chest as I carried her to the changing table for a fresh diaper.

With the soiled one in the diaper pail, I settled in the rocking chair and kicked my feet up. Kat lounged in the crook of my arm and started chugging her bottle like she didn't have a care in the world.

She was alert this morning, eyes looking up at me with a distinct gleam. Tufts of blonde hair pointed every which way. My girl must've been sleeping well.

"You know, one of these days you're gonna have to start

adding a little more to our conversations," I said as I looked down at her. "I've been carrying most of these talks. I know you're gonna have some good thoughts in your little head. I hope I'm around to hear them when you're bigger."

She just grunted as she suckled at the bottle.

Fuck. What if I wasn't here to see her grow up? What if I relapsed and fell back into darkness?

That's the thing about depression. No one talks about the fact that you're never cured. There are good days and bad days. And sometimes you hold on to the hope that, at the end of your life, the good outweighs the bad.

These last few months—I had been having a lot of good days.

That wasn't to say I didn't have bad days, but I knew that the good ones were more likely to happen now that I had someone to love. Maybe that was the key to it; finding a purpose that kept me going, even through the bad days.

All of the depression, the trauma, the survivor's guilt—I used to numb the pain with a bottle.

Now, I treated it with a different kind of bottle.

When Kat reduced her breakfast to droplets, I set her bottle aside and dabbed the milk dribbles dotting her lips with a burp rag.

"Good job, kiddo," I said as I gently lifted her and rested her upright against my shoulder. "Eating like a champ. You'll be rolling over in no time."

I fished my phone out of the pocket of my sweatpants and checked the app I had downloaded that detailed growth milestones.

A text that had come in while I was asleep caught my eye.

COLE

They want a headcount for the anniversary.
You in or out?

The "anniversary." It's what the families of my brothers called the date their loved ones died on a beach in Somalia. They always got together to share good memories and check in on each other. It was a nice thought, but I'd never been able to go.

Some wounds didn't need to be reopened.

SHANE

Working.

COLE

Figured. Same.

SHANE

Anything exciting?

COLE

Nah. I went up north and spent some time doing long-range targets. Got to break out the .300 Win Mag.

SHANE

You always were a half-decent shot.

COLE

Only second to you. I'm heading down your way. Keller's got me picking up some tech that he didn't want mailed. You got any half-decent joints to grab a bite in that cowtown?

SHANE

Might not be as fancy as your uptown ass, but it's a hell of a lot better than MREs.

> **COLE**
> Fair. Tonight I'm meeting up with some team guys in VA Beach, then I'm driving down to get the stuff from a Solomon Tech rep at a paramilitary training facility in Moyock. I'll be out of your way tomorrow night.

> **SHANE**
> Sounds good. I'll get off duty in the morning.

> **COLE**
> Work or not-your-baby-daddy duty?

> **SHANE**
> Work. And just for that, I hope that Mossad agent you work with kicks your ass in the sparring ring again.

And just for good measure, I took a picture of Kat up against my shoulder and sent it to him.

My alarm chimed, letting me know I needed to stop snuggling Kat, and get to work. Beth appeared in the doorway, wearing one of my t-shirts. There were red marks on her cheek from sleeping on a crease in the sheets. She yawned, stretching her arms out.

"Morning, sexy." Beth leaned on the doorframe and crossed her arms, smiling softly as she stared at Kat and me. "I'm not gonna lie. There's something irresistible about a tattooed man holding a baby."

I chuckled. "There's something irresistible about a MILF walking around in my t-shirt."

Beth bit her lip, pearl-white teeth sinking into the pout. "Pretty sure you've fucked me enough that I don't qualify as a mom you'd *like to* fuck anymore."

I stood, crossing the room with Kat still against my chest, and fisted the front of the t-shirt she was in. "I'll always want to fuck you, Mama."

I was expecting her to giggle or some shit. Maybe she'd be bashful and tell me I was lying. But instead, she blurted out, "Shane—"

Panic warred in her eyes.

Immediately I was on high alert. "What's the matter?"

"What if—" she paused, like she was worried about how I'd respond "—what if... I don't want more kids." Beth looked down at her feet. "What if I don't want to go through this again ... with anyone?"

"You mean, what if you don't want to have kids with me?"

Beth stared at the ground. "Yes. And it's not you—it's... It's just... I'm done. I don't want you to have these grand notions of more kids someday... And before you say I'll change my mind—"

"Thank you for telling me how you're feeling," I said, cutting her off. "But you don't have to worry about me."

"But what if you want—"

"A child?" I hooked a finger under Beth's chin and tipped it up until her eyes met mine. "As far as I'm concerned, I already have one. And she's enough for me. You're both enough."

32

BETH

"What a doll!" some little old lady cooed as she craned way too close to Kat's car seat for comfort.

Such was the case when grocery shopping with arguably the cutest baby ever born.

I gave Granny a polite smile and edged a little further down the deli aisle, hoping to shake her from my tail.

Kat's car seat took up almost the entirety of the grocery buggy, but it was worth it to not have to wake her to put her in the baby backpack. I only had a few things to pick up, and getting strapped into that thing was like getting into a straitjacket.

"They're so easy at that age. How old is she? A month?" the nosey woman asked, following me.

"Almost three months," I said with a thin smile. *Why did she think Kat was only a month old? Was she not growing fast enough? The new pediatrician was pleased with her growth. Kat wasn't quite up to where she should be, but the progress was steady and we were on the right track. Right?*

She reached into my cart, her hand going right for Kat's face. "What an angel—"

"Don't touch my baby," I clipped without a hint of the expected southern politeness.

She gasped. "Well, I was just—"

"Get. Your hand. Away. From. My. Baby," I said in the scary, punctuated tone that should have struck fear into the marrow of her bones.

I didn't care if I was making a damn scene.

Shoppers stopped in their tracks and stared.

I raised an eyebrow, daring her to test my goodwill one more time.

Why did strangers think that it was ever okay to touch a baby or a child just because they looked cute?

She huffed, grumbling about "this generation not knowing manners" and wobbled off to the cereal aisle.

From the lunch meat cooler, a mom with a double stroller and a baby on her back gave me a thumbs up.

I let out a breath and brushed my hair over my shoulder, feeling justified and pleased with myself.

Shane was meeting up with Cole for dinner tonight, and I was getting together with Layla, Caroline, and Brandie Jean for a quiet girls' night that would consist of final wedding details for Layla, and beginning wedding plans for Caroline.

I used to love hosting our girls' nights, but since Kat came into the world, my house was a constant wreck. Caroline was hosting all of us at her and Austin's place. She was adorably excited to have everyone over, and kept sending me a steady stream of texts asking if the food she was putting together was enough.

I grabbed a wheel of brie, snagged a jar of bacon jam, and beelined for the freezer section to grab a box of puff pastry. I'd throw it all together and bake it while Kat took her afternoon nap. I could manage one little charcuterie board and baked brie for four people. My phone buzzed, and I paused to read the message.

> **SHANE**
> I love you, Mama. Give my little tadpole a kiss for me if I don't get to see her before I meet up with Cole.

I couldn't help but smile. He was so good to me.

> **BETH**
> Were you able to sleep?

Shane and Austin had been on the same shift yesterday. Between a Ladies Auxiliary fundraiser that somehow involved ding-dong-ditching, a grease fire at The Copper Mule, and a gas leak near the elementary school, the boys were on their toes the entire twenty-four hours they were on duty. Shane was dragging by the time he made it home, and almost immediately crawled in bed.

> **SHANE**
> Took some melatonin. Out like a light.

> **BETH**
> What are you up to today?

> **SHANE**
> Austin's coming over to work out. Showering and meeting Cole at the Mule for dinner. You still going to Caroline's?

> **BETH**
> Yeah, I need to swing by my house and do a few things first. I'll see you tonight?

SHANE

Of course. My place? I want you to meet Cole.

Something inside of me glowed like a winter fire.

Shane wanted me to meet Cole. That meant more to me than he knew. In hindsight, it all made sense, but I was still a little jaded from Bradley keeping me at arm's length from his friends because I was his mistress.

BETH

I'd love to meet him. I won't be out with the girls too late.

SHANE

Don't rush. I can come pick up Kat after dinner if you want a little more time with them.

How had I gotten this lucky?

Kat blinked at me from the basket of the cart. I hunched over the handle and smiled at her. "How did we get such a good man?"

I steered the cart toward the front of the store, contemplating things like Father's Day and what Kat would call Shane when she started to form words.

"Well, there's the infamous Beth Hale," Patty the checkout lady said as she started scanning my random assortment of items.

I laughed as I looked in the diaper bag and fished out my wallet. "Why am I infamous?"

She craned over the credit card machine, eyes darting back and forth. "The whole store's talking about how you put that old bat in her place. Damn shame more mommas don't do that. I know I was scared as shit to stand up to those nosey, entitled grandmas when my youngins were babies."

I puffed out my chest just a little.

Patty scanned the last item and read out my total. While I swiped my card, she asked, "How's that sweet girl doing?"

"Better, I think," I said.

"Takes a while to get the hang of it." She nodded knowingly. "Focus on the days and the years take care of themselves."

I took my receipt, grabbed the three bags of cheese, fruit, and carbs, and tucked them in the basket beside Kat's car seat. "Thanks, Patty. See you next time."

The buggy bumped and bobbed over the asphalt parking lot. Kat gave me a gummy, wide-mouthed smile, thinking it was the coolest roller coaster ride ever.

My phone rang, and I grabbed it as I paused to wait for a minivan to back out of their space and drive off. "Hello?"

"Hey, sweetie. I hope I didn't wake you." My mom's voice was music to my ears.

"No, I just left the store, actually."

"How's Shane? Is he with you or is he working?"

My mom's love for Shane only increased after I told her that we were officially an item.

"Neither," I said as I spotted the back of my car and fished out my keys. "He's working out with your other child."

She sighed happily. "The five of you need to come visit. Austin's still got his house here in Beaufort. Find a weekend where he doesn't have renters and I'll make up the house for all of you. The four of you can have some fun during the off season and I'll snuggle my grandbaby."

There were days I missed living at the beach, but I had never loved my hometown the way Austin did. Falling in love with Caroline had made leaving Beaufort worth it for him.

Still, I couldn't wait to take Kat to the beach. I wanted to hear her giggle when her toes touched the water for the first time. I wanted to see her covered in sand like a sugar cookie. I wanted her to see the wild horses and experience the timeless magic of summer on the coast. Sun-kissed, salt-sprayed skin and wind-whipped hair.

I wanted Shane there. Beside me. With her. The three of us. I wanted to see Kat up on his shoulders. I wanted him whispering dirty things in my ear when Kat was distracted. I wanted to see him carrying her when she was too exhausted to stand after a day of playing on the beach.

I wanted it more than I had ever wanted anything.

I wanted forever with him.

"I'm hanging out with Caroline tonight. I'll have her talk to Austin and see if we can make it happen."

"And, you know, the holidays are coming up. Have you thought about Thanksgiving? I'd love to have everyone around the table. Does Shane have family he plans on visiting?"

I knew the CliffsNotes version of Shane's family history. His dad was never around and his mom struggled with drug addiction. She had suffered an overdose and died before he got out of the military.

"No, they're not in the picture," I said, keeping my voice as neutral as possible while I unlocked my car and popped the trunk. It wasn't my place to divulge those details.

"That's fine," she chirped. "He's my kid now too."

I tugged the cart a little closer as a car pulled up, waiting for a space to open up across from me. I trapped my phone between my ear and shoulder as I grabbed the bags and dropped them in the trunk.

"Shit—" the jar of bacon jam spilled from the bag and rolled across the trunk. I craned over the lip and reached for it, finally snagging it between my fingers and tucking it back in the bag.

"You okay?" she asked.

"Yeah, I was just getting my groceries in the car." I slammed the trunk closed and turned. "What were you—"

Everything stopped.

I was paralyzed. Horror abraded my skin, making me feel electric.

"Beth?"

My mom's voice on the phone sounded like she was a thousand miles away, shouting through an echoing tunnel.

I couldn't speak. I couldn't form a single word.

The shopping cart was empty. Kat's car seat was gone.

The parking lot was empty. No one was walking around.

My back was only turned for a split second.

"She's gone," I croaked. The momentary paralysis washed away, and panic set in.

"What?" Her voice was urgent. "Honey, what happened?"

"Kat's gone," I blurted out. "She was in the shopping cart and now she's—"

I was going to be sick.

"Call 911," she said with authoritative reassurance. "I'll call Shane."

———

"Beth!" Shane shouted as he jumped out of his truck, the interior ding-ding-ding sounding from the keys still in the ignition.

Blue lights filled the grocery store parking lot like it was the Fourth of July. Rubberneckers and onlookers lined the sidewalk as cops from two departments took statements, reviewed security camera footage, and started combing the area for my baby.

Abducted.

The word kept ringing in my head.

My child had been abducted.

Shane collided with me, pulling me into his arms. I was stiff as a board.

I blamed the shock.

"What happened?" he asked, frantic and shaken.

"Beth," Callum said as he pushed through the crowd. He was on duty today and had been one of the first units from the police department to respond.

I was shaking in Shane's arms, assuming that anyone in uniform was coming to give me news that the worst had happened.

He turned a tablet to face Shane and me. A black-and-white clip from security camera footage was displayed. It showed a car pulling up behind me while I was loading in my groceries. The driver got out, grabbed the handle of Kat's car seat without a moment of hesitation, put her in the back of the vehicle without securing it into a base or buckling it in, and driving off. The clip angle changed to the entrance and exit of the lot. As soon as the car reached the road, the driver floored it.

"The AMBER alert has gone out. Every law enforcement agency in the state has the plate number and a description. We're going to find her."

"Beth!" Austin bolted through the melee with Caroline at his side. He and Shane had been together when my mom called them while I attempted to talk to the 911 dispatcher.

The parking lot was pure chaos as Creekers poured in, ready to be deployed for the search.

"Bradley took her," I whispered as I stared at the footage. It was him, without a doubt.

"That's what we believe," Callum said. "Do you have any idea where he might be headed?"

Shane's arms tightened around me.

I shook my head. "I don't know anything about him." It was a harsh realization.

"What about his wife and kids? Would he go to them?"

I shook my head. "Julie's divorcing him. She kicked him out."

Callum's eyebrows rose. "Do you have her phone number?"

I nodded.

"Can you call her? Or have Shane call her? Tell her what happened. She may know of a place that you don't."

That's what this came down to? Julie and I had established some kind of truce, but I hadn't spoken to her since she brought her daughter over to meet Kat. Maybe we didn't hate each other, but I had been a nonconsensual part of the downfall of her marriage and break-up of her family.

"I can call her," Shane said.

I shook my head. "I need to."

One of the detectives stepped in. "Does Mr. Childers have your current phone number?"

I nodded. "Yes, but I have his number blocked."

"Unblock it in case he calls you with a ransom demand. Keep the line open."

My hands shook as I swiped through my phone, and did what he said.

"Here," Shane said, handing me his phone. "Call Julie."

We traded, Shane taking mine to watch for an incoming call, and me taking his, dialing Julie Childers's number and praying she picked up.

"Hello?"

"Julie?"

"Speaking. Who is this?"

I swallowed. "Beth Hale. I'm calling from Shane's phone."

There was a long pause, and she didn't make a peep. "I wouldn't be calling if it wasn't an emergency."

"What's going on?"

There was no use in burying the lede. The clock was ticking. "Kat was abducted. Bradley took her. Have you been in contact with him?"

She gasped, then a thud. Static shuffles filled the line. "Oh my god," she whispered when she came back. "No—I... I haven't seen or heard from him. Are you okay?"

Tears rolled down my cheeks. "He took her," I whispered as fear strangled my last bastions of hope. "Please—if you know *anything*—"

"Let me talk to the kids," she said. "If they've heard anything, I'll let you know."

"Thank you." I crumbled as I hung up the phone.

Austin's arms were around me as I handed Shane his phone back. "We're gonna find her."

"It's all my fault," I cried. "I shouldn't have turned my back like that. I was trying to get the bags in but they spilled, and I was on the phone with Mom and I just turned my back for a second—"

"It's not your fault. We're going to get her back," Austin said firmly. "You gotta believe that, kid."

"He's right," Shane said as his thumbs flew over the screen of his phone, texting someone.

A souped-up SUV with blacked out windows came ripping through the lot. Shane lifted his hand.

I could barely see through my bleary, tear-filled vision.

A grizzly bear of a man jumped out of the driver's side and slammed the door.

"Crowder!" Shane bellowed, making me jump.

The grizzly bear jogged over, engulfing us in his shadow. He was built like Austin, a tank of a human. "Hutch."

"Beth, this is Cole Crowder," Shane said.

"Ma'am," Cole said, nodding to me. "Wish we were meeting under better circumstances."

I didn't have the capacity to so much as greet him, but he didn't seem bothered by my silence.

"Cole does private security and personal protection for a company called Keller & Associates. He works situations like this a lot."

"I'm here to help," he said. "Any leads?"

Shane shook his head. "Not much, but we have a description and a plate number. The AMBER alert's out. Wheels are on the road looking for the car."

My phone rang, cutting through the mayhem. Everything went dead silent.

The detective in charge hustled to me. "Is it him?"

I shook my head. "It could be, but it's not his number."

"Answer it," Cole barked, taking charge. "Everyone shut the fuck up." Softening his tone, he said, "Put it on speaker."

With a trembling hand, I swiped across the screen and pressed the speaker button. "Hello?"

There was a long pause. My heart thudded in my chest, waiting to hear the disgusting sound of Bradley's smooth-talking voice.

"Miss Hale?" It was a male, but it wasn't Bradley. The voice sounded somewhat familiar, though.

"Yes. Who's this?"

I was bracketed by Shane and Austin, both of them tightening their arms around me.

The parking lot was silent enough to hear a pin drop.

"Josh. Uh... Josh Childers."

I could have been knocked over by a feather. Josh was Bradley's oldest, my former student, and had been taking his dad's infidelity harder than any of the other Childers kids.

I didn't mean to be curt, but I didn't have the capacity for small talk at the moment.

"Okay."

"My mom told me what my dad did. I got your number from Olivia."

"Have you heard from him?" Threads of hope wove together, giving me the smallest bit of strength.

"Yeah. I, uh... I'm on fall break. I was supposed to leave this morning to go to the lake house with him, but he called me a few hours ago and told me not to go up there."

Everyone jumped at the news, then froze, not knowing what to do with it.

"The lake house?" I said, trying to put together if it was the same place Bradley had taken me on one of our clandestine weekends. "The one on Lake Gaston?"

Josh's pause was weighted. "Yes."

At the single syllable, everyone sprang into action.

33

SHANE

"The house is on Lake Gaston, but it's across the state line on the Virginia side," Callum reported back to the cluster of bodies still surrounding Beth's open trunk. "We're working on getting in touch with the department who has jurisdiction of that area, but it's remote. They probably have fewer resources than we do."

Cole flicked his eyes to me, and it was like we were back in the Teams, running ops around the globe.

"It's two and a half hours from here. He can't be there yet," Austin said.

An hour and a half had passed since Beth made the 911 call.

"We've got roadblocks set up on our side of the state, and the Virginia highway patrol is doing the same on their side."

"He's not going to be taking the main roads," Beth said in a rasp. "He knows the area. He drove me there once and took a scenic route."

Callum gave me a look and lowered his voice. "What if you had a helicopter?"

Cole raised an eyebrow. "It's outside of your jurisdiction, but it's not outside of mine."

"I'm not law enforcement," I reminded Callum.

"Get me a helo and a pilot," Cole said as he stepped aside to make a call. "I've got the rest. I don't travel without costumes and party favors."

"How much jail time am I going to get for this?" I asked Callum.

His response was a terse grimace as he held his phone to his ear. "The less I know about what you're about to do, the better."

Beth's fingers dug into my arm. "What are you doing?" she hissed.

"I'm getting my daughter back."

Cole pocketed his phone and turned to Beth. "Ms. Hale, I need you to pay attention. You're going to get a call from a woman named Isla Davenport. She works at K&A headquarters. We're gonna be skirting some serious red tape, so she needs some information from you to get paperwork in our system that brings you on as a client. She's going to send you a backdated contract. Sign it on your phone and send it to her as soon as possible." His attention turned to me. "Isla's forging your paperwork. If worst comes to worst, you're now a licensed executive protection agent protecting your client. Whatever happens, you'll have the legal protection of the firm. Welcome to Keller & Associates. You ready to tac up?"

Callum got off his phone and stepped into the cone of silence. "AirCare agreed to go out of service. Odin's got the bird fueled up."

Cole crossed his arms. "You trust him?"

"He flew Apaches in Afghanistan in '04."

"Good enough for me," he said as he jogged back to his SUV.

My adrenaline was already pumping.

"Shane—" Beth grabbed my arm, tears in her eyes. "Please don't leave me."

Cole was already back to his SUV.

I pulled her into my arms and kissed her hard and deep. I rested my forehead on hers, wiping away the tears on her cheeks. "I will bring her back to you. I swear."

"But—the helicopter."

I knew what she was worried about. Ceiling fans made me think of crashing on the beach under heavy fire. What demons would being back in a helicopter conjure?

"I've done it once," I said. "Back when Layla was hurt. Don't worry about me, Mama. I need you to be strong. Stay by the phone. Stay with Austin. Follow the detective's instructions. You trusted me with Kat when you couldn't be with her in the hospital. I need you to trust me now."

"I love you," she whimpered.

I kissed her again. "I love you more."

Austin took my place, pulling Beth into his arms. Caroline came up beside her and held her hand. He nodded toward me. "Go get your girl. Be safe."

Gravel spit from under the tires as Cole roared into the parking lot of the AirCare base. Layla and AB were waiting outside, helmets in hand.

"How'd Fletcher pull this off?" I hollered at Layla.

"AirCare is a private company," she said. "We do what we want."

"And our business manager isn't here today," AB chimed in.

Cole got out and opened the back hatch. A mobile armory

lay before us. We scrambled, donning body armor, loading weapons, and pocketing backup ammunition.

I grabbed a rifle and slung it across my chest.

"When was the last time you fired a round?" Cole asked as he did the same.

I grabbed a sidearm and secured it in a thigh strap. "Archangel."

"That's what I thought." He tossed me three extra mags and locked the SUV. "Don't miss."

Layla and AB walked us to the airstrip. The steady *whump-whump* of the rotors made my heart stop. The smell of fuel roused the demons inside.

Kat. My baby girl. This was for her.

"You good?" Layla asked as she handed over her flight helmet.

Cole took AB's. It sported a *Calvin & Hobbes* sticker on the back that read, *Three to go, one to say no*.

"Let's spin up."

"No in-flight beverage service today, boys," Odin said from the cockpit as he put the wireless comms system Cole gave him into his ear. He had emptied the helicopter bay of the gurney, but left the medical equipment. As much as I didn't want to think about the worst-case scenario, if it came to it, I was glad to have the on-board necessities to save someone.

But the thought of it being the baby... I was scared shitless. Pediatrics—especially babies—was a whole different ball game from adult patients.

"I hear you were Army," Cole said to Odin through the mic on his helmet.

"Just like the old days," Odin chuckled as we lifted off. "Always giving rides to the Navy."

"What's the game plan?" I asked. If I kept talking, it would hopefully drown out the sound of the helo. The mental replay of screams of anguish. The hopeless feeling of certain death.

Cole moved to sit beside me in the bay and held his phone between us. "Isla just sent the blueprints for the lake house. Something tells me he'll park his ass on the ground floor."

"You've worked a case like this before?"

He nodded. "Yes. And I don't plan on losing my winning streak. Childers is a civilian. He doesn't think like we do. Shit like this is a little planning and a lot of rash decisions. He's not looking for the high ground. He's looking for the fastest escape route if he finds out he's been made."

"Where's our infil?"

"There's a main road in and a back road out." He swiped across the screen to an aerial map. "We don't want him to run or get in a police chase. My guess is that the abduction was half planning and half luck. He was probably following your woman, saw an opportunity, and took the baby. He got lucky that she was already strapped in a car seat, but he probably doesn't have a base or know how to strap it in without one. If he flees with her unsecured in the vehicle, that's one of the worst-case scenarios."

I nodded in agreement. "Stealth is the operative word."

Cole went back to the blueprints. "Odin drops us here." He pointed to the west corner of the lake house that faced the woods. "The only window on this side is in a bathroom. He won't be holed up in there."

I followed his logic. "We split up and insert at each ground entrance. You take the garage and I'll take the main."

"Odin will go back up and provide overwatch in case he runs."

"Copy that," Odin agreed.

"We clear each room, front to back, bottom to top," I said.

Cole nodded. "A-firm. Odin—keep an eye out and holler if you see local cops rolling in."

"Copy that," he agreed.

"What are the chances I'm about to get arrested for trespassing and murder?"

"If we take out the target, you might have to testify in court, but Keller's lawyers will have you covered. I swear to you, you won't touch a pair of handcuffs. Focus on the op and leave the paperwork to my team. Isla's good. She'll have forged documents detailing your fake career with K&A before we ever get on the ground. She'll hack into the fire and rescue station's digital records and change them to be what we need for continuity's sake. What happens on this op stays with us. The story dies with us."

I nodded.

"Remember why we called the HVT-hostage rescue op 'Archangel'?"

I nodded again. "Saviors and judges."

"This doesn't end the way it did in Somalia. We're gonna get her back, and we're all going home."

It took just under forty minutes from the time we lifted off at the AirCare base until we were hovering over the Childers' lake house.

An old sedan was parked in the driveway, matching the description of the one from the grocery store security footage. As Odin began his sneaky descent, I snapped a photo of the vehicle and sent it to Callum, confirming Childers's presence.

The jolt of the helicopter nearing the ground made my head spin.

"Stay with me," Cole said. "If you're not good, I need you to sit this one out."

I shook off the haze and did an ammo check on my rifle, even though I knew damn well it was at capacity. "I'm good."

I adjusted the tension on the Velcro closure of the tactical gloves I borrowed from Cole's stash.

Cole grabbed a handheld thermal imaging device and studied the house as we got closer to the ground.

"Got any heat signatures?"

"Two. One large and one small."

Thank God.

First floor. Just like I guessed." He set down the scanner and double-checked the blueprints. "Looks like they're in the kitchen. If you're going in the front, you'll make first contact."

The struts hovered an inch of the ground. Without another word, I rolled the door back and jumped out, staying hunched over and close to the ground as Odin lifted off again, peeling toward the tree line to hide the sound of the rotors.

"Comms check," I said.

Cole gave me a thumbs up, and Odin confirmed he could hear us as we circled the house. He stopped at the garage door, checking the handle. Surprisingly, it was unlocked. He snuck in as I rounded to the front door.

Cole's voice crackled in my ear. "Two, do you have a visual?"

It had been a long ass time since I'd been called that. I was out of practice and crossing my fingers that muscle memory took over.

Door number one was taking Childers alive and finding Kat unharmed. Door number two was putting Childers down. Waiting for the Virginia authorities wasn't an option. We didn't have time, and if Bradley felt like he was being cornered, he might choose door number three.

"Negative. Front door glass is frosted." I crouched, edging low along the front windows. There was a crack in the blinds, most likely from Bradley peeking through to make sure he hadn't been followed.

If he was smart, he would have parked the car in the fucking garage. Either he was an idiot, or he wasn't planning on sticking around for long.

And I wasn't convinced he was an idiot.

My calves burned as I pushed up on my toes, the bushes rustled as I peered into the window. I saw through the open concept living room into the kitchen. Bradley paced behind the island. Kat was still strapped into her car seat, but it was positioned at the same height as his center mass. "One, I have a positive ID. Baby is in a car seat on the kitchen island. Target is behind her. Watch your fire. Prepare to breach on me."

"Copy."

I slunk back to the front door, visualizing the entrance in my mind's eye. One hard kick to the spot right next to the doorknob and I'd be inside.

Ideally, Cole would be on my six and we'd have other bodies at the alternate entrances, but this was a fluid situation.

"Confirm ready to breach," I said, watching Childers's shadow move inside.

"Ready."

I took one step back, giving myself as much room as possible on the front step. "Three, two, one—" I slammed the sole of my sneaker into the door. It let out a deep crack as Cole rushed in from the garage entrance.

Kat screamed at the sound as I breached the front door.

Bradley Childers whipped around, beady eyes locked on me. He didn't even see Cole.

I stared him down through the sights of the rifle.

"Ground, you have company. State PD by the looks of it," Odin said through the patchy connection.

"Show me your hands," I barked over Kat's cries.

Bradley didn't move. He simply stared at me, daring me to flinch.

But my finger was already on the trigger.

A slow, psychotic smile crossed his face. "You."

"Hands!" I ordered.

Cole moved on smooth feet, keeping the barrel of his gun trained on Childers as he circled to the left.

"Get your fucking hands on your head," he barked.

"Really?" Childers cackled. "You're going to break into my house and shoot an unarmed man for what? A kid that isn't yours?"

"That's exactly what I'll do if you move an inch toward her without your hands up."

"Fine," he said all too agreeably, holding his hands out to his sides. "I'll put my hands up."

"Slow," Cole bellowed.

Sirens grew closer.

Bradley raised his hands another inch. There was something wicked in his eyes. It was a soulless gaze; the look of a man who had nothing left to live for.

I used to wear that look.

Not anymore.

"You think you're some fucking angel," he spat. "You're not. There are no good men. Only winners and losers."

"You're right about one thing." My sights never wavered. "I'm no angel."

His eyes flicked down to the knife block.

I kept my trigger finger steady. "Today I'm the archangel—the just hand of God."

Bradley lunged forward, grabbing a large knife. The blade hissed as it was drawn from the knife block.

"Hands!" Cole shouted.

But he didn't aim the tip of the knife at himself. It was pointed at my baby girl.

"Knife!"

Two shots rang out from my gun before Cole could finish the word.

Blood sprayed against the stainless steel front of the refrigerator, and Bradley Childers fell to the ground.

"Manual sedation," Cole said as he stepped in, standing on the knife still in Childers's hand as he made sure he was dead and not just down. "Effective."

"Justified," I said, breathless, as I passed him my rifle and rushed to Kat.

The gunshot could have ruptured her eardrums, but she was alive.

The visual of Bradley Childers raising a knife to the child he had fathered would be forever burned in my mind.

I pulled her from the car seat straps and cradled her against my chest as uniformed bodies swarmed the house.

It was a whirlwind of activity as masses of officers and first responders filled the first floor of the lake house. Through the front window, I watched Odin land the helicopter on the lawn.

Cole gave me the "shut up and let me do the talking" look until he had his boss, Grant Keller, on speaker phone.

Officers watched us like hawks as the legitimacy and reciprocity of the Keller & Associates armed security licenses were verified, but no one dared take Kat from me.

It seemed like hours had passed until we were finally given permission to leave the premises.

Cole precariously held Kat like I had just handed him a live grenade while I stripped off the bulletproof vest I was in and climbed into the helo. We loaded up and lifted off, leaving the carnage of what could have been behind.

The change in pressure as we took off made Kat cry, but in all honesty, I had never heard a more beautiful sound.

The sound of living.

34

BETH

Tick. Tick. Tick.
Tick. Tick. Tick.
Tick. Tick. Tick.

The only sound in my brother's house was the rhythmic *tick-tick-tick* of the clock.

No one spoke.

Caroline and Austin bracketed me on the couch. Callum, in full uniform, sat in an armchair. Even Brandie Jean was unusually quiet as she stood by the couch, too antsy to sit.

All eyes were trained on my phone as it lay face-up on the coffee table.

I didn't know what call I was waiting for. It had been hours. *Hours* since my baby had been abducted.

Was I waiting for a ransom call?

Was I waiting for another officer to show up at the door and deliver the most unspeakable news?

Was I waiting for a call from Shane?

What if Shane was hurt too? Would I hear from Cole?

Before I left the grocery store parking lot, I sat in Austin's truck and spoke to Isla, the woman who Cole told me would call. She gathered the necessary information from me about the situation and rattled off what I needed to do next.

Wait in a safe, third-party location. Keep my phone on. Don't speak to anyone about the situation. Don't lose hope.

That was easier said than done.

A phone chimed, and we all jumped.

"Sorry," Austin said as he eased off the couch. "It's Mom. She's driving up." He answered the call and stepped into another room.

No one else moved.

"Do you want some water? Or some tea, maybe? I have coffee, too," Caroline offered.

I just shook my head. "No." My throat was sore and raspy.

I stared at my phone, praying for the screen to light up with a call.

Nothing.

A stack of novels sat beside it. The one on the top caught my eye. *The Nature of Hope* by Whitney West.

"It's my favorite one," Caroline said softly as she reached for the book. A blue tab matching the cover stuck out from one of the last pages. "I always read the end first. I like knowing that everything turns out okay."

I took it from her and opened it with trembling hands. My eyes fell to the last paragraph.

No matter how dark the night is, morning always comes. The valley can be as deep as it wants, but hope pays no mind. It anticipates the climb ahead, and holds fast to the knowledge that the view from the peak is like no other.

When everything else crumbles, hope stays.

Hope is a caterpillar, bravely entering its cocoon and trusting that tomorrow will be better. It comes vibrantly, like the wings of a butterfly, painting the bleak present with promises of beauty.

That's the nature of hope.

Tears fell from my eyes and splashed on the page, soaking into the cream colored paper.

The book fell to the floor as Caroline pulled me into a hug. "They're going to find her," she whispered. "Shane saved me. It's what he does."

Across the room, Callum pulled out his phone. A fleeting look of something akin to hope flashed across his face, but he didn't say a peep.

Time passed at a snail's pace, but everything moved in a blur of motion as I stared at my phone.

Austin sat back down. Caroline got up. Brandie Jean stepped out for air. Callum stood at the window.

It was a haze of wash, rinse, repeat.

Thirty more minutes passed.

I didn't have any tears left. My head was throbbing and my mouth was dry. Still, I didn't move.

The screen lit up, and everyone jumped.

I scrambled, bones aching as I snatched my phone from the coffee table and answered the video call from Shane.

"Hey, Mama." His face filled the screen, smiling.

My stomach lurched. "Shane—"

"I got someone here who misses you." He tilted his phone down, showing me Kat, crying in his arms.

"Oh my god," I whispered before sliding off the couch and onto my knees.

The entire room let out a collective breath.

I couldn't speak as everyone crowded around me to get a peek.

"We're about to load up and head to the hospital for her to get checked out," he said. "She doesn't look hurt, but I want to make sure. Meet me there?"

"Yes," I cried.

"I love you," he said. "I'll see you in a bit."

I barely returned his I love you before the call ended. Austin whisked me into his truck. Caroline piled into the back with me, holding my hand the entire way as Callum escorted us to the hospital, lights and sirens clearing the way.

The wait was excruciating. We got to the hospital in record time, not accounting for the fact that Shane and Cole were twice as far away.

I nervously checked and double-checked my diaper bag, just in case Kat needed anything before the staff could get to her.

Slowly but surely, the lobby filled with Creekers waiting for the boys to bring my daughter back.

Layla and AB, still in their flight suits, showed up to wait. The Ladies Auxiliary poured in, filling the rest of the chairs. Off-duty firefighters and EMTs waited in the corner. Missy hurried over and pulled me into a hug as soon as she made it through the sliding doors.

Julie Childers had texted me to see if there was any news and, surprisingly, offered to pick up a meal and bring it to the hospital while we waited for the helicopter to arrive.

The smell of the garlic bread and chicken she brought pricked at my appetite, but I was too anxious to eat.

A police officer I didn't recognize strolled in and looked around before announcing, "Mrs. Childers?"

Julie looked up from her seat beside me.

The man stood off to the side, waiting until she came to him. They exchanged a few quiet words, and Julie clasped her hand over her mouth.

Something drew me to her.

She had sent her kids to stay with their grandparents while the situation unfolded and was on her own.

"Is there someone I can call to come be with you?" the officer asked.

I looked at Julie. "What's going on?"

Her face was ghostly white. "He's..." She stammered incoherently. "He's dead."

"Oh my god," I whispered.

And then it dawned on me.

My daughter was alive because the father of her children was dead.

I hadn't just wrecked a home. I burned it to the ground.

"This is not your fault," Julie said with resolve as tears rolled down her cheeks. She was adamant, shaking her head as she said it over and over again. "This is not your fault."

We clung to each other in the middle of the hospital lobby; unlikely shoulders to lean on.

Grief and gratitude warred in tandem.

"I loved him," she cried, tears soaking into my shirt. "I gave him everything, and for what? For twenty-five years to be nothing to him?" She gasped. "Why wasn't I enough for him? Why weren't our kids enough for him? Why did he do this to us?"

"I'm so sorry," I said again. There was nothing else to say.

It was my fault.

Julie shook her head. "*Us*, honey." She stepped back and wiped her eyes. "He did this to us. All of us."

The pungently sweet stench of peach and cherry blossoms neared. Brandie Jean joined our little group and put her hand on Julie's shoulder. "I know you don't know me, but what do you need?"

The emergency department doors parted and a nurse stepped out. "Bethany Hale?"

My heart leaped.

"Go," Julie whispered.

I ran to the doors, leaving the nurse in the dust as I darted down the bright white hall. *Where were they?*

I looked left and right, frantic to find them.

"Over here, honey," the nurse said, catching up to me. She led me around the corner. "We've got your daughter in one of the rooms. Figured you'd like a little more privacy."

I couldn't even muster a 'thank you.' I broke down as soon as she opened the door.

Heavy arms caught me as I crumbled toward the floor.

Shane was sitting on the edge of the bed holding Kat against his chest. I realized it was Cole who had his arm around me, leading me to the bed when my feet failed me.

My vision flooded with tears. Kat's crying was the sweetest sound.

Shane's eyes met mine. They were tired and weathered. "Hey, Mama."

I didn't know what to do. Did I hold her? Did I hug Shane? What did I say to Cole?

Shane shifted, and went to transfer Kat to my arms.

"I shouldn't touch her," I blurted out, terrified that I'd hurt her.

"Beth—" his voice was firm "—she needs *you*. Hold her."

Tears stung my eyes. I was shaking. I had failed her. I was the reason for all of this.

All the hurt. All the pain. The brokenness.

My choices had led us here.

She was better off without me. Everyone was.

"Please don't make me hold her," I whispered, sobbing. "I can't."

Shane was stalwart. "You need to. I'm right here. She needs you most right now."

Slowly, he shifted his arms, sliding Kat into mine. She was bundled up in one of the hospital swaddles. I was too terrified to breathe.

Then I was in Shane's arms.

He held me as I held Kat. I pulled her against my chest, weeping as fear, adrenaline, blame, and self-loathing roared through me like a flash flood.

"Thank you," I said in a blubbering mess.

His grip on me tightened.

"I... I don't know what I would have done if you didn't love her the way you do. I don't know how I'll ever repay you."

He pressed his lips to my temple. "You pay me back every day by being here. By giving me a reason to be here."

Kat settled against me, finally exhausted.

"That's the first time she's stopped crying since we found her," he said. "She wouldn't stop crying for me. She needs you. Don't forget that."

We clung to each other until a pediatrician came down to assess Kat's condition. Only after reassuring me over and over again that she wouldn't be taken out of my sight did I hand her over to the doctor.

"You're doing great," Shane whispered as he stood behind me. "I need you to stay strong for her right now. She needs you present."

My mind went back to Julie. Everything she was feeling. Was she still here? Had she told her children yet? How did someone even break that kind of news?

Something brushed against the back of my jeans and I spotted the thick strap of the empty holster. "Are you wearing a thigh strap?"

"Yes."

I looked at the floor and turned away from the doctors and nurses, trusting that Shane wouldn't let Kat out of his sight. "I know he's dead," I said quietly. "Julie Childers came to wait with me. The police tracked her down and gave her the news."

He lifted an eyebrow. "She's here?"

I nodded. "I... I need to know." I tangled my fingers in his. "Did you pull the trigger?"

"Yes." There wasn't a split second of hesitation.

There was no pride in his answer, but there was also no remorse.

"Beth, there's nothing that I wouldn't do for you or *our* daughter. Nothing."

I wrapped my arms around him, retreating into my safe haven.

While a hearing test was done to assess any damage Kat may have suffered from the gunshots, I texted Julie and asked if she wanted to talk before she went to see her kids.

Solemnly, she joined Shane, Cole, and me in the room and listened as they detailed what happened.

My gut churned as I imagined Bradley raising a knife to my daughter.

They may have shared DNA, but she was never his.

She was simply a pawn. A chess piece. Something to move and claim to get what he wanted.

And what he wanted was revenge.

Cole showed us photos of documents found in the kitchen at the lake house. Bradley had been trying to establish paternity.

It explained the break-ins with nothing taken. I had been staying at Shane's, and my house was clean. He wouldn't have found anything with her DNA.

A blank birth certificate—ready to be filled out and already sporting authorization by the office of the secretary of state—was next to fake IDs, bank bags of cash, and a DNA test kit. The nail in the coffin was the letter addressed to me. The envelope had been licked, but never sealed.

He claimed I had stolen everything from him, so he was going to steal everything from me.

There was no real investigation to be had. The evidence was damning in itself.

They say the truth will set you free, but I'm not convinced of that.

Truth hurts. It finds us at our most vulnerable moments and gets to the core of who we are as human beings.

Monsters wake up, put on their suits, and pretend to be saviors every single day. But it can only last for so long.

The truth will come out. It cuts to the quick, severing the façade of what we present ourselves to be.

In the end, maybe the truth is what saves us.

It forces us to expose the worst parts of ourselves. The truth demands honesty to identify the wound and heal the hurt.

I looked from Cole to Shane to Julie, and then at my own reflection in the mirror above the sink.

The scarred leader.

The recovering addict.

The scorned wife.

And me. The mistress.

There was a difference in us and the man who had been willing to hurt everyone in his path to feed his narcissism.

Truth.

Admitting to ourselves what and who we were. And deciding to do better.

35

SHANE

"Thanks, Ms. Bea. We really appreciate it." I took the covered casserole dish from her and went to close the front door, but she stopped me with a slippered foot jutting into the crack.

"Is there anything else y'all need? Someone to clean? You three wanna come over and join my bridge club? You know, there's a group of us that meet at the park on Tuesdays and take walks together. That might be good."

I forced a polite smile, but shook my head. "I appreciate the offer, and I'll call you first if there's anything Beth needs."

There were a lot of little old ladies I was apparently calling first.

Bea Walker nodded and backed away. "I see she and that sweet baby are in good hands. I'll leave you be."

"Thank you," I said quietly, not wanting to disturb Beth. She had finally dozed off about ten minutes before Bea rang the doorbell.

"Y'all are in my prayers and on my to-do list."

I waved her off and shut the door with barely a click. I had no fucking clue where I was going to put this casserole. The fridge was packed, and we had resorted to filling Beth's fridge and freezer at the townhouse to store it all.

We were just three people and, truthfully, neither Beth nor I were eating much. Beth's mom had come to town for a few days and stayed with Austin and Caroline when she wasn't with us. She had left just this morning to head back to the coast to care for Beth's granddad.

I peered under the aluminum foil to see what Bea had brought. Peach cobbler. Maybe I could coax Beth into a few bites of it when she woke up.

I snuck down the hallway and stole a peek in our bedroom. Beth was curled up on the edge of the mattress with her hand on the bassinet. I didn't mind Kat sleeping in the same room as us. In all honesty, it made me feel better having her close.

My phone buzzed with a text from Cole, checking in to see how things were. He had gone back to Rhode Island and was leading a new protection detail assignment.

He and I had different vices. I used to drown myself in liquor to numb the pain, and he would distract himself with work.

It scared me how easily those skills came back to me—the training it took to take a life without hesitation or guilt.

Nearly a week had passed since the abduction, and my therapist had been on my ass every day to come in for a session, but I couldn't leave Beth. Not for a minute.

Leaving her to rescue Kat was harder than any operation I had executed during my time in the military.

But it was different doing it for love, not just for duty.

We hadn't left the house apart from a doctor's appointment for Kat and slipping over to Beth's townhouse for reinforcements.

I was ready to say, "Fuck it," and empty out the damn thing. She lived over here most of the time anyway.

"Shane," Beth said softly from the bed.

"I'm right here."

"Will you lay with me?"

Truthfully, I was feeling a little antsy. All the sitting around made me anxious and agitated. The quiet was too much. Every little sound was amplified.

We had kept the curtains closed for privacy, but the darkness was creeping in, and I was starting to climb the walls.

Without arguing or grunting in derisive agreement, I stripped off my shirt, kicked off my jeans, and crawled in behind her. It's what she needed.

"I thought you were asleep," I said.

Beth shook her head. "Every time I close my eyes I relive the moment I turned around and she was gone."

I wrapped my arms around her and pulled her into my chest. She never let go of the bassinet.

Pressing a kiss to the back of her head, I said, "We're gonna get through this."

"It doesn't feel like it."

"Focus right here," I said with a yawn as I found her hand, laced our fingers together, and pressed it against her heart. "Right here."

Her gaze softened and, slowly, her eyelids lowered. I stroked my thumb overtop of her hand until her breathing was steady and slow.

I lay behind her for an hour, listening to each gentle exhale. Feeling her sleeping in my arms calmed me. I shielded her from her demons, and she strengthened me to fight mine.

When Kat began to stir from her nap, I slid out from behind Beth and picked her up. I settled against the headboard with Kat against my chest. Her eyes were bright today—blissfully unaware of everything that had happened.

Beth jolted awake, gasping for breath as she looked frantically at the bassinet.

"Hey—" I grabbed Beth's hand and squeezed tight. "I've got her. She's right here. She's safe."

Beth sat halfway up, stunned and shaken. "I just—"

"It's okay," I said, brushing Beth's hair away from her face. "I get it."

I looked at the time. "I've gotta pack everything up and get over to the American Legion to meet the group. Will you come with me?"

Beth looked up. "I don't belong there."

She was wrong, she just didn't know it.

"Please come. You can hang out with us, or I can get you comfortable in one of the other rooms. It'll be quiet. There's snacks."

"I'm not hungry," she countered.

"Please," I begged softly. "I don't want to leave you. Please come with me. Kat will be safe. It's a small group. No one will bother you. I promise."

Reluctantly, Beth agreed. I played with Kat while she showered before loading us all in the truck for the drive. Beth kept an iron grip on my hand.

I didn't bother hitting up the grocery store for refreshments. The food from the meal train the Ladies Auxiliary had organized for us was going to be put to good use. Kelsea had volunteered to pick up to-go containers, and the group would be divvying out heaping portions to give out to those in need. We were going to do what Brandie Jean had been doing the night before Caroline's transplant when she caught me outside the liquor store.

"Did you sleep last night?" Beth asked when I opened her door and helped her out.

I laughed. "Surprisingly, yes."

"Why do you say it like that?" she asked as she unfastened Kat from her car seat and slid her into the wrap that kept her safely tucked against her chest.

I chuckled as I shut the door and locked it. "I haven't slept in years. I don't know..." I dropped the tailgate of my truck and pulled the first cooler of casserole dishes out. "It's like ... going after Kat... It hit a reset button or something."

Beth adjusted one of the sides of the sling, making sure that Kat was supported by the fabric bands. "I feel so guilty for putting you in that situation."

"Why?"

She held onto the truck like it was a life preserver. "You took a life. For me. For her. I... I don't know how to reckon with that."

I dropped the other two coolers on the ground and slammed the tailgate shut. "Come here, Mama."

Beth took a step back instead.

I wasn't retreating this time. "Look at me."

She didn't.

Her back hit the side of the truck, and she panicked. There was nowhere to escape. Gently, I slid my hands down her arms. "I'm okay."

It felt like the first time I had said it in years and it wasn't a lie.

I *was* okay.

"I don't say this lightly, but on the practical side of things, I have a record of confirmed kills, Beth. I don't talk about it. I don't brag about it. It's not a trophy to me. At a point in my life, it was my job. I was trained to do it and I was trained to cope with it. So, believe me when I tell you I'm okay."

She nodded solemnly.

"I will always struggle with alcohol addiction. I will always have moments where I wake up and I'm reminded of the tragedy of losing my team—my brothers. But going after my baby girl? That was atonement." I tucked a lock of hair behind her ear and cupped her cheek. "I've had more certain death moments in my life than I can count. Moments where I shouldn't have made it out, but I did. And I'm choosing to believe that it's because my duty wasn't fulfilled yet." I rested my forehead on hers. "And I'm choosing to believe that we're going to have a good life ahead of us. I'm choosing to believe that tomorrow will be better. So I'm going to lay down tonight with that hope, and sleep."

Tears rolled down her cheeks. She came to me then, resting on my chest. "I can't shake this," she said. "And I don't know why. You did everything. You saved her. All I did was sit on a couch and wait."

She was hurting, but I couldn't help but smile. "That's love, Beth." I tipped my head down and kissed her. "That's love."

"It doesn't feel like it."

"You feel this way because you love her." I smoothed my hand over Kat's head. "And you love me."

"Love hurts," she said, closing her eyes.

I brushed my thumbs beneath her eyes, wiping away the tears. "Yeah. It does. But love does so much more than that, too. Because eventually the hurt will fade. You'll heal from it. And you'll realize that love is the thing that kept you going all along."

We made our way inside and found the room already set up. Kelsea, Daniel, and Odin had beat me to putting up the tables and getting the supplies for food distribution out.

Odin put his arm around Beth and dropped a kiss on top

of her head like she was his daughter. "Good to see you, Hon. Glad you could join us."

A few more bodies filtered in, bringing supplies for the project. Beverly led a pack of women from the Ladies Auxiliary who had volunteered to help take the plates where they needed to go. To my surprise, Julie Childers was the last one in.

Beth was deep in conversation with Kelsea and Odin while they arranged the buffet of dishes.

Kelsea took charge and started barking orders, forming an assembly line to get takeout containers filled, labeled, and bagged with utensils, wet wipes, and condiment packets.

I stood in front of a tub of chicken and pastry and ladled out scoop after scoop. I passed each container down to Beth, who added a slice of cornbread before moving it down the line for veggies.

Kat was snug as a bug in the wrap Beth wore. Her little legs kicked out like a frog hopping as Beth rocked from side to side.

It was amazing to see how much she had grown in the handful of months she'd been earth side.

I could barely believe it sometimes.

There was a time I thought all I'd ever be to her was a memory, but that fear was gone. I had seen her nearly every day of her life, and I planned on being around for as many days as time saw fit.

"Let me get that dish out of the way and put a new one in," Julie Childers said as she reached between Beth and Kelsea and swapped an empty vat of green beans for a new Tupperware container of broccoli salad.

"Oh—" Beth looked stunned. "Um. Hi."

"Hey," she said softly before looking up at me. "Mr. Hutchins."

"Just Shane's fine," I said.

Beth's expression softened. "How are you?"

Julie looked at the empty bowl in her hands. "I'm present. And I suppose it's as good as I can expect for now."

Beth nodded in understanding. "How are your kids?"

She sighed. "It's a lot to work though. It's been quite a year. First your news. And then telling them I filed for divorce. And then Bradley's arrest. And then what he did to your daughter..." her grip tightened on the bowl. "I don't even know how I feel about everything. But I'm keeping the kids close."

"That's good." Beth forced a small smile. "I'm glad to see you with the Ladies Auxiliary."

Julie let out a wry laugh. "I keep telling Brandie Jean that I don't live in Falls Creek, but she just keeps ignoring me."

I chuckled. "Yeah. She does that."

"Ma'am, let me take that dish to the kitchen for you," Odin said to Julie.

She looked up at him with wide eyes. "What?"

"The bowl, hon."

Julie stammered for a moment, then handed it over. "Thank you."

"Not a problem, Ms. Childers," he said.

"Julie," she blurted out. "Just Julie. I have a complicated relationship with my last name at the moment."

Odin chuckled. "Understandable. If it'll make things easier on you, just call me Travis."

I could have been toppled over by a breath. "His real name is Travis?" I mouthed to Kelsea.

She shrugged and replied with a silent, "I dunno."

Beth elbowed me in the gut. "I actually need to change Kat." Her eyes flicked between Julie and *Travis*. "Mind taking over for me?"

Trav—Nah. I'd stick with his callsign. He'd always be Odin. The pilot with the dog named Loki.

Odin nearly pitched the bowl across the room and jumped in, taking over my spot while Julie took over Beth's.

"What kind of trouble are you making, Dimples?" I asked when I found Beth changing Kat's diaper in one of the back rooms.

She looked up. "What? I was just asking if they'd take my spot."

"Liar."

She smiled to herself. "Maybe I saw an introduction happening and decided to facilitate a little more face-to-face time."

I kissed the top of her head. "Why's that?"

She fasted the new diaper and shimmied Kat back into her clothes. "Because once upon a time, I thought I had hit rock bottom. That I was too complicated to be loved. That I was too much of a pain in the ass for someone to tolerate. And you loved me anyway." Tears filled her eyes. "You healed a heart that you didn't break."

I wrapped my arms around her. "To be clear, you're still a pain in the ass."

She laughed.

"But you're my pain in the ass."

36

BETH

The autumn leaves were golden as Shane and I walked hand-in-hand through the low brush. I was bundled up in a United States Navy sweatshirt I stole from him, leggings, and boots that kept my toes dry as faded grass turned to mud.

"So, this is it, huh?" I looked around at the gaggle of four-wheelers parked along the bank. "The actual Falls Creek?"

I could hear the trickle of creek water rushing in the distance. It was serene.

He stroked his thumb over the back of my hand. "You've never been down here before?"

I shook my head.

Shane grinned. "If I had known that, we would've been down here making out for our first date."

"If memory serves, we *did* kiss on our first date."

"After our first date," he clarified. "Because I'm a gentleman."

"Yeah," I snorted. "Because what you did to me this morning was gentlemanly."

He just grinned and licked his lips like he could still taste me there. "Better watch your mouth, Mama. Do you really want all these nice folks to know you like having your hair pulled while I take you from behind?"

"Shush!" I hissed as I gently clapped my hand over Kat's perfect little ears. She was a fleece onesie with little frog feet, and the cutest knitted frog hat that Estelle Gould had made for her. At almost three months, she lifted her head off my chest to look around, and then immediately flopped back down on my boobs.

What a life it must be to be carted around and waited on hand and foot. The wrap I had tied around me kept her snug and warm against my chest. There was a bite in the air that invigorated me.

I loved Octobers. I loved leaving behind the heat of the summer. Autumn was an exhale; letting go of sweltering weight and breathing in crisp revival.

It was photoshoot day for the Ladies Auxiliary first responder calendar. The boys had been sneaking in push-ups and squats every spare minute they could.

On more than one occasion, I caught Shane doing sit-ups on the living room floor, holding a giggling baby against his chest.

I had ovaries of steel, but there was only so much a woman could do to resist when a tattooed hunk of a man was smitten with a baby.

Thank God for birth control.

"You're late," Austin said as we neared the creek. Caroline was bundled up and seated in a camping chair, sipping from an insulated thermos.

Shane grinned from ear-to-ear. "Wanna know why I was late?"

I smirked and raised an eyebrow at my brother, daring him to push it.

Austin groaned. "You two motherfuckers gotta cut that shit out."

"You're right," Shane said, that devilish smile hiding under a day's worth of stubble. He raised his hands in surrender. "I am a motherfucker."

Austin looked right at the sky and swore so loudly that every silver-haired lady in the vicinity collectively shushed him.

I cackled as I took a seat in the empty chair beside Caroline. "How's it going?"

She dropped her tumbler into the mesh cup holder and reached out with mittened hands. "I need some niece snuggles."

I pushed down part of the wrap that kept Kat tethered against me and shimmied her out. She squirmed as I handed her to Caroline.

"Come to Auntie," she said in a ravenous tone. "You're so precious I just want to smash you to bits." Caroline looked up as she settled with Kat. "Is it weird that I want to destroy your daughter because of her cuteness? I just want to smush her because she's so adorable."

I laughed. "Then we're both weird. I threaten to gobble up her fingers and toes pretty much every day. She thinks it's hilarious. I think I might be nearing cannibalism."

"It's your fault for having such a cute baby."

"When you and Austin have kids, they'll be so cute, I'll want to destroy them too."

Caroline cradled Kat's chubby cheek in her hand, smiling down at her. "I don't know if we'll have kids the old-fashioned way."

"Why's that?"

"My health," she said. "It could be too much. We've talked about starting the process of getting approved for adoption once we get married. It can take a while, so we figured getting the ball rolling sooner rather than later would be smart."

I nudged her with my shoulder. "However it happens, whenever it happens—you'll be amazing parents."

"What about you and Shane? Is my sweet niece going to get a brother or sister?"

Kat grabbed a handful of Caroline's cream-colored curls and yanked.

Caroline hissed as I reached over and pried Kat's vise-grip fist open. For such a little thing, she was surprisingly strong.

"You know, I think Kat might be an only child," I said as I saved Caroline's curl from infant wrath.

"I can see that," she said as she entertained Kat with her mittens. "Shane's so good with her."

"Yeah." My gaze wandered to the creek's edge where a pop-up tent had been erected. A few representatives from each department made up the twelve men of the calendar shoot.

Shane and Tommy represented the EMS crew. Austin, Elijah, and Marcus were the designated firefighters. Callum, Wyatt, and Lucas were there for the police department. Someone from AirCare had volun-told Odin—*Travis*—that he would be participating. He leveled up the whole crew with the silver fox thing going for him. Two dispatchers and the town manager rounded out the group.

Shane's eyes found mine and crinkled at the corners as he smiled at me while he half-listened to the photographer's directions.

I was a lucky woman. Not many men would—not just voluntarily, but excitedly—become 'dad' to a baby that wasn't biologically his. But from my view on cloud nine, Kat was the light of his life.

Guilt stung at me from time to time when I thought about the fact that I didn't want to have more children.

Even if I wanted to go through pregnancy and parenthood for a second time, walking through mental hell with postpartum depression was a whole other ball game.

Sure, there was no guarantee that it would happen with another pregnancy, but what I knew was that I needed to be fully present for my daughter, and that meant knowing my limits.

But as I looked at the future with Shane and *our* daughter who held his name as her middle name, I didn't feel incomplete. Not in the slightest.

I felt blessed.

Brandie Jean flung mud from the tires of her hot pink golf cart. She hopped off the bench seat and grabbed a bedazzled bullhorn that had *DIRECTOR* emblazoned on the side.

"Here we go," I snickered to Caroline.

"Am I late?" Layla was out of breath as she jogged across the grass. She looked over at the tent of still-clothed men. "Oh, good. I was worried I had missed it."

"Nope—no one's stripped yet," Caroline sang with barely contained excitement.

"Hey," I teased. "You're marrying my brother. Don't forget that."

She giggled. "Doesn't mean I can't appreciate the fine men that serve this town."

"Cheers to that," Layla said as she grabbed a spare chair and pulled it over. She dropped down and reached for Kat. "Oooh! Let me see the baby. She's so cute I want to eat her up."

"Right?!" Caroline said as she carefully passed Kat to Layla. "What is it with baby cuteness and wanting to squeeze them for it?"

Layla pressed her cheek against Kat's and hummed happily. "I swear, this girl is going to be the death of me. I might actually be disappointed if Cal doesn't get me pregnant on our honeymoon."

"Alright, y'all!" Brandie Jean shouted through the bullhorn. Everyone jumped. "Mr. January. Front and center."

"Callum is January," Layla said with a grin as she sat up straight in anticipation.

"Why do you look so excited?" I asked. "Don't you see him shirtless all the time?"

Layla snorted. "Of course I do. But watching his cranky ass pose in front of a crowd of little old ladies? Priceless. I told him if he behaved himself and didn't complain that I'd reward him later."

"Why do I have a feeling you're not talking about taking him out for ice cream?" Caroline said.

Layla grinned. "Because you're not as innocent as you used to be. I'll lick that man like a damn popsicle."

I gasped and cautiously snatched Kat out of her arms. "Watch your innuendos in front of my baby."

Caroline laughed. "Like you haven't done worse."

I bounced Kat in my arms, watching her eyes light up as I cooed. When I looked up, Callum was shirtless.

"Well, hello, Officer," I mumbled to Caroline.

Dark tattoos wrapped around bulging muscles. He was in his uniform pants, and had his belt full of equipment resting extra low on his hips, but that was it. From those V-cuts up, it was all bare skin.

"Yeah," Layla smirked as she chewed on her fingernail, watching as he posed against a parked Falls Creek Police cruiser.

Callum had a pair of handcuffs dangling from the tip of two pointed fingers. His other hand rested suggestively on his belt.

Brandie Jean waved her arms and bolted out of the seat. "Hold up! Someone grab the oil!"

Callum looked terrified.

"I'll do it!" Mavis Taylor shouted from the on-hand crew of Ladies Auxiliary members.

"Nope!" Estelle Gould said, as she elbowed Mavis out of the way. "I'll oil him up!"

Maribel Gonzales, the eighty-something year old librarian, grabbed the back of Estelle's hair and yanked.

I shrieked in horror.

The beehive went flying.

Estelle gasped, palms grappling at her head.

Callum had almost snuck away from the cruiser when Brandie Jean caught him by the arm and dragged him back.

"You gonna save him?" I asked, looking over my shoulder at Layla.

"Hell no. I should have brought popcorn. This is his worst nightmare." She laughed. "Grannies gone wild."

Estelle, wigless but holding a bulk bottle of baby oil over her head like a trophy, broke free from the pack and marched toward Callum.

"Go easy, Stella," he said like he was trying to talk down a grizzly bear.

"Easy my wrinkly ass." She slapped a shiny palm to his chest and worked the oil between his nicely defined pecs.

More hands appeared, working over his arms and shoulders. Callum managed to wriggle one arm free to keep a sure hand on his gun. The other was protectively placed in front of his crotch.

He looked longingly at Layla and mouthed, "Save me."

She shook her head and snapped a picture on her phone.

"Alright!" Brandie Jean hollered, shooing the vultures away. "You've had your fun. Get your phones and take pictures like your grandkids taught you. I want a social media blast so powerful it'll scare the ink out of the printing presses."

"What are we 'sposa put the pictures on again?" Bea Walker called.

"My grandkids call it the 'Gram. It's short for 'instant graham.' Like a microwave s'more or something. Those whippersnappers are always taking pictures of their food to put on it," Estelle said.

"That's right!" Marilyn Dreese said. "'Cause you gotta do the hash browns on it."

"Hash*tags*," Brandie Jean corrected.

"Like 'hashtag food porn'! For the graham cracker app!" Ms. Tinsley said with excitement. "That one's real popular!"

"Not hashtag food porn, and it's Instagram—not the damn graham cracker app!" Brandie Jean snapped. "Take notes during the next meeting. I don't stand up there just to hear myself talk."

"This is better than TV," Caroline said with a laugh as she slurped from her travel mug.

The photographer dismissed Callum, who ran back to the tent like his ass was on fire.

A handful of other victims—*volunteers*—were oiled and photographed before it was Austin's turn.

Caroline let out a piercing wolf whistle as he was directed to pose next to a tree.

"Oh God," I cackled. They had him dressed in the lower half of his turnout pants with just suspenders over his bare chest.

Someone came at him with oil, and Caroline was out of her seat, fighting the grannies off.

"Vultures, all of you," she scolded as she grabbed the oil and slathered him up herself.

They made eyes at each other as she worked her hands over his chest and arms.

I looked at Layla. "I'm gonna throw up."

"Pretty sure this is payback for all the times you answered the door wearing nothing except Shane's clothes."

"That was *once*. This is pornographic!"

Layla howled. "It's Caroline. Let our sweet little moonbeam have this."

"You know he used to be skinny as a stringbean, right?" I said. "Not this GI Joe shit. I have pictures. Someone has to keep him humble."

Caroline skipped back to the chairs with a giddy look on her face.

"Satisfied?" I asked with a judgmental, yet good-natured note in my voice.

She smirked. "Not in the slightest. But I will be later."

"You know, I should be furious at my brother for corrupting you, but you're going to be my sister-in-law and I can't possibly be mad at that."

"Mr. August! You're up!" Brandie Jean called.

"That's Shane," Caroline whispered.

My heart skipped, and I quickly shimmied Kat into the baby sling.

Those little old ladies weren't laying a finger on my man.

Before I got out of the chair, Caroline gasped.

I frowned. "What's the matter?"

Her eyes welled up with tears, and she pressed her fingers to her lips. Her gaze was locked on Shane's body, but it wasn't full of lust.

She stared at the kidney donor scar that warped the tattoos on his abdomen. "I've never seen him shirtless."

"Come on," I said, grabbing her hand.

Caroline followed me through the crowd. Shane was seated on the open edge of the back of an ambulance.

Shane's expression softened when he saw me dragging her along.

Like he knew, Shane stood still as a statue as Caroline gingerly touched the slight ridge of skin.

It was framed by smaller scars—bullet wounds and shrapnel marks.

They told a story of choices, change, and perseverance.

I was yanked out of the way as the photographer snagged a photo of the two of them.

Austin appeared beside me, watching as Caroline stood next to Shane and lifted the edge of her sweater just enough to show her scar. The two smiled at each other as the photographer snapped away.

Without a word, Shane turned around and showed off the kidney tattoos on his lower back—one detailed and crisp, the other in gray and white ink.

But that wasn't what I was enamored with.

There was a new tattoo on the back of his shoulder, tucked in among the bone frogs.

It was two new frogs.—a big one with a tadpole beside it. The artwork was still covered by a clear aftercare bandage.

Caroline scurried back to Austin and me, slipping under his arm to watch the rest of the shoot. I was vaguely aware of Austin kissing the top of her head, but the tears in my eyes blurred my vision.

Kat let out a warning cry before immediately cranking it up to glass-shattering decibels.

I looked at the time. I had just fed her. Maybe her diaper needed to be changed? I patted her bum. It felt fine...

I rocked back and forth, trying to sooth her while Shane finished posing with a stethoscope around his neck.

"I think she's had enough of being outside," I said to Austin. "I should probably head out."

As soon as he was dismissed from the set, Shane ran over, not concerned in the slightest that he was only half dressed.

"Come here, baby girl," he said with concern marring his McDreamy face. Shane took her out of the wrap carrier and rested her against his chest, dropping a kiss to her rosy cheek. Kat immediately settled and went to sleep. "Come to Daddy."

37

SHANE

I sat on the front steps of my house, listening to the soft rustle of the leaves as I stared at an empty driveway.

Unease crept at me.

Sitting in an empty house made me antsy, so I resigned to waiting on the steps.

The late fall sun was bright but cool. I closed my eyes and inhaled the breeze, counting down the minutes until Beth would be back.

She went to the American Legion with me for the support group this morning, then left with Kelsea for lunch and an afternoon spent in Chapel Hill. I had offered to bring Kat back home, but Beth insisted that she could handle going out and about with her.

A few hours without my girls and I was going stir crazy. I wanted them back. Safe. Protected.

I had been handling the aftermath of Kat's abduction as best as I could, but something unhinged came out in me when I didn't have them near.

I trusted Beth more than anything, but I didn't trust the world with souls as beautiful and delicate as theirs.

A text from Cole lit up my phone. He was on his way to a new assignment overseas with one of the other protection agents he worked with—a woman he couldn't stand.

That was a recipe for disaster.

Responding to him distracted me enough for two minutes to pass and for Beth's car to roll up the driveway. She parked, but instead of getting out, she sat in the driver's seat and closed her eyes.

I waited it out, trusting that she was okay and she'd come to me when she was ready.

After ninety seconds of controlled breathing, she climbed out.

"Hey, Mama."

"Hi."

"How, uh... How was lunch with Kels?"

She looked down at the boots on her feet. "It was good. We went to a Mexican place near campus. Ran into some of my colleagues."

Shit.

It was no secret that the university had been under intense scrutiny after the ordeal. One of their professors not only cheated on his wife with his former teaching assistant, but got her pregnant, threatened her multiple times, and eventually kidnapped her baby in some sort of sick revenge plot.

"How was that?"

She sighed and leaned against the car. "Makes me think of January when my maternity leave is over and I'm back in the classroom." Her gaze drew to the car seat in the back of the sedan. "It's going to be weird not having her with me every day."

I leaned in, sifting my fingers through her soft tresses. "Have you thought about what you're going to do for childcare?"

I had an answer on the tip of my tongue, but when it came to Kat, I always let Beth lead.

"I have a few thoughts," she said noncommittally, dancing around the subject.

I leaned in and grazed her lips with mine. "Hmmm. What are those?" I murmured.

She bit her lip, taking it away from me. "Well, Austin and Caroline have offered to help on days that he's off or afternoons when she's done teaching."

"And on the days they can't help?"

She kicked at a piece of gravel. "I've been thinking about it..."

"Ask me," I whispered against her lips. "It's okay to ask for help. I want to help. I want the responsibility. Just *ask*."

She rested her forehead on my sternum and exhaled. "Would you be willing to keep her while I'm at work?"

"Yeah, Mama."

"Hopefully, it won't be too much. A lot of the courses I teach are online and I can work from home, and—"

"No excuses. No rationale. If this is going to work—if *we're* going to work—I need you to believe me when I say I'm in. I'm all in."

"I believe you." She looked up at me. "I do. I know you'd do anything for her and for me. You went—" Her voice broke. "You went after her when I couldn't. You've always been there for her when I couldn't be. And it makes me feel guilty to keep asking you to be there for her so I can be off somewhere else."

I shook my head. "That's not it at all." I cupped her cheeks. "She needs you to do all those things for yourself. She needs to see it. She needs to see you taking care of yourself and getting your doctorate and kicking ass as a professor. She needs to see you being great. That's what will make *her* great."

"Speaking of taking care of myself..."

I tilted my head, curious but quiet.

She took a deep breath. "I think I might be ready to talk to somebody..."

"You mean like—"

"A therapist. Or a counselor. Or a psychiatrist," she rambled. "I guess—I mean—I have good days. More good days than bad days now. But the bad days are still there, and it's hard to get out of that dark place when I get in it. When I was at lunch with Kelsea, she was telling me how she struggled with these thoughts after her son was born, and she recommended a lady who really helped her talk through it all."

My eyebrows lifted. "Yeah?"

"Why doesn't anyone talk about how common this is? Feeling like you're alone... It makes it even worse because you feel like you're the only one and everyone's judging you."

I pulled her into my arms and held her tight. "I don't know. But I'm glad you're feeling up to going to see someone. And I am so fucking proud of you."

She laughed, exasperated, and wiped her eyes. "Thanks, baby."

Damn, I loved hearing her call me that.

I opened the backseat and unfastened Kat, who looked like she was five seconds from screaming if she didn't get to sleep. "Hey, tadpole. C'mere."

The first wail nearly busted my eardrum.

Beth sighed and shouldered the diaper bag. "I probably kept her out too long, but I was having such a good time with Kels. It's going to be a pain to get her to go down."

"I like a challenge. Leave her to me. You need to call your mom back. She called me and wanted to know if we were coming down to the beach for Thanksgiving."

We divided and conquered once inside. I mixed Kat a

bottle while Beth changed Kat's diaper and attempted to get her to settle. When that didn't work, we swapped, with me rocking her as she sucked down the formula while Beth, despite my protests, tidied up.

"There you go," I said softly as Kat's eyelids slowly lowered. Her head was conked back and she snoozed in a blissful milk coma. "Defeated by your appetite once again."

I laughed quietly to myself as I eased out of the rocking chair and laid her in the crib. After a quick check to make sure the baby monitor was on, I snuck out and pulled the door.

Beth was in the bedroom with a laundry basket of clothes. Her phone was trapped between her ear and shoulder as she stood at the end of our bed and riffled through the basket.

"I think that's fine. I'll talk to Austin and see what he and—"

She clammed up as soon as I slipped my hands beneath her shirt and started unfastening her bra.

"You there, sweetie?" her mom asked through the phone.

Beth stammered. "Um—yeah—I—"

I cupped her breasts, fondling them in my palms. My dick strained at the front of my jeans, and I pressed it into her ass.

"Beth, honey—"

"I'm here, Mom," she said before silently gasping when I rolled her nipples between my fingers.

Her knuckles turned white against the laundry basket.

"Anyway," Mrs. Hale said. "You talk to Austin about sleeping arrangements at his house and let me know what Shane likes to eat."

I grinned like a devil as I slid my hand into her leggings, beneath her panties, and teased Beth's wet pussy. "Beth knows what I like to eat," I said loud enough for her mom to hear through the receiver.

"Well, hi, Shane!" she exclaimed. "How are you, honey?"

Sliding two fingers inside of her, I cupped Beth's pussy in my hand and stroked her inner walls.

Her knees went weak. I had accessed the master controls on Beth's body, turning her into putty.

I used my one-handed grip on her breast to keep her upright against my chest. "I'm good, Mrs. Hale. I hope you are too."

Beth slammed the phone into the basket of clothes so I couldn't hear the response. "Why are you making small talk with my mother while you're inside of me?" she hissed before picking up the phone again. "Mom, I'll call you back. I think Kat's crying."

Dirty little liar.

"Okay, sweetie—"

Beth hung up. "Please make me come," she begged.

I chuckled as I pinched her clit between my fingers. "Look at you asking so nicely. I like that."

"Shane," she whined, eyes screwing shut.

"Here I was, about to give you a reward, but I think I like fucking with you just as much as I like fucking you."

I stopped teasing her pussy and pulled her leggings down to her knees. With one hand, I grabbed her hair at the base of her scalp, keeping the tension firm. Goosebumps erupted down the back of her neck like a volcano.

"Feet apart. Arch your back."

She braced against the laundry basket, pushing her ass up toward me.

I tugged on her hair, bringing her ear to my lips. "That's my good girl." I smoothed my hand down her ass. "I think this ass would look prettier in pink, don't you?"

Before she could utter a sound, my palm clapped against her lily-white ass. Beth gasped, throwing her head back.

"Yes," she hissed as I soothed the sting away with my hand.

"You like that, don't you?" I said as I spanked the other cheek.

She whimpered, exhaling sharply. "Yes."

"Atta girl." I tugged on her hair again, and slid my fingers through her wetness, teasing her clit on the way. "Look at you—dripping for me."

"Please," she gritted out. "I've been horny all day. Please just—"

"Ah, ah, ah—" I pushed my thumb, coated in her arousal, into her mouth.

Beth let out a muffled cry as I played with her breast again.

"You make me so hard." I ground my erection against her bare ass. "So fucking hard. I want to tie you to this bed and fuck you until the only thing you can say is my name."

Beth nodded desperately.

"Are you going to be good for me?" I growled in her ear.

"Mhmm—"

My smile curved, slow and villainous, against the shell of her ear. "Then get on your knees."

She dropped like a rock, immediately hitting the floor with her leggings still binding her knees. I unzipped my fly and lowered my jeans. My cock sprang out, bobbing in front of her.

Wide green eyes looked up at me, innocent and seeking.

I trailed my knuckles down her cheek. "So pretty." I thumbed her lip. "All of you—so fucking pretty. Open that mouth for me. Suck my cock until I tell you to stop, and then I'll fill that pretty pussy with my come."

She worked the flat of her tongue along the underside of my cock before taking it between parted rosy lips. Her mouth was warm and silken, pulling at my cock with perfect pressure. I grabbed her hair and pushed her head into me, forcing her to take my length.

She sputtered, releasing air before swallowing and swirling her tongue around my shaft.

"God Almighty—" I groaned "—you're so fucking good at this."

Her hand crept up and squeezed my balls. I threw my head back and swore at the ceiling. Her fingers wandered, teasing the sensitive skin behind them as she edged further and further back.

A low groan ripped out of my chest. "Fuck—yes—"

The dynamic had shifted and she knew it. I had her on her knees, but she had me in the palm of her hand.

Her index finger pressed against my asshole, sending erotic lightning lancing through my spine as she teased the nerves there. The head of my cock hit the back of her throat, and I nearly lost it.

"That's enough," I barked, pulling her head back. She wore a mischievous grin.

I left her on her knees long enough to toss the laundry basket onto the floor.

I kicked my jeans off and ripped my shirt over my head before making her clothes disappear like a Las Vegas act. I had her sprawled across the bed before she could blink.

"That's it," I soothed. "Let me see all of you."

Beth closed her eyes and rested her cheek on the comforter as I started at her ankles, kissing up her legs and nipping at the softness of her thighs. I gripped her legs and spread them apart. "There you go, Mama. Open these up for me. Let me kneel before you and worship."

Her back arched off the bed as I lapped at her pussy like a dog.

"Shane," she said in a whisper. Her toes curled and her fingers fisted the bedding. "Oh, God—"

I chuckled. "I'm the one praying at your altar, but if you want to give me your reverence, who am I to say no?"

I traded my tongue for my fingers, sliding them inside to keep her on edge as I stretched over her and kissed every inch of her stomach. She flinched and squirmed as I pressed wet kisses to her stretch marks and her navel. I pressed my forearm to her collarbone, keeping her still.

"Please just fuck me already," she begged. "I need you inside of me."

"And I need you to stay still while I praise the body that carried my child." I kissed her waist. "I will keep both of you safe." I kissed her hip bone. "I'll provide for you if you let me." I kissed the right side of her stomach. "I'll never raise my voice with either of you." I kissed the other side. "To me, your daughter will never be anything but mine." I lapped at her navel. "I will love you both until my dying breath, and then I'll keep loving you until I see you again."

"Shane..." I looked up and found tears in her eyes.

"Say yes."

She licked her lips, trying to catch her breath. "To what? You haven't asked me anything."

I grabbed a condom from the stack I kept at the ready on the bedside table, tore into it, and rolled it on. "Say yes to life." I slid into her slowly, memorizing every inch. "That we'll take it slow, and we'll figure it out. And you and me—" I grabbed her hands, lacing our fingers together as I held them over her head, against the mattress "—you and me are gonna live happily ever after."

Her head tipped back into the bed, opening up her throat. I lavished it with kisses. "I love you so much, Beth," I whispered gently, even though my balls ached with anticipation.

Her eyes welled up with tears. "I love you too." She

wrapped her arms and legs around me, keeping us as close as two people could be. "Thank you for loving me."

"You make it easy."

I braced my hands against the bed and pulled out before sheathing myself once again.

She was ecstasy.

I memorized every desperate breath and plea she whispered as I drove in and out of her heat. I pushed away from the bed and knelt on the mattress, lifting her hips and making her levitate as I fucked her harder and faster.

Her tits bounced as I pistoned into her cunt. Blonde hair splayed across the sheets like golden rays of sunlight.

She was everything to me.

My whole world fit under one roof. I was one lucky motherfucker.

"Shane," she said with a trembling voice. "I—I'm—"

"Come for me, beautiful. Give me everything."

We collapsed into each other, breathing heavily with smiles on our faces.

For all the heartache. For all the struggle. For every moment we survived to get to the living.

It was worth it.

38

BETH

The sea breeze floated in through an open window in Austin's house on the water. The curtains billowed as the currents brought in a late-season storm.

"So, are we ever going to talk about this?" I asked as I traced my finger along the tadpole tattoo Shane had inked on his body. We should have left Beaufort to drive back to Falls Creek an hour ago, but my mom babysat Kat this morning so I could show Shane where I grew up.

Of course, that turned into an hour of sex, a quick drive into town for breakfast at Jokers, my favorite bar, and then more sex when we were supposed to actually be packing our things.

Remnants of yesterday's Thanksgiving feast still lingered in the form of elastic waistband sweats for Shane and me wearing the maternity pants I had pulled out of my closet for the explicit reason of eating my body weight in mashed potatoes.

Thanksgiving in Beaufort was exactly what I needed. Shane, Austin, Caroline, and I took over Austin's house for three days. We spent our time hanging with my family and taking Shane and Caroline to our favorite spots. The nights were spent playing cards and shooting the shit.

Kat was surrounded by all her favorite people, and even got to meet her great granddad.

As much as I loved being back, there were hometowns, and then there was home.

Shane was mine.

Austin and Caroline were figuring out how to split holidays. They seemed to be doing well managing Caroline being an only child and needing to spend special moments with her parents, while still getting to visit our parents on the coast.

My mom's solution was simple: everyone comes next time. Us. Austin and Caroline. Caroline's parents. Hell—she even told Shane to extend an invite to Cole Crowder for the next holiday.

I loved her for it.

Austin and Caroline had left after my mom's midday Thanksgiving feast to get back to Falls Creek so they could spend the rest of the long weekend with her family. As soon as they departed for the drive inland with parting instructions to not burn the place down, Shane and I christened every surface we could think of, lasting into the wee hours of the morning.

Now, it was actually time to go.

Shane rolled over and pulled me into his chest. "Are we ever going to talk about what?"

I smiled, pressing a kiss to his sternum. "The new tattoo you never told me you got."

He nuzzled into my hair. "I don't know what you're talking about."

"I saw it the day y'all did the calendar shoot. And I've been waiting for you to bring it up."

He chuckled. "Mama, you know you're supposed to ask if you want something."

"Just tell me."

Shane slid his hand up my leg. "Yeah. I got a new tattoo."

I rolled, pulling the sheet up to my chin. "It's a tadpole."

"That it is."

"Will you stop being all vague and *I'd tell you, but then I'd have to kill you*?" I made the remark with my best neanderthal man voice.

"If you're asking if my tattoo is for our girl, then yes." He tipped my chin up and kissed me. "I've never gotten a tattoo that represents where I'm at now. Only my past. I wanted it to be her and I."

My heart swelled. What else could I say? I was one lucky girl. "What about me?" I looked up, meeting his smiling eyes. "Do I get a place on your body?"

"You already do."

I looked at him quizzically. I knew every inch of his body better than my own. I had spent hours poring over his tattoos, admiring the muscle and ink.

Shane pulled his left arm out from under the covers and laced his fingers with mine. "I've got you right here, Mama." He wiggled his ring finger against our clasped hands.

He had the letter 'B' tattooed where a wedding ring would go. It blended in with the rest of the tattoos that covered his hands, but the ink was far more crisp.

"Mark my words, I'm gonna marry you one day. It might be far off, but I promise you—I love you, and I'm gonna make you my wife."

"I love you too—*wait*." I reared back. "Why would it be far off? There's a perfectly good courthouse we can go to right now."

"Because I'll marry you on one condition."

"Isn't it usually the woman who makes the conditions?"

He squeezed my hand, showing off the letter tattoo again. "I'll marry you as long as you finish your degree."

My heart sank. I'd been debating if it was too much. My maternity leave ended in just over a month, and then I'd be juggling motherhood, school, teaching, and squeezing an hour or two of sleep in there every other night.

"You're holding me hostage?"

He pecked the tip of my nose. "Incentivizing, darling."

I rolled my eyes at his sarcasm.

Even though I was annoyed, Shane drew me in for a long, slow kiss. When he pulled away, he rested his forehead on mine. "Get your degree. Become Dr. Hale. Do it for yourself. And I swear to you, the next day I'll make you my wife. I have no problem being known as Dr. and Mr. Hutchins. But that degree and that honor is yours and yours alone. Even if it's only for a day, I want you to know that you earned it under no one's name but your own."

"But what if I want to skip being Dr. Hale and just be Dr. Hutchins?"

"I'm setting the rules this time because I know you can do it. And until then—" He lifted his hand and showed me the tattoo again "—My love for you is just like this tattoo. Public and permanent."

I closed my eyes and wormed my way back into his warmth. "But it could be years, Shane. *Years*. And not just a few. Like—Kat will probably be in first grade by the time I'm done. Do you really want to wait that long?"

"I'll wait as long as it takes. I want you, but I don't want you to give up on yourself for me."

———

I was wistful on the way home. I couldn't wait to get back and start decorating for Christmas.

Decorating Shane's house for Christmas.

I smiled to myself because he didn't know what was about to hit him. I *loved* holiday decor. His little shotgun ranch was going to be so fucking festive. My mom had sent us packing with two of her infamous wreaths—one for my front door and one for Shane's.

But at what point would we just have one door?

One home?

On one hand, it felt too soon to move in together, but on the other hand, we were already living together. Our romance bloomed out of one of the scariest days of my life. It came out of nowhere.

A year ago I was devastated and terrified. I looked ahead at the next eighteen years of my life and saw struggle and loneliness. I believed that I was too unlovable. Too complicated. Too messed up. That I had too much baggage.

But there had never been a single day of loneliness.

There had always been Shane.

I looked across the truck cab—the place where he had taken a knife to the compression garments that I thought I needed to wear to hold everything in and make him be attracted to me.

But he cut it off and held me instead.

Shane's eyes darted to the clock on the dash, then back at the road.

"You got a hot date or something?" I teased.

He smirked. "Nah. Just ready to be home."

"Then why are you taking the long way around?"

He rounded the bend leading up to The Lookout. Someone else was parked on the shoulder today, but there were no bodies visible in the vehicle.

Pretty standard for The Lookout.

Shane and I had our fair share of fun there.

The tires ate up the miles as we finally made it into town. He slowed past The Copper Mule and looked longingly at the patio.

"You hungry?"

He shook his head. "Just thinking about the first time I saw you."

I racked my brain to try and remember it, but I couldn't quite place it."

"I thought we met at the Filling Station."

He shook his head. "We talked there for the first time. But it was way before that. I was at the Mule with Layla and Lauren from the police department, and you and Austin showed up. You had just moved here and he was visiting you. Layla got up from our table and Austin introduced you two."

I blinked. That day felt like it was a hundred lifetimes ago.

But he was there. I remembered it as soon as I closed my eyes. Shane had been there that day, and every moment since.

We passed the community center and the elementary school, laughing at all the time we spent together at Ladies Auxiliary fundraisers. He recalled our whispered conversations during the Charity Date Auction that forced Layla and Callum to pretend to be engaged to each other just to get out of it. We talked about the Winter Warm-Up where Austin and Caroline had suspiciously won the same prize.

Fine. Now that they were together, I was willing to admit that Brandie Jean convinced me to bid on the weekend stay at the Ballentine House and give it to Austin.

At every turn, pieces of our story would forever be engraved in this tiny town that I had grown to love with all my heart.

Shane turned onto his street, slowing as he neared his

driveway. Richard the cat sat on the front stoop, staring angrily at the cars, motorcycle, and truck piled into the driveway.

"Are the guys coming over to work out?" I asked. As far as I knew, Austin and Caroline were supposed to be with the Tyrees, and Callum, Layla, and Gran Fletcher were spending the day with the Mousavis.

Shane just smiled. "Nope."

My heart ramped up as I saw bodies hustling around inside. I grabbed his hand. "Shane…"

Kind eyes met mine as he put the truck into park.

"What did you do?"

"Not me. I didn't do a thing."

I sat frozen as he came around and opened my door, helping me down before getting Kat out of her car seat.

He took my hand and led me up the walk.

"Why does this feel like a proposal is about to happen?" I was already getting misty-eyed. "You literally just said I'd have to wait five damn years before you'd marry me."

Shane chuckled. "This is more than a ring, Mama." He let go of my hand and opened the door. "This is the rest of our lives."

Boxes filled the living room. Boxes of *my things*. Boxes of Kat's things. Kitchen appliances and decorations were in huge bins. Among the boxes were Callum, Layla, Austin, Caroline, and Brandie Jean.

I should have known.

I smelled Love Spell as soon as we got out of the truck.

"Surprise!" Caroline shouted in a panic. "Please don't be mad! We were just following instructions."

I blinked, not quite believing what I saw. "You moved me into your house."

My entire townhouse—minus the big pieces of furniture—was sitting in Shane's living room.

"Caroline and I left early yesterday so we could pack everything up. BJ, Cal, and Layla helped us move it all today," Austin said.

And was that? I sniffed. "Why does it smell like paint?"

Shane pressed a kiss to the side of my head. "I may have teamed up with my other half to give you a little surprise."

Caroline bounced up and down.

I looked up at him. "I thought I was your other half."

He shrugged and steered me toward the nursery. "Yeah, well, Caroline has my kidney, so..."

I looked back and gave my future sister-in-law a wink.

Shane opened the nursery door, then stepped back.

I gasped.

Galaxies.

A new mural had been painted over standard beige walls, but it wasn't the forest theme Caroline had painted back at my townhouse. It was ... It was so much more.

A sign hung on the behind the crib that read, *Katherine Shane*. The bear he had made out of his EMS shirt was tucked in the corner of the crib.

I cupped my hands over my mouth, not quite believing my eyes. The whole room was done in stars. A moon mobile hung over the crib. It felt like standing on the edge of the universe, about to leap into the unknown.

There was one detail that didn't quite match the theme—a black-and-white afghan that had been crocheted. Each square had an alternating mathematical symbol. Plus. Minus. Multiply. Divide.

"Gran made it for you," Callum said.

Shane tucked Kat into one arm and pulled me into his side with the other. "You named her after Katherine Johnson, right? The mathematician who helped astronauts orbit the earth?"

I laughed in spite of the tears running down my face. "You remember me saying that?"

He chuckled. "Of course I remembered. You told me that when nothing else makes sense to you, math does."

I barely remembered telling him that. Then again, I was about to pass out when he asked me where I got Kat's name from.

"Thank you," I whispered in utter disbelief.

Shane squeezed my hand as the rest of the crew gathered around. "Life isn't always going to make sense. We'll celebrate together when it does, and we'll lean on each other when it doesn't. Through the hurt. Through the healing. Through waiting on the things that save us and make life worth living. We'll hold strong to the belief that there's purpose in all of it."

EPILOGUE
SHANE

Peals of laughter filled the house as half of the town crowded in our kitchen and watched Kat smash into her first birthday cake. Green frosting went flying everywhere. It splattered across the high chair and stuck to the microwave.

Kat's eyes went wide, shocked at the chain reaction of the buttercream explosion. She froze, assessed, then raised both arms as high as they'd go and slammed them into the demolished frog cake. A maniacal belly giggle reverberated from her as she squished and squashed her fingers in the mess of cake and icing.

Beth stood by my side, recording a video on her phone while I was on picture duty.

Kat dove in headfirst, sticking her entire face in the cake.

I laughed as I snapped a burst of photos. "I think she's gonna have a sweet tooth."

"She comes by it honest," Beth said with tears in her eyes.

Wrapping paper, gift bags, and tissue paper were all over the place. The balloons outside had wilted in the August heat, but Kat was hitting the peak of her first-ever sugar high.

Olivia Childers was in attendance, standing between Kat's grandparents. Julie had politely declined the invite, but only because she was supervising a weekend at their new lake house, where Odin wanted to spend some quality time with her boys. They were taking it slow, but things seemed to be going well for them.

Beth and Julie usually managed to meet up for lunch once a week between the classes Beth had taught over the spring and summer to catch up on life.

"Thanks for having me over," Olivia said as she checked her phone.

"Do you need a ride home?" I asked.

She shook her head. "Mr. Travis is coming to pick me up. He and Josh are driving back together from the lake so they can take me out on the road with them. I need to get some hours in for my driver's license."

"How—uh... How's that going? With him and your mom ... hanging out."

Olivia laughed. "I know they're dating. It's fine. I guess it's still weird sometimes, but he's nice. I like his dog. But I guess it's probably weird for me to be hanging out here, too."

I knew what she meant. I felt guilty every time Olivia or one of her brothers came over to visit with Kat.

I was the reason their dad wasn't alive. But if the choice was between him or my daughter, I'd make it every single time.

Life wasn't always full of easy choices. Sometimes there was no outcome where everyone got to win.

Guests started to say their goodbyes and filter out as Beth lifted Kat out of her highchair and immediately deposited her into the sink to get all the frosting and crumbs sprayed off her.

Kat babbled an endless string of 'dada, mama,' over and over and over again.

Austin and Caroline took care of covering the leftovers and getting them into the fridge while Beth's parents started taking down the banner that read, "Hoppy Birthday, Kat."

Olivia said goodbye with quick side hugs for Beth and I, and I rolled up my sleeves to help Beth. She was elbows deep in soapy water as she gave a still-giggling Kat a quick scrub.

"A whole year," I murmured as I bracketed her between my arms. "We made it a whole year, Mama."

She paused, keeping both hands on Kat as she used her shoulder to brush a strand of hair out of her face. "I can't figure out if it's been ten years or ten minutes."

"The days are long, but the years are short."

Kat's giggles softened, and her head did the tired-baby wobble.

"She's about to crash," I noted.

"That makes two of us," Beth said before lowering her voice to a whisper. "Is it bad that I'm glad my parents are staying with Austin and Caroline? I just want to sleep."

I chuckled, "Nap time as soon as we have an empty house."

I grabbed a towel from the linen closet and unfurled it so that Beth could deposit a squirming, pink baby into it. I wrapped her up like a burrito and carried her into the nursery.

Life was better than it had ever been.

I had a family. A good woman and a daughter. The Hales had brought me in as one of their own without so much as a second thought. Austin and I were back to being thick as thieves after he finally accepted that I was in it with Beth for the long haul.

Caroline and I were closer than ever. Every fear I'd ever

had about confronting rock bottom was unfounded. She had become my sidekick. It was nice having her near—especially with what I had up my sleeve.

Beth popped her head into the nursery as I was fastening a clean diaper around Kat. "Everyone's heading out. Are you okay with meeting up with them for dinner at The Copper Mule before my parents head back to Beaufort in the morning?"

"Yeah, that's cool," I said as I pulled a clean onesie from Kat's dresser drawer and worked it over her damp skin. She was already crashing. "Come on, Tadpole," I said as I held her against my chest, bouncing between my feet to keep her on the track of a solid nap. Her head rested against my shoulder, little breaths tickling my neck.

Beth smiled softly as she leaned against the doorway. "She's out."

"Is it bad that I don't want to put her down? That I just want her to stay this little forever?"

She laughed under her breath. "If she could change her own diapers that'd be nice."

I smoothed my head over the wisps of honey blonde hair covering her head. She had graduated to wearing the occasional hair clip to keep the strands out of her face, and it made my heart seize.

She was growing up too fast.

I wanted to slow down time. Hell—I wanted to stop it together.

I'd been with her since her first breath, and it would still never be enough time.

Beth and I still had our respective bad days. Days where we didn't want to get up. Days where it was hard to see past the mental haze. But sometimes it's easier to show up for others when you don't have the energy to show up for yourself.

For Kat, we opened the curtains and got going every day. And, like clockwork, the haze always lifted.

The next day was always better than the last.

"Come on, Daddy. Put her down so we can nap," Beth said.

"Fine," I grumbled as I lowered Kat into her crib and made sure she was comfortable.

Before Beth could head to the bedroom, I grabbed her hand and dragged her through the house. She squeaked, stumbling over the carpet. "Shane!" she hissed. "I thought we were napping. Trust me, I need a nap or I'm gonna get really cranky."

"One second, and then we will."

As I pulled her into the living room, Beth skidded to a stop. "What's going on?"

"I have a present for you," I said, cool as a cucumber in December. "Don't get me wrong, I love celebrating our girl and seeing her roll around in cake like a pig in mud, but I think we should have a little celebration of our own. We made it a whole year, and she's still alive and in one piece."

"Cheers to that," Beth said as she flopped down onto the couch.

I grabbed a gift bag that hadn't been destroyed by our one-year-old and handed it to her. "This is for you, Mama."

She tilted her head and gave me a quizzical look as she pulled the tissue paper out. "I feel bad. I didn't get you anything."

"Nah. Just open it."

I sat on the edge of the coffee table so we could be face-to-face.

Beth pulled out the Mason jar I usually kept on the end

table in the living room. Yesterday I told her I was moving it so it wasn't in the way during the party, but that wasn't the case.

Beth looked up, clearly confused as she studied the jar full of sobriety chips.

I leaned forward and picked up the first chip from the top. "Three months sober." I picked up the next. "One day sober." And the next. "Six months sober." And the next. "One year sober."

One by one, I picked up each chip and keychain and read off the period of sobriety that it celebrated.

"The past isn't much of a gift, but for me it is. If I had given up then, I wouldn't have you. You're my gift. Our daughter is my gift. Every day after one of these chips that I get to spend with you is a gift. And I promise you one thing—I don't take any of those chips for granted. They're not the finish line; they're mile markers. I still have a ways to go, but I don't want to do it alone." I dumped the rest of the chips out. They fell to the floor like confetti, but I caught the small velvet box that was at the bottom.

Beth's eyes turned to saucers, and she clapped her hands over her mouth.

My heart stopped, nerves building like a chemical reaction about to explode. I opened the box and pulled out the ring I had been saving up for. "I want every breath I take to be with you as my wife."

"Shane," she whispered as she wiped away glistening tears.

I slid off the coffee table and got down on one knee. "Will you marry me?"

Her hand shook as I slid the ring on, then kissed it.

"It's so beautiful," she said with a laugh even though tears were sliding down her face.

"I took Caroline with me to pick it out."

Beth threw her arms around me and slid off the couch into me. "Thank you for loving me. For loving Kat. For wanting us."

I kissed her, tenderly at first, then deeply. "I always have. I always will."

BONUS EPILOGUE
BETH

"I think you take the cake for longest engagement," BJ said as she fastened my veil in place. "You've been engaged longer than my last two marriages."

To be fair, both of her most recent husbands had been on hospice.

"Hey, that wasn't my choice," I pointed out. "Shane refused to marry me until I graduated."

Layla floated by, a vision in pale pink, as she toted her youngest kid—a baby boy named Kellen—on her hip. She spoke to him quietly in Farsi before sending him down the hall to where the men were getting ready. Her oldest, Asal, was sitting in the corner in her flower girl dress, as she played on a tablet and munched on carrot sticks.

"I swear he was about to come out of his skin at commencement yesterday," Caroline said with a laugh.

The months leading up to our wedding were some of the most intense and stressful that I had ever experienced. But I was a lucky girl. I had Shane by my side every step of the way.

He waited outside the room as I defended my dissertation. He waited with me, holding my hand as my work was evaluated behind closed doors. He cried happy tears when the doors opened and they requested for *Dr. Hale* to come back in the room.

True to Shane's promise all those years ago, I had spent a grand total of twenty-four hours as Dr. Hale. Now, I couldn't wait to become Dr. and Mr. Hutchins.

"Beth," Kylie Solomon, the wedding planner's assistant, said as she popped her head in the room. "Are you ready for your first look?"

I turned to BJ for reassurance, and she gave me a nod. "You look so beautiful."

"When are you gonna settle down for the long haul?" I asked her.

Currently, there was no ring on her finger. BJ just shrugged. "You know me. I always find someone."

I took a fistful of white tulle in each hand and made my way down the hallway of The Taylor Creek Inn.

Shane and the boys had been sequestered as I made my way down to the lobby and out to an ivy-covered courtyard.

Kat stood in the middle of the cobblestone pavers in an age-appropriate maid-of-honor dress. Her hair was curled and pinned into place, and I had given her permission to get a light dusting of makeup from the makeup artist doing up the rest of the wedding party.

My sweet six-year-old was growing up too fast.

"I can hear you, Momma," she giggled as she stood with her back to me.

I rocked my hips, swishing my dress back and forth. "My dress is kinda loud, isn't it?"

"Can I turn around yet? Can I see?"

I waited as my wedding planning wizards, Hannah Jane and Kylie, fluffed the train and laid my veil in place. The photographer clicked away, snapping photos of our first look.

Shane was adamant that he wanted the first time he saw me in my gown to be when I walked down the aisle. He was old-school like that, so I decided to steal a moment with my daughter.

I picked out my dress in the presence of Layla, BJ, and Caroline. Kat had seen it on the hanger, but she hadn't seen it on me.

"You ready, sweetie?"

She giggled as she held her hands over her eyes. "Yes!"

"Turn around."

Kat whipped around and stood stunned, then gasped. "*Mom*," she whispered reverently. "You look like a princess."

Everything was princesses to Kat. It had only escalated when Austin and Caroline gifted her the *Pretty Pretty Princess* board game. Shane was often subjected to being dressed up in the plastic tiara and pretend jewelry. *And he smiled through every minute of it.* He was the frequent subject of her manicure attempts, and wore messily painted nails to work quite often.

I smoothed my hands down the glittering tulle that flared out in a dreamy silhouette. "You think so?"

Kat couldn't stand still any longer. She bolted to me and leaped. I caught her and managed to stay upright on my high heels. "Daddy's gonna think you're so pretty."

I laughed. "I hope so."

She smoothed her hands down my long waves. "Your hair looks like mine."

I gave her the tightest hug I could. "That's because you're my girl. And I love you farther than the stars."

"I love you even farther," she said. "Is it time for cake yet?"

I laughed and spun her around. "Not yet. But I promise you'll get the first piece."

Cake tasting was, arguably, Kat's favorite part of wedding planning. Frankly, it was the favorite of all three of us.

I walked hand-in-hand with her as we were ushered outside to meet up with the rest of my bridesmaids for pre-ceremony photos. Kat thought she was hot stuff since she was one of the "big girls," and took her maid-of-honor duties very seriously.

The afternoon flew by in a rush of *"pose here"*, *"smile here"*, and *"go here."* By the time we were lined up, ready to walk the waterfront aisle to the outdoor ceremony space, I didn't care about all the pomp and circumstance.

I just wanted to see my husband.

Brandie Jean went down the aisle first, followed by Layla, then Caroline. Asal, Layla and Callum's daughter, made her trek down the aisle with a fierce frown on her face as she took flower petal placement very seriously.

Kat was next, giving me a kiss on the cheek before heading down the aisle. I peeked around the corner of the floral arch and watched her run at a dead sprint to Shane. He let out a loud laugh as he caught her in his arms.

Austin, standing behind Shane, picked up Kat's bouquet as it fell.

I let out a shaking breath as I blinked away tears, not wanting to ruin my makeup just yet.

"You found a good one," Hannah Jane said.

I gave her a nervous smile. "He's the best."

"Alright, Dr. Hale," she said with a smile. "When you come back down the aisle, you'll be Dr. Hutchins."

"Shane told you to say that, didn't he?"

She winked. "Like I said, you found a good one."

The music swelled and I took my place at the end of the aisle, holding on to my dad's arm. I tried to remember everything Hannah Jane had told me during the rehearsal. *Walk slower than you think you should. Keep the stems of your bouquet just below your belly button. Look at Shane.*

The last one wasn't hard, but fighting the urge to bolt down the aisle like Kat had done was nearly impossible. Everything was a blur as my dad kissed my cheek, then took a seat beside my mom. I gave my bouquet to Kat and Shane took my hand.

The officiant spoke over us, talking about the meaning of love.

Shane was all choked up. "You look like a dream, Dimples."

"You think?"

He looked dangerously sexy in a black suit and tie. The boutonniere pinned to his lapel was classy and understated. Everything was picture perfect except for—"

"Why are you wearing one blue earring from *Pretty Pretty Princess*?" I whispered. It was dangling from the side closest to the preacher, so it wasn't visible to the crowd or the photographer.

He grinned from ear to ear. Keeping his voice quiet, he said, "Kat gave it to me this morning. She said Caroline told her about the "something borrowed, something blue" saying. She told me to wear it so I'd have something blue."

"And you actually wore it during our wedding?"

"Mama, you should know by now that I'd do anything for the two of you, including wearing a game-piece earring."

I squeezed his hands. "What did I do to deserve you?"

"Nothing. And that's the point. We chose each other because we wanted to. Not because we had to."

The preacher ended his speech and, thankfully, moved on to the vows.

Or so I thought.

"Before Shane and Beth exchange their wedding vows, I'm gonna give the floor to Shane."

I cocked my head and gave him a very clear "what the fuck is happening" look with my eyes.

This was *not* in the plan.

Shane let go of my hands and took a step away from the officiant, looking around me. He crooked a finger, "Come here, Tadpole."

I looked over my shoulder and found Kat's eyes just as surprised as mine. *So, she didn't know this was happening either.*

Shane lowered to one knee as Kat joined us at the altar. Austin discreetly handed him a box.

Ah, so there were multiple conspirators.

"I love you, baby girl," he said, looking her in the eye.

Kat swished her dress back and forth nervously.

"I've been with you since you were born, and the first thing I ever said to you was that I loved you. That will never change."

I cupped my hands over my mouth as I watched the scene unfold.

"I love you too, Daddy," she squeaked.

Shane grinned. "I know. But I'm about to say some vows to Mama. I'm gonna promise to love her as long as I live, and I'm promising the same to you. I will always love you. I will always be here for you. I will always protect you." He opened the box and pulled out a small, heart-shaped locket. "Mama gets a ring, but this is for you, so that you can remember that promise."

With trembling hands, he unlatched the necklace and fastened it around her neck. Without a second thought, Kat dropped her bouquet and mine, and leaped into Shane's arms.

It was everything I could have ever dreamed of.

They were everything I could have ever dreamed of.

Shane stood and kept Kat on his hip as he took my hand

again. Caroline jumped in, scooping up the fallen flowers and discreetly handing me a tissue.

There wasn't a dry eye in the house.

If I was being honest, the rest of the ceremony was a blur. It was a good thing the officiant fed me my vows line-by-line, because I couldn't have remembered them if I tried.

He pronounced us man and wife, and made the declaration to kiss the bride. Kat jumped from Shane's arm to Austin's like a flying squirrel just in time for Shane to dip me all the way back in a movie-worthy kiss.

Our guests cheered as we made our way down the aisle.

Dr. and Mr. Hutchins.

As soon as we were back through the floral arch and the bridal party was making their exit, Shane stole me away to the side. "One more thing," he said, reaching into his suit jacket, pulling out a folded stack of papers, and handing them over.

Carefully, I opened them. My heart stopped.

PETITION FOR ADOPTION.

The papers fell and I looked up. Shane cupped my cheeks. "She is wanted, Beth. Always."

I nodded fervently. "I'll talk to her about it as soon as we leave for the cruise."

Shane cupped my cheeks, wiping the tears from under my eyes. "She's the one who told me she wants it. She wants her last name to be the same as ours."

I went willingly into his arms, whispering I love yous and stealing a moment with my husband before the chaos of a wedding reception and our family honeymoon.

"Thank you," I said quietly. "For choosing to make it to tomorrow."

WHAT TO READ NEXT

Check out *100 Lifetimes of Us* and get to know Shane's best friend Cole as he supports the leading man, Miles, in this spicy bodyguard romance!

AUTHOR'S NOTE TO THE READER

Dear Reader,

I've never written a book that was this hard to get through. It made me vulnerable in the most uncomfortable ways. I felt the weight of Beth's mental battles the same way I experienced them years ago.

If I'm being honest, most of what I wrote in this book, I have never said out loud because I was ashamed. But like Shane tells Beth, calling someone is always better than keeping it to yourself. Even if you don't think it's a big deal or you think it'll pass, tell someone. Get it out there.

Here's my promise to you:

I promise you that tomorrow will be better. I know it doesn't feel like it. You're in the tunnel, and it's pitch black. I've been there. I know how fucking dark it is. But I'm standing at the other side and I promise you—*I promise*—there's light.

Keep fighting for tomorrow.

XO,
—Mags—

PS. Because you're super cool, let's be friends!

Want to spread the love? Tell others what you thought of this book by leaving a review on Amazon and GoodReads (I'll do a literal happy dance if you do)!

ACKNOWLEDGMENTS

To Landon: We made it through. Here's to the good days.

To Melina joon: I can't believe it was actual YEARS ago that we chatted about the vague idea of Layla's story. Now here we are at the end of the series. You are the cornerstone of these books. The heart. The love. The soul. I'm so grateful to know you. Keep doing incredible things for the world.

To Mikayla: If I get kidnapped with anyone, I hope it's you.

To Mandy: You're the sweetest confidante and encourager, badass excavator driver, and fierce mama bear.

To Nicole: If anyone comes to save me and Mikayla, I hope it's you. I cut the power to the woodchipper.

To Kayla C: Thank you for being the most quietly reliable presence! I'm so grateful for everything you do! Keep kicking ass!

To Crosby: Thank you for being a badass PA and not running for the hills when I said, "I need help, but I have no idea what to do with you!" I'm so eternally grateful for you and everything you do!

To My Hype Team: Thank you for your enthusiasm and encouragement! You all are an imperative part of my book team and I'm so grateful for every recommendation, video, and post!

To My Sensitivity Readers: Thank you for sharing your experiences and helping me build these characters. You are invaluable!

To My ARC Team: You guys are the greatest! Your excitement and support astound me on a daily basis. You make me feel like the coolest human being alive. I'm so grateful for each one of you. Thank you for volunteering your time and platforms to boost my books!

To My Readers: Because naming all of you one by one would double the length of this book: You all are the reason I keep writing books. I'm thoroughly convinced that there's no greater group of people in the world than my real-life poker club. Y'all are amazing human beings! Thank you for loving these characters and getting as excited as I do about their stories! Thank you for your hype, encouragement, and excitement!

To The Starbucks Baristas: You never talk to me or question why I'm sitting in the corner 40+ hours a week. Thanks for that.

To The Formula Company Representative: You gave me sample cans in the lobby of the pediatrician's office and that helped me breathe.

To Our Pediatric Nurse: You're an unfrosted Pop Tart. I hope your pillow is always warm, that you hit every red light when you're late, and never find a good parking space again.

ALSO BY MAGGIE GATES

Standalone Novels

The Stars Above Us: A Steamy Military Romance
Nothing Less Than Everything: A Sports Romance
Cry About It: An Enemies to Lovers Romance
100 Lifetimes of Us: A Hot Bodyguard Romance
Pretty Things on Shelves: A Second Chance Romance

The Beaufort Poker Club Series

Poker Face: A Small Town Romance
Wild Card: A Second Chance Romance
Square Deal: A Playboy Romance
In Spades: A Small Town Billionaire Romance
Not in the Cards: A Best Friend's Brother Romance
Betting Man: A Friends to Lovers Romance

The Falls Creek Series

What Hurts Us: A Small Town Fake Engagement Romance
What Heals Us: An Age Gap Romance
What Saves Us: A Small Town Single Mom Romance

ABOUT THE AUTHOR

Maggie Gates writes raw, relatable romance novels full of heat and humor. She calls North Carolina home. In her spare time, she enjoys daydreaming about her characters, jamming to country music, and eating all the BBQ and tacos she can find! Her Kindle is always within reach due to a love of small-town romances that borders on obsession.

For future book updates, follow Maggie on social media.

- facebook.com/AuthorMaggieGates
- instagram.com/authormaggiegates
- tiktok.com/@authormaggiegates

Printed in Great Britain
by Amazon